The Countess

The Countess

Janice Law

PIATKUS

Copyright © 1989 by Janice Law

First published in Great Britain in 1989 by
Judy Piatkus (Publishers) Ltd of
5 Windmill Street, London W1

British Library Cataloguing in Publication Data

Trecker, Janice Law
 The Countess
 I. Title
 813'.54 [F]

ISBN 0-86188-849-9

Phototypeset in 11/12 Compugraphic Times by
Action Typesetting Limited, Gloucester
Printed and bound in Great Britain by
Biddles Ltd, Guildford & King's Lynn

To Jerry

Author's note

I have long been interested in the European Resistance Movements of World War II and, particularly, in the career of the Polish born Strategic Operations Executive (SOE) agent whose activities I have borrowed for this novel.

Most of the events in this book occurred; but if the events are factual, the characters are fiction. Their beliefs, background, ideas, personal relationships and fate are the responsibility of the author and the brave women and men who inspired them are quite separate – and doubtless far more admirable – than these fictional creations.

Chapter One

A Holiday in Zakopane – 1929

'Dr. Klimosky says,' the Countess began for the fifth time of the evening, and Jozef let his eyes slide away from her plump, anxious face to the black-coated waiters hurrying self-importantly back and forth, the expanse of damask that spilled over his lap, the trolley of desserts – a perennial subject of the children's speculation – and the regulars of the hotel dining room. There were the Blochmanns, blond, heavy, red-faced, engaged in their chief activity of the day, the demolition of vast piles of heavily fragrant sausages and cabbage. Next to them, nearest the waiters' station, was the Sarkowski family, father, mother, grandmother, three tall daughters and the boy, perhaps eight, all keen skiers. Their faces were tanned and burned from the wind, and the conversation drifting over in disjointed snatches was all of runs, lifts, tours and spills. The young people laughed, and the oldest girl, plain but vivacious, smiled at the next table where four young skiers, still in ski-pants and heavy sweaters, were rehashing their runs between anxious glances at the menu. Jozef wondered if they had enough money for their dinners and whether they had been staying out at the hostel or up in one of the guides' huts to save money.

No question about the funds of the Polowitzs at the other side! Pan Polowitz, whom the children called Monsieur because he was always speaking French, was a mine owner from Silesia up to visit his wife, who spent the winter months in the sanatorium. On nights when Madame Polowitz preferred to remain there, Monsieur ate with Pan Tomzewaki, another sanatorium 'widower', a banker from Posnam. Then there was the elderly Colonel Leschke, an official with the Ski Federation, accompanied by a pretty, dark-haired secretary whom the Countess refused to meet. Jozef thought this a pity, since she was charming and her casual flirtation with Mitrowski and his blond friend, the two best skiers around, had raised Jozef's hopes that she might be approachable. There were, after all, not many younger people at the best hotel in Zakopane, which catered to the rich and sedentary; to the relatives, in short, of the town's sanatoria patients.

'... the new vitamin therapy,' said the Countess, and Jozef hastened to agree. He did not need to pay much attention to her, knowing her conversations by rote. They began and ended with André and he had only to nod his head or to murmur, 'Yes, Countess,' for her to be satisfied. Probably she knew he did not listen, perhaps she knew she was a bore; she was not unintelligent. Looking now at her rather heavy face, Jozef wondered whether she had once been attractive, whether she might still be attractive now were it not for her obsession. She was calling over the waiter – André's meat was over-done, or not done enough, or too tough – there was something every night. The waiters were deferential, eager to please: Jozef knew they merely added an extra dinner to the bill. André said nothing, and Jozef thought, He is a saint. The boy was pale – the mountain air that flushed his sister's cheeks left him white and sallow. He was thinner, too; the wrist resting lightly on the edge of the table was all bones, and, where the cuff had been pulled back, Jozef could see the faint network of blue veins. André was being worn down by patience and by cures.

'It is all right, Mother,' he said softly with a smile to the waiter. 'The cutlets are perfectly acceptable.'

The Countess sighed. 'I know you think I fuss too much, but Dr. Klimosky is very strict about your diet. We've promised him when we eat out that all is to be in order. I know you think I'm a foolish woman.'

'I don't think that,' André said. His voice was always soft, as if he was startled by its new depth. 'If Dr. Klimosky's food was as good as this, he wouldn't have to be so strict.'

'Amen,' said Elizabeth. 'That pudding you had for lunch was like glue. I thought I tasted Daddy's last hunter in it, too.'

André laughed, his drawn face momentarily alive.

'Elizabeth,' said the Countess, 'how often have Mademoiselle and I told you about topics for the table?' At her side Mademoiselle obediently nodded her head. This was the newest Mademoiselle, the fourth or fifth she'd had, the second during Jozef's tenure. Mademoiselle Emilie did not look to have any more staying power than the others. She was nearly fifty, short of both breath and sight, deficient in humour and energy, content to eat at a good table, sit in a comfortable chair, collect gossip for her relatives in Alsace and sympathise with the Countess. Her neck was goitrous, her dark eyes protruding. She looked like a myopic frog, and Jozef wondered if there was an unlooked for streak of humour in the Countess that she should engage so listless a person as duenna and instructor for her daughter.

'*Pardonnez moi*,' Elizabeth said, '*je suis désolée*.'

Mademoiselle sighed at this patent insincerity and André sniffled and whispered, 'Poor old Dobbin,' so that Elizabeth giggled.

'*Quelle infante*,' said Mademoiselle crossly, and it was true. Elizabeth had scarcely grown in the two years Jozef had lived with them. She was still small and delicate in appearance, her body straight and flat, although now, studying her face, he could see that it had lengthened, that the cheekbones were higher and wider, the lines of jaw and chin more definite. Her long black hair, braided during the day for skiing and skating, was allowed down for dinner and its thick waves shaded her face and rippled over her shoulders, bony under the thin party silk. She was very vain of her evening dress; when he came with André's chair to collect them for dinner, he would often hear her complaining to Mademoiselle that the sash was not right, that she hated the white childish socks, that she was ready for silk stockings and real party shoes. But that was ludicrous. She looked nearer eleven than thirteen, though there were moments when he could see glimpses of the woman she might become, something about the turn of her head, or the pattern of her heavy hair against her forehead, or a sudden thoughtfulness.

'Did you see Adam again?' she asked, leaning close to him so that the Countess could not hear.

'No. He had taken a party out – up to the hut, I think.'

'I hope he will say we can go tomorrow. It can't get warm so soon, can it?'

They had put off a run to the Five Lakes district for most of the holiday, but now even Adam, their guide, had to admit Elizabeth was strong enough to manage. Jozef was proud of that; he had trained her in only one thing perhaps, but he had done well. The guides were astonished by her stamina, by the wiry strength of her slight, childish body. It came from making her climb up the hills, from rationing the luxury of the cable car and the *téléphérique*, until he was sure her legs were strong.

'We will see. The *foehn* wind may come – it is very late in the season.'

'You are such a pessimist, Pan Jozef. It will get cold tonight, and be beautifully frozen tomorrow so we can ski to the lakes.'

'And if not, there will be fog and you will see your third halo rainbow and never die in the mountains,' Jozef teased.

'And I will be fourteen before I see the Lakes, and Czeslaw will torment me dreadfully when we see him.'

'It will be good to see your cousin again.'

'Yes, although he is very cruel to me,' she said with a smile. 'I don't see why he has to go to school anyway. You could teach him everything, couldn't you?'

'If he's to join the Uhlans, he will need to learn to work with other boys.'

Elizabeth made a face. 'I'm glad I don't have to go to school – since they wouldn't let me join the Uhlans, anyway. Though I ride just as well.'

Jozef smiled, but now her attention, always wavering, shifted to Max, their waiter. Had he saved her one of the cream-filled cakes? One of the chocolate ones? They went so fast – she was sure the Blochmanns ate more than their share. Max laughed and promised to set one aside this minute, for she was a favourite with the staff – with the guides – with, Jozef sometimes thought, everyone except her mother and Mademoiselle. But that was unfair. Elizabeth did not seem to mind that her brother was the centre of their mother's life. She wished only to be free to run about as she pleased, to spend the day on skis or in a fast sled. Her wants were simple: had she been born a guide in the mountains, she would have been content. They had that in common: a passion for the emptiness of the mountains, for the pure, cold air, for the crunch of skis along the runs, for the pines and spruce black and blue against the snow. And then, childlike, she loved all the festivities of the resort — the skating competitions, the ski jump and the bob sled run, the torchlight parade of guides on skis, the evening outings on the sleds.

'We can go to the skating exhibition tonight, can't we? They are going to dance, and Max said they would have lights; it will look very pretty. André can go, too. Don't you want to, André?'

'Dr. Klimosky expects us back,' said her mother.

'It would do André good. They're to do a waltz and a mazurka on skates! Think of it. I would fall in a minute.'

'It's very late,' protested Mademoiselle, disinclined for any exertion.

'It's all right. I'll take them,' said Jozef, who enjoyed these special evenings, the earnest gaiety of the visitors, even the professional cheerfulness of the guides and the waiters. Later, standing with Elizabeth at the side of the outdoor rink, he had a fleeting memory of walking along the street in Zakopane with his father's heavy silhouette blocking the brilliant winter sun. He remembered happiness, excitement. They were going to see the ski jumpers at the old jump, pitifully small by modern standards, but a great and novel excitement then. He could see the exact contour of his father's jacket against the intense sky, hear his mother's voice, saying, 'I don't suppose it will be *too* dangerous, do you, Georg?' His father's laugh, then oblivion. It teased him that he should remember this trivial moment with such vivid force when so much else was lost — his father's face, his mother's eyes, important events and significant conversations.

'Oh, look, Pan Jozef. They're putting out the lights. We'll see the torches now.'

The rink went dark and the stars emerged in the cold night sky. Around them the crowd stamped their feet, chafed their hands and exchanged jovial remarks about the fortitude of the dancers in their short skirts and tights, before a little flaring light at the far end brought cheers, disturbing the horses waiting by the sleds.

'How pretty,' Elizabeth exclaimed.

The skaters wove towards them on the ice, their torches like arctic fireflies, yellow and orange against the black night, the blue snow. They becan a complicated series of interlocking loops, flying lights in orbit, until, passing close, a face, an arm, a red or blue skating costume, was suddenly illuminated and Elizabeth cheered one of their friends. Beside her, Jozef applauded. He was sorry to be leaving, to be going back to the winter-locked estate, to the stained brown and yellow snow of the farmyard, to the pinched misery of the villages.

'They are wonderful, aren't they?'

'Yes. Very good.'

'We'll get some medals at the next Olympics, I'm sure we will. Though our skiers are better. But skiing *is* the best, isn't it?' She turned excitedly, and exclaiming 'Look, there's Adam,' pushed through the crowd towards the guide, who stood tall and handsome in white shirt and trousers, his embroidered sheepskin coat left open to show the wide belt. The Gurals were nothing if not elegant, even if their fine jackets stank of badly cured hide and their white clothing picked up every spot, every soil.

'It is getting cold, isn't it, Adam? We'll be able to go tomorrow, won't we?'

'We will see, Little Countess. I hope so. It's not just you I've promised.'

'A whole party to go? That will be such fun!' said Elizabeth, delighted with the prospect of a grown up trip.

'Well, Countess, watch the weather. This clear night, see, is hopeful,' he said, stroking his grey-streaked moustache. 'That means frost, but it will be as God wills.'

'As always and forever,' she said politely, 'but we can hope, Adam.'

'So man lives,' he said sententiously, 'and woman, likewise.'

'Adam has hopes, Pan Jozef,' Elizabeth said as he joined them. 'I know we will see the lakes tomorrow.'

'If you get to bed promptly tonight,' said Jozef, who checked the time for the morning. After a little ritual gossip with Adam, he steered Elizabeth towards the hotel.

'Adam's laughing, but I really want to go before I'm fourteen. I'll have something on Czeslaw, then. He's always best and first in everything.'

'He is the oldest.'

'And the best,' she admitted candidly, 'but he is an awful tease. This will show him, won't it?'

'You'll be a real skier, certainly. But don't tell Mademoiselle; she will only be worried.'

Elizabeth made a face. Behind them, the hotel lobby glowed, the cheerful clutter blurring to a rosy mosaic. 'Goodnight, Pan Jozef,' Elizabeth said. Without waiting for him she ran inside, careless of the old ladies who might be tottering up the steps, her long hair flying, the ribbons that were supposed to keep it neat, dangling limp and defeated over her ears. At the top of the stair she turned and waved: she knew his habits well, understood he must occasionally walk at night. To the Countess's question, she would say casually that Pan Jozef had stopped for a coffee. In actuality, he would be wandering the quiet, icy streets, listening for the faint scratchings of memory and outwaiting the loneliness which, waylaying him along the hotel corridors, sometimes sent him to a woman who kept rooms in a shabby hotel near the railway station. Neither the Countess nor her daughter needed to know about that.

The late morning opened with an astonishing pink, gold and lavender sunrise that spilled over the blue and purple snow and turned it to a white of blinding, unbelievable purity and brightness. Despite his dark glasses Jozef's eyes stung and even when they reached the shadows of a long file of spruce, he kept his head down against the light, watching the tips of his skis and the smooth rolling motion of the older Sarkowski girl just ahead. Suzana was her name, and though he had always thought her very plain with her big nose and bad teeth, he had to admit she had beautiful legs. The long swelling curve of hip and thigh in the tight grey skipants was undeniably attractive and when she turned, as she did occasionally, to see if he was keeping up, her smiling face seemed to him fresh and open. Being a tutor could be a miserable business, Jozef thought, though Miss Sarkowski did not seem to mind his status. She was rather shy and awkward with young men and always pleased with his somewhat formal attentions: the polite greetings, the move to hold her chair, to open the door or to stand in line for her *téléphérique* tickets. The shifting of her weight from one muscular leg to the other, the alternate rise and fall of her round buttocks, sent intimations of a host of other little attentions through Jozef's mind, and the worst of it was his suspicion that, were he to drop his ski poles and reach out to caress one of those long and sturdy limbs, Miss Sarkowski would react with the purest delight.

Irritated by this distraction, he dug his poles into the snow and moved up aggressively. He and Miss Sarkowski had been lagging somewhat to the rear, behind her younger sister, Katya, and far behind Wlad Mitrowski whose effortless glide aroused even the guide's admiration. At the very front was Adam, his white clothes blurring against the snow, and beside him Elizabeth, for they were the firmest of friends and, since the going was soft and perhaps dangerous further on, he wanted the girl beside him.

In fact, they were taking this trip a little against Adam's best judgment. Despite the cold clear night, it was obvious that the thaw was approaching and he had agreed to take them only if the party got up well before the sun had any chance to soften the drifts high on the mountain. He had made it clear that if conditions looked dangerous they were to turn back at once, and despite Wlad's sarcasm and the protests of the young Sarkowskis, all had agreed to this. But now Jozef could hear Wlad talking to Katya, telling her the guide's caution was all nonsense and that he could take her to the lakes if Adam turned difficult.

'I know what he'll do. He'll get a bit tired – no wonder since he's a shade over fifty, my father knew him here before the war – then he'll sniff the air and say he smells the *foehn* or sees a ghost or whatever' – Katya laughed – 'and it'll be back to the hotel in time for lunch. I know these old fellows.' Jozef had to laugh, too, for he had the Highlander's dialect down perfectly, even to the long, characteristic pauses. 'I'm right, eh, Goralski?' the boy asked.

Jozef shrugged. Since his illness he felt less at home with such robust and athletic types. 'You pay him for his expertise,' he said. 'There's no science of avalanches.'

'Ah,' said Wlad, 'different for you. You've got the child to look out for. Though she's a fine skier. More wind than some of us, I'd say.'

The girls laughed, and not for the first time Jozef cursed Mexico and all its fevers. 'You'll do as you please,' he said. 'For myself, I've never been afraid of common sense.'

Wlad made a face and, feeling like a pedant, Jozef moved along the trail towards Adam and Elizabeth. It was his job, he thought, that had made him older than his years and robbed him of the youthful brio that distinguished Mitowski. He heard the girls' voices behind him, full of laughter and promise, and felt an uncharacteristic jealousy: that Mitrowski fellow was a damn fool, and the Misses Sarkowski the silliest girls in creation.

Jozef's disposition was not improved by what soon became a steep, exhausting climb, but by mid-morning they had reached the ridge that ran to the lakes. Adam pointed to a snow and ice-covered pond, sunk in a circle of peaks. 'Black as coal in summer,' he told Elizabeth. 'Deep too. You let down a line there, little Countess, and it will never reach the bottom.'

At the moment, frozen solid and buried amid feet of snow, the lake looked little different from the rest of the terrain. Still, to mark their arrival, they stopped for a while and took off their skis. For the first time that season, the snow was wet enough to make snowballs, and Elizabeth, Katya and Wlad hurled arsenals at each other, shouting and laughing. Then Adam opened his knapsack for the chocolate and hard, dry sausages he carried and the rest took out flasks of brandy. Max had given Elizabeth a thermos of coffee, instead, but Jozef poured a little brandy into her cup so that she could toast the day with the rest.

'This is wonderful, isn't it? Would Mother bring us again in the summer, do you think?'

'Maybe.'

'That child is spoiled,' Suzana said in an undertone, and Jozef felt oddly resentful. Elizabeth took no notice, for now

Wlad was demonstrating something with his skis: he was going to do a slalom run down towards the lake for her benefit. The child watched with rapt attention, the hood of her jacket back, her face red with the wind. Jozef noticed that even with the braids she was extraordinarily pretty. The big, rather ungainly Misses Sarkowskis saw it, and, with an uneasy sensation, Jozef realised that Wlad Mitkowski did, too. She is just a child, he thought, yet he had a perception of change, a sense of her being on a balance point between one thing and another. Annoyed with himself, he spoke to Katya. 'Are you next?'

'It's far too steep for me! Wlad is a crazy man.'

Below them Wlad swooped back and forth like a hawk, his skis sending up steep plumes of white, until, reaching the narrow beach of the lake, he pushed into a sharp turn and stopped in a shower of snow.

Elizabeth clapped her hands and waved and the Misses Sarkowski, not to be outdone, laughed and shouted encouragement to him as he began toiling back to the ridge. Adam waited until he had reached the top, then cut short the exclamations of admiration with the news that they had to press on if they wished to follow the usual trails.

Overhead, the sun was warm. They unbuttoned their jackets and stuffed them in rucksacks, and on the upgrades, stopped to wipe the sweat from their faces. A few miles along the south face of a slope, Adam hesitated. Wlad had been correct. The guide looked all round, signalled for quiet, then tested the air with his thin, flaring nostrils. The others waited, cleaning balls of snow off their poles. 'A bit of melt here,' Adam said after a minute.

'Sun's strong on this side, that's all.' Wlad's tone was brisk and confident. 'Good enough for a run yet.'

'I'm not wanting to disappoint you, sir, but I don't like the look of the valley. It's always dangerous for avalanches and I'm not venturing further – not on this crust. Especially not with ladies in the party.'

The Misses Sarkowski groaned, and Wlad stamped one ski on the crust. 'Not a crack, not a break anywhere! This slope is as sound as a rock.'

'You wouldn't be presuming to tell me anything new about

the mountain, would you, sir?' On the mountain a guide's word was law, and the old Gural was not used to rebellion.

'I'm saying that I have eyes as well as you,' Wlad answered, 'and a watch as well.'

'What would that be meaning, sir?'

'It means if we go back now, you can fit in another party for this afternoon.'

'Come on, Mitrowski,' Jozef said, 'Don't play the fool. If Adam thinks the slope's unsafe, forget it.'

'Do you see a bulge? Hear any shifting? Listen, I've skied the Tatra since I was old enough to buckle my skis and I haven't been caught yet. Now if you, Goralski, want to go back, it's understandable. But I say we can go on.'

'Not with me, sir,' said Adam.

'We'll find our own way home.'

Adam looked at him, then at the young Sarkowskis. 'The young ladies intend to go?'

'I think you're being a little bit cautious, Adam,' Katya began.

He raised his hand and cut her off. 'Think what you like, miss, but I'll not guide you again on the mountain. Nor you, neither.' He nodded at Wlad.

Suzana looked distressed, but it had gone too far to allow either side to back down. Although Jozef tried again to smooth things over, Wlad and the girls turned their skis and headed diagonally along the track. Adam's face was flushed with anger, and he pushed off down the hill, stopping however at a little rise to shout back, 'Stay high and descend one at a time. Do you hear me, sir?'

There was no answer, and waving Jozef and Elizabeth ahead of him, the old guide began their descent. The late snow wore a thin, icy crust, and whatever disappointment Jozef and Elizabeth had felt in not managing the final peaks was erased as they swept across the empty drifts, muscles straining on the turns, the blood beating behind their eyes on the steep.

They were on a long open slope, racing the wind, when Jozef heard Adam shout, 'Faster! Faster, Countess!' and turned, his eyes watering, and heard the sound, a dull, hollow booming that rose over the crunch of his skis and the whistle of the wind. Elizabeth, too, had turned. 'Go on,' Jozef screamed, 'it's not safe!' He crouched low over his skis, stiffened his ankles as he turned slightly, then, lifting his poles, shot straight down the great chute of the mountain. He could see Elizabeth ahead of him, the red cap and sweater like drops of blood against the snow. A little flat momentarily checked his speed, then over the crest he saw the valley spread out below, heard Adam shouting a warning, and, in a mixture of terror and exhilaration, Jozef dropped into a tight crouch and let gravity and the mountain take him. Behind him the roar increased like an express train, and when he glanced back, he saw Adam outlined against a wall of white. Ahead of him the mountain lurched dizzily towards the village. 'Left, left,' he shouted. The last thing he saw was Elizabeth veering toward a little group of trees, before the snow bulged in front of him, bucking like a horse, and the avalanche hit him in the back like a huge wave. It rolled him off his feet and tumbled him like surf; the universe went white, then red with pain, then black, and Jozef was buried in the thunder.

Everything was dark. He thought it was morning, morning in his room at the estate, but when he tried to move, Jozef found himself immobilised and panicked with the cold wetness in his eyes, his mouth, his nose. He screamed, remembering, and flung his arms up in supplication. Mother of God, he was buried! After the roar, in the thunder. He cried again in animal panic, but his arms were moving, flailing, and there was a dim light in the darkness.

Like a swimmer emerging from the depths, Jozef struggled upward. His legs were caught, and he slid one hand down the side of his body. He touched a boot top; remembered, as if it were some date in Assyrian history, that he had been skiing, that he was in the snow; and gasping, floundered into brightness. One hand broke through the crust into the blue light, and clean mountain air poured into his lungs. Jozef closed his eyes, stunned by colour after blankness, then struck out, pulling wet snow on to his face, into his eyes. The blue space was big enough for him to breathe, and he was exhausted. His lungs burned and one leg was still rooted in the snow. Trapped under a ski, he supposed. He had been skiing. With Elizabeth. Then he was awake and his heart was breaking. Where was Elizabeth? He cried out, calling her name; in anguish, he demanded her of the saints, and when there was no answer, tore himself in a frenzy from the drift and scrambled out on to the scarred track of the avalanche.

Nothing. He turned, frantic. The sky was perfect, blue and clear. Below and to his left, the trees in the little grove were black, a few broken off, showing the white of their heart wood. The snow, gouged and scoured, was without movement, without sound. He was quite alone, and his heart opened within him, astonishing him with the unimagined emptiness of desolation. He got to his feet, his blood beating in terror, and called her name. Silence, nothing, no one. She was gone, erased from the face of the earth. It was not true! He would be calm, systematic. He was alive, she might be, too. And the others. He shouted. If only he had one of his poles. One probed, that was how it was done. And there were dogs, too, trained for rescue. He wiped the sweat, snow and tears from his face. Systematic. She had been ahead and to the left. He would walk and call. He would hear her through the snow. After all, he was alive. He knew that because of the fierce pain in his right ankle. She might be, would be, must be, too. Shouting, he staggered forward.

He found Adam first, or rather, the old guide found him, crawling out of the snow further down the slope. His face was bloody, but he was in better shape then Jozef and immediately laid out the pattern they must walk.

'The others, did you see the others?'

'We will find the little Countess first,' he said, and Jozef loved him. It was on the second sweep across the slope that he saw her cap, blood red with the white eagle Marie had knitted into the design. 'Adam.' He could barely speak.

'Shout, then listen,' Adam commanded. Once, twice. The third time, the guide put his hand on Jozef's arm and nodded.

'Where? Where?' His own ears, ruined by city life, were not so acute. The old guide froze, concentrating completely on the wind, the silence. Perhaps it was only the rustle of the settling snow, the far off cry of an eagle. Then Jozef knew, knew not heard, knew in his leaping heart, in his parched mouth. He floundered forward, heard a sob and fell on the snow like a dog, flinging it to either side with his hands. He touched fabric – a coat – red, soaked. Adam was on the other side of him, scooping away the snow, then she stirred and, forgetting everything, Jozef seized her arm and wrenched her body from the drift. Elizabeth was half conscious, her face ashen, blue around the mouth, her hands limp. Jozef clasped her in his arms, her cold face against his cheek, and it was a moment before Adam could unfasten his grip, check her pulse, chafe her bare hands.

'Something hot. She must have something hot,' he said. He patted the snow, plunged his arms again and again into the drifts. 'The rucksack. It's not still on her?'

Jozef shook his head. He took off his coat and wrapped it around her. A moment later, Adam found the sack. The thermos was dented, but there was a little coffee still inside. 'Hold her head.' The dark liquid dribbled out of the corner of her mouth.

'Drink, Countess. You must drink.'

The child choked, coughed. 'More,' Adam said. 'The heat, Countess. You must have it.' She swallowed and her eyes opened. Jozef bowed his head, the buttons of her little coat sharp against his forehead. 'You are on the mountain,' Adam said. 'There was a snow slide – a small avalanche.'

She looked stunned. 'Are you hurt?' Adam's strong hands touched her arms, her legs. Elizabeth shook her head.

'I couldn't breathe. I couldn't move.'

'Move your legs.'

She sat up, one arm around Jozef's neck, and pulled up first one leg, then the other.

'Thanks be to the Virgin and all the saints! They have preserved you, Countess,' said Adam. He crossed himself and the others followed suit.

'We must get her off the mountain,' Jozef said. 'And we must get help for the others.'

'You help the Countess. I will go on ahead. They will have heard the avalanche in the village.'

But when Jozef got to his feet, he could barely walk, and the three of them staggered down together, the two men trying to warm the child. Elizabeth was barely conscious when Adam began to shout and wave to the skiers climbing the slope from the village, and Jozef ws almost sick with the pain in his ankle. Then blankets, sleds, clear, fiery vodka, coffee, the crisp commands of the guides in the patrol and the reassurance of expertise, before the earth tipped precipitously and the sleds, pulled by their rescuers, descended.

Chapter Two

When they returned home from Zakopane a week later, the Countess was both anxious and exalted: the nearness of the disaster had shaken her soul, but Elizabeth's deliverance was surely miraculous. She immediately began making plans to take the child to the great shrine of the Virgin at Czestochowa; she spoke of dedicating her daughter to the Virgin; in unguarded moments, even a vocation for Elizabeth did not seem implausible, although these hopes rarely survived the child's presence. Still, the Virgin could accomplish all things and in the holiest shrine in Poland, Our Lady might touch her daughter's heart. Temporarily neglecting André, the Countess consulted the priest, wrote to the monastery, ordered a new dress for Elizabeth, and stirred the household into a religious fervour that touched them all. Even Jozef.

He had discovered passion on the mountain, awkward, unsuitable but unmistakable. Had Elizabeth died in the snow, his heart would have shattered like glass. He had known that instantly; the depth of his feelings was only confirmed at the station in Zakopane, where he watched the two long coffins loaded on to the Warsaw train. Katya Sarkowski had survived; plain Suzana, with the beautiful legs, and Wlad Mitrowski had been buried too deeply, too long. In the smoky chill of the station Jozef shivered at the power of the avalanche, which, in an instant, had not only erased the lives of the strongest of them but had sprung open his heart and rearranged his existence. Even when they were safe at home on the estate, he would feel sweat on his face when he thought of the snow, the dark coffins, or of Elizabeth's coat, half buried in the drift. He loved her so much it seemed he had never loved before and the radiance that emotion gave the world both delighted and appalled him. She was a child and in his care, and their miraculous salvation had led him into temptation. It was not hard to feel the Countess's fervour, to share her gratitude, to hope that the Virgin of Czestochowa might somehow restore the balance of his heart.

In the meantime, he was happy, with a guilty, nervous, giddy happiness which surely that old rebel, the Count's widowed sister, Madame Anna de Bonheur should have noticed. But Madame Anna had taken to her bed at the beginning of the winter, and the shock of her beloved niece's accident had not done her failing heart any good. They had been home over a week before she had strength enough to summon him to the chill, bare room which suited her ascetic soul better than the opulent disorder of the rest of her brother's house. Jozef found the old lady lying propped up on her bed with a wolfskin rug over her legs. Her skin was as white as the sheets; her large cold eyes as light and clear as water.

'Pan Jozef Goralski,' she said. He bent to kiss her hand, but she seized both of his instead. 'Pan Goralski,' she said again, and stopped, her thin cheeks quivering.

'I am early,' Jozef said to spare her embarrassment. 'It is not yet the *l'heure de la conspiration*'.

The old lady smiled then, patted his hand and lay back on her pillows. Jozef often accompanied Elizabeth to visit her aunt, always in late afternoon; the time, according to Madame Anna, of confidences and conspiracies. 'At my age, I cannot keep so strict a schedule, Pan Jozef. But have some coffee, please. Though it's a pleasure now denied me, you have a cup and remind me of Warsaw.'

She gestured towards the pot of thick, strong coffee that conjured up for her memories of certain smoky coffee houses, of hasty conversations under the violins, of cryptic orders and notes passed in folded newspapers. In the partitioned Poland of her youth, Madame Anna had lived dangerously and bravely. In her great and feeble age, she lived for Elizabeth, her devotee and pupil. When Jozef was settled with his cup, she spoke again. 'So. You are going on the pilgrimage?'

'I have much reason for gratitude, Madame de Bonheur.'

'You will light candles for me.' She gestured toward the drawer by her bed and Jozef opened it and gave her the purse. 'And something for the monastery.'

'Of course, Madame de Bonheur.'

The old lady closed her eyes for a moment. 'When we lived in France, my husband and I used to attend mass at Val-de-Grâce. A Queen of France enlarged it when she was delivered of an heir. I think I will have a mass said there.'

'Most suitable, Madame de Bonheur.' But thought Jozef smiled, he felt uneasy. In her love and anxiety for Elizabeth, Madame Anna always tried to extract promises from him, spoken or implied. Now, when his feelings were confused and intense, he felt vulnerable and sensed the hard, clever old woman would press him.

'I was not wrong about you. I knew my Elizabeth would be safe with you.'

'Thanks to Our Lady.' Jozef was not devout but he regarded the events on the mountain as only slightly less miraculous than did the Countess.

'Even the saints have their instruments,' she said, struggling to sit up. Jozef jumped to straighten her pillows, and to his surprise, she took his hand again. Her own was very soft, the flesh without muscle, the joints like marbles lying under the skin. 'My sister-in-law is unrealistic,' she said, her face close to Jozef's. 'She is not without hope of giving Elizabeth to the church.'

Jozef shook his head. 'Elizabeth is sincerely pious but –'

'"But" – that is right. When I am dead there will also be talk of sending her to a convent school.'

'Not for a long time yet, I trust, Madame.'

Madame Anna's face tightened along the cheekbones and she gestured for silence. She knew her time was short. 'Elizabeth has been raised too freely, that I admit. To speak plainly, my brother is too lazy to discipline the children and my sister-in-law cares only for her son.'

'I've had little experience teaching girls,' Jozef said carefully.

'But to put her in a convent without her horses and her pets! Can you imagine anything worse for a child who has run as wild as a savage? The sisters would send her home or break her spirit. They would no more see her possibilities than her parents. You must stand against this,' she said so passionately that Jozef was disconcerted.

'Madame de Bonheur, I will do all I can, but you know my position.'

'Ah, you speak like a servant! But of course they tell you nothing. One a fool and the other in her dotage! Consumption runs in our family, Pan Goralski. I have been spared to die slowly of old age and a worn out heart, but my brother is afflicted with the early stages. You may believe it, healthy though he looks. His cigars and wine and peasant girls cannot keep him from coughing. And when I see Elizabeth so like him!' She touched her heart, then burst out: 'The country, clean milk and good air keep her strong. I won't have her shut up in a school in the city. Nor tormented to enter the church. Especially not that, Pan Goralski. She is destined elsewhere, I am sure of it.'

'And I as well, Madame.'

There was silence while she rested. Jozef looked at the photographs and portraits that were, with her crucifix, her only ornaments – Marshal Pilsudski and Alexandra, Monsieur de Bonheur, old soldiers on their chargers, old brigands with revolvers, serious young women with fanatics' eyes – until he felt the old lady studying him. 'I believe you love Elizabeth,' she said.

On the mountain his heart had opened on to emptiness as if pierced with a knife. 'Elizabeth is fourteen, and I am her brother's tutor,' he said, but his voice died in his throat. It was an unspeakable subject, an unsuitable conversation.

Madame Anna's face was immobile. What Jozef had taken for coldness in her was ruthlessness, was the capacity for passion. For the legions she had wrapped bands of cartridges around her waist and caried ammunition and dynamite in a carpet bag. She was a woman who feared neither means nor consequences. 'It is a risk I will take,' she said. 'I do not fear human love for Elizabeth. It is the other, it is the love for unreachable things, that we must beware of. There is in our family a great lover for the unreachable. And then there is the Countess with her love for the Church, and for her dead infants like saints in a shrine. We are much in need of ordinary human kindness, Pan Goralski.' She dropped back against the pillows and closed her eyes. 'I am out of breath' she whispered.

Jozef bowed and kissed her hand.

'If you would send Elizabeth to me in a little, I want her to have my ring.' She touched the black mourning ring that lay heavy on her withered finger. 'The women of our family have worn this ring since the failure of the Rising in '63. I believe it is time for Elizabeth to wear it now.'

'Of course, Madame de Bonheur.'

'*Au revoir*, Pan Goralski.' She looked at him from beneath her almost transparent lids. 'You will not forget.'

'No, Madame de Bonheur. *Au revoir*.'

At dinner, Elizabeth was wearing the ring proudly, although it covered her knuckle and drooped to one side whenever she rested her small hand on the table. When her mother saw it, she took the meaning at once and wondered and fussed if it were wise to go. But the arrangements had all been made to be in Czestochowa for the Feast of the Annunciation and, with Elizabeth well drilled and catachised, they departed for the shrine.

This was the pilgrimage season and Czestochowa was crowded with the devout, many of whom had walked for days, some carrying heavy crosses in the cold and slush. Spring was still undecided: it was the time of year Jozef liked least, when the cleanness of winter dissolved, when the earth turned to slop and mud, when all the ordure, human and animal, of the winter was revealed in every yard and forecourt. The streets of the city were filthy, the sewers overflowed with the thaw, and a clammy chill hung over the town, so different from the bracing cold of Zakopane. They had taken a horse cab at the station, but Elizabeth insisted on joining the procession of pilgrims. While the Countess and André rode on ahead to the monastery, she and Jozef walked beside a group from Lodz who carried a crippled girl on a pallet in their high, canvas-covered wagon. The others went on foot, sometimes singing lustily, the men taking turns carrying a tall, heavy cross. On the steep avenue before the

Monastery of Jasna Gora, they broke into a hymn to the Virgin, their voices so unexpectedly sweet and vibrant, so full of faith and longing, that Jozef was glad they had walked in spite of the wet and dirt. It was along this pilgrims' route that foreign armies besieging the holy place had been driven off, and every stone, every wall, bore testimony to human steadfastness and faith. Looking at the worn, earnest faces of the peasant pilgrims, their cheeks red and cracked from the wind and cold, Jozef felt the passionate fervour of his countrymen as a living spirit. And the next day, in the soaring white and gold monastery basilica, jammed with the other pilgrims near the altar, he felt, for perhaps the first time in his life, a genuine religious emotion.

The Black Madonna over the altar was uncovered; her dark face, severe and Byzantine, was, like her infant's, framed in gold, and a jewelled military cloak was fastened to her shoulders. He could feel the heat from the altar candles, which blazed about the icon so that the Virgin and child glowed in gilded brilliance as if clothed by the sun. The smoke of candles, the perfume of incense and the scent of flowers and pine bows rose to the Madonna, rose to the great mural of the Queen of Heaven, rose to the dense, white, twisted pattern of the ceiling like thoughts in some gigantic brain. From the corner of his eye, he could see Elizabeth in her white dress, her dark hair covered by a lace scarf. Her expression was rapt and her lips moved with the words of the Mass. '*Aqnes Dei, qui tollis peccata mundi* . . .'

Would his sins be taken away, Jozef wondered? Around him, he could hear the whispers of the congregation, could see their tears. The peasants touched their foreheads to the cold, dirty stones, and the smell of crowded humanity about him was filled with anguish and with hope. Could he be saved? The Virgin's eyes were cool, serene, rather worldly and unshockable like Madame Anna de Bonheur's, but her mouth was gentle, her long, oval face wise. Was he to have wisdom? Love? Temptations? Suffering? Was this how she would save him from a meagre, selfish existence? Jozef had an awareness of his total insufficiency, and in a moment of piety and resignation, he bowed his head to the stones and left his fate to the Virgin.

* * *

They returned home to Madame Anna's deathbed, solemn farewells, funeral rites. The old lady was laid in the crypt to the accompaniment of the Chopin funeral march, the tears of the peasants and a universal realisation of the old order passing. Aware of the fragility of his happiness, Jozef held his breath for weeks after, but there was no sign from the Count or Countess that any change was planned. The children went on with their lessons, the ponies got their heavy coats clipped and their shoes renewed for the riding season. As the mud began to dry, André took the dogcart out on the roads and the forest trails, while Elizabeth raced her mount ahead of them, shouting like a hussar and, when Czeslaw was with them, taking such fences that Jozef felt his heart turn over.

As spring advanced and there was no word, he began to think that they might go on this way indefinitely, that he could survive on intense and unsuitable emotions which nonetheless filled him with joy. His life was preposterous, yet he could not bring himself to leave the one creature who gave him happiness. The days grew longer, the countryside more beautiful, his existence more secure. He decided Madame Anna had been wrong, entirely, and it was only with the Countess, who held the keys to his happiness, that Jozef was at all uneasy. He feared her impersonal piety, sensing even a certain brutality under her serenity. Sometimes he thought he caught her studying him, as if she was aware there had been a change since the avalanche, and he disliked the mornings when he was called to see her, particularly if she was working on her list of the deserving poor and sending the maids back and forth, packing hampers with food and medicine. That meant that he and the children would be dragged from one stinking hovel to another, to lug the Countess's baskets of bread, cabbages and cloth, and dole out cough syrup to the pre-tubercular. Through the largesse of the Countess, Jozef had come to know all the miseries of rural life: the mothers half dead with child bearing, the families with tuberculosis, the children sickly with rickets, swollen glands, eye infections, dysentery and malnutrition. He was disgusted by the spectacle. And angered, too, that the Countess's piety made all serene. Even admitting that she was genuinely kind, genuinely loved, quite genuinely admired, Jozef often found her incomprehensible and unsympathetic.

'Good morning, Jozef,' she said. Despite the smile, her face was without expression.

'Good morning, Countess.' She cares nothing for happiness, Jozef realised. Not for her own, not for Elizabeth's, certainly not for mine. That thought made him rebellious, and when his eye caught the red and yellow splendour of the tulips beyond the window, he cast about for some excuse.

'How are you today?'

'Very well, Countess, but I think Elizabeth should stay at home if you are going visiting. I think she has a bit of a cold. Mademoiselle mentioned it,' he added, too quickly, as if she might doubt his word.

'Very well,' the Countess said, unperturbed, 'but I would like you to go, Jozef.' She smiled slightly as if he had given her an idea. When he went outside after lunch, he found they were going alone. The Countess was preparing to drive the horse herself.

'Would you prefer that I take the reins, Countess?'

'Thank you, no, Jozef.' She gestured for him to get in, and they set off on the straight flat road. Flocks of larks, finches and rooks swept this way and that across the fields as if drawn by the fast moving clouds overhead. It was a day of sun and shadows with bits of blue sky, like shattered glass, reflected in the puddles. At the crossroads, they turned towards the north hamlet, where a peasant woman was recovering from a difficult delivery. On an earlier visit, Jozef had made the mistake of mentioning the number of children playing in the yard. The Countess had been angry and at some pains to lecture both him and Elizabeth on the duties of maternity. This time, after he carried in the supplies, he was told to wait with the horse, and he passed a quarter of an hour exchanging such conversation as he could with the thin and dirty children. Leaving the convalescent, they went to dress an injured forester's leg. Their final stop was to see a peasant sick with dysentery. The woman met them at the door and kissed the Countess's hand.

'How is he?' The Countess asked.

The woman's face was strained and yellow. 'He is having trouble eating.'

'You've fed him the soup?' The Countess's voice was sharp. The man had been given only old turnips and porridge last week.

'Nothing else, Countess.'

She nodded to Jozef to bring her basket. It was a low thatched cottage with thick walls and even though the door and the small windows were wide open, Jozef nearly choked on the stench. The Countess stepped around a pail of slops and went to the man lying half conscious on the bed. His face was pale and thin, with a film of sweat across his forehead. His youth surprised Jozef. From the woman's appearance he had guessed the couple were in their fifties, but now he saw the sick man was thirty at most. The Countess laid her hand on his forehead. 'He still has a fever.'

'He mumbles and talks to himself,' the woman said. 'He was shouting something awful last night.'

The Countess asked how much soup he had had and how much fluid. She gave the man some medicine from the doctor and repeated the directions three times because the woman was illiterate and would have to memorise the dosage. 'And he must keep taking fluids even if the bed is soiled,' the Countess said severely. 'Soup and tea are even more valuable than the medicine. He must drink.' The woman wiped her eyes with her apron. 'And if he dies, Countess? What will we do if he dies?' She looked around her distractedly. There was a baby in the crib near the stove and four barefooted children peered in at the windows.

'It is God's will,' said the Countess, 'but if you can get him to drink he has a chance.'

The woman kissed her hand, half in tears again. The Countess stopped at the doorway to cross herself before a crude lithograph of the Sacred Heart. 'Pray to the Virgin,' she said.

She had been brusque with the woman in the cottage, but when the Countess got into the cart, she sat staring straight ahead for a moment before she touched the horse with the whip. Her lips were a thin line. Jozef asked if the man would live, and she shrugged. 'If she will feed him the soup and the medicine. You see how they live. They will put children with dysentery in the barn to save the mess.'

Jozef said nothing.

'It is a hard life for the women,' the Countess added unexpectedly. 'They would die without their faith.' When he did not at once agree, she turned to look at him. 'You were a student. I know how students think, how they are all half-Red. You think it is our fault the peasants suffer and you seek their salvation in education and Bolshevism.'

'Education would certainly not make them any more miserable, Countess,' Jozef said, but he took her meaning. In the coffee houses the talk was of 'elevating the peasant'. The actuality was less pleasant, he would give her that.

'The Saints preserve them,' she said, 'and God help us all if they ever lose their faith. The women especially. I do what I can, you know,' she added in a low, angry voice. 'We have not the wealth of the Radziwills.'

'There are many alive who would be in their graves without you, Countess.'

'But this is not why I am talking, Jozef. It is Elizabeth I am thinking of. She will have duties; you see their nature, you can understand the necessity for faith and self-discipline. That is why the Count and I have decided to send her to school.'

The blow had come when he had least expected it, and it was all he could do to murmur, 'Elizabeth's faith is surely not in doubt, Countess.'

'Out of deference to my sister-in-law, I did not press to have Elizabeth sent to the convent earlier. Now I think it is of the essence. This is no reflection on you, Jozef. The Count and I are grateful beyond words for your devotion to her. We would have lost our daughter in the avalanche otherwise.'

'Perhaps,' said Jozef, playing his only card, 'you would want to consider another instructor for André as well.'

The Countess tightened the reins and the horse stopped. She gave him a close, shrewd look that made him fear his emotions had betrayed him. 'We are not talking of academic matters. Open your eyes, Jozef Goralski. Is Elizabeth ready to take on this work? Is she ready for a home and family of her own?'

'She is a child,' Jozef whispered. 'Can she not have a childhood?'

'Woman's duty is not all pleasure by half,' the Countess

said drily. 'Elizabeth has run wild too long already. It is not knowledge of books she needs, but knowledge of her role in life. She is not being prepared for the Uhlans, although when I see her on a horse, I think she is better prepared for a regiment than for a marriage.'

'Madame de Bonheur,' Jozef said carefully, 'was concerned about her health.'

'Elizabeth is in excellent health,' the Countess said. 'And there is something else. She is a young woman now. Though I find no fault with your discretion, she should have a woman to instruct her.'

Jozef looked away. He had known this and yet he had allowed his happiness to rest on the child. 'When will she leave?'

'I want her to start next month. Before the summer holidays.'

'So soon!' he exclaimed.

'So late, rather,' said the Countess.

Chapter Three

The little Countess learned deception at the convent, not in the sense of lies and strategems but the deep deception of the heart, the deception of perfect self-control, of perfect conformity. This the good sisters neither intended nor perceived, rejoicing rather in their pupil's beautiful manners, her air of distinction, her perfect French. They saw the transformation of the wild little girl who had already been sent home from one convent before she arrived at their door as proof of God's blessing on a religious education, and it would have been perverse of them to ask how deeply those lessons went. But without this question, they did not know the little Countess.

To Elizabeth the Convent of the Sacred Heart had seemed a castle out of a fairytale, a puzzle, a challenge. She had expected to escape, if not by her own action, by some wonderful coincidence. But her indulgent, impractical father already had the cough that signalled the recurrence of his tuberculosis, and the little Countess waited in vain for her reprieve. When it did not come, she made a different escape and became a model student; a transformation that astonished everyone, even herself. On her name day, when she was seventeen, Elizabeth looked in the mirror and saw a distant acquaintance.

The unfamiliarity was not simply because they were forbidden mirrors at school. She felt that she looked at her mother's dreams, at an evanescent image of convent life. This Elizabeth wore her hair in a braid, was very clean, spoke only when spoken to, and knew the days of obligation better than the pedigrees of her horses. She sat through meals without giggling, walked in a line with other young ladies, conjugated French verbs without error and made petty sacrifices during Lent. She did not run along the top of the high convent walls, as she had done during her first week at the institution. So far as even the eagle eye of Sister Ursula could detect, she was perfectly modest, able to dress and undress and wash herself without revealing so much as the hem of her drawers. She was polite to everyone, but not familiar, and though it was noticed that the little Countess never blushed or seemed at a loss in male company, these occasions were too rare to arouse concern. Even her mother was pleased. As Elizabeth studied her face, she wondered how long it would be before the real Elizabeth emerged, not just for the holiday hours when she could ride or ski, but in ordinary, spontaneous life.

She leaned forward and breathed on the cool glass so that her face dissolved in mist: there was Elizabeth, and she was impatient, with the kind of restlessness she sometimes felt riding with her cousin and his friends from the regiment or watching the tall blond boy who delivered potatoes and sacks of turnips and onions to the grocery store near the convent. She should have wondered if this was sinful; she should have known that leaning out of the window or loitering towards the back on their daily walk in order to see the handsome delivery lad was at very least an occasion for temptation. Had she been asked in religious class, she would have answered perfectly. She knew the occasions for sin, but unlike some of her friends who tormented themselves over petty faults or were thrilled with the forbiddenness of little transgressions, Elizabeth had a defective notion of sexual sinfulness. Nor did she have an awareness of the otherness of the male half of the universe. She felt at home with men, loved her father, André, Czeslaw, and Jozef, just as she loved riding, the outdoors, skiing, dogs and horses. Standing before her mirror on her name day, she was as natural a creature as she had been when she entered the Convent; her scrupulous manners, the disguise that had been the price of her survival.

Now she was ready to leave. She had completed the school's French courses, could read German as well as speak it, wrote her native language correctly and in a fine hand. She could do simple algebra, could just manage embroidery, and knew many fine points of Catholic doctrine. She expected her freedom, but at their interview, Sister Margaret was thoughtful and non-commital, and Elizabeth began to feel uneasy.

Sister sat with her back to the window, very still and dignified, her fine high forehead shaded by her veil. Of all the women in the convent Elizabeth admired her most. She was by far the cleverest, most powerful and aristocratic personality, and Elizabeth had taken her almost from the start as a model, as the very pattern of her salvation. This was disingenuous, yet at fourteen the Countess had been taken from everything she loved and understood and put into an environment hostile to her liberty. In the early days, she had remembered the courage of Madame Anna, imprisoned for gun-running and conspiracy, and wished that she, too, suffered for Poland. Although she prayed for patience, Elizabeth had even considered putting her trust in Our Lady and risking the sheer wall outside the dormitory window. It was in this state of mind that she had had her first interview with Sister Margaret.

'The Virgin has shown you great mercy and concern,' Sister Margaret said.

'I am under her protection,' Elizabeth replied, for the mountain rose in her imagination as it did in Jozef's: a division between one sort of life and another.

'And she will care for you and seek to guide you.'

'Yes, Sister.'

'She has brought you here for a reason.'

This the little Countess had refused to answer, but Sister Margaret's cool, clear voice continued. The Virgin's mercy brought with it obligations, gratitude, service. She spoke of the well-known sacrifices of Elizabeth's kinswoman, Anna de Bonheur, of the needs of the country, of the Church. As she talked, her large eyes seemed to peer into Elizabeth's rebellious and untidy soul.

'I am not used to the city,' she said.

'We are rarely used to what we are required to do in life,' said Sister Margaret. 'It is the purpose of education to give us fortitude.'

'Is it the Virgin's will that we suffer?'

'Never,' said Sister, 'but we endure suffering with her help.'

Elizabeth had looked at the handsome figure before her; even in her grey robes Sister Margaret was elegant. Her heart is protected by the way she holds her pen, by the fold of her veil, thought Elizabeth. She straightened her back like the sister and let her face grow still. Sister Margaret had taken this for assent and let her go. Three years later, sitting opposite the attractive young Countess, Sister Margaret wondered if her victory had come too easily, yet it would have been difficult for her to define why she felt uncertain or why, indeed, she would have assessed Elizabeth as a remarkable personality. The girl was not brilliant academically, merely alert and able. She was a leader, although regrettably not one with a religious vocation, and she had, despite a small, even delicate frame, a great deal of vitality, mental and physical. But what did all this amount to? It was rather that with Elizabeth one sensed potential, talents of personality and character, embryonic but indubitable. Without being disobedient or eccentric, she gave the impression of a powerful will and unusual self-confidence. She had the makings of a formidable personality but was as yet without focus. Sister Margaret decided this was what was missing. She smiled at the girl. 'You have done well in your languages. Sister Domenica is pleased.'

'Thank you, Sister Margaret. Now may I ask your permission to write to my parents, since I have finished the programme here at the school.'

'You are — how old?'

'Seventeen.'

Sister Margaret smiled benevolently. 'A delicate age. Between school and marriage.' She smiled again. 'Some of our pupils find it advisable to spend another year with us, working with the younger students. Most find it an excellent preparation for training children of their own.'

'There will be children at home, Sister Margaret,' said Elizabeth.

'Yes, your position in life will make you responsible for the people of your estate. Your mother, I believe, does much charitable work.'

'Yes, Sister, and with my father ill, I know I am needed at home.'

Sister Margaret inclined her head. It was an ambiguous

gesture, at once benevolent and cautionary. 'Your mother, like me, has certain reservations about a young woman of seventeen making her debut in the world.' She drew a letter from the fold in her habit.

Elizabeth felt a sudden fear, edged with anger. Not another year! 'Mother thinks only of others,' she said, knowing Sister Margaret had a good nose for rebellion. 'But she does too much. She will need my help.'

Sister nodded and let Elizabeth continue.

'Besides, I have worked hard to finish all the courses.'

'Education is more than intellectual training. The will, also, must be disciplined. It is only through the most perfect self-control and self-discipline that we have freedom. I refer now to freedom in the world as well as within the convent.'

Elizabeth said nothing, knowing that the more she protested, the weaker her case became. She must appear to submit, although she wanted to leap up and slam out of the room. But the Sisters had taught her well; she sat with her hands folded, her feet tucked neatly under her chair. Sister Margaret noticed and approved without being satisfied. Perhaps, after all, she sensed deceit. 'You would help Sister Domenica with the beginning French classes and continue your work in German.'

'I wish to discuss this with my family, please, Sister.'

'You have my permission to write, of course,' said Sister Margaret. She unfolded the letter and pushed it across the desk.

One glance told Elizabeth her case was hopeless. Her mother spoke of sacrifices, of 'her own good'. When she was excused, Elizabeth ran to her room, tears of rage in her eyes. Another year! It was so monstrously unfair that the very thought of it made her feel ill. She had done everything they asked, and still they were dissatisfied, as if they wished to alter the very contours of soul.

Elizabeth felt the cost of deceit, of continued conformity, as a stabbing pain, and when the other girls were preparing for dinner, she quite honestly claimed to have an upset stomach. But after they were gone, she went down the back stair to the chapel, a high, narrow room of white-washed stone with oak benches, stained glass windows and a lovely gilt altarpiece. In an alcove to the right was a carved and painted statue of the Virgin, a figure ancient, elegant and sympathetic. Elizabeth knelt before it and begged Our Lady's mercy. It had been a point of pride with her that since the mountain she had never prayed for anything for herself, never asked the Virgin for more than her blessing. Now, her face white, she begged for her release, wet the front of her blouse with tears, fell upon the stones like a peasant.

The blue of the Virgin's mantle was as brilliant as her ultramarine robe when Our Lady had reached through the snow to lift Elizabeth clear. The Virgin's head had been haloed in fire, her face serene and golden, her robe so intense that it gradually dissolved into the mountain sky and the sleeves of Jozef's jacket. Elizabeth would remember that until the day she died, and in the chapel with the fading spring sun lighting the glass and picking out the gems in the Virgin's crown, she felt again the mountain wind, the terrible breathlessness, the clarity of that vision.

The pain, she only felt as she rose from the stones. It was on the left side, level with the point of her hip, a tearing pain that took her breath away. I have sinned, thought Elizabeth, to have called on Our Lady to let me leave a convent. Then it receded, leaving a memory in the flesh. It was not the first time she had felt it, but when she went to check her calendar, she was puzzled that it was two weeks before her period. Although she was not one to make a fuss over cramps, when it came again, very hard and sharp, she was frightened.

'Alexandra, Alexandra! Katya!'

Her roommates were still at dinner. The upper floor was quiet and deserted. Elizabeth lay down on her bed and told herself that she was behaving like an infant. Then the pain returned, horrifying, and she sat up. A vile sourness filled her mouth and spattered the coverlet before she could reach for the chamber pot. When she could breathe again, she staggered to the bell rope and pulled it with all her strength. It jangled fiercely, like the pain that tore into her side, then Elizabeth sank to her knees, as the edges of the room wavered black.

Sister Ursula was called, and Sister Claude, who handled

medical care, and then Sister Margaret telephoned the doctor. The other girls looked out of their rooms when Elizabeth was carried to the ambulance, and the veils of the young sisters flared like wings as they ran down the stairs beside her stretcher. In the hospital, there were consultations and an injection that left Elizabeth floating several feet above her bed, watching the preparations below. The Countess arrived in her black gloves and travelling hat. She sat down on the edge of Elizabeth's bed and took her hand. 'Be brave, darling.'

They had told Elizabeth nothing.

'It isn't my appendix?'

'Something like. It won't be a long operation.'

'But what, Mother?'

'They think it's a cyst. On the ovary – the female organ.' The Sisters would never have been brave enough to tell her, and even her mother was embarrassed. Elizabeth would have been baffled had she not grown up on a farm. She remembered watching the chief cattleman cut an ovarian tube in a groaning cow. The operation had been bloody and frightening. Her eyes turned wary.

'They will put you to sleep,' said her mother. 'They will use gas – you won't feel any pain.' Despite this comforting intelligence, her mother wiped her eyes.

'What's wrong?' Elizabeth asked. 'Nothing's happened to Daddy or André, has it?'

Her mother shook her head. 'You're so young,' she said. 'So young.'

When it was over, they talked around her bed. Elizabeth was lying in a vague whiteness as cold as the mountain and unable to ask for a blanket. The voices said: 'We can't be sure, Countess. The other ovary may be affected as well. We left it, of course – at her age.'

'She might have children?' asked the Countess. 'It's not impossible?'

'By no means. Her chances, obviously, are reduced by half. As for the right side – well, we can't be sure yet.'

'She is so young.'

'Sadly, this is often the time, Countess. It was impossible to do anything else but operate, you understand.'

'Doctor, I don't blame you. But at her age. My poor girl.'

Elizabeth tolerated the anaesthesia poorly and took pneumonia. For a long time, she was feverish and wandered in a murky whiteness that was sometimes the corridors of the school and sometimes the mountain. Voices came and went. One day they brought a priest, and Elizabeth struggled to confess. But after asking his blessing, she could not remember what it was she had done wrong, what mistake she had made.

'Lord, have mercy on us.'

'Christ, have mercy on us,' murmured the nursing sisters and her mother.

'And lead us not into temptation'

'But deliver us from evil,' Elizabeth whispered.

'Save thy servant.'

The white mist returned, then she heard the blessing and felt the drops of Holy Water.

In May, Elizabeth went home. The doctors and nurses all came to say good-bye to the little Countess, who presented the hospital chapel with a fine statue of the Virgin. Her father and mother brought bouquets of flowers from the estate and some of the nurses followed them to the door and waved from the hospital steps. The Count wrapped her up in a travelling rug, and big Jakob, his factotum, carried her onboard the train. Her mother's eyes were wet.

'It will be good to have you home. André and Jozef will be waiting. They wanted so much to come, but we were afraid it would be too much for you.'

Elizabeth pressed her mother's hand. When they left the city, she could see the fields green with the early hay, and she asked her father to open a window so she could smell the grass and wet earth and flowers. 'I thought I'd never get out,' she said. She wondered about Zofia and whether she would make the special pancakes she enjoyed, and about her horse, which Czeslaw had promised to ride, and the dogs and all her favourites, but when they arrived in the carriage from the station, she was so exhausted she had to be put to bed.

In a week, however, the little Countess's natural vitality

began to assert itself. Despite her mother's objections, she got into the dogcart and let André drive her all over the estate. From then on, she insisted on a drive every afternoon, and one day when André had some essays to prepare, she asked Jozef to take her instead.

It was overcast and humid, with a hint of a storm. Over the woods, the clouds were low and purple-bellied, and when the wind blew, the leaves showed their silvery underside. Elizabeth leaned comfortably against the cracked leather seat and listened to the horse's rhythmic trot. She had had little chance to speak to Jozef since her return. She had to rest a great deal, and he had been busy preparing André for some university examinations that he was to sit as a special student. Then, too, their relationship had undergone a change. She was no longer his pupil, no longer a child. There had been a detectable awkwardness between them since she entered the convent, an awkwardness she was only now beginning to understand.

Beyond the wood, the land sloped into a field white with clover and early daisies. 'It looks like snow,' said Elizabeth. The bees amid the flowers made a low hum that reminded her of some half forgotten hospital equipment. Without thinking, she said, 'In the hospital, I dreamed of the mountain.'

Jozef looked at her. 'I have dreamed of it as well.'

'Then it is sure. A miracle needs witnesses.'

Jozef nodded. 'I do believe that, Countess.'

'You used to call me Elizabeth.' She spoke quickly; it was an accusation.

'You are grown up now.'

'And everything has changed.' She looked away over the flower strewn fields. 'Everything changed after the mountain.'

'I have thought that, too,' Jozef said softly, and wondered how much he had betrayed during the time when he was so much in love with her.

'I can tell you something? Ask you something?'

'Anything, you know that.' He omitted her title and she was glad.

'When we went to Czestochowa to thank the Virgin, I decided never to ask her for another thing. I could not, I felt.'

'Yet she is most merciful.'

'I sinned when I asked her to let me leave the convent.'

'It does not seem a very terrible sin,' Jozef said carefully.

'That is because you are a freethinker and perhaps a Communist — though you hide it from Mother.'

Jozef was surprised. He had been careful never to discuss politics with the children. 'I believe in what happened on the mountain,' he said. 'Whatever else, I believe that we were saved by the mercy of the Virgin. We would never have found you in the snow otherwise.'

'Then you understand I should not have asked more. I should not.'

Jozef shrugged. It was true he was not religious and had difficulties understanding the feelings of those who were. What surprised him was that the child he remembered as being feckless and pleasure-loving should have made such a decision at fourteen.

'When I was sick, they used to stand by my bed and talk. I remember Mother crying,' Elizabeth continued.

'Your mother blamed herself because you were not at home, but were taken ill among strangers.'

'My mother was crying because I may not be able to have children.'

'Elizabeth, I am so sorry!' Jozef said. For propriety's sake the Countess had told him very little of her daughter's illness and the extent of the disaster came as a shock. He fumbled for a reply. 'It was no fault of yours. Such little biology as I have taught you, must tell you these things happen.'

She looked at him curiously. 'You mistake me, Pan Jozef,' she said, giving him his old name. 'The Virgin heard my prayer and changed my life. I know now that I am under her protection forever.'

Chapter Four

'Do you think it's all right?' Elizabeth asked as she tied the sash. Clothes that looked perfect when Josephina finished sewing them at the estate, had a way of looking ordinary in Warsaw.

'It's delightful,' Cousin Félicie said. '*Charmante.*'

'Mother preferred the rose to a real red. She is afraid I will look *de trop.*'

'Never, darling. Now leave it, before it's stretched. I don't know what more you need anyway. There are officers simply camped in my salon, and Czacki's bringing someone. If you attract any more we won't have room.'

'Poor Félicie! I'm afraid I'm nothing but a nuisance.'

'Don't believe it for a minute. Now had your dear mama come, it would not have been fun, though you know I love her dearly and absolutely worshipped her mother, which means – I'm not sure what.' Félicie rolled her blue eyes, patted her hennaed hair and took out a cigarette. 'Your mama does not wholly trust me, darling, so you're on your honour. Remember that.'

Félicie Halpern was a big, angular woman whose fluffy, girlish manner concealed a shrewd brain and a good heart. Her position in the family was ambiguous despite her rich husband, four children and an unblemished reputation, because she was considered unconventional and 'advanced'. The truth was she had fallen between the generations and married too early. Though her eldest son had reached his teens, she still felt young enough to flirt with handsome officers, and her sympathies, political and emotional, were all with the younger generation.

Elizabeth's arrival had provided her with an excuse for leaving a guest list top heavy with her husband's friends at the Polytechnic. Now scientists and technicians brushed elbows with Czeslaw's pals, young cavalrymen mad to ride and hunt, and certain bohemian pals of Félicie's like the journalist, Czacki, and his young protégés. Unusually for a Warsaw gathering, their politics were as varied as their interests, resulting in loud and sometimes heated arguments. Czacki used to say that he could get a week's columns out of an evening at Félicie's, but the household's excellent cook and Karol Halpern's good store of Hungarian wine kept the parties merry.

This easy, slightly raffish setting was not one the Countess would have picked for Elizabeth, but she had realised during the fitting of the rose evening dress that the neighbouring landowner's boy would not do. He had grown dull; Elizabeth, if anything, more lively. What had seemed a possible match at twelve was a frank impossibility at past seventeen. She had seen something else, too, while arguing with Elizabeth that scarlet was unsuitable: her daughter, though not a beauty, was a striking young woman. Something had to be done. The convent would have postponed the decision, but since Elizabeth was adamant about not returning, it was necessary to make the best possible match and, given the circumstances, to make it early. Somewhere in between the pinning of the peplum and the marking of the hem, the Countess decided on Warsaw. A little calculation revealed that the only possibility was Cousin Félicie, and after some delicate family negotiations, Elizabeth was installed in a tiny bedroom in her cousin's handsome apartment on Nowy Swiat.

Soon, thanks to Félicie's afternoon and evening soirées, to Czeslaw's regimental friends and her own charm, the young Countess was dashing about with some of the most eligible men in Warsaw. In the autumn, there were elegant parties in the best districts, and less elegant but very cheerful gatherings with the students who hung around the theatres, and long afternoons in coffee houses thick with smoke, gossip, laughter, politics and flirtation. Sometimes she went to the country with Czeslaw and his friends for riding but not for shooting, for she still loathed the whole business of driving game to slaughter. Even this eccentricity didn't matter; she attracted men as easily as she breathed – rich, poor, student, soldier, socialite – they all showed up at her table in the coffee house, haunted Cousin Félicie's, and, after she went to work for Czacki, developed an interest in the press.

Félicie, with a mixture of amusement, admiration and envy, attributed Elizabeth's success to her dainty and feminine appearance. But there was something else: released from the convent, restored to health, protected – she was convinced – by divine intercession, the young Countess was bouyant with vitality and good nature and confidence. She was irresistibly enthusiastic and, because of her convent training, capable of subordinating her own interests to those of her companions. With the exception of shooting, she was able to be happy with any activity and interested in any topic, and more than one young man lost his heart before he realized that the young and charming Countess was simply being pleasant, was simply making life enjoyable.

To these unfortunates, Félicie was always understanding. She had just the right blend of sympathy and humour, so that disappointed suitors had a tendency to continue at the Halpern salon for *tête-á-têtes* with a kindly Madame Halpern. This troubled no one; not her husband, who referred to them cynically as 'the walking wounded', and certainly not Elizabeth, who was on good terms with almost everybody and who was, in any case, herself always turning up with strays of either the two-legged or four-legged variety. She was happy because she took no one seriously, not even herself. It was this which fascinated, and annoyed, the journalist Czacki.

'Madame Halpern! And Countess! Were I but a poet I would be inspired!' He strode forward into the salon and kissed their hands with so much bombast and flourish that everyone laughed. Czacki was a journalistic showman, forever presenting the new and astonishing to his readers with all the flair of a first-rate conjurer. He was a man interested in truth but passionate about novelty, and his professional life happily coincided with this pursuit of fashion. He liked people and things so long as they held some mystery for him; as soon as he had converted them into the well-balanced paragraphs of his mildly heated prose, Czacki grew bored and looked for the next sensation. At the moment, the Halpern household was only relatively new, but Elizabeth was both novel and unpredictable.

'I have someone for you to meet,' he said, kissing her hand again.

'You are such fun, Pan Czacki. You know everyone,' Elizabeth said. 'And everyone in Warsaw has heard of you.'

Czacki smiled broadly. When he had first met her, seeing only her innocence and her avidity for life, he had envisioned guiding her, had anticipated a certain gratifying hero-worship. He had given her a little job writing occasional pieces — 'Scenes from Country Life', 'Our Modern Peasantry', 'The young Society Set' — without any real expectations; but her eye was sharp, people liked to talk to her, and both her writing and her character were more formed than Czacki had anticipated. He had published the articles and changed his tack. Now he told her with subtle flattery that her mind was too good to waste: he talked to her of serious issues and encouraged her to learn about politics, factories, the 'real' Poland. But giddy with the social round, the Countess took only so much direction, and Czacki had taken the unusual step of introducing her to some of his other protégés. The first, Janusz Bronski, a handsome university graduate with an interest in labour questions, had proved too serious and overbearing for the little Countess. The other was a spur of the moment inspiration whom he had invited just that day.

'Countess, this is my dear friend Charles Litowski — '

'Lord,' Félicie cried coming up to kiss the newcomer, 'it's English Charlie!' Which rather spoiled Czacki's surprise but made the young man very welcome. His hand was shaken all round, his tweeds — indeed very Saville Row — admired, his genealogy — related to the great magnates, the Potockis — whispered. Félicie's children's tutor had been Charlie's; they were distant cousins; there were other connections. Elizabeth listened with half an ear: English Charlie had a beautiful profile, fine, large eyes, and a long, sculpted mouth. His back and shoulders were wide but graceful, and the angle of his chin on his strong neck, perfection. She could feel the whisper of her blood in her ears and over its murmur, Czacki's voice.

'He's called English Charlie because he went to Oxford and

became an English gentleman — listen, even his Polish has an accent. He goes abroad for his clothes and his dogs.' Czacki nodded, a wicked little smile on his lips. 'If he weren't so nice, Charlie'd be ridiculous, but he is very nice and rich enough to be eccentric.'

Elizabeth absorbed all this like Holy Writ. He was wonderful with an impossible, artificial perfection. He was ridiculous, possibly crazy: it didn't matter.

'I see he's impressed you,' Czacki said drily.

'How do you know him?' she asked. Oh, she was stunned; her interest transparent. She had to know his location, his parentage, where she might meet him again. And yet none of that mattered. He might have been a gypsy: his hands were still beautiful and something about the way he moved, the way his shoulders shifted under the soft grey tweed, was irresistible.

'Dear, I know everyone. His father's important in the Catholic Action movement. Litowski *père* is not my *beau idéal*, but Charlie's all right. You have a rival, Charlie,' he said now, beckoning the young man across the room. 'Come and talk to Countess Elizabeth. She writes for me sometimes — when I can get her out of the social whirl. Charlie's part of my private intelligence service, English branch. But he's not as good a writer as you are, Countess.'

'I'm sure he's very much better,' Elizabeth said. 'I'm just a beginner, Mr. Litowski.'

'Oh, please. Charlie to my friends.'

Czacki smiled: they were a matched pair; two geniuses of the salon, two virtuosos of idleness. He watched the tilt of her head, the way English Charlie laughed, the way they lifted their tea cups, turned to include others in the chitchat, then returned to the table, selected sugar biscuits and considered each other's eyes. Had he been younger, Czacki thought, he'd have fallen for her himself: she had a dainty leg, pretty hair, a very strokable neck. He sipped his tea and decided they did look nice together. And afterwards, when they were the latest gossip, when Charlie danced all night with her at a ball at the Sapieha's, when they were seen almost daily driving in his beautiful Mercedes, when they would come to the paper together with her copy, with his gossip, Czacki would remark,

'Of course, I introduced them. I knew who would suit the little Countess.'

And those who wanted to get on the good side of him, would say, like the Countess, 'But of course, you know everyone.'

That winter, just after Elizabeth's eighteenth birthday, English Charlie came with her to the estate for a visit. The older Countess had met him once, briefly, in Warsaw, but this was a formal visit, a sign that the young couple were serious. Or so it seemed. English Charlie had not only failed to raise the question of marriage with his mother, he had not yet introduced Elizabeth to her, and he was vague about when that crucial meeting would take place.

'You don't know Mother,' he said.

'The point I'm making, dear.' She leaned away from him in the car and sat up very straight.

'Don't be snippy. It's got to be practically a *fait accompli* or she'll make trouble.'

'You don't want me to meet her.'

'I don't want to push her for a decision too soon.'

'Sooner or later,' she said and set her mouth in a thin line. They were too alike. They had exactly the same talent for concealment, for creating the perfect surface. Elizabeth understood; it was one of Charlie's attractions that he was, in a sense, self-created and she still thought him wonderful. He could make her head spin, but she wondered sometimes how strong he was, and if he was as strong as she.

'Well, it will be later,' he said haughtily. 'When I think the time is right.'

They were in heavy traffic near the Saxon Gardens, but Elizabeth reached for the handle anyway and opened the door. A horn blared behind them, Charlie stamped on the brake and swerved, and a horse carriage bolted out of their way. Elizabeth jumped out and, furious, Charlie got out on his side as well, ignoring the horns and the shouts of carriage drivers behind him. Elizabeth put up her chin and told him to go to hell, then she ran into the Gardens, weeping with fury. She adored him, could not live without him, would be sick before evening if he didn't call, but her instincts were sound:

his autocratic mother — glimpsed so far only through the photos in his drawing room and the remarks of some of Félicie's friends — was the obstacle to their happiness. Charlie hoped to ignore that fact and, in the meantime, to secure Elizabeth, whom he saw had an impulsive and passionate temperament, as his mistress. Elizabeth, who rarely failed in a contest of wills, had other ideas.

When he caught up with her near the War Memorial, Charlie was very cold, very English — he even had his umbrella in his hand. But he had come, and Elizabeth decided to speak first. 'It is because I love you.'

He knew that was true, but he recognized a will like his mother's and turned sulky. 'You don't have confidence in me. You don't believe I can arrange things.'

'I know what is proper,' Elizabeth said. 'I promised Cousin Félicie I wouldn't do anything scandalous.'

Charlie laughed in spite of his anger. 'You just stopped traffic on Marszatowska Street. Suppose we'd had an accident.'

'I do have confidence in you — see. You're an excellent driver.' She wiped her nose, furious now that her eyes must be red.

'Well, it was stupid.'

'And you're stupid not to see why I must meet your mother. If you are serious.'

'Of course I'm serious. I love you! We've gone over this before.' Then they were yelling again, both of them quick and angry, until he said, 'We shouldn't be arguing near the monument.' When he turned correct and English, she hated him. She strode down the path, thinking, Let him stay, I don't care; let him come, please! I can't bear it.

Charlie did not follow her this time, but he did come later to the apartment, where sensible Cousin Félicie suggested that he visit Elizabeth's people first. If they were agreeable, then Elizabeth must meet his mother. 'How stupid I was,' she said, when he kissed her in the hallway.

'But delightful.' He managed to kiss her again before he heard Vincenty, the butler, coming to let him out. Maybe she was right; he couldn't go on courting her for weeks and months. She was intoxicating and there were too few chances to be alone in Warsaw, unlike the estate, which, though shabby by Charlie's standards, had a wonderful silence and freedom. The snow was deep when they arrived early in January, and they travelled around the farm in a sled, wrapped in motheaten furs. When he kissed her then, her lips were cold and her hands on his neck burned like ice, but in the old manor house that smelled of wood ash and burning pine they were left almost as much alone as they were outdoors.

'Do you want to see the schoolroom?' she asked.

He pressed her fingers. They'd prowled through the stables and barns, through the vast attics, through the now abandoned kennels, and everywhere there had been a corner, a shadow where for a few moments they could fall into each other's arms and exchange increasingly serious and adept caresses. The schoolroom promised to be dismal and unheated, but private.

'Yes.'

She opened the door and the dogs that followed her everywhere ran in, their claws rattling on the bare wood. Elizabeth did not embrace him immediately, but looked around curiously, nostalgically. Sensing her mood, Charlie released her hand and examined the maps and pictures yellowing on the walls: maps of the modern and ancient republics and the Congress Kingdom, a map of Europe and one of North America, pictures of Pilsudski and Paderewski and Napoleon, and several childish drawings, curling at the edges, including one of a fat, yellow cat. Elizabeth had signed it with a bold scrawl. 'I didn't know you were an artist.'

'Oh, I remember doing that. That was Imbir. I loved that cat. Isn't the writing awful! Jozef made me draw because he thought it would help.'

He touched the side of her neck gently. 'It must have. Czacki says you're very good.'

'Czacki's a flirt.'

'I wouldn't know about that.' It was satisfying that everyone liked her, but it sometimes made him, not jealous, but wary. He rested his chin on her hair and felt the subtle shift of her weight, the slight adjustment in her stance that brought her hip against his thigh. Her responsiveness always delighted him; he knew that she would make him happy. He knew, too, that he should speak formally to the Count, but he was afraid, a little, now that he had seen their estate. The debts would be enormous, and what had liens and what was profitable only that Jew Weisenov would know. He knew what his mother would say, and yet when Elizabeth slipped her arm around him, he kissed her forehead and then her lips.

The day was fading; the shadows across the snow were blue, as blue as the very edge of the iris of Charlie's eyes, which curved like some distant, mysterious planet. Did he love her? He said so, whispered it over and over again, but feeling she had to know for sure, Elizabeth pressed closer to him, as if his flesh would reveal all his secrets.

'Dearest,' he said, 'dearest.' His eyes were closed, giving his face a blind, vulnerable look, and Elizabeth felt a pain that was neither true pain nor pleasure in the very centre of her body. He held her closer and they stumbled together against the wall where the old smudged drawing of Imbir the cat hung. Imbir who had haunted the schoolroom and jumped in at the windows and run along her desk and spoiled her papers so that Pan Jozef was cross. She felt the paper crumble against her shoulder, felt Charlie's breath on her neck, felt his hands touching the collar of her blouse, felt, for a few dizzy moments, his lips on her naked breasts. She was holding him like that, when the door opened and her heart jumped as nimbly as Imbir had, and she felt the blood rush into her face and some pain, too, because it was Jozef.

'Excuse me,' he said. 'I thought the room was empty.' The door closed softly, but Elizabeth drew away from Charlie, straightened her camisole and buttoned her blouse.

'We're practically engaged,' he said, stroking her hair, but the opportunity was lost.

'It's time to feed the dogs,' she said briskly. 'I don't see them enough as it is. They'll forget me.' She was irritated and guilty because it had been Jozef. If it had been Pytor or Zofia or anyone else, she would have laughed with Charlie, but Jozef was different. 'You know,' she said to Charlie later, 'he saved my life.'

'Very appropriate for a tutor,' Charlie said, so Elizabeth did not tell him about the mountain or the miracle, and the

45

next day, when Lev Weisenov arrived for a consultation on her aunt's bequest, she invited not Charlie but Jozef. No one else was there, not even her parents, and she asked the old man why.

'Oh, Countess, I had very specific orders from Madame de Bonheur. Very specific.' He rubbed his hands and huddled nearer the fire.

'We will have coffee,' said Elizabeth, 'you look frozen. This could have waited till milder weather.'

'Not a day; it was Madame's wish that this be settled as soon as you were eighteen. There is some land now and full control of your funds when you are twenty-one. If God spares me, I will see that done as well, though if I am gone, Madame had a man of business in Cracow who will instruct you.'

He opened his leather case and drew out the documents. Both Elizabeth and Jozef were surprised at the amounts.

'I can clear some of the debts on the estate,' said Elizabeth.

'Begging your pardon, Countess, that is one thing you cannot do. Your aunt was very specific about that. The funds are in trust for your own use, and as you can see,' he said, pushing across a document festooned with legal stamps, 'you are restricted in how you can use your principal. The interest, yes, if you wished, but not the principal. This is to protect you.'

'Yet,' said Jozef, 'you also handle the estate's business. There could be a conflict of interest.'

'I trust Pan Weisenow,' Elizabeth said quickly. 'We would have been ruined a dozen times over without him.' She was annoyed with Jozef and wondered if she had made the right decision. They hadn't found anything to say while waiting for Weisenov.

'Pan Goralski is perfectly correct,' the old man said, 'but I have reasons for gratitude, personal gratitude to your dear aunt. I can assure you, your interests will be sacred.'

'It goes without saying, Pan Weisenov. But I am willing to help my parents. I am surprised at my aunt.'

'Countess, forgive me, but your family has been in a delicate way financially since ever I knew them. Your aunt, may God keep her soul, had not enough to clear the estate debts, but enough to keep you, dear Countess, from want. I can find some little monies for you to help the estate, but the rest must stay invested. It was your Aunt's wish, given these uncertain times, that the investments be continually updated.'

He handed a list to Elizabeth.

'Why do we not put it all in Polish bonds?'

Weisenov touched his thin beard and exchanged a glance with Jozef. This was delicate. As a Jew his patriotism was suspect, and the easiest course would be to agree, with a few flattering words. But he had promised Madame de Bonheur, who had saved his sister's boy from deportation. 'Your aunt left you a good number of Polish bonds, but it is considered wise, Countess, to have your investments in different places. Don't put all your eggs in one basket.'

'Pan Weisenov is giving you good advice,' Jozef said. 'Money has little to do with sentiment.'

'Better if it did,' said Elizabeth, and both men were afraid she would try to overrule them.

'Your aunt arranged things as she thought best,' Jozef added. 'She had a great deal of business sense.'

'And I have none, I know. Well, what's this? I think we should sell the German stock.'

'It is not very high now but a better price than a year ago,' said Weisenov.

'They are trying to ruin us and they shouldn't have our money.'

'Very well, Countess. You will make some profit. But it must be reinvested.'

Elizabeth's impulse was to invest it all in Poland — in the mines, maybe — but she remembered Czacki saying there was a great deal of unrest. He predicted serious strikes. Then she had an inspiration. 'What do you think, Jozef? You agree on the Germans, don't you?'

'I think your aunt would have agreed.'

'But where to put it? Do you remember telling me about America, Pan Jozef? About the Polish people you stayed with in Chicago and Detroit?'

'That is where to put your money, Countess. Stocks are low there now, but so great a nation must recover economically,' Weisenov said.

'Well, Pan Jozef, pick something for me. I would trust you

with anything,' she said, looking him in the eyes. 'Anything.'

Jozef's face grew serious. After a moment he said, 'What about meatpacking? People must eat after all. There's a big company called Armour.'

Weisenov nodded. 'I will get the man of business in Cracow to buy this stock.'

'And automobiles. You should buy General Motors, Elizabeth.'

'Ah,' said Weisenov, 'a man of the future. I am agreeable, Countess, these are good suggestions.'

When they were finished, Elizabeth rose and shook their hands formally. 'Thank you for your kindness. You will make me a rich woman. Rich enough, perhaps, to marry English Charlie.'

She was teasing, but as soon as she spoke, she saw Jozef's face and regretted the joke. It was not easy to know what to say to Jozef, now that her affection for him was complicated, now that she was in love with Charlie. 'Forgive me,' she said, taking his hand for a minute. Then she hurried from the room and ran upstairs.

Chapter Five

The road was straight, but narrow and muddy, and the big Mercedes launched itself over a string of ruts, wallowed into a gully, then churned out again, sending the road bed flying. Over the straining motor and grinding gears came an obligato of youthful laughter that increased to shrieks as the big car slewed left, then right, threatening to land its passengers in the ditch as first Charlie, then Elizabeth seized the wheel. They bounced up and down along the ruts, laughing until tears came into their eyes, before Elizabeth suddenly braked and the Mercedes settled back on its haunches like a stubborn horse. 'I see a cart,' she said, pulling the big car well to the side. 'We'll frighten the horse.'

'What a good girl,' Charlie teased, but Elizabeth was not to be drawn, and the Mercedes crept decorously toward a bony grey drawing a loaded manure cart.

'Jesus Christ is Lord,' called the driver, a thin, toothless fellow, sunburned and wrinkled like an old apple.

'Forever and ever,' Elizabeth and Charlie replied together, as the hot, wet, ammonia smell of the cart engulfed them. It was spring, and everywhere the same smells of mud, raw earth, manure.

'Whew,' said Charlie, 'get a move on,' but Elizabeth waited until the old horse was well clear, a tender caution Charlie decided was delightful. He reached over and steered the Mercedes to the side. Elizabeth giggled. 'I was doing well,' she protested, but not too strenuously.

'You're doing marvellously. Put it in neutral.' While she was occupied with the gears, he put his arms around her. The high blue sky was crossed by fast moving clouds, and with the engine off they could hear the water running everywhere, murmuring secrets. Finches fluttered through the shrubby growth at the roadside, and big rooks wandered self-importantly about the new sown fields or rowed themselves with hoarse, resonant cries towards the forest. Elizabeth lay against the leather upholstery and locked her hands behind Charlie's blond head. She loved him; it was marvellous; they were on their way to meet his mother.

As soon as the car drew up in front, Antoni, the butler, came limping out to greet them and a row of chambermaids curtseyed from the steps. Elizabeth admired the fine white stone house and the garden, Madame Litowska's chief vanity now that Charlie's brother had assumed control of the estates. 'You'll have to see his home,' Charlie said when they entered the high, marble-floored hall. 'He's got everything, almost, except my first boar.' He pointed proudly to the trophy, then led the way to the main reception room. There were oriental carpets and good pictures and, awaiting them on the threshold, a large, red chow with suspicious eyes and a blue tongue lolling between prominently displayed teeth. 'Damn,' said Charlie. He took a step forward, but the dog growled. 'Mother! Mother, call Khan.'

There was a sound from within but the dog did no more than twitch one of its ears. Elizabeth stepped forward and extended her hand.

'Careful,' Charlie said. 'He's a marvellous watchdog, but no good with strangers.'

Elizabeth clucked her tongue, and Khan studied her with wary eyes. 'Good boy. Come here.' To Charlie's surprise, the dog came forward, careful and stiff-legged. Elizabeth clucked again and dropped to one knee. Khan sniffed her small fingers gently, and she smiled and stroked the animal's thick woolly coat. 'A fine dog, aren't you?' she asked, and Khan wagged his tail.

'Ah,' said Madame Litowska from the doorway, 'I see your friend is talented.' Madame was straight, well-made and elegant. Her round face had high, prominent cheekbones and a little pointed chin. A famous beauty in her youth, she had aged as gracefully as a pretty, self-centred cat.

Elizabeth stood up, one hand on the dog's head. 'How do you do, Madame Litowska?'

'Countess.'

Charlie went forward to kiss his mother, who stood for a moment with her arm around his waist. 'I see now why Charlie has stayed in Warsaw,' Madame Litowska said. 'It was kind of you, Countess, to bring him home.' Her smile was dazzling but cold, and Elizabeth was warned.

'He promised me the pleasure of meeting you as soon as I learned to drive,' Elizabeth said, 'and here we are.'

'You will whiten my hair,' Madame said to Charlie. 'Come, we need not stand here. We will have coffee.' She snapped her fingers to the dog, but it hesitated beside Elizabeth and Madame noticed. 'You can speak to dogs, I see.'

'All animals,' Elizabeth said simply.

'Indeed,' said Madame Litowska. 'When I was a girl in the dark ages they said witches talked to animals.'

'And did they answer?' Elizabeth asked.

Charlie laughed nervously. 'It's pure love in Elizabeth's case. I even have to hide my guns when she comes to visit. I'll call for the coffee, shall I? We're so thirsty and cold. It may be spring, but the wind is chilly.' He ushered the ladies into the main salon where Elizabeth examined the paintings. Charlie showed her one of his father, and she exclaimed, 'How handsome,' which pleased Madame Litowska. While she and Charlie reminisced, Elizabeth studied her as she had once studied Sister Margaret. Madame had beautiful clothes, magnificent jewels, a personality *trés formidable*; she was a woman of the great world, and at their meetings at lunch, dinner, and bridge, Elizabeth was on her mettle. She made sure to sit as Madame did without touching the back of her chair, to bid carefully at cards, to keep from yawning when the conversation turned, as it so often did, to the Litowskis and, especially, to the shining elder son, Michael.

In compensation, there were splendid horses to ride and the beautiful little estate to explore. The weather was perfect, mild, and sunny. Except for meals, Elizabeth and Charlie were never indoors. They occupied a realm of their own, composed not of fields and woods and farms but a purely mental landscape suffused with erotic delight and anticipation. They had tumbled into a fairy kingdom and in their pleasure in each other, in the spring, in good horses and fine weather, they ignored any sign of hard times.

On Saturday morning, Elizabeth walked in the garden after breakfast while Charlie visited his mother. Khan was with her, trotting along the paths alert for field mice, and she amused them both by breaking off little twigs and throwing them into the shrubbery which the big dog attacked with relish. She was just beginning to tire of this game when the butler appeared: Charlie had had to drive into town on an errand, but would be back for lunch. In the meantime, Madame Litowska wished to speak to her.

Though Madame was still in her robe, her hair was perfectly done and her face, freshly powdered. 'A charming day, Countess.'

'Beautiful,' said Elizabeth, glancing out of the long French windows at the yellow, blue and white spring bulbs, 'but your garden must be lovely at any time.'

Madame Litowska inclined her head gracefully; a lifetime of compliments had not jaded her. 'I am saving this for Charlie. It is delightful — on some mornings I'd even say, "perfection" — but as one gets to a certain age, country living becomes arduous. I have an apartment in Warsaw and a villa outside Cracow. I like the theatre in winter.' She touched the chair opposite as a signal for Elizabeth to sit down, and poured her a cup of coffee.

Just then Khan came into the room, shook the dampness off his woolly coat, and swaggered up to greet the ladies. 'You've made a conquest,' Madame remarked, 'one among many.'

Elizabeth rubbed the dog's head and said nothing.

Madame studied her for a few seconds and then took a sip of coffee. When she set down the cup, she said, 'You must understand, Countess, that it is impossible.'

'I beg your pardon, Madame,' Elizabeth said, flushing. 'I don't understand.'

'Your face tells me that you do. You are in love with my son and hope to marry him. I'm doing you the kindness of telling you that is is impossible. He will not marry you.'

Elizabeth felt her chest contract. 'You seem very sure,

Madame. What then was the purpose of this visit?'

Madame gave a coquettish little shrug. 'Hope. You know men, or — ' she gave Elizabeth a shrewd look ' — you soon will. They are unlike us; they are creatures of dreams, of hopes.'

'Charlie wants to get married.'

'And to marry you, Countess. You have not been deceived. But you are misinformed, I think, about my son's situation. Charlie must marry well.' She waved her hand. 'I know your family is good. After all,' she said with a malicious smile, 'many families have some Jewish blood. We are liberal minded, and of course your father's people have served the Republic nobly.' Again the smile. 'But I will speak plainly: Charlie must marry wealth, and your family's situation — ' She raised her eyebrows.

'You expect a dowry?'

Now Madame laughed. 'I expect an income for Charlie sufficient to run this place. And I would hope for some land or some sound investments.'

'Are you marrying him or selling him?'

'Your distress will excuse your rudeness this one time. I will ask you a question: will my son be happy as a clerk somewhere, working in a business, living in a little flat in Warsaw? I cannot support him. You cannot, Countess, so it is settled. For Michael, I might have considered; for Charlie, I cannot.'

'Charlie is not here. What has he to say? What has he to say to me?' Elizabeth heard her voice rising and gripped the arm of the chair.

'Charlie is gone.'

'You sent him off so that he could not contradict you.'

'I told him this morning.' Madame's voice was flat. 'He will be back this afternoon — to drive you to Warsaw.'

'He left? Knowing?' Elizabeth demanded, but the pain in the back of her throat told her it was true.

'He is fond of you,' Madame said not unkindly. 'Probably he is in love with you, but he knows nothing can be done.'

Elizabeth's anguish turned to fury. She stood up abruptly. 'I won't wait for him.'

'This is childish,' said Madame Litowska. 'People must live within their means.'

'You speak like a peasant with one cow,' said Elizabeth. 'You are afraid of hardship and he is afraid of facing me.'

Madame Litowska rose. 'Do not dare speak to me in this manner.'

'Then have the chauffeur drive me to the station. If that is inconvenient, I'm sure there is a horse free.' There were tears in her eyes and on her face, and though Madame was furious, the car was summoned. Elizabeth waited an hour and a half for the Warsaw train, and until she heard the rumble of the engine, she expected to see the Mercedes roar up to the depot and Charlie run from the car to tell her it was all a mistake. When the train arrived, its plume of smoke sweeping over the fields, its wheels like the thunder of heavy cavalry, she was stunned. She had no vocabulary to encompass such a defeat, and alone in a first class compartment, she whispered to herself, over and over, all the half heard, half forgotten expressions from carters with a broken wheel, peasants with a foundered horse, from miners whom she'd seen with Janusz, desperate and out of work, shouting profanely in the streets, from toughs of the university quarter tipping over some Jewish merchant's stall. There was a world of violence and anguish she had not understood until now, when she was overwhelmed with anger and hatred and disappointment and misery. The train had almost reached the suburbs when her fury shattered like a window struck by a rock, and she put her face in her hands and wept. In the station, she wrote a note to Cousin Félicie and mailed it at the box outside. Then she went down to the platform and waited for the first train for home. She never wanted to see Warsaw again.

Back on the estate, Elizabeth was miserable and restless. She rode morning and afternoon, helped with her mother's charities, drove about with André, played bridge with Jozef; nothing distracted her. Letters came in Charlie's flamboyant hand which she returned unread after agonies of curiosity and self-pity. She was suffocated with regrets and with too recent memories, and when Jozef suggested a trip to Zakopane, she felt such a longing to be in the mountains that she was amazed she had not thought of it herself. This time, of course, there would be no fine resort hotel.

She took the money she'd earned from the paper, bought new hiking boots and a sleeping bag and went off to stay at hostels where the bunks were full of fleas and the poor students lived on dry sausages and bread. Other times she stopped with the Gurals and accompanied Adam, his brother, Wojcik, and his young nephew, Kasimir, into Czechoslovakia for tobacco and cigarettes. They crossed in the short spring nights, alert for the sounds of the frontier patrols, and returned to sleep away the mornings in the village. The Gurals were glad of an extra porter and often, camped out in the hostel, Elizabeth would see Adam or Kasimir striding up the hill. 'God bring luck, Countess!' 'God give, Adam. Tonight?' And they would rendezvous at dusk to set off on paths marked by the feet of generations of smugglers.

These trips were a tonic for Elizabeth: she loved the high, white spring nights, the camaraderie of the Gurals, the black spruce forest with the rustle of a fox or a boar in the undergrowth, the shadows that flickered across the streams like the water sprites the Gurals still half believed in. Even the danger; perhaps, especially that: a guard's challenge, a rifle shot across a glen, a precipitious descent with a heavy pack — these made her heart pound and dissolved the mist of apathy that had descended on the Warsaw train to keep her from the taste of life. Sometimes, returning in the early morning hours, the Gurals would stop to build a fire and enjoy some of the restorative brandy that was the Countess's usual gift. They would lie about the fire, their heads on sacks bulging with loose tobacco or lumpy with boxes of cigarettes, the good tobacco smell mixing with the scent of mountain grass and the resinous breath of the spruces. Then Adam, the oldest and spryest of them, would stand up and pound rhythmically on the ground with his hatchet-tipped mountaineer's staff. The young men would groan and protest their weariness half-heartedly, but the Countess would take up the rhythm, clapping and stamping her feet, until first one, and then another of the smugglers would begin the *zbojnicki*, the Robber's Dance, squatting and jumping like Cossacks and leaping over the fire in celebration of their success, their freedom. Such a life restored her soul.

Elizabeth loitered in the mountains until the evening when

the radio in her usual Zakopane café broke into its programming with the Funeral March. The crowd fell quiet and listened as the state shuddered and pronounced Marshal Pilsudski dead. Elizabeth was stunned. Her father's hero had guided the country as long as she could remember, and now, without warning, he was gone. She toyed with the cutlery on the café table and remembered her father's panegyrics to the Marshal. He used to recreate the great man's campaigns on the dining room table, the condiments standing for Polish and Cossack cavalry, the big pepper mill for a Ukrainian stronghold. As children, she, Czelsaw and André had never tired of hearing about the battle for Warsaw, and in harsh glare of the café, she remembered her father's face by candlelight, his eyes fierce and serious above the thick moustache, the sabre scar white against his cheek, as he laid out the Polish and Russian forces before Warsaw. He could move the glassware about to show how, risking all, Pilsudski and weakened the thin Polish line before the capital to send out a flanking manoeuvre, guessing that the long lines of the Reds could not be strong in every place. The children would lean forward in anticipation to hear how the cavalry had crossed the marshes in the night, every nerve strained for the sounds of enemy patrols, and in the dawn flung themselves on the rear of the Russian lines, screaming, lances ready, their red and white banners beribboning the plains, the white eagles of the Republic flying in the wind of their charge. Those had been the great days, and now in the café, people forgot differences and disillusionment, crossed themselves and murmured a prayer for the Marshal's soul. Some wept, and Elizabeth, who for weeks had thought of nothing but herself and her own sorrows, thought of her father and hurried to the station.

The Marshal's funeral was set for that Friday, and the Count ordered his old military trunks opened. If he had the faults of his class, the Count had preserved its virtues. His hands shook and his cheeks were gaunt, but he appeared to the family in his Legion uniform, the uniform he had worn at forty-five when he had charged with the Uhlans. Elizabeth smiled for him, though her heart contracted at the sight. How pale he was, how thin! It was a bad sign that he had lost so much weight, and André whispered that the old man had coughed blood while she was in Warsaw during the winter. But there was no question but that he would go to the funeral and then to the salute on the Mokotov parade ground. 'I can't march, but I'll be there. Some of us old chaps have to be there. Right, Elizabeth?'

Her mother gave her a look, but Elizabeth knew her father would rather die than fail his old commander. 'I will go with you, but then we must come straight home.' The Count gave a crisp, military nod and straightened his shoulders. 'All right?' he asked.

'Fit to command any company.'

'Once,' he said gently, 'but I'll see the Marshal off. Poland will not have such a man again.'

The coffin was carried to the Mokotov and placed on a mound blanketed in wreaths while muffled drums beat like a grieving heart. The red and white flag on the coffin shivered in the approaching storm as if at the precariousness of fate, as if the great dreamer it covered still dreamed – and who could imagine what he might dream for Poland now? First he had dreamed the Polish army out of a rifleman's club and a horseless cavalry, and then he dreamed the Polish Republic out of the rubble and slaughter of the Great War. After this success he dreamed the secret, quixotic dream of commanding the Polish Army in battle. He was fifty-three when the chance came, and he took that army all the way to Kiev and back and saved Warsaw at the eleventh hour. For such a man, many faults can be forgiven, much misery forgotten; so now, from the length of the parade ground, units of foot and cavalry from every regiment of the army approached his bier. The pride of the nation stepped forth with magnificent horses, the light coats of the greys pale against the dark sky, a splendid equestrian spectacle – how obsolete only certain men in Berlin truly guessed. The pounding of the horses' feet brought forth thunder, and the funereal clouds were split by streaks of lightning. The crowd stirred. – What now? They thought – and looked over the vast eastern plains whence came their enemies. The Count stood stiffly at attention, tears on his face, and Elizabeth took his arm.

The Uhlans' lances flickered like points of fire against the storm and rain came spattering down. Over the Count's protests, Elizabeth put up an umbrella.

'What is a little rain?' he asked angrily.

'You'll catch pneumonia,' Elizabeth said.

The 7th Uhlans distracted the Count, who searched his old regiment for Czeslaw and his friends. The rain pounded on the umbrella and the Count shivered with cold and weariness. By the time the ceremony was finished and the storm cleared, he was white with exhaustion, and when Elizabeth saw Czacki in the crowd, she did not hesitate.

'Countess! My pleasure. And Janusz's too. We've been desolate without you. How do you do, Count? We have seen a sombre pageant. A true memorial to a great man.' Czacki tested his headlines and studied the Countess. So she was back, lovely as ever, though the old man looked ready to drop.

'I must find a taxi or a carriage for my father,' she said in a low voice. 'It's too far for him to walk to the streetcar.'

'We have transport. May we offer you a lift, Count? Please, let me insist. We've missed your daughter: one of the ornaments of Warsaw society.' Czacki sent Janusz to get their driver; he had prudently hired a car to take him to the station and then on to cover the reaction to the funeral train.

'And are you back, Countess?' he asked when they were all squeezed into a vehicle of great age and dubious origin.

'For the funeral only,' she said.

'You're not going to hide in the country! You're as bad as the Litowskis. You gave them such a fright, they've sent Charlie to Canada.' He gave her an appraising look: the stories of the breakup had been fascinating and had lost nothing in the retelling. 'You need to get writing again. You could do me a favour.'

'Whatever could that be?' Elizabeth asked irritably. Next to her father's grief, Czacki seemed shallow and cynical, and he knew Charlie and so reminded her of all she'd rather forget.

'Janusz is going to Paris for me, but he can't take the position immediately. You could go for a couple of months, couldn't you? My dear, it's the City of Light! And Janusz will help you out, go over the information he wants you to get. As I told you before, he's a substantial sort. You'll find him interesting.'

Chapter Six

After Elizabeth returned home, Czacki wrote her letters retailing the latest gossip and begging her to reconsider Paris. Replete with malice and with flattering complaints about his boredom in her absence, his letters were as frequent as a lover's, but Czacki had realised early that the Countess was not for him. Instead he now wished to select whom she would have, and he was determined it should be one of his protégés. So he began to tempt her interest, subtly mentioning Janusz and teasing her for sticking in the country at 'this time of interest and crisis'.

'He is full of nonsense,' she said to Jozef, as they walked across the new mown fields. The hay was coming in and the sky was crossed by innumerable larks and swallows and small insects that sent up a humming column of ecstatic life. Now and again the vibration of the summer — the birds, the insects, the sun, the heavy wagons, the light breeze — would set up a sympathetic tremor in her soul and she would remember Charlie and the taste of first, innocent passion. 'He says,' she continued, 'that Slawek will be out and that Smigly-Rdyz is to be a power. Huh!'

As prime minister and organizer of the pro-government bloc, Walery Slawek was Pilsudski's political heir; Smigly-Rdyz, who had taken Kiev and commanded at Warsaw in 1920, was the Marshal's successor as Inspector General of the army.

'What does he base that on?' asked Jozef, who was much more politically interested and astute than Elizabeth. He enjoyed Czacki's gossip even as he was irritated by the man's ridiculous flirtatiousness and pretension.

'He says Slawek has been deeply depressed since the Marshal's death. Let's see: "His love for the Marshal being the passion of his life, 'Faithful Walery' has scarcely survived the loss of his friend and idol."'

'That sounds ready for the typesetter,' Jozef observed.

'He always sounds that way; he even speaks in leads and paragraphs. "It has been observed that the PM is barely able to fulfil his duties and begs off official functions. Worse yet, my dear —"' at this Jozef winced — '"the Faithful One does not show the lust for power essential to political males."'

'There could be something to that; it cannot be easy to assume command after having been number two man for so long. And if not he, the party will have to find another figurehead.'

'The Marshal was no figurehead.'

'No, but your friend Czacki may be right. They may try to give the country a strongman who looks like the Marshal — to be under the control of the politicians, of course.'

'He is so cynical,' said Elizabeth.

'I suspect it is his line of work.'

'He wants me to work for him. Shall I have to become cynical, too?' There was a playfulness in her voice, almost a flirtatiousness.

'Never,' he said, 'you're too light-minded.'

She laughed and gave him a little push; he might have been her contemporary, a boy she knew, instead of her old tutor. 'Don't be a tease. Shall I go? Go to Paris, I mean?' She was serious now and took his arm. He was the only one who understood her; it always came back to that, to that and to the mountain, almost forgotten now save in dreams.

'Do you want to?'

'I think I ought to get away. I don't know if I'm interested in Polish immigration to France or whatever it is Czacki wants, but I want to get away.' She hung her head and bit her lip. She had spoken to no one and now it burst forth: 'I loved Charlie so much. I cannot bear his loss.'

Jozef put his arm around her as if she were ten again, the recipient of some petty grief. The Countess looked at him in anguish, and for a moment they were close once more.

Jozef rested his chin on her hair. 'There will be others; there are others who love you.'

She drew back and met his glance, but her love for Charlie had left a vacuum in her heart. 'You are always wise,' she said. 'I can go for a month or two.'

'Most young people would give their eye teeth to go to Paris,' he said, resuming his bantering tone. 'It will be an education in itself – all you never learned form me.'

Elizabeth laughed and pressed his hand. 'I wish you were coming. You and André, too. Then I know Paris would be fun.'

Before she left, her father gave Elizabeth some money and told her to not to waste her time on journalism, but to learn how to dress, order a meal and drink wine. She had been touched by this foolish extravagance and promised to do her best. Though she still drank wine sparingly, Elizabeth had haunted the couturiers, and in her black and white Chanel suit she looked like an elegant Parisian. The French were charmed with her chic and delicate appearance, and her interviews were always a great success. Czacki received a stream of short pieces on the styles of the capital, on the notables of the day, on the doing of various celebrities, Polish and French. These were fun; this was the Paris she loved; the elegant, sophisticated, beautiful Paris of fine food, great art, beautiful buildings and ornate gardens, the Paris of daydreams where she was greeted in Polish.

'Good afternoon, Countess.'

The white sand walks, the brown and gold leaves of the Tuileries came into focus. 'Good afternoon, Jakub.' She smiled and the old man stopped sweeping and leaned on his broom.

'It is a fine afternoon, Countess, and perhaps a special one?' He nodded and she understood he had noticed her new suit.

'Maybe. I am to meet someone from home.'

'Ah,' said Jakub sadly, 'from Warsaw. In spite of all this,' he gestured toward the trees, the statuary, the pools, the triumphal arch, 'I was happier on the Vistula.'

'But it would be a terrible thing not to be homesick at all,'

Elizabeth said and the old man laughed.

'That is right and you are a patriot,' he said. 'A pity you don't smoke; then you would be a philosopher, too.'

At this hint, Elizabeth opened her purse. 'My friend left these,' she said, handing over a few cigarettes.

The old man winked, knowing quite well that she bought them for him, for the pleasure of his company, for the sound of a true Warsovian. He appreciated the Countess, enjoyed her humour, saw, despite her gaiety, that her soul had a touch of melancholy. 'Thank you, Countess. And thank your noble friend. When one is far from home, memories are sweet.'

'Sweeter than those, I should think.' She wrinkled her nose at the Gauloises.

'Tobacco is one of God's little gifts, Countess. Not to be scorned.' He tucked the cigarettes carefully into his blue overalls and picked up the broom.

'*Dowidzenia, Jakub.*'

He moved slowly along the path, sweeping the leaves and litter, an old horseman too arthritic to ride, an old peasant too weak for heavy work, an old man with no land. There were so many of them, and this was the side of Paris she hated: the exploited misery of her countrymen.

Every afternoon well-dressed children came with their parents and nurses to play in the gardens, and dozens of them were running here and there on the wide, softly dusty avenues. The air was mild; autumn was only present in the leaves, brown and gold like ancient coins, and in a certain violet softness along the horizon. Summer was finished; the Parisians had returned and with them, Czacki's favourite journalist, Janusz Bronski. Frowning a little at the thought, Elizabeth selected a chair near the Orangerie where she could watch the stollers approaching up the wide stone steps. She had not been waiting long when she heard a low, masculine voice behind her. 'Countess?'

She turned around. 'Mr. Bronski! I expected you from the other direction.'

'I hardly knew you. You've gone native,' Janusz teased. He remembered Elizabeth as a frivolous teenager; now she seemed elegant, even sophisticated, and he was caught off-guard.

'When in Rome. Besides, I promised my father.'

Janusz laughed. 'How very *ancien régime*.'

'He gave me good advice. I can go anywhere here; the officials expect it and the working men appreciate it. This is a curious country.'

'Not to be understood in a day,' Janusz said sententiously. 'I'm looking forward to a long stay. The immigration question will take time to investigate.'

'If you mean our people that is easily told,' the Countess said abruptly. 'Our poor countrymen sleep in filth and load coal for a few francs a day when they are lucky, and beg in the streets when they are not.'

'You've been to the hostels? To the employment brokers?' Janusz asked. There was a note of resentment in his voice: this was his story and he was prepared to be annoyed if she had already sent something to Czacki.

Elizabeth laughed. 'You needn't leave this park to see the situation. The streets of Paris would be knee deep in dirt if it weren't for East Europeans.'

'Anecdotal material is not enough,' Janusz said. 'You've found me a list of hostels and homeless shelters? I'd told Czacki that was essential.'

She produced a leather notebook and ran her finger down the entries. 'I also spoke with the employment minister and some union officials. I told them you might follow up my visit.'

'I'll have to,' Janusz said. 'Although the stories you sent back to Czacki weren't bad. He's used them all.'

'Not all,' Elizabeth said drily. 'One about the French border signs that prohibit "gypsies, Poles, Bulgarians and Rumanians" never saw the light.'

'It was naive to expect him to print that. You must appreciate our political situation. The French alliance is vital.'

'But apparently our alliance is not so vital to the French.'

'They are worried about jobs,' Janusz said. He spoke brusquely and a shade impatiently like a busy instructor with a dull or disinterested pupil. 'You should realise their own people are out of work. We're coming out of a worldwide depression.'

Elizabeth glanced around at the magnificence of the

Tuileries. 'Their soul is set on their comfort,' she remarked, and thought fleetingly and bitterly of the Litowskis. 'Their fine food, their great art and beautiful buildings, their elegant clothes.' She stretched out one arm and examined the fine, handsewn braid and the ornamental buttons. She loved the beauty and luxury of it and at the same time was repelled by all it stood for.

'Ah, a Savanarola in Chanel!' Janusz was irritated, the more so because she piqued his curiosity. And why? She was ignorant. He could tell from her expression that she was uncertain who Savanarola was.

'When you've been here for a while, see what you think,' she said. His superior air was insufferable, particularly when his accent was so poor. 'Of course, once your French is better, you will pick up more of the nuances.'

'I trust my Polish will be good enough for the workers,' Janusz replied, stung.

'But maybe not your manners. The Polish workman is a gentleman, whatever the intelligensia might be.' She tore the page out of her notebook and handed it to him.

'I could find these on my own,' he said, crumpling the paper. 'I don't need some dilettante's help.'

'Czacki's orders; but do what you like. I won't waste my time.' She turned quickly and walked down the broad curving steps towards the metro. She'd write to Czacki. Perhaps she'd go home. Better yet, she'd stay. There were other papers and her French was perfect – even the French journalists said so. She was cross enough to draft the letter twice and then, the next afternoon, still wondering if it was strong enough, left it on her desk while she went to a reception for a Polish violin virtuoso.

'My dear you're here,' said her hostess, 'and with your little notebook! Not something on our gathering for Mademoiselle L!' Her bright blue eyes were round and seemingly disconcerted, and Elizabeth hastened to reassure her.

'No, no,' Elizabeth said quickly. 'Just Mademoiselle L.'s concert schedule – and a few words from her on the joys of touring France.' Despite this reassurance, she thought her hostess looked a shade disappointed. 'I could, of course, add that she was interviewed at a charming private gathering given by – '

'Ideal! Quite sufficient, and not a word more. Now promise, Countess, because I have a very handsome surprise for you.'

'You can rely on me, Madame.'

'I am sure, Countess. And now for my surprise.' She led the way into the throng and touched a man's sleeve. 'Here you are!' she said to him. 'Just as I told you: the most fascinating young woman in Paris.' She turned back to Elizabeth. 'Countess, this is Janusz Bronski. He's been promised so long I thought he would never come!' She beamed with the pleasure of a significant introduction, and there was nothing Elizabeth could do but express delight. Janusz responded with an ironic bow.

'I know you two will have so much to talk about,' their hostess burbled. 'Now, Countess, he knows no one, so you're to take him in hand! I leave you in the best of care, Mr. Bronski.' She positively radiated good will, and Janusz gallantly kissed her hand.

When she was gone in a trail of greetings and compliments, there was an awkward moment. Janusz cleared his throat.

'She and Czacki think along the same lines,' Elizabeth said.

'Quite incredible how they could both — '

' — make the same mistake?'

'Exactly, this is ludicrous.' There was another awkward silence.

'She will be mortified,' Elizabeth said at last, 'if we can't at least think of something to say.'

'You had plenty to say when we last met.'

'I could say the same about you. Of course I was wrong then,' Elizabeth said. 'I thought you were the professional. I thought you wanted to get a really good story about the Polish question.'

'You're a good example of a Polish question,' Janusz said, starting to get hot again and not much caring whether their hostess heard him or not.

To his surprise, the Countess laughed out loud. 'This sounds like "The Journalists and the Polish Question",' she said.

'No, it's "Unemployment and the Polish Question",' Janusz snapped, but his expression changed subtly.

'"Society receptions and the Polish Question"?'

'Frivolous. That never was a Polish Question. The classic Polish Question was "The Elephant and the Polish Question".'

They both laughed, and Janusz said, 'I am sorry about yesterday, really. I was just tired and – I don't know – out of sorts.'

This was generous of him, and Elizabeth felt some major concession was required. 'I was sick of hearing about you from Czacki. Do you suppose he means to fire me now that you're here?'

'Not for a while, I shouldn't think. He told me you got the best interviews. That's honest.'

Elizabeth put out her hand. 'No more arguments then until we get back to Warsaw.'

'Agreed.' He looked around the salon and signalled to the waitress for some tea. 'You know, Czacki actually gave me an advance for expenses,' he said when they had both been served.

'You are favoured!'

'What about dinner after this? For truce negotiations. You could tell me a good restaurant and I could tell you how to investigate the immigration problem.'

'A good dinner?'

'A very good dinner. On Czacki.'

'I'll meet you at eight,' said Elizabeth.

In the next weeks he dragged her to all the hostels, doss houses, shelters. They spoke to workers, priests, Salvation Army matrons, government officials and beggars in the street. Elizabeth could type and every day she transcribed the notes in their tiny office and prepared final copy. While she worked at the machine, Janusz discussed social policy, and they usually argued back and forth until she began making mistakes and sent him out to buy crêpes and a bottle of Vittel.

'Of course, at home, it's mostly the woman,' she remarked one afternoon.

He looked up.

'Who get the worst of poverty. If a man has a job or some land, he's happy. The women have a dozen pregnancies and die at forty-five. Here it's the men who are utterly broken down. It looks worse because we're not accustomed to that.'

'One's natural; one's socially caused,' Janusz protested. 'Unemployment's preventable. We could restructure the economy to absorb more of our labour.'

'French women don't have such big families.'

'They are not truly Catholic,' Janusz said, a little shocked, for on religious and ethical matters he was deeply conventional. 'But we could provide jobs for our labour. If we break the Jewish monopoly in trade and retail businesses, and in the learned professions.'

'Many Jews are poor enough,' Elizabeth said. True, her relatives were wealthy but they had been Catholic for two generations.

'I don't blame them as much as the *schlacta*. This fear of soiling your hands with money. It's got to stop.' He slid from his habitual perch on the edge of his desk and walked to the window, where he stood thoughtfully with his hands in his pockets. Bronski was a big, solid man, taller than Charlie and more muscular. The French women whom she knew said he was *magnifique* and *trés beau,* judgements which, on closer acquaintance, Elizabeth could not entirely share. He was virile and able, but she still remembered Charlie, who was fun.

'The peasants don't want a shop. They want land.'

'Land hunger, yes. To be resisted. There the large landowners are correct. Efficiency is essential and the big estate is far more practical than dwarf holdings. No one debates that.'

'Efficient, practical, you'd have us all German,' Elizabeth teased. She had not liked what she had seen of Germany: the omnipresent swastikas, the casual arrogance and the aggressive, almost hysterical patiotism and anti-semitism.

'Listen, you don't have to go along with the nonsense of the *volk* and the Nuremburg Laws to see they're on to something. A few years ago they carried their money in wheelbarrows. Now they're dangerous because their economy is disciplined and strong. That's why I've supported the government and the BBWR, right or wrong. Poland's got to have a strong economy and a disciplined political life or it's right back to 1773.'

'Our army's too strong for that,' Elizabeth said confidently.

'Yes, but, as Napoleon said, the army travels on its stomach. And we're poor.' He sighed and sat down at his desk and began to cite statistics. Elizabeth resumed typing, the keys making a satisfactory clatter. She was not particularly good with her hands, never having had to do any manual labour, and she was proud of having conquered the machine. Janusz, in contrast, picked out the keys painfully, but she had refused to become his secretary entirely. No matter how he badgered and teased, she never did anything but retype notes and final copy. Janusz was clever, well-educated and domineering, and Elizabeth felt she had to stand up to him.

'You'll come?'

She hadn't been listening, having been absorbed in the fate of an ex-miner who had walked from Silesia to Paris in search of work. She looked up. 'Sorry. I have to concentrate when I'm typing numbers and things.'

'I said I have to visit my aunt in Dieppe. You said you've never been to the sea. Would you like to come?'

'To Dieppe? *Quelle enfante*!' Madeline exclaimed and took Elizabeth's arm. 'You had us fooled with your convent manners.' She gave a throaty laugh. 'What about this one, Annette, eh? *Formidable*!'

'And here we've been putting runs in our stockings trying to catch his eye. It is too bad of you, Elizabeth,' Annette said.

Madeline and Annette worked in the neighbouring office of a silk importing concern. They were both lively, attractive young women, mad for boyfriends, movies, cigarettes and all things American. Elizabeth liked their friendliness and independence and rather envied their disregard of convention.

'Oh, nonsense. I'm only going to meet his elderly aunt.'

'His aunt!' Madeline shrieked. 'We are done in, Annette. *L'enfante* has struck a coup, indeed.'

'She is right,' Annette said, 'and lucky you. He is so handsome. And rich, yes? I am sure.'

'I've told you he's just a friend — just a colleague. It's a chance to see the water, that's all.'

Madeline shook her head. 'We will go to a café and have a drink and enlighten *l'enfante*. To have so much style and so little sophistication is a tragedy.' She put her hand to her heart in a pantomine of deep emotion, but said nothing more until they were comfortably seated. Then Annette, who was privy to any intelligence Madeline possessed, began.

'He is serious, of course, the *beau* Janusz.'

'He doesn't even like me much,' Elizabeth said, 'and I certainly don't care a lot for him.'

'*Quel dommage*! But when a man like that takes a convent girl visiting, it's a sign.'

'A man like what?'

The two Frenchwomen rolled their eyes.

'Well, dear,' said Madeline, 'I'll take you at your word that you are only a friend and tell you that he has a mistress.'

'So soon?'

'Ah, the innocence of her! Yes, it's true,' Annette chimed in, 'for we've seen him going into a *maison particulière* in the Rue de General Lanrezac.'

'And with a blonde! Quite attractive.'

'A little dumpy,' said Annette, who resented the competition.

This was another side of Bronski, and Elizabeth was curious.

'It goes to show,' said Madeline. 'And now a family visit.'

'Most likely a trial run,' said Annette.

'Oh, most definitely,' Madeline agreed. 'He has turned serious and is looking for a marriageable girl.'

'But having had so many that weren't marriageable,' Annette continued, making a wry face, 'he's not sure of his taste.'

'*Voila*! The aunt. A visit to Dieppe.'

'That's it! – unless he hopes for an intimate rendezvous.' Madeline raised her eyebrows.

'Perhaps I shouldn't go, Elizabeth said, and then could have bitten her tongue. She sounded so priggish. In Warsaw even Cousin Félicie was considered 'advanced'; here in Paris, she would be the most conventional of matrons as Elizabeth was considered a country innocent.

'Ah, *mon Dieu*!' Madeline exclaimed. 'What is life without experience? And those shoulders and those Slavic eyes. My dear, I'd go in a minute.'

Elizabeth laughed. 'All right, I'll go. For the experience.'

Chapter Seven

Elizabeth stood on the wide shingle beach at Dieppe and watched the murky ocean rolling and surging, its forward tentacles slithering, with a soft and sinister murmur, through the stones. She loved the power of it, the wet, salty, fertile smell, the restless, opalescent light, the unending boom and whisper of the surf. To Josef, she wrote, 'I have seen the sea at last,' and stopped. She was not good when it came to psychological nuances, to inner currents. There are tides besides the ones which roil the surface of the deep, and the little port town with its cold November beach had given her intimations of them.

She and Janusz had taken an early train from Paris to Rouen where they stopped to see the cathedral and the Tour de Jeanne d'Arc, the saint's English prison. Both were dark with the soot and dust of the ages, but the carved front and astonishing rose window of the cathedral were splendid, and inside the radiant glass stained the worn stones of the floor and dyed Our Lady's robes in purest blues and reds. The tower, black and claustrophobic, made Elizabeth shiver. 'I'd hate to be shut in here,' she exclaimed. 'How she must have longed for freedom!'

'And you?' Janusz asked.

'I could not stand it.'

'You like to be free.' It was neither a question nor a statement, and she caught just a hint of the *double entendre*. She could not read his eyes. He'd been irritated on the trip because she'd entered into a long conversation with an old lady who was returning to her farm after visiting grandchildren near

Paris. The old lady had described her geese and sheep, numbered her chickens and their breeds, spoken of an orchard which had borne a fine crop that year. Janusz was bored – although he'd been silent enough before – but Elizabeth was delighted. The woman had the true love of the soil, and, longing as she was for the country, Elizabeth could almost smell the orchard, heavy with fruit, could almost see the dusty yard filled with fat, clean chickens. They talked on – horses next, Normandy being a great horse breeding area – and Janusz lit his pipe.

He had thought how unfortunate it was that the very things which intrigued him about Elizabeth should also annoy him. Her sociability was wonderful for his work. She charmed everyone; even the immigrant workmen liked her, accepted her title, admired her fine manners – which reminded him that no change was likely from a nation of eighteenth-century aristocrats.

Then there was her promiscuous sympathy. The old lady, now. A well-off peasant who perhaps could read, perhaps not. Dried up, ugly as sin. He knew that she and Elizabeth would be thick as thieves in a few more miles. She was one of the better ones. Every beggar in the arrondisement knew the Countess, as did the stray dogs and the thin, suspicious cats that hung around the courtyard at the office and waited for their daily milk. It was the smile, of course, that made her almost a beauty, that and a perfectly genuine interest in and concern for other people's wishes, which made her break off her examination of the prison now, and take his arm.

'I enjoyed this so much. What a wonderful idea! But you'll have things you want to see. We should go.'

She took a pleasure in life that made her sweet, and when she was sweet, Janusz forgot all he disliked about her. They stopped at a café near the station for a bowl of fish soup and bread. He talked about some ideas he had for articles, about his desire to go to London, about himself, in short, and she gave him all her attention, all her enthusiasm. London would be wonderful, but wasn't English hard! Because they each knew a smattering of words and place names, they amused themselves by making up sentences. 'Hello. Waterloo? I want a room –'

' — for the cat in Leicester Square — '

'Is your seat — '

' — excuse, please. Good-bye. Taxi.'

'For Piccadilly . . .'

It was only when he added 'and Savile Row' that her eyes flickered momentarily at the thought of English Charlie and his fine London suits. So she had loved Charlie and had not forgotten him yet, Janusz thought. But she might. He glanced at his watch. 'Time for our train.'

The cloud lifted as suddenly as it had appeared. 'I can't wait to see the sea,' she said.

Janusz's great-aunt was French, immensely old, stooped and eccentric. Her face was pale and flaccid, devoid of life except for the alert, amused eyes, like bright beads sunk in the lines and pouches of her skin. This aunt loved gossip and news of any kind, and to its collection and dissemination she devoted her remaining energies. The telephone linked her to a selection of cronies as ancient as herself, while news of the younger generation was supplied by Simone, her tall and handsome cook-housekeeper. The old lady digested the latest information in her high, dark bedroom until dinnertime, when she descended to the lower floor in a tiny lift. The dining room faced the Channel, and Elizabeth could hear the mysterious boom of the surf beyond the thick velvet curtains.

'It must be a beautiful view,' she said.

'I've seen wrecks,' said the old lady. 'Some Dieppoises used to live on the flotsam, there were so many ships lost in the Channel. When I was a girl there were still sailing ships. Lovely things. And of course, all the fishing boats were sail powered.'

Simone came in with a huge tureen of mussels, redolent with garlic.

'These are gathered from the rocks offshore, Countess. You're never had them? Ah, Simone can do them justice.' The old lady beamed. She'd had famous dinners once with twenty, thirty, forty guests at a time. In the isolation of age, the banter and compliments of the young people were a tonic.

'You'll take the Countess to the church,' she told Janusz. 'It's very interesting. The beach will be too cold. You want to come in July, Countess. Ask Janusz to bring you then. If I live until summer, you will be more than welcome.'

'I thought you planned to live to be one hundred, Aunt Claudia.'

'It's getting close, nephew. When I outlived my husband,' she told Elizabeth, 'I wanted to die. If I could have died with Stanislaw, I would have. But I didn't. So, as I hated his brother, begging your pardon, nephew, I outlived him for the inheritance. I quarrelled with my sister; there was nothing for it but to outlive her and all her family. Her last child died a year ago. What am I to do? I am ninety-six and only my dear Janusz is left. You will take my reason for living from me,' she said affectionately and patted his arm. 'Now,' she said to Elizabeth, 'tell me about Paris. Tell me about my nephew. Even if it is scandalous, it is all right.'

'I should have told her the gossip about you,' Elizabeth remarked the next day as they walked through the narrow streets toward the church of St. Jacques. 'It would have done her heart good.'

'Would it? And what might that be?'

'It's said you keep a mistress.'

'Then it must be said Czacki pays me more than he does,' Janusz said, without denying it. 'She'd have liked that. She's a terrible old person, isn't she?'

'I like her. I think she's *formidable*.' Elizabeth gave him a shrewd look, and Janusz was not pleased.

'Some things mean nothing,' he said.

The old church had been built by masons of extraordinary skill and invention. Gargoyles leapt to the rafters and writhed along the buttresses, and every pillar and column supported a mass of grotesque and vigorous life. Elizabeth found the effect disconcerting and, as if to dispel unseemly thoughts, lit candles before the Virgin. Their soft light flickered warmly, but the immense nave behind lay in gloom like some vast engine whose workings were mysterious, whose purpose, unknown. Elizabeth was glad to get outside again, to be along the sea front, where all ambiguity was blown away by the wind that raced in off the Channel to chap their faces and tug their coats. The tide was out, but once they reached the shingle they could see the surf, boiling and pounding, and a line of whitecaps stretching halfway to the horizon. Elizabeth ran across the shifting pebbles to the wet, stained edge and hurled a rock that broke the satin front of a wave and sank with a low plock. The wind whipped the tops off the breakers and skittered the foam inland. She had to jump back from a rapidly advancing wave, but the sea was wonderful: rhythmic, powerful, a beautiful pale green under the slate-coloured sky. Against the stark white of the cliffs and the buff and grey of the town, Janusz's black coat and long red scarf were vivid accents. Otherwise, the whole shore beyond the harbour was deserted.

They returned across the shingle and walked along a strip of grass to the base of the cliffs. Elizabeth was surprised at their softness.

'It's chalk. Schoolroom chalk. You can write with it.' Janusz found a board among the washed up seaweed and, when they sat down out of the wind, he wrote her name on it in block letters. Then he took out his pipe, but Elizabeth soon jumped up again and scrambled on to an outcropping of rock at the edge of the surf. Though the water boomed up around her, she was undeterred by the spray and the slippery wrack, amusing Janusz with her almost childish pleasure. She was not like Leila, his friend in the Rue de General Lanzerac, who would have found the shore in November frightful. But Elizabeth did not belong in the city or, perhaps, did not belong under too many restraints. That was the thought which teased him, which made him notice her unusual prettiness, which aroused him. He had grown tired of the semi-professional attentions of Leila and her predecessors, yet he knew himself well enough to know that any replacement would have to satisfy his passionate temperament. He sensed that in Elizabeth's blithe and fearless independence he might find what he wanted, and he watched her clamber back ahead of the incoming tide, now lunging hungrily at every crevasse in the rock.

'It's coming in,' she said. She was breathless from the wind, which swirled her thick, wavy hair across her red cheeks.

'Of course,' he said. 'All those rocks will soon be underwater. It's called the tide.'

'Don't be condescending, it's so beautiful to watch.' She

brushed away her hair impatiently and tried to fasten it with a clip.

So are you, Janusz thought. 'You will be cold,' he said. 'We should go back.'

'It's only three-thirty.'

'It will be getting dark in an hour. And you're shivering already.'

She stuck her hands in her pockets and hunched her shoulders. 'It's the wind.'

'You need a scarf.' He unwound his red wool muffler and slung it over her head and around her neck. 'To match your red nose,' he said.

Elizabeth tossed her head and tried to escape, but Janusz drew up the ends and pulled her against him. He wound the scarf once, twice about her neck and folded the ends across her face. 'Better?'

'I'll look like an Arab and now you'll be cold.'

He shook his head, pulled the scarf away from her mouth and kissed her. The stones were loose and uneven and Elizabeth slipped, so that he put his arms around her and kissed her again, surprising her with an eager intensity quite without playfulness or tenderness. He was not like Charlie, not at all, and what he offered was a sensation as powerful and impersonal as the rolling surf. As they walked back in silence, his arm flung across her shoulders, Elizabeth wondered if in that emotion she would forget Charlie, forget love, forget happiness – but she had no opportunity to find out. When they reached the aunt's house, Simone told them that a great friend had visited unexpectedly and Madame wanted a little party, perhaps cards. Their presence upstairs was required immediately.

The next day it rained. They had walked to the harbour in the morning drizzle because Elizabeth wanted to see the fishing boats, but after lunch it began to pour. The wind was still from the sea, and the rain lashed in sheets against the high windows of the parlour. There was a telescope mounted on the seaward side of the room, a relic of the late, beloved Stanislaw, and while Janusz read, Elizabeth strained her eyes trying to pick out the horizon, which wavered clear for an instant, only to be buried in another spatter of rain. 'I think it's letting up,' she said. She was always restless and bored when she had to stay in without some work.

Janusz looked at the glass, streaming with water. 'You'd be drowned in an instant,' he said, and returned to his book.

'I think there's a ship,' she said a few minutes later. 'Yes, and it's in trouble. You should see it pitch. I'm afraid it will sink.'

He closed his book. 'Most likely you've got the focus wrong again.' Janusz found Elizabeth's mechanical ineptitude rather endearing.

'It's perfect. I can see the mast. Oh, now I've lost it. There it is. The waves are so high.'

She stepped back so that he could have a look. 'Do you see it? It won't sink, will it?'

The field of the telescope was a boiling grey surface, and he was about to say that she was seeing things, when the stubby fishing boat came bouncing into view. It was labouring through the heavy sea, its bow rising and plunging like a frightened colt. 'He'll be making for the harbour. He's not too far out.'

'Will they be all right?' Elizabeth persisted, and now her tenderheartedness, which sometimes irritated him, seemed charming to Janusz.

'Oh, I think so. They are very skilful sailors.'

She leaned in front of him, still anxious, and put her eye to the scope. 'He is moving along now, isn't he?'

Janusz pulled one of his aunt's small wine-coloured sofas to the table and sat down. 'We'll watch him. If he gets into trouble we can phone to the harbour master.' He reached for her hand and drew her down beside him.

Elizabeth adjusted the telescope, turning it slightly to follow the ship, a tiny dark shape in a swirl of greens and greys. The sky and sea had lost any definite boundaries and the ship floundered between them in desperate confusion. She was aware, too, of the same storm enclosing the room, separating them from the rest of the world. Janusz reached over and laid his hand on the back of her neck. 'How is he doing?' he asked softly. He might have been asking if she loved him, if she wanted him.

'He's still making headway.' His hand seemed to have

gathered an electrical charge for she could feel a prickling down her spine.

'As long as he's not wallowing. If a ship gets going from side to side, it's in trouble.' He stroked her back.

'I don't think so, but you'd better look.'

He leaned over and rested his chin on her shoulder. The ship had nearly reached the point of land which marked the entrance to the harbour. 'He's almost at the point. You know where the seaman's church is.'

'May Our Lady protect him,' Elizabeth said, and crossed herself. 'Can you still see him?'

He shook his head. 'The angle may be wrong.'

'Let me look.' The thick dark curls swept against his cheek. 'No, he's still there. Is that the entrance?'

Janusz smelled faintly of tobacco, tweed and shaving soap. 'Yes, yes, see, he's at the mouth, anyway. You can just see the tip of the mast over the harbour mole.' He put his arm around her shoulders and drew her nearer. 'Do you see?' She fiddled with the scope and her hair fell forward, away from the nape of her neck.

'Yes, I think so. Yes, there it is. He'll be safe now?'

Janusz bent and put his lips to the back of her neck. 'I'm sure.' He slid his arm around her waist.

'I'd like to be on a boat,' she said casually, but Janusz detected the nervousness in her voice.

'I've been on ships,' he said. Her skin was very soft and she smelled delicious and her silky hair tickled his chin.

'What's it like?'

'You have to do it. It's kind of like this, with the rain all around, and the sound of the wind, and no land in sight.'

She looked at the water streaming down the tall windows; his aunt's parlour might have been at the end of the earth. The fog was coming in faster and thicker and though there were windows on three sides of them, they seemed completely enclosed. She could feel his breath against her throat and she felt her heart's rhythm alter, as if, like the ship's engine, it had changed gears.

Janusz pushed the telescope away and touched her face so that she turned towards him. The French girls were right: he was not so handsome as Charlie but more powerful, with symmetrical and cleanly shaped features. Against the murky red velvet of the sofa, his dark hair was as shiny as an animal's pelt. He was dark like her, as dark as Charlie had been fair, and dark, too, in the sense of being unknown to her. She did not understand what he was thinking, could not imagine all he knew. He was not innocent like her and Charlie and that was an attraction, too. When he kissed her, she did not draw back. Then he did, his face a little flushed. 'You're so nice.' He ran his hand down her neck, over her breast and down on to her hip

'Am I?'

'Yes, yes.' He lifted her on to his lap and as he did so, her skirt slipped over her knees and she did not bother to straighten it. His hands on the silk stockings were nice, his touch smooth yet strong — and knowing. Yes, that was part of it. They began kissing again, and she stroked his face, his wide, muscled shoulders. He was right; it was like the sea, was like sinking into something vast, rhythmic, mindblotting, ferocious — especially ferocious, like his hands tearing at her, like his mouth. 'Darling, darling,' he said, pleading, so that Elizabeth saw he was lost, too, on the same tide. 'I won't hurt you, I won't, I swear,' he said. She could feel his heart beneath his ribs, could taste, faintly, tobacco on his tongue, could feel, when he moved her hand down, the appalling readiness of his body.

He pushed her against the velvet, against the exuberant Victorian curve of the sofa arm, until she was arched like a diver. She could see the ceiling, wavering dizzily, and tried to sit up, but he was too strong, too eager, and kept kissing her all down her body, opening her clothes neatly and quickly as he went, like a machine. She began to laugh, but then he slid from the couch and pressed his mouth between her legs, and all laughter stopped and there was only ferocious hunger, the irrationality of the sea and of the rain, of the beings that in normal life were Janusz and Elizabeth.

She left that same evening, while he was dressing for dinner. She gave Simone a thank you note for the old lady, took her case and found a cab along the front, near the hotels. Within minutes of reaching the station, Elizabeth caught a train, and when she got into Paris, she booked a seat for the early morning train through Berlin to Warsaw. She went to Cousin Félicie's again and earned money by writing articles for Czacki. In the Warsaw afternoons, she went to the coffee houses or visited the cavalry officers. At the weekend she went home to ride. Janusz did not write; she did not expect him to, did not miss him, did not want to see him, though she was often bored. Her confessor was severe, but his penance, ineffectual; her convent training had given her a perfection of manner, not of belief, and for almost the first time since her illness, she thought seriously about what had happened to her. She asked an embarrassed Félicie and a cautious Warsaw doctor if she could have children. They were not sure, but it seemed that she would escape the life she had feared, the life she had seen in the peasant women, whose freedom and health were destroyed with pregnancies. But what sort of life was to be put in its place? When she had loved Charlie, the obvious answer was a life with him, and every other consideration was secondary. Now she loved no one, but she was paradoxically aware of how passion could fill one's life and that raised questions she found difficult to answer.

Just before Christmas, there was a ball at the Radziwill's, and they went in a party – the Halperns, Elizabeth and Czeslaw and several other young people. These affairs were all alike, bringing together the same set of people and differing only in the decor, the jewels of the hostess, the gowns of the season. The ball at the Radziwill's was no exception, until, doing a mazurka with Czeslaw, Elizabeth looked across the room and saw English Charlie dancing with a tall girl as blonde and good-looking as himself. The golden couple turned momentarily toward's her; Elizabeth saw his happiness and felt her heart die.

'Too many foxtrots,' Czeslaw teased as she faltered. Then he took another look at her and stopped. 'Are you all right?'

Elizabeth bit her lip. 'I'm fine. I just got out of step, that's all.'

But when the music ended, she excused herself. She had an impulse to leave, to speak to Charlie, to die on the spot, and, distracted, bumped into someone as she was leaving the ballroom.

'Do excuse me,' she said and started away.

'Elizabeth.'

It was Janusz.

'You left me with some explaining to do in Dieppe,' he said.

For a moment, she thought she might burst into tears but recovered herself. 'Your aunt must have enjoyed that.'

'She did, as a matter of fact. The old devil! You're invited back, of course. She was entertained. I was criticised.'

'It's was no one's fault.' She started to leave.

'You owe me a dance, at least. A waltz?' He took her arm, but Elizabeth did not move. 'Everyone's here tonight. Even Charlie.' He waved and Elizabeth caught another glimpse of the blond couple whirling across the floor. The woman was laughing. 'The Litowskis have let him come home at last. They did you the compliment of a six month exile. I should dance, if I were you,' Janusz added quietly. 'It will be noticed.'

Elizabeth was tempted to pick a quarrel but, of course, he was right. She could not be seen to be distressed as if it had been her fault. 'It would be my pleasure,' she said formally.

'That's right, that's the spirit.' He held out his arm. 'It's what I admire most about you, besides your lovely face and beautiful legs.'

'So your aunt has taught you flattery,' Elizabeth said as they began to circle in the waltz.

'My aunt despairs of teaching me anything. She fears I have no skill with *l'amour*.' He nodded to some friends and, as they passed Charlie and his companion, said, 'Smile and he will envy me forever.' Then they glided away, rustling through the silks, the satins, the taffetas and brocades of the ballroom. The crystal facets of the chandeliers spun rainbows on the floor while the violinists, sweating behind their stands, added a gypsy plaintiveness to the strains of old Vienna. 'We'll have something to eat, now,' Janusz said, 'and another dance and then I'll take you home. I've a car, so it isn't any trouble. Czacki may send me to Berlin next if I can improve my German. You're fluent, aren't you? You could help me. Would you?'

Elizabeth's face was blank. 'If you wish,' she said, 'but now, please, I must leave.'

Janusz planned to stay in Warsaw for some time, and Elizabeth met him whenever she went to the newspaper. He appeared, too, at her favourite coffee houses and came to pay formal respects to Cousin Félicie. Though she would have preferred only casual meetings, his persistence gradually wore her down. He persuaded her to coach him in German, sometimes at Cousin Félicie's, sometimes, when she was in an especially good mood, in his apartment. These sessions frequently ended with her in his arms, the record player blaring a German language lesson to deceive his landlady. On weekends when the roads were passable, he began driving her to the estate. When they were not, he sometimes rode the train with her, hoping for an empty compartment. Her parents regarded him as eligible, as potentially a man of influence, and by spring, both the Count and Countess were pressing Elizabeth to make up her mind to marry him. They saw a good match for her, possible loans for the estate and connections for André lost if she did not decide soon.

'What shall I do?' she asked Jozef. She confided in him now that her father's illness and her brother's invalidism had reduced their interests to their own concerns. When she was in Warsaw she wrote him so often that Janusz noticed and was jealous.

'Marry him or break off with him. That is only fair.' Jozef did not like her pale cheeks, her quietness. 'This uncertainty is not good for you,' he added.

She nodded. 'I'm not in love with him,' she said, 'but it is hard just to break off.'

It was almost, although she did not say this to Jozef, as if Janusz knew she didn't love him and didn't care, as if he wanted to prove he could hold her by the force of his personality alone. He had the power to make her forget Charlie and he planned to use that to steal her volition. It was ridiculous. 'I do like him in some ways, you see.'

Jozef understood. His own life with its professional celibacy and holiday dissipations had followed a similar pattern. 'There are other fish in the sea. See someone else. You will find someone suitable. Or go back to Paris.'

'I believe he would follow me.' She was oddly dispirited, and it was that passivity, so foreign to her nature, which worried Jozef most. In compensation, she was often reckless. He knew she drove Janusz's car frightfully fast and on several occasions he had seen her putting her father's big stallion at dangerous fences. Whenever he thought of these incidents, he cursed English Charlie, who had broken her heart.

'Get away elsewhere, then.'

'I wish I could go to America, to the jungle, to Greece and Rome and all the places you told us about. But I promised Adam I'd see him in the spring. I'm off to Zakopane. Janusz can wait a few days for his answer.'

Chapter Eight

It was early spring in the High Tatra and water was running everywhere out of the body of the earth. Each slope had its little rivulet, while on the tops of the hills there was the sound of moisture percolating through the soil. The new grass was a sour green, vivid against the black spruces, and all day the sky had shifted restlessly from blue to grey. Towards dusk, when the clouds thinned and the sky above the spine of the Tatra turned a clear lavender pink, they set off through the forest, past streams bubbling with water sprites and perhaps *skorzaty,* evil creatures of bad luck. The horses moved in and out of the shadows, dark and light, and the smell of resin and damp and humus was touched with their warm odour. Each of the Gurals led one or two extra mounts. The men's white trousers and shirts were hidden under long dark cloaks, and Elizabeth wore a thick black sweater and dark jodhpurs. She rode a nice little gelding, a real mountain pony, small, but tough and nimble footed, and led a fine chestnut mare of the same stock.

Above the tree line, the moon was a cold white cusp against the indigo sky, and Kasimir, Adam's shy, handsome nephew, reminded him that they had hoped for clouds and mist. The old man just nodded his head; there would be cloud; he could feel a dampness. The others shrugged, trusted his instincts, and urged their mounts up into the high, stony meadows. Somewhere a bird cried; otherwise there were only the sounds of the horses' feet, the jingle of their bridles, the quiet, slow voices of the mountaineers. Trotting along in the column, Elizabeth was happy; she could have ridden forever under the wisp of moon and the ridge of the Tatra like the bewitched in a legend. But, of course, this was only an interlude. When she got home, it would all begin again: her parents' suppressed anxiety, the observations about her father's health, the estate debts, her brother's needs. The priest would disapprove of her life and advocate marriage as the true vocation of a Catholic woman. And Janusz, if he was still speaking to her, would press for an answer. Czacki planned to send him to Germany, and Janusz saw that as an opportunity. 'Berlin is the most important place a journalist can be at the moment. Like it or not, fascism is the vital force in European politics today, and the Reich Chancellor is riding the tiger.'

Elizabeth had listened and said nothing. She had told Jozef she did not think she could live in Berlin, but she had not discussed this with Janusz.

'Your German is perfect. I will say that for your old tutor –' he always described Jozef as 'old', although the tutor was only eight years his senior, precisely the same as the gap between Janusz himself and Elizabeth – 'and with you to translate, I could write some really valuable articles. There's nowhere, except maybe Russia, that we more need accurate information about than Hitler's Germany.'

She tightened her legs so that the pony picked up its gait a little. She would rather stay in the mountains, which was childish, and earn her living smuggling, which was reprehensible. Soon, she knew, she would have to grow up, marry, fulfil some of those unsolicited expectations, but for now there were the mountains and some men who were interested in frontiers and passes.

She had met one of them in Zakopane during the skiing season when she was first happy with English Charlie. His name was Evelyn Martins and he had known Charlie at Oxford. He called Charlie 'old boy' and 'sport', and they spoke English together. He did not say much to Elizabeth until Charlie and Jozef left to take André to his room. Then, after an awkward silence, he cleared his throat and said, 'Well then, Charlie tells me you're a mountaineer,' in perfect Polish.

Elizabeth laughed. 'No one's a mountaineer except the Gurals.'

He gave her a sharp, steady look. 'But you have skied here since childhood? And visited summer and winter?'

'Oh, yes. I have loved the Tatra ever since Jozef taught me to ski. And you, do you ski?'

Martins smiled. His eyes were small and dark and he had a very large nose. He reminded her of some intelligent ground animal – an otter, perhaps, or an ermine – a creature that looked much and said little. 'I saw you today, watched you ski. Beautifully, if I may say so.'

Elizabeth inclined her head. He was not the first man to admire her skiing and she knew what such compliments were worth.

'My guide said you know the mountains, know the Gurals.' He examined her quizzically from beneath his thick, arched brows.

Elizabeth shrugged. She had learned some of the Gural caution.

Martins lit a little green cigar with fussy care. 'They're smugglers, of course, always have been.' He smiled to show he meant no harm.

'Are you a frontier agent, Mr. Martins?'

He gave a sputtering chuckle as if this was a very good joke, drew on his cigar and wiped a flake of tobacco off his tongue. 'Not in the sense you mean, no. The passage of tobacco and horses back and forth is none of my business. We Britishers are free trade men anyway.' Another smile; he was a genial man.

'Then your interest must be skiing.'

'There you are wrong, Countess. I am a wretched skier. I was born for the south, for trade winds rustling in the palms. No, I'm here on business and my business is frontiers.'

Now it was Elizabeth's turn to look puzzled.

'We live in what the Chinese would call interesting times, Countess, and your fair country is in perhaps the most interesting position of all: to the east, Bolshevism; to the west, Nazism; to the south, a variety of small, new and dubious republics. In any conflict, Poland will be one of the focal points, hence the interest of His Majesty's Government and of my service.'

'Which is?'

'Secret and official.'

'And what are you interested in, Mr. Martins?'

'Roads, dear Countess. Trails in and trails out, crossing points, frontier fortifications, guard posts – the lot. A pair of open eyes would go a considerable way towards helping a sedentary man file his reports.' Again the lazy, genial smile, but Martins was alert enough to spot Charlie and Jozef in the doorway. 'Our companions return. Did I mention that His Majesty's Government pays for its information? Quite well. Do please think it over, Countess.'

When she found him *bona fide*, she had begun to work for him. On one trip or another, she had surveyed a good part of the Polish-Czech border and she could find her own way over a fair bit of the Tatra. As she followed Kasimir along the trail, she thought that this trip would be especially interesting to Martins since horsemen were apt to attract the attention of the frontier guards.

Adam's meterological instincts were proved correct near the Czechoslovakian border. The air turned warm and moist, and they began picking up patches of fog. Adam sent two men ahead to reconnoitre, but there was no danger. They cantered across the last open stretch between Polish and Czech soil and were soon safe in a patchy wooded area. A mesh of narrow, spongy trails led to the mountaineers' village where they stayed for three days, visiting the Gurals' relatives and bargaining with the horse traders.

The mountaineers enjoyed these long sessions, the careful examinations of teeth and hooves and legs, the admiration of their fine stock, disguised though it might be in faint praise. They liked, too, to see who would be taking possession of animals that had shared the family home. Then there was a wedding in the offing, plans to be made, and new fiddle to be heard. For two nights the village was full of merriment; on the third, a cousin led them to a trail slightly east of their previous crossing. There had been a shower earlier; the trees dripped water and the horses' bodies steamed in the damp. Where the wood thinned out, the villager turned back, followed by whispered farewells of 'God lead you' and 'Stand with God', before the Gurals moved off in a straggling line.

They travelled through broken patches of forest and

meadow until they reached an open grassland rising gradually towards the north. A blurred shadow along the crest of a hill indicated the mass of the Tatra, half lost in the mist. Adam held up his hand. The muffled figures reined in their horses and sat silent, studying the all but undetectable sounds of the night. Adam looked at his nephew. The boy glanced east uneasily, but when Adam consulted the others, they nodded and moved forward. They were halfway across the field when Adam suddenly wheeled his mount to the left, and Elizabeth's heart jumped with excitement, almost with joy.

She touched her pony with her heels and they sprang forward, diagonally up the hill. The frontier guards were on the ridge above, their horses at the gallop, but the Gurals were already in flight, hunched low over their ponies necks, their long black cloaks whipping behind them. There was a shout and the explosion of a shot, as loud in the silent mountains as an avalanche, but they gained the crest of the hill while the frontier guards were trying to turn their charging horses. Adam yelled for them to scatter and spurred his horse straight on.

Elizabeth veered west with Kasimir's grey pounding beside her. Another shot, still close, and she glanced behind to see three frontier police in pursuit. She dropped lower on her horse's neck, urging it towards a grove of spruce. They had almost reached the trees when her horse stumbled. Elizabeth felt her stomach turn over and struggled for balance, but the nimble pony regained its stride. With the Czechs and the disgrace of capture close behind, she saw Kasimir's grey disappear into the grove to her left and urged her horse towards the wall of trees. At the last minute, the forest opened, revealing a little rutted track crossed by a fallen spruce. She steadied her mount to set its feet for the jump, then rose in the stirrups as the valiant creature hurled itself forward into the misty darkness. One hoof clicked against a branch, but they raced on over ruts and stones. Ahead, Kasimir waved his arm and pointed left again. The trail split into two, into three, parts and they charged down the narrowest track, crossed a glade, and stopped, breathing hard, their blood pounding.

There were shouts as the Czechs galloped up and down the logging trails, and Kasimir said, 'They will be here in a minute.' He led the way through the brush to a steep and slippery incline. At the bottom, a vertical mass of rock rose darker and higher than the trees. Kasimir slid off his horse and signalled for Elizabeth to do the same. They picked their way around the edge of the rock, then he touched her arm and pointed. A shadowy fissure split the rock nearly from top to bottom, the entrance to a high, narrow cave. Into this they led the horses and waited, listening to the horsemen in the wood above.

The cave was damply rank and the horses shifted their feet uneasily on the dirt and pine needles. Kasimir and Elizabeth had to stroke the animals' necks and whisper softly to distract them from the sounds of their fellows up in the clearing. Behind them, all was darkness, but the moon had risen above the clouds and lent a feeble radiance to the grey mist at the mouth of the cave. Elizabeth was conscious of every sound, every sensation: of the faint shifting of the ponies' feet, their comforting scent, the touch of their manes, the smell of the cave and of the forest, the sounds of the approaching horsemen, the pattern of Kasimir's breathing, the light that illuminated one side his face. 'They're coming,' he said.

They could hear the rattle of the guards' equipment, the crackling of brush: the Czechs were circling at the back of the clearing, searching in the murk for their trail. Elizabeth stroked the pony's moist, bristly muzzle, then Kasimir put his hand lightly on her arm, and she caught the sound of his indrawn breath. 'One,' he said.

She heard the unsteady descent of a single horse, the snap of branches, and an exclamation of anger and disgust as the guard yelled up to his companions. He had the hoarse voice of a man who has spent too many nights in the mist and rain. An answer from the clearing above produced a burst of profanity from the slope, then the sound of the horse scrambling back up to the clearing. A few loosened stones bounced against the rock.

Elizabeth moved slightly, eager to be out of the cave, but Kasimir stopped her. 'They will circle beneath us; one track leads that way,' he said, and they had not waited more than five minutes when they heard the hoofbeats again. Kasimir put Elizabeth's hand on his pony's bridle and slipped to the mouth of the cave, his cloak folded like the wings of a giant bat. Below came the jingle and creak of bits and saddles. Kasimir stood listening until the sounds of the guards faded, then he returned and took his pony's reins, touching Elizabeth's hand as he reached for the bridle. 'We will ride fast along the middle track,' he said. 'They won't venture much more than a mile inside the border.'

'Your uncle and the others? What about them?'

'I'm sure they're safe. They'll expect us to make our own way home.' He held her horse so she could mount, then swung into his saddle. Elizabeth could feel, rather than see, his smile. When she had met him with Adam, he had always been silent, a fair, sturdy youth almost paralysed with shyness. In the darkness, with the blood pounding in their ears and the frontier guards within reach, he was more natural, a wild, reckless creature like herself.

As soon as they reached the track, they put the horses to a gallop, and by the time Kasimir judged they were quite safe, the animals were beginning to slow with weariness. They walked them a bit and gave them water at a narrow stream, but the hardest part of the journey lay ahead, and when they passed the tree line and found the ground unfamiliar, Kasimir admitted they would have to wait until light. They stopped in a meadow littered with massive boulders and tied the horses on a line to a rough evergreen shrub. The mist had been left behind in the forest. Up here the moon and stars were visible again, lighting the stones and the meadow and the bare, otherworldly ridge of the Tatra. Elizabeth leaned against a rock. The adrenaline still raced in her blood, and she felt that she could do anything, could fly like an eagle, had been born for the mountains.

She caught the glint of Kasimir's eyes as he loosened the ponies' saddle girths and, when he saw her watching, he smiled a soft, feral smile like the greeting of some mountain creature. He had lost his awkwardness in the cave. When Elizabeth stretched out her hand, he reached for it eagerly and stepped against her. The narrow cusp of the moon swam in his eyes and his long hooded cloak held the darkness of the mountains. Elizabeth laughed with the sudden unexpectedness of it and saw a way to keep her independence forever. His hands were cold when he touched her face, but his mouth was warm and she could feel his heart leaping like hers with the joy of danger and freedom and flight and desire. He kissed her with passionate eagerness, then dropped to his knees, slipped off his long cloak and threw it behind him on to the damp grass. A moment later, they were rolled in each others' arms with blackness all round them.

It was after this trip that Elizabeth agreed to marry Janusz Bronski.

Elizabeth had refused to have the lights on, so the curtains were still open and the golden twilight swept in through the long windows and rippled pink and mauve across the surface of the large pier glass. A flock of rooks were settling for the night in the elms, and every few minutes a scrap of black whirled a shadow across the mirror, unsettling superstitious Marie, who had been seconded to Elizabeth for this important occasion. 'Let me do your hair, Mademoiselle.'

Elizabeth sighed and pulled irritably at the neck of her gown, her polished nails disarranging the ruffles. 'It's not right. I hate this dress.'

'Mademoiselle, it is perfect. *Très charmante.* You are just nervous. That is natural, but Monsieur Bronski will be charmed.'

'It's the red. I don't like it.'

Marie shrugged eloquently. Of course, red was unsuitable for an engagement, but the silk was lovely, and the embroidery, magnificent. 'You would have it, Mademoiselle.'

'I knew you didn't like it.'

'I only said, Mademoiselle, that it was unconventional. For you, it seems perfect.' She picked up the hairbrush, but Elizabeth showed no interest in getting ready. Through the open windows, Marie could see the tall trees at the edge of the lawn, darkening in the twilight. 'The lanterns are lighted, Mademoiselle. It is very pretty. Your papa has outdone himself.'

Elizabeth sat on the bed and said nothing.

Marie raised her curved black eyebrows. Though the young Countess was often fussy and eccentric about her clothes, she was usually cheerful and full of fun. 'Ah, look, the musicians are here. I love to hear musicians tuning up.' She leaned out the window with a smile, her delight in an entertainment momentarily erasing her anxiety. The young Countess did not seem happy, and a pretty girl like her –

'It is a beautiful night.' Elizabeth's voice was soft and wistful.

'A night for romance, Mademoiselle.'

Something about her voice reminded Elizabeth of Annette and Madeleine, the two French women who had admired Janusz. If they had not, would she have gone to Dieppe? Life might turn on a word, she thought, and began twitching irritably at the sleeves of the gown.

'It will be all stretched out of shape. Let me fix – '

'Leave it for a moment, Marie. I don't feel well.'

'It is just excitment.'

'I will call you in a few minutes, Marie, then you can do my hair.'

'You cannot be late this evening, Mademoiselle. Not this evening.'

'I will call you, Marie.'

'It is nothing. Just nerves. A little breathlessness, perhaps?'

'Yes, that is all,' said Elizabeth.

'You will look *très charmante*, Mademoiselle.'

'Yes, Marie.' She gave a sudden smile, gentle and warm. '*Au revoir*, Marie.'

'*A bientôt*, Mademoiselle.'

The latch of the door clicked and Elizabeth put her hand to her throat. She would be sick, she was suffocating, it was all impossible. Guests were arriving in the hall below and out on the lawn the gypsy musicians took up a song, stopped, tuned, began another. It was too late! She had left it too late! She had given her word, yet every sound of the party filled her with horror, and it was her own fault, her own cowardice. How she hated that realisation: one may be undone in a moment, in a moment of trying to do the honourable thing. She pulled furiously at the ruffles, tempted to rip them off, and realised that thought was her enemy. Whenever she abandoned her instincts she went wrong, and all her instincts now said, this is impossible.

Elizabeth rubbed her hands together and began to turn her

aunt's ring over and over. Aunt Anna had known about instinct. She could hear the old lady's clear, precise voice: 'On the run, I trusted absolute strangers with my life at a moment's notice, and I was never wrong.' There was a corollary to that, namely that there were some one knew well who were not to be risked. Like Janusz.

She stood up and went to her dressing table, opened her jewel box and began taking out the valuable pieces, seeing what it would feel like, what the plan would be. There was a sound in the trees as the rooks were disturbed, and their black shapes flashed like cinders across her mirror, flashed in sweeping arcs like the trajectory of swallows – or of a whip.

She had cantered over the fields after Janusz, who had gone to see the new carp ponds. He was interested in all aspects of the estate and had already hinted he would be willing to see to the running of it, an idea which she knew had pleased her parents. The day was warm and sweet with the smell of the new hay, and at every field she had to stop and accept the greetings and congratulations of the peasants. She'd been happy; her mind was made up – if there were doubts, hesitations, some shrinking of the heart, it was but childishness. Her course was right, and, as though racing toward its consumation, she'd slackened the reins and put the horse to a full gallop. From the top of the hill, one saw the land stretched out in the endless fields, broken only by the shallow glitter of the carp ponds and the winding dirt road. But what she saw was one thing only, the curve of Janusz's arm, the descent of the whip, the terrified dance of Mysz, the gentlest beast in the stable.

'Stop that! Stop that!' she shouted. Janusz turned, then struck the mare again. She cantered down the hill at him, horrified. 'You're never to beat her!'

His face was flushed. He knew her love of animals and he was furious that he had given into his temper, that she had caught him unawares. He sensed that this was a thing she would not excuse in him and spoke roughly. 'Don't dare order me like some hired man. That damn horse tried to throw me. You've got them spoiled.'

He raised the whip again, determined to show who was master, but Elizabeth jumped in the way and seized Mysz's bridle. The horse threw up her head and danced back, favouring the right foreleg. 'She's been hurt! If you rode better you'd have known that.' It made Elizabeth sick to see a carter beat his horse in the street; she would not have it with her own.

'I might have broken my neck, for all you care! Do you care?' He caught her arm. There was something in her which he could never touch, some little particle of independence — of indifference — which made all the rest of her compliance unsatisfactory. Without that spark she would not have attracted him, yet its presence pushed him to demand her complete surrender which would be, for him, her love. 'What a fool I am to love you so. You don't care, do you? You care more about some damn horse than me,' he burst out, for in his own way he loved her. But his fingers tightened on the riding crop and she saw it was impossible. There was a hardness in him that revolted her. If she married him she would always see it, and it would destroy all she felt for him. She should have told him then, standing in the field with the larks singing and the horse shivering and the two of them baffled and furious. But instead, she had let herself be dragged into a noisy, pointless quarrel, into one of their sweet, pointless reconciliations. His subtle intelligence was like a net, flexible and insinuating, flung over her life. And she, who feared captivity more than brutality, had seen how she was caught in her own promises, by her own honour. He sought to envelop her, but she had given her word, and though she said many angry things she did not say the chief thing: that marriage would be a mistake for both of them.

Now there was laughter from the servants, hurrying to lay out the buffet. One was singing in a rich baritone and the musicians began following him plaintively. Elizabeth wrapped her jewellery in a scarf and stuck it into a handbag. She stood up and glanced in the mirror. The dress was a pillar of fire; she found the fastening and the gown rustled to the floor like a red ember in the twilight. When she had finished changing, she picked up the bag and stepped on to the balcony. The sunset was red gold and the fir growing at the side of the house, almost black. She climbed over the balustrade, reached into the tree for a branch and swung down to a lower limb. She and Czeslaw had done it a thousand times, and the raspy, sticky bark and the scratch of the needles brought back poignantly the summer twilights of her childhood. Elizabeth dropped to the ground, her hands sticky with pitch. The deep shadows at the side of the sprawling house hid her until she was halfway to the garage.

'Good evening, Countess.' Jozef had taken to calling her 'Countess' since her engagement. A little ripple of pain began at the back of her throat; she would lose them all, even him.

'May I offer all my good wishes and prayers for your happiness.' Behind the light, ironic tone there was pain – and brandy. Jozef was not a great drinker, and even in small doses spirits went to his head.

'She looked down at the ground in silence. When she raised her head, she said, 'I have made up my mind.'

'Ah,' said Jozef, and his face grew sad. He had known for some time and had waited for her to know, too.

'Would you find Thaddeus for me?' She straightened her shoulders and spoke briskly. 'Ask him, please, to take out the car. You could say you have changed your mind, Jozef, that you plan to leave for Vienna tonight. I know there is a late train.'

'He will wonder,' Jozef said slowly, sensing a decision, hating its precipitateness. Elizabeth had a way of sweeping others up into her plans.

'But he will take out the car. I will be on the road at the top of the drive. Tell him to stop.'

Jozef said nothing.

'I cannot do it,' Elizabeth said. 'I do not love him and I must get away.'

'I cannot leave for Vienna tonight,' Jozef said carefully, but his heart was already jumping like a caged thing.

'You have wanted to leave. We could go to Greece and see the islands of the sun. Homer's wine dark sea, the groves of the goddesses, all those things you taught us. We can leave for them tonight,' she said, and realised that this was what she wanted.

He had no reply.

'How long we have talked of them, dreamed of them?' she said reflectively, and looked over the fields beyond the trees.

She loved nowhere on earth more, and the beauty of the edge of the steppe entranced her. 'But you will still ask Thaddeus. Please. I will be at the gate whether you come or not. But say good-bye now, Jozef, if you must stay. I will miss no one as much as you.' She took his hand in the shadows and raised it to her lips.

'My darling Elizabeth,' he said. The rooks were crying in the trees, the gypsy strings wavered softly, the guests, the servants, the family talked and laughed and bustled importantly, and Jozef felt the corporate life and body of the estate, which he had loved, for the last time. 'I would go with you to the ends of the earth.'

In the train, she wept and then, seeing them sitting there forlornly in the half lit compartment with only Jozef's bag for luggage, she began to laugh.

'This is madness,' he said. 'We have no money.'

'I brought all my jewellery. I'll sell it until my dividend cheques arrive. I hope Greece will be cheap.'

'We must at least have enough for the tickets,' he said, opening his wallet. Their fares took nearly every penny, and when they were settled in Vienna the next day, Jozef went out to sell one of Elizabeth's rings while she composed a letter to her parents.

The squares were deserted in the heat, the trees powdered white with dust. After he sold the ring, Jozef stopped for a beer before walking slowly back to the old-fashioned hotel, showy in high Viennese baroque. As he climbed the wide marble stairs, past the gilded stucco cherubs and garlands of the lobby, past the tapestries faded to dusty maroon, past the enormous crystal chandelier refracting the afternoon into a thousand spectra, Jozef recognised the baroque aspects of his own situation. Tired from the heat, he almost expected the lobby, the stair, the long mauve and gold corridor to dissolve, leaving him to awaken in his own room, a bit the worse for wear after Elizabeth's betrothal party. But that would have been terrible, too.

He unlocked his room. The windows were all open and the sheer undercurtains pulsed back and forth in the hot breeze. He tapped on the connecting door, but there was not a sound and he turned the handle. Elizabeth was lying on her side asleep; he took that in, and also the golden whiteness of the sun pouring on to the bare floor, and the white lacy coverlet and sheets and pillow and walls, and against them, Elizabeth's dark head and the pale satin of her slip. Her arms and legs were bare, palest gold against the white, and Jozef felt his heart stop. He loved her beyond reason.

'Elizabeth.' No answer. He stepped to the bed and hesitated, aware of her near nakedness, the smooth curve of her hip, the soft proximity of her breasts. Then he sat down beside her and laid his hand on her bare shoulder. 'Elizabeth.'

Her eyes fluttered but she was still asleep in the whiteness, and Jozef felt his heart torn with fear, relief and joy, and remembered the brilliant certainties of the mountain. He touched her skin with his lips and took the first faint taste of her body. She opened her eyes, smiled and put her arms around his neck. 'Darling Jozef,' she said.

He lay down next to her, naked in the white sunshine, and took her into his arms while the hot Viennese breeze washed over them, drying their bodies and consuming their hearts. They were never to be quite so perfectly happy again.

Chapter Nine

Nîmes 1939

They wound up in Nîmes with its ruins and its opportunities. Jozef taught French to émigré Poles and rudimentary English to nervous Jews. Elizabeth wrote pieces for Czacki, sometimes travelling as far as Lyons or Paris to get information, and he recommended her for a job translating propaganda pamphlets which supplemented her dividend cheque. At first, when she still hoped for a reconciliation with her family, they lived in a hotel near the station. But though the Count and Countess sent on trunks of clothing, they refused to answer her letters, and at last, despairing of rootlessness, Elizabeth asked her bankers for permission to invest in a pink stucco house a few blocks from the gardens. It came with Madame Rozier, a plump, nosy, energetic window who cleaned and cooked dinner in exchange for rooms for herself, her cat and her spry fox terrier. They moved in the week Elizabeth learned her father was dead, and from that time she did not mention going home again.

Instead, she tried to cultivate a pleasure in France. She liked the cafés, the films, the lively discussions that sometimes brought back the smoky coffee houses of winter Warsaw. But she disliked French politics and hated the chilly rationalism of the French soul. Her communications with Czacki, both public and private, became increasingly pessimistic. Even the great social success of the Polish Ambassador that summer and the splendid military display along the Champs-Elysées did not raise her spirits. She missed her family and her own country and, away from both, was struck by their vulnerability. The new rumours, of course, were absurd, yet they made her so restless that she abandoned her work and went down to the café to wait for Jozef.

'I was afraid that awful woman had made away with you,' she said as he stepped into the rosy shadow cast by the café awnings.

Jozef wiped his face with a handkerchief and sat down heavily in the cane chair. Morning and evenings in the Languedoc were delightful, but the August afternoons were hot and humid. 'They are leaving in a week. The packing company was there. What a circus!'

'Lucky England,' Elizabeth said drily. She had met the Blomfedders; Madame with her impossible French, her endless stream of orders and exclamations, her unsuitable furs and curious hats had made a particularly deep impression.

'She has recommended another family, though. They are to call me.' Jozef smiled as he signalled the waiter for a beer. He enjoyed teaching and had considerable tolerance for the vagaries of his clientele. 'Hermann, the smallest boy, will do well. He has a good ear. He will wind up as the family's translator.'

'Most likely your work will be wasted and they will shift again. Madame will be discontented anywhere.'

'Nonetheless, I think they're wise to go.'

Elizabeth looked serious. 'Really?'

'As you yourself have observed, the French are not fond of Jews.'

'Still, the protection of French law, the power of France, what have they to fear here?'

Jozef shrugged. 'The French smell trouble, and dislike foreigners. I said to your friends the Levinsohns, too, that I thought Britain or America a better bet.'

Elizabeth had mixed feelings about the refugees. Certainly they had every reason to leave the Reich, but they brought with them the smell of fear and, too often, hid their terrors under the arrogance of money. She wondered about the poor left behind. 'Your honesty will cost you pupils,' she said softly.

He gave a short laugh. 'Herr Hitler will keep me well supplied. It is not often he does us Poles a good turn.'

'Jozef,' she said after a moment, 'there is a rumour in the

press today that the German Foreign Minister has gone to Russia.'

He gestured for the paper and she showed him the story.

'It makes no sense. It could only mean – '

'A bluff, I would think,' Jozef said, although even that raised a chill. 'Probably put out by the Russians to get the English back to negotiating. I can't see the Reds with Hitler.'

'Everyone feels something is going to happen. Everyone. Even Pierre, the waiter here. Everyone is waiting. It may be something completely unexpected.'

'Better hope it's not a rapprochment between Hitler and Stalin,' Jozef said.

'If it happens, we must go home. I don't want to be an exile.'

'A status half the world aspires to,' he said lightly, the beer beginning to restore his spirits. He was still thin, but his face was tanned and the scattering of grey in his hair was not unbecoming. His lady pupils thought him attractive, and told him he was distinguished in a gushing way that sometimes angered Elizabeth.

'I just want it understood.'

'We can leave anytime and get work in Warsaw,' he said, though it would have pained him to sell the house, the first property they had ever owned. He counted on her dread of returning without a reconciliation with her family. 'Write to Czacki, if you like.'

'We will see,' she said, waving to someone across the café. 'There is Maurice. Maurice, have you seen the late editions?'

He came over and kissed her cheek and shook hands with Jozef. Maurice was somewhere in his twenties, a schoolteacher with olive skin and the black almond-shaped eyes of the south. After a few pleasantries, he and Elizabeth plunged into a discussion of the news, while Jozef had another beer and settled comfortably in his chair. He did not mind listening to Maurice. Though she collected strays of every persuasion, Elizabeth was always admired by men of substance; more so, it seemed, since their marriage. And why not? She was lovelier than ever, stylish, amusing, friendly. A good companion. A good wife? Time would tell.

Maurice was now defending his country's commitment to

Poland. One of the few — if he was sincere. His father had died at Verdun; he would, Jozef thought, have had reason for scepticism. Maurice raised his glass and offered, *'Vive la France et la Pologne.'* Jozef drank, too. He quite liked Maurice and, because of Elizabeth's reservations about France, saw the Frenchman as less of a threat than, say, Jerzy, the good-looking Pole who worked in Avignon as an engineer, or playful Osip, his friend.

Now Elizabeth was laughing. She had a beautiful laugh and that was something important in a woman, Jozef decided; it showed a capacity for enjoyment. But at that thought, his mouth turned down, he answered Maurice perfunctorily and took another sip of beer. It was he, after all, who lacked the capacity for enjoyment — at least with the creature he loved most. He glanced out into the street where pedestrians and cars swam like motes in the falling sun and the little cafés were visible only by the brilliant flashes of their awnings. He was lucky she stayed with him.

Their escape, at first, had been marvellous, an illicit and extended holiday where all the rules might be safely bent. They had married in Vienna, for he had refused to compromise her reputation further, and gone from there into Italy. To Venice, first, staying in the cheapest *pensiones* and hiking from one small village to the next until a letter came with money from her banker. Then they went to Rome and travelled south to ancient Syracuse where the captive Athenians had died in sun-struck quarries. The heat, the excitement of escape, of her, kept him bewitched, and, although Jozef had tried to hide it from Elizabeth, he often felt vaguely feverish, as if his old illness might recur. They walked for miles every day or rode up and down narrow trails on thin donkeys. He remembered the landscape as white and blue: dust, sky and sea; simplicities that dulled the mind and sharpened the senses.

They reached Greece in late autumn, a land of mountain villages, poor as Galicia, oppressed by tradition and religion. In little Greek Orthodox churches, Jozef implored Byzantine Madonnas to forgive him, and, a moment later when he reached the brilliant sunshine, turned apostate. He was not truly a believer, yet he had been imbued with a sense of sin. Between love and lust there was an unbreachable gulf, and although he had struggled since the mountain to eradicate desire he had been unsuccessful. Even as Elizabeth's teacher, as her guardian, his love had been tainted. Just how tainted had been revealed to him under the brilliant Mediterranean sky, in a hundred sun-washed rooms, in a year of nights black as velvet. He was feverish with sun, with heat, with passion, like a man in an unending and inescapable erotic dream, and it woke in him revulsion. He loved her as nothing else on earth, desired her with passionate intensity, and yet, in cooler moments, he almost regretted ever having touched her, almost wished not to sleep with her again.

In the spring, a division grew between them. He could see she was hurt; she had, somehow, escaped the inhibitions and guilts which should have been her birthright. The good reports from her convent school now struck him as bitterly ironic. She had escaped their net completely; she smiled easily at the young mountaineers, at stocky Professor Theopolis with his ill-fitting suits and his antique coin profile, at the muscular fishermen who ferried them between the islands. She thrived on their admiration, was amused by jokes delivered in the ragbag of tongues which serves as the patois of the tourist trade. Sooner or later, he saw, the right one would come — unless she was indeed like him and it was rather the right situation that was required — and she would be gone.

But it was he who left; in justice he would remember that. The quarter where they lived in Athens was very poor and cheap, the finest building a better class brothel, impossible to miss. Jozef wandered out one night on the excuse that he couldn't sleep, but Elizabeth was no longer a child and she guessed almost instantly. The china basin and pitcher in the room were white with a mauve floral design, and when she threw them to the floor they had shattered to bits.

'It is impossible,' Maurice insisted. 'Impossible.' He was a leftist, perhaps a communist, certainly a socialist. For him, the Soviet Union was the home of the Revolution, the hope of the world. Alas, that the Revolution had been born in Russia, the Mother of Oppression, the arch-enemy of hope and freedom. 'Stalin will never reconcile with Hitler, never.'

'They have certain things, certain interests in common,' Elizabeth said. 'They both hate Poland.'

'You Poles are too self-centered,' Maurice exclaimed.

How true! He, Jozef, had been too absorbed in his own sufferings to see how young Elizabeth was – just twenty-two when they found themselves in Greece. He had betrayed her trust twice; in imagination when she was a child, in reality when she became his wife. She had found a vase that went the way of the wash stand crockery and sworn like an Uhlan, tears of rage on her face. She drove him to such a pain of loss and desire that he caught her wrists and trapped her, struggling, in his arms. 'I loved you too long,' he shouted. 'I married you too late. I love you too much.'

She tried to strike him, but only succeeded in knocking off his glasses. They shattered on the tile floor, and she put her hand over her mouth and turned away from him. When he saw she was crying, he took her in his arms and in a flood of emotion made love to her. Yet though their marriage was imperfect and, sometimes, unhappy, they loved each other. He could not sleep if she wasn't beside him, and when he came into the café or met her unexpectedly in town during the day, her smile was radiant. Someday she might find a man who loved her both ways and leave with him. Until then ...

'Will they fight?' she asked Maurice. 'That's the question, isn't it? Is the will there to stop Hitler?'

'When it was Czechslovakia,' Maurice said, 'your government went along.'

'Out of stupidity and greed,' said Jozef, who had little patience with the *Sanacja* régime.

'Of course, nothing is certain until we know the news from Moscow,' the Frenchman said, willing to talk around the question. They all had the smell of the future in their nostrils, the whiff of exile and disaster, and like the other refugees and émigrés, the soldiers and the ordinary French people, they lingered on the sunny café terraces, savouring the pleasures of one of the best summers on record. Elizabeth and Jozef talked of leaving, stored some furniture, packed some bags, but they were still sitting in their favourite café when the panzers rolled into Poland over the hopes and illusions of the Thirties. Elizabeth haunted the newstands and considered one plan after the next for getting home to her family; then the Red Army invaded from the east, and she admitted they would not get back. Disgusted with the French refusal to attack the Rhineland, she announced that she was going to London. They left the house in the charge of Madame Rozier, the housekeeper; Jozef dismissed his pupils, and they set off for the city of arrivals and departures, the war room to be of exile and empire.

Their hotel in Kensington was a dark way station in this surreal landscape. Children were being evacuated to the countryside, and a dwarf army appeared at every tube and train station, their names pinned to their little coats, favourite toys clasped in their hands. Civilians wore gas masks slung on their arms instead of umbrellas, and labourers piled sand bags around the doors of public buildings. The silver barrage balloons hung moored on the edges of the city like silent leviathans, and back gardens sprouted Anderson Shelters that reminded Jozef of digging the trenches in front of Warsaw almost twenty years before. He wondered if they had had to dig trenches this time or if aerial bombardment necessitated something more elaborate like the anti-aircraft emplacements that were appearing in all the London parks. Though the island's preparations for meeting mass destruction depressed Jozef, the contrast with France was striking, and Elizabeth was encouraged. She took a liking to the British and was convinced they would fight.

'Yet they seem as unready as the French,' Jozef said. He could understand enough of the press debates to see that the military was woefully unprepared, and even the childrens' evacuation haphazard. The Poles, in all innocence, had supposed the British to be the possessors of a mighty war machine; it was now obvious that they were barely equipped to defend the home islands, never mind the wide open Polish plain. Although he admired their bluff confidence, it made Jozef cynical and suspicious.

'They have the will. They're our only chance,' Elizabeth said so passionately that he did not have the heart to discourage her. She was restless and miserable without word of her family, and she chafed against the enforced idleness of London. She spent her days frantically studying English and searching the bureaucratic labyrinth of Westminster for Evelyn Martins. Jozef doubted she would find him, but one afternoon she came home excited. That night she got out their best evening clothes and the bulk of her remaining jewellery. Dressed in yards of white satin and pearls, she looked magnificent. 'They will listen, won't they, Jozef?'

Before he had been certain she would be disappointed; now he was not so sure.

'I think it's likely,' he said, and though she was nervous in the taxi cab, Elizabeth was transformed when they arrived at the party, a smoky drinks in hand affair at a fine Georgian house. She asked for Martins in a tone that brooked no denial. They were put in the care of a soft-faced young Lieutenant with a tall, gangling frame.

'Dreadful crush, but we'll find him. Are you hoping for news of a relative, Countess? A soldier, perhaps?'

'My husband and I are here to offer our work, Lieutenant. Is that right, Jozef?'

Her pronunciation was already good but she was still easily confused by English synonyms.

'Services,' Jozef said.

The young Lieutenant raised his eyebrows. 'There is some talk of reforming Polish units in France – '

'You will see we will be useful in other ways,' Elizabeth said. 'There is Mr. Martins.' She touched the lieutenant's arm and nodded.

'Ah, Countess! And Pan Goralski, am I correct? Such a pleasure,' Martins said in French. 'How I missed you and your wonderful reports and suggestions.' He kissed Elizabeth's hand. 'I am so glad you got here safely.'

'We were staying in France. We could not get back home.'

'No, no. Very wise. And now you are here.' And then he looked at them shrewdly, trying to estimate how much help they would want and what it might cost.

'The Countess and I wish to do whatever we can for our country's allies,' Jozef said stiffly. His wife was sincerely, if naively, idealistic and this man did her wrong if he thought they had come for favours.

'Undoubtedly,' Martins said smoothly, 'but what – isn't that the question? There will be some sort of Polish corps formed, but for you – ' He hesitated delicately. The plain fact was that Jozef looked a trifle old for the army and the

105

admirable Countess was, unfortunately, a woman.

Elizabeth was amused by his lack of imagination. 'We will do whatever is required, of course,' she said in Polish. 'Civilians will be needed, linguists, people who are unafraid to come and go, who can speak languages, who are determined to die usefully.'

There was a little pause and in that silence Jozef glimpsed something new in his wife, a balance of determination and resignation that he was to recognise later in others of his countrymen, in other irregulars. She was determined, he realised, in a way neither this man nor his masters could stand against, for she was concentrated absolutely on her goal and willing to pay whatever price. He had not realised that until now and it made him fearful for her.

'After all, there is no army in Poland now – or in Czechoslovakia or Austria, is there?' she asked Martins.

'Some say it will go no further.'

'The *sitzkrieg*'? Jozef asked. 'What do you call it?'

'The Bore War.'

'Do you believe that, Mr. Martins?'

'Not I, Countess. But your proposal?'

'To go back, of course. There will be a Polish Resistance. It is a foregone conclusion. They will need information, money and, above all, the knowledge that Britain will fight. If they could learn of your preparations, hear of Mr. Churchill's speeches, be assured that you will never bargain with the Nazis ...' She smiled at him as if Martins were personally responsible for barrage balloons and Anderson shelters and ack-ack guns in St. James Park. Jozef saw the agent's face grow reflective; Elizabeth was in her element.

'His Majesty's Government would want information,' the Englishman said.

'And you'd get it from as far behind the enemy's lines as possible.'

'There are some people who might be interested,' Martins allowed. 'I have a contact in the foreign office. But they will want to know how you intend to get into Poland.'

'There will be snow in November,' Elizabeth said. 'I plan to ski over the mountains.'

Chapter Ten

Budapest – Winter 1939

Elizabeth knocked the snow and slush from her boots, shook off her coat and glanced into the main room of the apartment where Jozef was sitting huddled next to the ancient porcelain stove. He had a blanket flung around his shoulders and his papers blanced on a board on his lap. 'Any luck?' he asked.

'Just some more information from the Consul. I am amazed at the number of our people who have escaped. Whole companies. He told me today of two pilots who hired a bus to take their group from the internment camp right into Budapest.'

'The Hungarians have been very good.'

'Yes, but I'm not sure how long it can continue,' Elizabeth said as she rubbed her cold hands in front of the stove. 'Alojzy said today that his hotel is full of Gestapo. They are travelling around Hungary quite openly.'

'They will be everywhere. The Nazis think they're the kings of the earth at the moment.'

Elizabeth sat down on a baggy, ill-sprung chair and stretched her cold feet nearer the heat. Except for that halo of warmth and drying wool, the whole apartment had the musty cold smell of old stone and plaster. 'I'll freeze to death before I find a guide,' she said. 'The Gurals will only go to the Polish border, and the people who know the Czech side aren't to be found.'

'Come spring there will be more crossings,' Jozef said easily. 'Not everyone is fit for the Tatra on skis.'

'It will be too late by spring. And in the good weather there will be more patrols. As you say yourself, the Germans are everywhere. They'll soon have control of the Czech border police.'

Jozef shrugged. It would suit him as well if she never found a guide. 'I left you some coffee. But don't drink it all,' he added as she went into the tiny kitchen. 'Someone's coming.'

'You didn't mention that.'

'A few surprises keep you from being bored.'

'You're a wonderful man, but he's not a guide, is he?' Elizabeth asked, returning with the coffee cups. 'I won't forgive you if he's a guide, when I walked through most of Pest today, looking.'

'No, he's not a guide, but he may be worth knowing. We'll see.'

The knock came while they were drinking their coffee, and Elizabeth jumped up to answer the door. The hand lettered card outside read "Jozef Gorman, Teacher of Languages", and the tall man asked for Pan Gorman.

'Come in, please. Jozef.'

'Ah, Lieutenant Zermoski, good to see you again. This is my wife, Elizabeth.' The visitor bowed. 'Marek Zermoski,' he said. 'My pleasure to meet you.'

The Lieutenant limped noticeably; otherwise he was impressive, a powerfully built man with dark eyes and strong features. His face was wind-burned and his large hands, red from the cold.

'Come in by the stove,' Jozef said. 'And have some coffee. It's such cold weather.'

'At home,' the visitor said, 'we'd say this was an open winter.'

'Everywhere is cold in exile.'

'Yes, how true. It is the dampness that really bother's me.' Merek Zermoski stretched out his right leg as if it were stiff.

'Were you wounded?' Elizabeth asked.

'Shrapnel in the knee. They wanted to take the leg, but I had other ideas.' He showed his strong, white teeth as if to suggest the folly of crossing his wishes, and there was a moment's pause before Jozef said, 'You had a proposition?'

The Lieutenant looked from Elizabeth to Jozef.

'My wife would have to be involved,' Jozef said. 'You see our accommodation.'

'Yes, Well,' he said decisively. 'I have some "parcels" I must hide. May I leave them here?'

'Parcels?' Elizabeth asked.

'Two airmen and an artillery sergeant. Normally, I'd run them right to the border, but the car is broken down and we're waiting for a part. My hotel's resident Gestapo will certainly report three visitors. One or even two is explicable – my partner has put it about that his tastes are unnatural,' Marek said, his expression amused, 'but three is pressing their gullibility and the hotel's tolerance.'

'We have room, Jozef.'

'Certainly. Bring them at once if you like. I always have people coming and going.'

'Good. They will be here tonight.' Marek stood up and shook their hands. 'We will have to postpone our English lesson, Pan Gorman. When the car is fixed, I will call and make an appointment. That will be the signal to have them ready.'

Men came regularly. Elizabeth and Jozef got some extra mattresses and learned to make a cheap but filling stew. When Jozef had his pupils, the "parcels" hid in the bedroom, playing silent games of cards or reading the books that Elizabeth found in the secondhand shops. Since many were still in uniform, she bought overcoats, jackets and trousers at little second hand shops and outdoor markets in the poor quarters. Bundled in a cheap, shapeless coat, a package of worn clothing under one arm, she was ignored even by people who had been introduced to Elizabeth Gorman, the Anglo-Polish journalist. The effectiveness of this simple disguise gave her confidence, and one day when she saw a man leaning weakly against a lamp post, it seemed safe to stop and see if he needed help.

'Are you hurt, sir?' she asked in Hungarian.

When he turned, she recognised Marek Zermoski, but just barely. His face was grey, his eyes dull with pain.

'I will be all right, madame, thank you,' he said. 'Just an old complaint.' He turned away, then glanced back at her. 'Pani Gorman? I wouldn't have known you. What are you doing here?'

'Out shopping.' She half unfolded the coat she carried over her arm. 'Less conspicuous than full flight uniform. He had not even removed his insignia!'

'I am sorry. He had been warned to ao that at least,' Marek said. 'But I was not up to escorting him.' He gave a smile which turned into a grimace.

Elizabeth took his arm. 'What is wrong?'

'The usual. The surgeons couldn't get all the metal out of my leg. It's never healed right.'

'We should get a cab.' She looked around.

'No, no, just help me to the tram stop.' He flung one arm across her shoulder, and Elizabeth held his waist to steady herself.

'All right?'

'Yes, it helps to take the weight off.' He spoke cheerfully, but she could see the pain in the thin lines on either side of his mouth. When they got into the tram and sat down, Marek stretched his sore leg and leaned back in the leather seat with a sigh. 'I'd be in France now without this. I got away from the camp without the slightest problem. Guard winked on the way out and said, "Nice day for a walk." They didn't take a cripple too seriously. That was good. The bad was that our people have naturally wanted to get the able bodied out first.'

'You are probably more useful here,' Elizabeth said. She unfastened the hateful brown woolen scarf and shook out her long wavy hair. 'Who knows what will get done in France? I think the English a better bet.'

'Perhaps I'd better stick with your husband's lessons,' he teased, but as the cars lurched over some frozen points his colour ebbed and his knuckles went white. When they got off near his hotel, Elizabeth insisted on stopping for tea with rum. After a couple of glasses, Marek ran his hand over his face and through the dark, untidy hair that tumbled on to his forehead. 'That's better,' he said. 'The cold is bad and the walking. Otherwise, I'm perfectly healthy.'

Elizabeth smiled. Used to smart officers like her father and cousin, she found Marek's appearance slightly raffish. Despite his impeccable manners, there was something – the too long hair, the faintly slanted Tartar eyes, the contrast between the boldly modelled head and thin lipped, sensitive mouth, or perhaps simply the expressiveness of his features and his amused amber-flecked eyes – that was not, as Martins would have said, *pukkah*. He had the face of a bandit chief, and Elizabeth sensed a spiritual cousin.

'So what are you here for? Or shouldn't I ask?'

'You shouldn't ask,' she said.

'I will anyway. You've managed to meet every Pole in Budapest.'

'Not the right one, yet.'

He raised his eyebrows. 'I'd had had hopes,' he said, and she laughed. He had a playful, irrepressible streak that reminded her of Charlie.

'I need a guide. Someone who can find his way through the Czech side of the Tatra. Someone who knows the safe houses and where the guards are likely to patrol.'

Marek looked thoughtful. 'In mid-winter?'

She nodded. 'Safer, in some ways. By spring, who knows what will have happened.'

'Jozef, too?'

'No. He was a good skier, but his health is poor. And he does not really approve.'

Marek shrugged his shoulders. 'He is a brave man but none of this appeals to him. Unlike you and me.'

'What are we like?'

'We were made for this. It's the air we breathe.' His eyes became hooded, secret. 'We were bored before, and now we live. It's as simple as that.' He studied her across the café table: the ridiculous coat, the frayed sweater, the mismatched gloves, the magnificent hair and eyes. His was a susceptible nature; a certain flirtatiousness was as natural to him as breathing. And it was pleasant to talk of the past, of people they had both known, of places they had ridden, of coffee houses, of parties, of Warsaw as it was before the newsreels captured an unknown city, filled with smoke and falling stone. He remembered that her elopement had created a great scandal; that piqued his interest. People said she was sweet but wilful; she said herself she intended to cross the Tatra in the dead of winter. Now and again she brushed her hair from her eyes with a restless, impatient gesture. 'It's late,' he said.

She glanced outside at the street lamps swimming in light

snow, the tram lights reflecting in black pools of slush.

'Have dinner with me. I can drive you home and pick up our parcel in one trip.'

She smiled again. 'I will call Jozef,' she said.

He kissed her in the car. It was parked in an icy little courtyard beside his hotel. She took his arm as they crossed the ice, afraid he would fall. 'Is it hard to drive?'

'Not so hard as walking.' His mouth was tight. He opened the door and she slipped into the freezing interior. Then Marek swung himself into the car and put the key in the ignition. The starter ground, then died, once, twice, before the engine caught. 'It stalled one night halfway to the border. Fortunately, one of the parcels was a mechanic. It just needs warming up,' he said as the motor sputtered unconvincingly. 'I really need a truck.'

'I might be able to help with that.'

'A woman of many talents.'

'The British have money.'

'I don't care where I get one from, so long as it runs.' He put his foot down and the engine raced long and loud in the snow muffled courtyard. 'There,' he said as it settled into a smooth hum, 'we're off.'

But first he leaned over and kissed her.

'I don't like it,' said Jozef.

Elizabeth looked up from ineffectually repairing a rip in a heavy wool jacket. 'What?'

'Do you remember that Henryk fellow? Linde was his last name.'

'He came over and spoke to us in the café the other night.'

'That's right. He wants lessons in French.'

'So?'

'"I know of your work," he says to me. "Of course I want to do all I can."'

'What did you say?'

'As little as possible. I said my pupils were usually satisfied. He kept trying to bring the conversation round to the war.'

'Maybe he is all right.'

'I thought about that, though I'm sure he's German — one

of the *Volksdeutsch*. Then Marek said something tonight, when he took the pilot. He said he'd seen Linde around his hotel.'

'That I don't like,' said Elizabeth. 'Marek's hotel is no good at all. It's full of able-bodied Poles and anti-fascist Hungarians, one of the first places the Gestapo would put under surveillance.' She did not say she had been there. She did not say that on the way to his room, Marek had nodded towards a man in tweeds and whispered, 'Our German friend.'

'Linde's persistent. He's coming tomorrow evening for a lesson. I've put him off twice, but I don't want to be too obvious.'

'I will warn Marek.'

'But tell him to come. We must decide about Linde. If he's all right, we'll just put him off. He can go join the corps in France if he's a patriot. If not – '

Elizabeth looked up sharply.

'This is not a game, my dear. If he's a German trying to infiltrate, we've either got to get rid of him or move our base of operations. Marek will see that.'

'Budapest is the only possibility.'

'Yes,' said Jozef. 'So, we will decide tomorrow.'

The next night was terribly cold, and the slush and water of the streets turned to black ice, hard as iron. Jozef stood in front of the stove, rubbing his hands together, and said, "Now is the winter of our discontent".

Elizabeth went into the kitchen. She had learned to make coffee and could boil eggs, but Jozef cooked the soups and the stews for the 'parcels'. She started some water, her fingers stiff with cold. They had been waiting quite a while. 'Maybe he won't come.'

Jozef didn't answer.

She stepped to the doorway and spoke more loudly. 'I said, maybe he won't come.'

'If we're right, he will.'

She returned to the stove, impatient and apprehensive. She hated violence and cruelty, and that hatred was one of the things that made her fearless. She had not hesitated about the 'parcels'; when the time came, she would not hesitate to put on her skis and head north; but this business with Linde was something else again. He was up to no good and their only recourse was obvious; she still hoped he would not come.

There was a knock and she waited, the coffee pot in her hands. She heard the creak of Jozef's chair, the sound of the bolt being drawn back. 'Ah, Pan Linde. I was afraid you would miss your lesson.'

'The tram switches were frozen.'

'Come in, come in. Will we have some coffee? Elizabeth, another cup.'

She brought everything in on a tray, and Linde jumped up and made a fuss of helping set out the cups and the plate of biscuits. He was short but stocky, with a very red face, light grey eyes, and an air of good fellowship that did not quite conceal a prying shrewdness. 'I will leave you to your lesson,' she said.

'Do not let me inconvenience you, Madam Gorman. Stay, if you like by your fine stove.' He grinned and rubbed his hands. 'I know quite well these lessons are only part of your interests.' He nodded briskly. 'Oh, you needn't say anything yet. But in these sad times, patriots must find their way to each other.'

'And also earn their living,' Elizabeth said drily. She gave Jozef a look and retreated to the bedroom. From the living room came the sound of their voices droning through the French alphabet. She could hear Jozef correcting Linde's pronunciation carefully, making him repeat the sounds over and over, a familiar repetition grown sinister. She had hoped Linde could be left to Marek, but Jozef had insisted on coping alone and, to her surprise, Marek had agreed. 'He was a soldier, he knows about such things,' she argued with Jozef.

'He was an engineer and is no more fit than I am. Neither of us is armed.'

'If Linde is armed, you won't have a chance.'

'And Marek will?' Jozef gave a thin smile. He did not miss much and he had not missed the new gaiety Elizabeth had shown since the Lieutenant came on the scene. But this was to be his job, and Elizabeth, though rarely thwarted by masculine pride, had had to let the matter rest.

In the other room, she heard Jozef say, 'Thirsty work,' and

Linde's jovial agreement. Then he opened the door and looked in.

'We thought we'd go and have a drink. Don't wait up, we might meet friends.' They exchanged glances and Elizabeth mouthed the words, 'Be careful.' Jozef nodded and closed the door. She heard them putting on their boots and coats, then the sound of the latch. From the window she saw the two figures leave the circle of the street light and disappear into the thin sleet. Elizabeth lifted the phone and dialled Marek's number.

'They've gone,' she said.

'I'll be there in an hour or so.'

She replaced the receiver. Fair or not, if anything happened to Jozef she would blame Marek.

He arrived before eleven and sat down, still bundled in his coat. 'Do you know where they went?'

Elizabeth shrugged. 'He said he knew a place. By the river, I think.'

Merek nodded.

'I wanted you to meet them there,' Elizabeth said. 'I thought it would be safer.'

'But not so secure,' Marek said calmly.

She jumped up, annoyed, and stood warming her hands at the stove, her back to him.

'Your husband can take care of himself. He told me he spent years travelling: Mexico, America, the islands.'

'And ruined his health,' Elizabeth said. 'When he came to us first he was half dead from fever.'

Marek narrowed his eyes. In the dim, yellow light, Elizabeth seemed very lovely.

'You don't always think about him.'

'I love Jozef,' she said, 'For always.'

'And me?'

She came over and touched his shoulder lightly. 'For sometimes,' she said.

He reached for her hand, but she drew away and went to sit on the other side of the stove. 'We should have gone too. If Jozef drinks anything but beer, he will be lost.'

Around midnight, Marek fell asleep in his chair, and Elizabeth covered him with a blanket. In the silence, she could hear the soft hiss of the coals, his quiet breathing, the occasional gusts of wind that swept off the Danube to rattle sashes up and down the Buda hills. The walls exuded dampness, and she hunched her shoulders against the chill and buried her hands in the pockets of her sweater. Marek turned in his sleep, his handsome profile drawn with exhaustion, and Elizabeth felt her irritation slide into tenderness. After their first, chance meeting in Pest, she had seen him often — there was always some excuse. It was foolish, but she could not pass his favourite coffee house without checking the usual table. 'I have the new parcels' documents,' he said one day. 'Do you want them?'

'When are you planning to take them to the border?'
'Tomorrow.'
'All right.'
His expression was sly. 'The documents are at the hotel.'
Marek noticed the Gestapo agent as they got out of the elevator, and though Elizabeth was glad she had kept her scarf fastened and her coat collar up, her folly felt like wine, so intoxicating it made her fearless. Marek unlocked the door to a spacious, faded suite. 'Where's your friend?' she asked.

'Off to pick up some others. His last run, I'd think.'
Elizabeth gave him a look.
'He's been questioned twice. He'll be deported. I'll have to find somewhere less grand.'

Through the mesh under curtains, Elizabeth saw the city, black, grey and white, accented by the spiky silhouette of the Parliament buildings. Pest looked unreal. Insubstantial. She leaned against the casement, felt the roughness of the flaking paint, the chill from the glass. When she turned around, Marek was standing against the door, his hands in his pockets, watching her, and in that moment Elizabeth saw quite clearly how her life would fragment. She was the Countess, she was Pani Goralski, she was the journalist Elizabeth Gorman, she was the anonymous woman who shopped at the cheapest stalls; they all had to survive. She felt the rhythm of her heart and went to him. He put out his hand, brushed back her scarf and pulled her against his big, strong body. She felt the cold of his face, the rough texture of his coat, a sudden tension in his shoulders. On the other side of the door, there were German voices. They drew apart, listening. Then Marek slid the bolt closed.

He started unbuttoning his coat, but eager, reached for her again. Elizabeth felt a delicious recklessness, as though with one touch she could obliterate this beautiful, dangerous, alien city, the voices in the halls, the 'parcels', the documents, even their insubstantial, assumed selves. She put her arms around him and drew his mouth down against hers.

That had been the first time. Now it was twenty to one on a cold, damp Budapest morning. She told Our Lady that if anything had happened to Jozef, she would never sleep with Marek again.

She must have dozed, because she heard the key first, hitting the panel, the door knob, rattling uselessly around the edges of the lock. She jumped up, touched Marek's shoulder and ran to fling the door open. Jozef was standing unsteadily on the threshold, looking pale and sick.

'My darling,' he said, and stumbled forward so that she had to catch him.

'Marek, help me!'

'Fine,' said Jozef. 'Had nothing but beer. I'm perfectly fine.'

'He's dead drunk,' Marek said, and Jozef giggled.

'Linde's dead drunk,' he said. 'Or drunk dead, if you prefer, Marek. Or do you prefer Elizabeth?' and he giggled again.

'He'd better have some coffee, some soup,' said Elizabeth.

'He ought to be sick. Throw up some of it.'

'Good idea,' said Jozef. 'Very sick.' He belched and looked greenish.

'Heat the coffee,' said Marek. 'And get some bread or something.' He grabbed Jozef by the shoulders and began dragging him towards the bathroom. Elizabeth went into the kitchen. Over the bubble of the water, she heard Jozef vomit. By the time the coffee was ready, the two men were in the living room, Marek sitting in one chair, Jozef lying on the floor wrapped in a blanket.

'The Tenderloin,' he said in English. 'Chicago.'

'He's thrown some up,' Marek said, 'but he's still got a lot of alcohol in him.'

117

'He's right, my dear. I haven't been so drunk since Chicago. Wonderful music. Negro men playing pianos and horns 'til sunrise. You would like Chicago, Marek.'

Elizabeth knelt down beside him with the coffee. 'Drink this.'

Jozef made a face but managed a few sips.

'Better?'

'Better than Linde. The bastard.'

'Where is he?' Marek asked.

Jozef struggled to raise himself on to one elbow. 'We went out for a drink. There's a bar near here. By the river. Tough crowd. Like Chicago without Negroes.' Jozef took another drink of coffee and lay down flat on the floor. 'The bargemen drink there, and the thieves. Some good Poles. May Our Lady preserve them.'

They crossed themselves.

'Linde likes brandy, the bastard. He's a Kraut, for sure. I'm broke.'

'In a good cause,' Marek said, and patted his shoulder.

Jozef rubbed his head which was beginning to pound as if he had a fever. 'I had beer. Nothing else. Linde drank like a pig.' Jozef gave a little giggle that changed to a cough. 'I've killed a man,' he said.

Elizabeth sat back on her heels. 'What happened, Jozef?'

'Linde passed out. I bought drinks for my friends the bargemen, the thieves. They said, "Your pal's passed out." I said, "He's a Nazi spy."' Jozef coughed and sat upright. 'They said, "We'll not have Nazis here. Chuck him in the snow." So we hauled him out to a snow bank and drank to the friendship between Poland and Hungary. I'm going to sleep now,' Jozef said, and he fell back on to the floor and closed his eyes.

Chapter Eleven

The guide proved to be a will o' the wisp who led Elizabeth through the back streets and salons of Budapest. He had just arrived – or just left; he had been arrested, warned, had abandoned the business. Fey and elusive, he was often promised, but dark and dirty flats, lonely tram stops, seedy hotels did not reveal him. He seemed destined to be pursued as avidly and inconclusively as a dream, until, one afternoon at a party in the Hungarian Relief Headquarters, Elizabeth heard the single word 'Zakopane' and saw a lean, fair man with curly hair and eyes light and clear as water: a Highlander for sure. His name was Stefan and when he stopped flirting with a pretty relief worker, Elizabeth asked when he had left the Tatra.

'First snow. I decided I wasn't going to teach SS men how to ski.'

'The Germans are in the mountains?'

'They love the mountains. We Highlanders are to be honorary Aryans.' He gave a bitter laugh. 'They'll not win us over that way.' He lit a cigarette and drew in the acrid smoke, his eyes narrowed. Elizabeth saw that he was not quite so young and candid as he looked.

'Would you go back?' she asked. 'If you had a reason?'

The clear eyes turned wary. 'Some go back and forth,' he said. 'Some do, I've heard.'

'Do you know anyone who takes people across? To the Polish side?'

'Not now. The snow's four, five metres deep all over the Tatra.'

'One can ski the Tatra now. Conditions may be worse in the spring.'

'Worse before they get better,' he agreed. 'Who wants to go?'

'I do.'

'Let me offer you a dance instead. The passes in mid-winter are no place for a woman.'

Elizabeth slipped into his arms, neither annoyed nor offended. She had looked so long for a guide that she had not the slightest doubt he could be persuaded to do as she wished. 'I'm a very good skier,' she said as they circled the floor.

'I would think nothing less, but the trip needs either an expert or a fool.'

'You came out.'

'I'm one or the other, depending whom you ask,' Stefan said, 'and I crossed before the weather turned bad.'

'There will be a break in the weather. When the break comes, I will be ready.'

He had the mountaineer's dislike of being contradicted. 'You will not have a guide,' he said.

Elizabeth gave him her most beautiful smile. 'Do come and see us,' she said. 'My husband teaches languages. If you are thinking of going to France he could advise you. You would be welcome any time, no matter what you decide about my suggestion.' She spoke then of Adam and of other friends in the Gural villages, and they talked about Zakopane, about the trails and their favourite runs. Stefan thought Elizabeth a charming woman, despite her dangerous ambitions, and he began to show up at the apartment for tea with rum and little cakes and conversation. But even when it transpired he had already made a couple of trips, Stefan remained adamant about not taking her over the Tatra.

Elizabeth ignored this detail and went ahead with her plans. She laboured up and down the Buda Hills carrying a heavy rucksack to strengthen her legs, and hired a forger to prepare the work permits, ration cards and personal credentials needed in Poland. Still Stefan resisted, though her attention flattered and amused him. She suggested that he was a man of insight and character, a patriot, the next thing to a hero, and she did all this with such cheerful confidence that when the weather improved the first week in February, the guide began to weaken. The sky turned a real mountain blue over Budapest; Elizabeth said it was a sign, and Stefan said they might chance it.

She wrapped her documents in oilskin and hid them in her rucksack, along with a stout leather money bag from London, letters from various Polish politicans in exile, propaganda leaflets, and a change of city clothes. Stefan's held food for four days. They took the train from Budapest to the former Czech town of Kosice, where they stayed with a local school teacher, a man with Highland connections. Before dawn the next morning they headed toward Slovakia, Stefan's friend leading the way. The moon sailed over a sky mottled with round grey clouds like slabs of ice in the black Danube, and by its pale silver light, they moved swiftly, their skis cutting through the light crust with a clean, swish, swish. On the bank of a tiny stream they halted and listened, their breath curling in the frosty air. The teacher pointed across a rutted field, swept bare by the wind.

'The Slovaks won't be patrolling at this hour. Keep straight on for two kilometres and you'll come to the first Slovakian village. There's a train at eight for Poprad and the Polish border. But don't loiter about the town. Get into a café if you're delayed.'

They shook hands with him, and he said, 'Go with God,' like the Gurals, reminding Elizabeth of earlier crossings, of boisterous parties, of silent dawns and twilights hiking through the mountains. Stefan waved, then dug his poles into the snow and set off smartly. Elizabeth knew he would try to tire her out and discourage her before they reached the mountains. He did not dream how seriously she had been training on the Buda Hills, exercising until her lungs caught fire, until even Jozef had admitted that she was ready.

By the time the weak red sun began to light the east, they were on the platform, skis in their hands. The farmers around them were bundled to the eyes. They stamped their feet and rubbed their chapped hands, while the stationmaster's dog barked monotonously from a shed near the track. Stefan and Elizabeth waited quietly in the blue shadows until the train steamed up like a dragon to take them to the last station in Slovakia.

The safehouse Stefan used lay within sight of the Polish border, and from the cheerful and familiar greetings, Elizabeth was sure that he had crossed often, that his given profession of ski instructor was a mere euphemism. The next morning, they made ready in the darkness and drank coffee laced with brandy before stepping out on to snow crackling under fifty degrees of frost. Before dawn tne landscape was purple. As the light intensified, the snow faded to lavender and then to a rose pink unbelievably vivid against the blue evergreens. These thinned out near the border where there was a slope before the foothills hunched themselves into mountains and the track lay uphill, mile after mile of steady climbing. Stefan stopped, wiped his red nose on his glove, and looked at Elizabeth. He had given up hope that she would turn back, but with the Tatra rising above them, its ridges thrown into bold relief by the sunrise, the snowy peaks already white in the first rays, he hesitated. The old mountaineer at the safe house had thought him mad for taking her, and, faced with the great expanse of snow and rock ahead, Stefan had a moment of doubt.

Elizabeth ignored his unspoken question and looked up and down the valley. There was not a sound; the air that burned into their lungs carried nothing but the wind, and after the restricted and ambiguous existence of Budapest the vast emptiness of the mountains exhilarated her. The rainbow hues of the snow and the crystalline mountain sky filled her with happiness. She had not the slightest hesitation. 'It will be all right, you'll see,' she whispered. Stefan dug his poles into the snow and pushed off. Their skis flew over the dry, powdery crust, hurtling them forward into blue and rose over a field paved with diamonds. For a moment Elizabeth had the impression that they would be borne up above the mountains and land like falcons on the banks of the Vistula. But the walls of the Tatra rose steeper and steeper, the land tilted upward, and, as the snow turned blinding white, their flight slowed. 'We're in Poland now,' said Stefan, and he led the way up the first ascent, along a track that passed through a dense grove of spruce.

The storm came on the second day. At two the sky was clear,

still brilliant as the sun dropped. Within half an hour, the wind had shifted; the air seemed to thicken and fast moving clouds turned the sky to lead. They were both tired, their thick shirts damp under their heavy sweaters, their muscles aching from climbing splayfooted up the slopes. They had stopped, planning to rest for a time and then push on towards a hostel at the far end of the next valley. But when the first flakes whipped across the pass, Stefan said, 'We cannot wait.' Elizabeth checked her watch; they should have had several hours of daylight. Now they might lose visibility at any time, and if the storm trapped them on the heights, they would die of exposure or fall from a precipice. They started up a steep and rocky incline, where the mountain winds had wiped rocks here and there clean of snow. The storm snuffed out their breath and lashed their faces with stinging needles of ice. It decapitated the mountain peaks, and the bold black and white of the jagged terrain sank into a pearly grey swirl of wind and snow. Every step became an effort, and the patches of ice and rock made them swear under their breath. In the lee of a jagged outcropping, Stefan stopped, panting. The thin track wound up along the face of a ridge and, where the snow had been blown away, the going looked icy and treacherous: they would not manage the hostel.

Elizabeth wiped her nose and struggled for breath. 'Is there anywhere nearer?'

'What?'

'Shelter? Anywhere nearer?'

Without answering, Stefan slid off his rucksack and offered her the brandy. The alcohol ignited her throat, leaving her mouth and face rigid with cold. She handed the flask back. 'How much further can you go?' he asked.

'To Warsaw.'

He patted her shoulder. 'We must try to manage this ridge. There is an old guide's hut on the other side. If we can find it, we will make Warsaw.'

Elizabeth fell twice, hitting ice and floundering into deep snow that stole like cold fire down her neck and up under the cuffs of her ski mittens. Stefan damaged one of his poles on a rock and they had to refasten the ring with a scrap of rawhide. By this time, the track was visible only a few yards in front of them and it was almost impossible to breathe in the wind. The upgrades were torture, their weary legs crying out for rest, but the descents were worse, the world sliding away into a swirling, sunless void that might conceal an abyss as easily as the track. Stefan went first, and once again Elizabeth marvelled at the skills of the mountaineers. He had what old Adam would have called a sense of the mountain, moving forward cautiously, but steadily, and probing delicately with his poles when he was uncertain. They climbed for what seemed an entire afternoon, hours and hours of exhausted misery to reach the top of the ridge, where the unimpeded force of the wind rocked them back in their bindings and drenched them in snow. They appeared to have reached the edge of a vast cauldron, a witches' brew of storm that clawed its way through their clothing and dried the sweat on their bodies, making them shiver uncontrollably and bite their lips to stop chattering teeth.

'The valley,' Stefan yelled over the wind.

'Do you know where the hut is?'

He gestured straight down, wrapped his scarf more tightly around his mouth and pushed off.

Elizabeth followed, watching the snow divide under her skis, trying to keep the ice from getting into her eyes. The wind seemed to be supporting her, holding her back from the descent, and the whistling and roaring around them was like the avalanche. She asked the Virgin to be with her at the hour of her death, lifted her poles and dropped into the white blindness of the valley.

The first trees appeared like mountain spirits, a darkness behind the swirl of snow and Stefan let out a whoop of joy. They floundered into the trees, not even looking for a path, and flung their arms around the scaly trunks. The great branches rose and fell in the storm, dusting them with snow, but they were too tired to care. After a few minutes, Stefan said, 'The hut is on the main logging road,' and they began searching along the timberline for the trail. Finally they found an opening in the trees and a few hundred yards further, a low stone and timber hut. The snow had drifted up to the sills of the two small windows, and the door, stuck in a thick layer of ice, did not yield until they had dropped their rucksacks and put their shoulders to it. Then it opened to a dark cabin, scarcely warmer than the woods outside, but furnished with a stone hearth and a supply of logs. Stefan arranged the kindling and struggled to light a match. Elizabeth shut the door, latched it against the wind and collapsed on the floor. She did not move until the flames were leaping high above the logs, washing the rough walls with orange light. Then she crept over to Stefan's rucksack and pulled out the flask. 'To Warsaw,' she said.

'I'll be thankful to see Zakopane.'

'To Warsaw and Zakopane,' she said. Stefan took a drink and began cutting off chucks of dried sausage with his knife. They shared these, some dry bread and a few bits of chocolate, then sprawled half asleep by the fire, glad to be inside, thankful to be alive. Outside, the wind shrieked around the eaves and sent sudden swirls of snow slapping against the shutters. They put their boots to dry by the fire and wrapped their cold feet in their blankets. Elizabeth put her head on her rucksack and closed her eyes. A wood mouse ran about in the rafters, and below, the fire crackled, its sour wood and ash smell filling the hut, which shivered in the wind like a ship at sea. Elizabeth dreamed of the ship at Dieppe, struggling towards the harbour, plunging desperately up and down on the waves, while its captain cried for help over the storm and she sat in Janusz's arms. 'Help us, help us,' the boat cried in a human voice, and Elizabeth swam to the surface of her exhausted sleep. The wind was howling, the windows rattled, a fine layer of snow sifted through the cracks between the logs. She closed her eyes and was almost asleep again when she heard the sound. This time she sat upright, and her heart jumped: someone was outside in the storm.

The fire was only a mass of embers. Elizabeth threw on another log, before she stuck her feet into her ski boots and struggled to open the door which, unlatched, tore out of her hands and banged against the outside wall. A shower of snow blew into the room. 'Hello,' she cried. 'Hello!'

Stefan woke up, his voice hoarse with sleep. 'What the hell are you doing?'

'I heard someone.'

The storm had buried every landmark. Beyond the fringe of

trees about the hut, there was only the white chaos of snow.' Elizabeth was out of the doorway before Stefan caught her arm. 'Get back inside.'

'There are people out there. Can't you hear them? We're coming, we're coming!' she called, twisting out of his grasp and plunging into the drifts. He stumbled after her in his bare feet and caught her around the waist. 'Get back inside!'

'They'll die! Let me go! Here,' she called over the wind. 'Here!' She kicked at his legs and tried to twist free as the snow drenched their faces and whitened their hands.

'You'd be lost before you've gone five metres,' Stefan shouted. They struggled for a moment, half blind, still half dreaming, the voices ringing in their ears like some nightmare song, then he seized one of Elizabeth's legs and turning, half off balance, lifted her towards the doorway. She reached out to stop herself on the door frame and gave a cry as her hand was torn on the rough edge. Stefan dropped her and she rolled on to the doorstep and into the cabin. Behind her the door slammed and the latch rattled.

'I know they're out there! You don't care. You're no real mountaineer if you leave them in the snow.' She tried to get to her feet, but Stefan seized both her arms before she could reach the door and forced her to her knees.

'You're not going anywhere. I promised to take you to Zakopane and by God I will, but I'm not going to commit suicide on a whim of yours.'

'Whim! There's someone out there — maybe more than one. And I can tell by your face you heard them too.' She started to get up again and this time, exhausted, he flung himself against her so that they both sprawled on the floor.

'I was bringing airmen out when you were still partying in Budapest. Do you think those poor bastards are the first to die? Do you think we can save them all?' He shook her so hard her head banged against the boards. 'You're wrong. We can't save them — even if we die ourselves. It's that kind of war,' he said more quietly, his voice dropping towards despair, and Elizabeth saw that he had learned this cruelty, that he had heard other voices in the snow, and stopped trying to tear herself free. Stefan released her and looked at her seriously. 'You're not Countess Elizabeth anymore who can make things change. People die and you can't stop it, and if you can't stand that you'll be no good back home.' He went over to the fire and fiddled with the logs, his face drawn, his feet blotched white and yellow from the cold. There was no sound now but the wind.

After a moment, Elizabeth threw her blanket to him. 'Wrap up your feet,' she said. 'You look as if you've a touch of frostbite.' She lay down, shivering, with her head on her rucksack and listened to the storm. Stefan stretched out beside her, wrapped his feet in one blanket, then threw the other over them both. 'You'll see,' he said. 'Even staying alive is a victory.'

The next time Elizabeth woke the air was still and there was light around the edge of the shutters. When she opened the door, the grey sky was lit through clouds thick as frosted glass, but the storm was over. She could see the trees, the outline of the peaks, the forested valley. She scooped up a handful of snow, let it melt in her mouth and felt the water run down her chin, then she walked into the trees. By the time she returned, Stefan was back with an armful of wood to replenish the hut's stock. He dumped the logs in the bin beside the fireplace, then opened his rucksack for another hunk of the tough spiced sausage. 'I want to get down the valley,' he said. 'It looks like more snow and the hostel's better equipped.'

They set off after breakfast and were barely out of sight of the hut when they found the woman. She was lying in the snow, her hair frozen to the drift, ice about her mouth. Elizabeth felt the rich sausage in the back of her throat and threw up in the snow. Stefan knelt beside the woman, quite young and pretty in her ski jacket with fur trim, but when he touched her shoulder, he shook his head. He did not touch the child, a boy of perhaps twelve, still with a small suitcase strapped to his back, and when they found the man further on, it was Elizabeth who covered his face with a scarf since his dark eyes had frozen open. Elizabeth wondered if they were city people who were not used to the mountains. 'They must have had a guide,' she said.

Stefan shrugged. 'Nothing is as it used to be.'

Elizabeth spat the sour taste of shock on to the trail. 'It will snow,' Stefan said. 'We must get to the hostel as soon as we can.'

She folded her hands deliberately and, though their faith was unknowable, said, 'Eternal rest grant unto them, O Lord.'

Stefan bowed his head. 'And let perpetual light shine upon them.'

'May they rest in peace.'

'Amen,' said Stefan. They made the sign of the cross, then dug their poles into the deep, soft snow and moved down the valley.

Chapter Twelve

The train was full of women, that was the first change: peasant women in head scarves and muddy boots, smartly dressed city women, some in furs, and underfed housewives in wornout men's coats, all with bundles and baskets which they kept protectively under their feet. The city people sat alone, silent and nervous, but the peasants were more expansive. They sized up the others with shrewd, hard eyes and talked among themselves like horsetraders at a fair. They had cabbages, turnips and potatoes; one spoke in undertones of a pig just slaughtered. Although they feigned indifference, the Varsovians pricked up their ears with interest and envy. Food was their consuming passion, and even the poorest of the peasants' crop was worth the jolting, shuddering journey over the damaged roadbed. The track was lined with bomb craters, and every town had ruined houses and signs of shelling, but Elizabeth had expected that. What she had not expected, what the newsreel could not show, what she had glimpsed only in the hut with Stefan, was the human atmosphere of fear and bitterness and hatred and defiance and loss – loss beyond imagining, which took shape for her unmistakably as they pulled into Warsaw.

    It was a raw, bleak day, the sky dark behind the pale stone of the city, and, as they drew near the centre, she saw the devastation: the buildings sheared off, apartments punctured and opened, wallpaper and bits of furniture still incongruously intact despite absent ceilings and gaping floors. The familiar streets, now pitted and filthy, had taken on a geography of their own, marked by mountains of rubble and dark pools flooded from ruined pipes. In Central Station, the light streamed down on to the tracks from between the twisted girders of the roof, and the passengers exited along a windy plywood corridor that wound through the ruins. On the next platform, German troops were embarking, tall, healthy-looking fellow in grey uniforms, singing like schoolboys. Elizabeth felt such a wave of anger and hatred that she stopped in her tracks, her face frozen. The other passengers pushed around her, indifferent to the Wehrmacht, and she had to force herself, like the others, to walk slowly, to look as if she had seen all this before, as if she had already taken in the extent of the disaster. By the time she stepped out on to Jerusalem Avenue, Elizabeth was shivering with the strain, and here she stopped again, unable, for a moment, to absorb what she saw.

The wind off the Vistula rushed over the pavement, sifted the earth from the rubble and floated it in marled patterns at ankle height. Every square was littered with uprooted paving and ringed by splintered trees, and there were barricades about the still unfilled bomb craters. All over the centre of the city, shops and offices and churches stood gutted or else chewed about their roofs and attics as if by some giant rat; others, standing as if unharmed, on closer approach revealed murky shafts floored in mud and banded by layers of twisted girders. Their former inhabitants lay under the paving: candles burned for them on certain corners and forlorn bunches of real and paper flowers covered their unmarked graves. There was smoke in the air and sewage and an acrid smell of stone dust that made Elizabeth's heart jump. Surely Mother and André were safe at the farm, but what of Félicie? The Halperns' apartment was only minutes from Central Station, but after a moment of agonising temptation, Elizabeth turned north through Tlomackie Square, plastered red and black with German information posters. She soon found the big, ugly apartment building she was looking for, but continued past it around the block. Though the neighbourhood was so quiet the Germans might have been beyond the moon, in the nervous shock of her arrival every detail struck Elizabeth as ominous. Her home was now enemy territory and it took a moment before she could control her pounding heart and enter the lobby. Her contact was in apartment three; she had a long, chilly, silent wait before a thin, unshaven man wearing a thick overcoat, gloves, a hat and slippers answered the bell. His dark eyes glanced at her nervously, then his face settled into a studied indifference. 'Good afternoon.'

'Good afternoon. Is Juliusz in? My name is Marysia. I have a message from his Cousin Bastia.'

'His cousin in Gydansk?'

'Yes.'

'Please come in.' He shut and locked the door behind them before he stuck out his hand. 'Welcome, welcome. I'm Juliusz. The others will be here by three. We had almost lost hope.'

'Our trip took longer than expected. The weather turned bad.'

'We did not think you'd make it. Come, sit, you must be tired,' he said, gesturing towards a room dark with furniture of all different sizes and styles. Chairs and tables were squeezed promiscuously together or stacked on top of beds and bureaus to be, in turn, surmounted by bric-a-brac in unstable piles that exuded a stale and unwholesome odour of decaying velvet and horsehair. Elizabeth caught a glimpse of herself in a dresser mirror, her hair wild, her face burned dark from the mountain sun and wind. Juliusz pushed aside a bureau and lifted a set of fire tongs to make room for her on a chair thick with dust and impregnated with the smell of tobacco. He rearranged a desk, a low chest and a small table in order to pull up another for himself. 'I sell furniture,' he said, showing the wide gaps between his teeth. 'There is so much to buy now.'

'But who has money to spend?'

He gave a soft, cynical laugh. 'You'd be surprised. There is always money in wartime.'

'How true,' said Elizabeth. She opened her rucksack and produced the heavy leather money pouch. 'From friends in London.'

He felt its weight, then disappeared with it amidst his stock. The bell rang twice as he was returning, but though Elizabeth gave a start, her host was unperturbed. She heard the rattle of bolts and latches, then two men in business suits followed him into the room.

'The representatives from the Peasant's Party and the Christian Democrats,' Juliusz said. 'Our courier, Marysia.'

Elizabeth stood up and shook their hands. She gave each man a large sealed envelope from his Budapest Headquarters.

'Were there any verbal messages?'

'Yes,' said Elizabeth. 'I will need perhaps an hour with each of you. I have questions for you to answer. I am prepared to take your replies when I return to Hungary.'

'Excellent,' Juliusz said, 'excellent.' He looked at each of them. The Christian Democrat arranged to meet her the following day. Juliusz cleared a little more space amidst his stock and left her to report to the Peasant Party representative.

The sun was low when Elizabeth left the furniture dealer's. Though she longed for even a glimpse of Félicie's apartment, Elizabeth knew she had to reach the safehouse before curfew and went straight to the tram stop. With half of every car reserved for Germans, the trams were terribly crowded. Two passed without stopping, and after an hour had gone by, Elizabeth considered walking, then realised with a fright that there was not enough time. The other people waiting were tense with the same repressed anxiety. They stood frozen, clutching bags and parcels, or walked up and down irritably. It was almost dusk before the right car arrived, and then they began a slow and halting progress, lurching over the defects in the track, stopped by pedestrians, by carts, by a detachment of troops, a thousand and one petty delays as the hands of Elizabeth's watch raced inexorably forward. It was close, very close now to curfew, to the danger time when people were stopped and arrested — or shot — on the street, and, at each stop, tardy travellers clutched their belongings, scanned the street, then hurried home, even those limping, even those with canes and heavy bundles.

Elizabeth felt her stomach clench. When she finally reached the right area, darkness had fallen and the sound of tramping boots send her diving into the nearest apartment lobby, fearful she would be spotted as an outsider, as a courier. She waited until the soldiers passed, then slipped out, searching for the number in the unlit street. Just at curfew, she found she was on the wrong street, began again and at last found her way up the rickety stairs of the tenement by lighting matches.

She spent the next three days in the maid's alcove of a fourth floor flat owned by a cavalryman's widow. Then, her first round of meetings over, she packed her rucksack and left. She had wanted no contact with her family while she was staying in a safehouse and now, for the first time, she approached Nowy Swiat Street.

The fine apartment buildings were blind with boards and plywood, but as Elizabeth neared Félicie's block, her anxiety lifted. She had allowed the shock of the occupation to worry her unnecessarily: the house was intact, with even a few panes of new glass winking in the weak February sun. Inside the ornate door, she discovered that the inhabitants had multiplied by three at least, the newcomers' names scrawled on cards stuck beside those of the original tenants. But the Halpern's name was still on its accustomed brass plate, and when Elizabeth went up the wide marble steps and rang the bell, Vincenty opened the door.

The butler had grown old since she had stayed with Félicie for parties and for English Charlie, but his parchment-coloured face broke into a smile. 'Countess!'

She put her finger to her lips. 'No titles, Vincenty. How are you?'

'Surviving, miss, surviving. There are many worse off. 'He held the door for her. Like Juliusz, he wore gloves, and a thick woollen sweater under his dark jacket.

'And my cousin and her family? Are they all well?'

'The children are safe in the country, thank God.' But before he could continue, Félicie came into the hall, wearing a fur coat and high boots.

'I knew that voice!' she exclaimed and Elizabeth was swept into a cloud of fox fur. 'How did you get here? No, don't answer! I know better, but why did you come, Darling, when we thought you were safe abroad?' She released Elizabeth and wiped tears from her face. 'God, you've been out in the snow. You're as black as an Indian. Don't tell me – '

Elizabeth hugged her cousin. 'Yes, that's how I came – and how I'll go, too, I'm not staying long. Look.'

She pulled out her documents. 'I'm a distant relative – father's side – Anna Dabrowska. I work as a translator for a leather exporting business in Kielce. That's an essential work classification, so I am exempt from forced labour.'

'Dear God,' said Félicie.

Vincenty repeated her name. 'Miss or Mrs. Dabrowska?'

'Oh, Miss, Vincenty. One husband is scandal enough.'

The old butler laughed. 'It is good to have you, miss, whatever your name. I will tell cook.'

'Thank you, Vincenty.'

'And tell her to heat up some of that soup,' Félicie called. 'I'd kill the fatted calf for you, dear, but I'm afraid today it's all starved horse. Come in here. We managed to get a window fixed in the drawing room, lucky us, and so we all pretty much live there.'

She opened the door. There were five beds arranged around the stove and a general air of disorder. Félicie shrugged. 'If there's heat, we all get the benefit. Vincenty's a marvel at scavenging fuel.' She wrapped her fur around her tightly, and Elizabeth noticed the lines in her face, the bones visible in her wrist. She must have betrayed the thought for Félicie said, 'We must all look the worse for wear, dear. The Germans aren't giving us much.'

'There were women in the train carrying bundles of food.'

'How we live. The black market or runs to the country. Your mother tries to send us what she can.'

'How is she, Félicie? You know she will not write to me. Not even a word about Czelsaw. I've prayed she would stay on the estate.'

'She is well enough. And there is no news of Czeslaw, nothing since mobilisation. It is a question of your brother. If his health declines, she is determined to bring him to hospital in Warsaw.'

'She must not, Félicie. It is said the Germans kill the crippled.' Elizabeth looked away. 'I hope that is just propaganda, but —'

'I believe they would kill anyone,' Félicie said in a flat voice. 'I have seen men shot in cold blood on the street. But your mother won't listen to reason. You must try to see her.'

'I will. But it is so good to be here, Félicie. I could not wait to come.'

Tears came into her cousin's eyes again, and she wrapped Elizabeth in a furry embrace.

* * *

People crowded into the pleasant warmth of the coffee house where they could open their coats and wrap their chilled fingers around a 'large', a 'small', or the hopeful 'large small' coffee. Elizabeth bought hers and looked for a chair, then gave up and remained standing near the counter. In the hubbub of voices, in the laughter, the joking banter, it was almost possible to believe this was the old Warsaw. No Germans visited this shop, and if one could avoid looking diagonally out of the miraculously repaired window, one need not see the heaps of rubble, the posters with the twisted black cross, the grey-coated troops marching arrogantly along the pavement. Instead, warm from the profligate steam, one could inhale the fragrant coffee, admire the quasi-military coats and high boots sported by the younger men, and listen to the news of the city. Deprivation gave a special edge to even the simplest pleasures, so that a cup of real coffee, some cheap music, even the momentary warmth of the café made one a poet on the nerve ends of the universe. Elizabeth closed her eyes and thought of her friends, of Czeslaw, Janusz, the wild students, Charlie – where were they now? When she opened them, the one man who might know had appeared as if by magic. Czacki, her old editor, was standing beside her at the counter. He gave his order, felt her glance and turned.

'Well,' he said. 'Long time! I heard you were married. What are you calling yourself now?'

Elizabeth smiled; Czacki was never surprised. 'Anna Dabrowska.'

'Ah,' said Czacki, trying to remember who Dabrowska might be. Elizabeth rescued him.

'A precaution only.'

'And very wise. So, you have learned discretion and returned for a visit.'

'A brief visit.'

'The best kind nowadays. There's no change but for the worse. You've seen the paper, I suppose.'

The Nazis had taken it over and filled the pages with German propaganda, official announcements, warnings, threats and reports of reprisals. 'Yes. I am very sorry, Czacki.'

He laughed and slapped her on the shoulder. 'Don't be

sorry. One cannot be a conventional journalist in these times. Lack of paper for one thing — if you can believe that one of the world's great forests suddenly cannot supply enough pulp for newspapers. There's no respectable perch for a real journalist these days. We've had to go elsewhere.' He winked at her and sipped his boiling coffee cautiously. 'Ah, there's a table free. Grab it, you're quicker than I am.'

Elizabeth noticed how stiffly Czacki walked, his left arm held rigidly by his side.

'Honourable wounds,' he said. 'Gained in the battle of Warsaw. We were magnificently foolish.' He lowered himself into the hard chair and raised his cup. 'To your visit, my dear.' They talked of the destruction, of her trip, of his 'new venture', which Elizabeth correctly guessed was one of the underground newspapers. She could not bring herself to ask about her friends. Their names were on her tongue again and again; each time, she hesitated, fearing he knew the place of their graves. She still had not asked when she left the coffee house with him, taking his arm along the rough paving. Though his hair was quite white, Czacki seemed in fine form, as if the disasters of the invasion had been a stimulus. 'You're here on business?' he asked.

'Yes.'

'And you intend to leave again?'

'Yes.'

'Good. There are people you ought to meet.'

Elizabeth could not help smiling. Once it had been labour leaders, young intellectuals, Janusz Bronski she'd had to meet. This time, it was a different kind of surprise. They took a tram down to Burakow Street and got off near the Chemical Institute. Czacki led her down a side street and tapped on the door of a basement flat.

There was a sound within, the little spyhole slid back, then the door opened. The man was square and sturdy with a bold jaw and a hawk nose. His thick, stiff hair was cut short, giving him a military appearance strengthened by a scar down the left side of his face, but no military man would have been dressed in such dirty, rumpled garments. His striped trousers bagged out at the knees over a pair of riding boots. On top were a variety of shirts and sweaters in half a dozen colours and a heavy green laboratory apron. His extraordinary costume made him look quite different, but Elizabeth remembered him by his eyes, palest grey with a fine black line around the iris. He was one of Karl Halpern's friends.

'Hello, Professor,' she said.

'Countess.' He gave a stiff, formal bow and let them into the apartment. 'This is a great pleasure,' he said and invited them in with a gesture that encompaseed a workbench littered with pipes and electrical devices, flasks, heaps of books, and, alone amid a room that was more workshop than living room, a fine crimson velvet sofa.

'I have brought what you were looking for,' Czacki said.

The Professor turned his bright, cold eyes on Elizabeth.'Where have you come from?'

'Budapest.'

'Recently?'

'Two weeks ago.'

'My congratulations. And you are going back?'

'Quite soon.'

'You have a reliable means?'

'For anyone who can ski or can hike well, yes. For others it would be difficult.'

'Czacki and I have no ambitions to travel, eh? But for the young ones, there needs to be some system.'

'One of the purposes of my trip,' Elizabeth said. 'There are now guides and safehouses. And people in Budapest, quite a number of them, who are prepared to help with papers, transport, and lodgings. Our people will be welcomed in the West. The British, especially, are prepared to work with them.'

'The British had done better to bomb Berlin,' the Professor said sharply, 'and saved us the trouble of walking half the way to London.'

'They were poorly prepared,' said Elizabeth, 'but they have been making the strongest efforts. I was in London until late November. They have turned their parks into artillery stations and are preparing their citizens.'

'While we die,' said the Professor angrily, but Czacki interrupted.

'Let us not argue policy. The Fraternity has wanted a

courier and the Countess is willing to take messages and to set up a line into Hungary. We have common ground, whatever our opinions.'

'Yes,' said the Professor, 'though you're the next thing to a Red and our Countess is an Anglophile. Well, this is the situation,' he said, and for the next half hour he discussed The Fraternity, a gathering of resistants connected with the Chemical Institute where he had taught before the Nazis began exterminating the Polish intelligensia. Now the Professor worked as a custodian, handyman and mechanic while organising sabotage and the evacuation of military personnel to the West.

'He is an eccentric and a bigot,' Czacki said as they walked toward Burakow Street two hours later, 'but a good man. I know. The Fraternity has helped some of my friends. They got one of my best typesetters Aryan papers, and they've helped a few others get West.'

'You don't need to convince me, Czacki. We've got to organise and act together.'

'Yes, individual initiative sometimes does more harm than good. The Nazis shot over one hundred people in Wawer for the murder of two Germans non-coms just after Christmas. You look surprised. That's only the beginning. It's of the utmost importance that people realise no rapproachment is possible. No collaboration. No fraternisation.'

Elizabeth realised with alarm that his voice had risen. 'For God's sake, Czacki, you're supposed to be a member of the *underground* press.'

He closed his mouth and shook his head gloomily. 'The clandestine life does not always suit me. And you? Are your papers good?'

'I believe so. Good as they can be.'

'You'll soon find out,' he said as their tram came into sight. 'They usually stop this one. Prussian efficiency, you know.' He gave her a look of bland sophistication, touched with mischief, but Elizabeth was glad he had warned her, for two stops down the line the tram was halted and a pair of German officers came on and demanded papers. They glanced perfunctorily at the first few passengers' documents, but just as Elizabeth was beginning to relax, they found something suspicious and a young man was hustled off the car. After that, the officers progressed with horrifying thoroughness, and when the woman in the seat in front of them was also seized, Elizabeth was sure her time was up. Czacki wore an expression of absolute indifference which she tried to copy, though her mouth had gone so dry and she felt she'd never get a word out.

'*Urkunen*!' A black-gloved hand appeared before her, and Elizabeth handed over her papers. She had an impression of grey wool and gilt buttons and a heavy revolver, and then the documents were miraculously lowered and she asked the Virgin to remember Pavel, the forger, with his beautiful handcarved stamps. Czacki put away his documents and gave her a sidelong glance but said nothing until they left the tram in the centre of the city.

'What will happen to them?' she asked. 'The man and the woman who were taken away.'

'Forced labour, probably. Concentration camp if they're at all suspicious. Is your German still good? Use it if you have to and bully them. They're afraid of rank. There are tricks in every trade,' he added.

'And you know them all, Czacki. Do you still know where all our friends are?' she blurted out, hating his sophistication when her nerves were all on edge. 'Charlie and Janusz and the law students? What has happened to them all?'

Czacki's face was flushed with the cold. 'Wilk is dead; his friend Danka was deported to East Prussia. Janusz was wounded, but not badly. He is working in Cracow.'

'And Charlie?'

Czacki did not answer for a moment, and Elizabeth understood that the news was bad. 'And Charlie?' she asked softly.

'His unit was overrun. He is dead.'

'Where?'

'In the East. The Russians seem to shoot the officers. His valet brought his papers and personal effects back. A mad thing to do in itself, don't you agree? I hate that sort of feudal loyalty.' Czacki's face was strained.

Elizabeth took his hand for a moment. 'No wonder the city seems dead.' She turned and started stiffly toward Nowy Swiat. Her youth was over.

In the fourth week of her stay, Elizabeth went to the estate. She got to the village station by late afternoon and a farmer gave her a lift in his sleigh as far as the driveway. She stood for a moment in the road, one hand on the iron bars of the gate, listening to the departing sleigh. There was no moon, just the remote brilliance of the stars and their faint reflections in the fresh snow that cloaked the yard and fields in immaculate white. At the top of the drive, the house was black against the night sky, its snow-covered roof a clean white trapezoid. Everything was still, and it passed through Elizabeth's mind that this all might vanish, that even now the house might be insubstantial, a dream mansion from one of Zofia's old stories. Then came the thought, keen and almost unbearable, that she might never return, that so much of what she loved was already lost.

She leaned on the gate, opening it with a grating creak. A dog barked near the house, and Elizabeth gave a low whistle. She heard the watchdogs' feet on the ice before the low black shapes swept across the snow like wolves. She waited, slapping her leg gently with her free hand. Several of the older dogs knew her and began barking and whimpering in delight; the younger ones stood with teeth bared and the hair crested along their spines until calmed by the sound of her voice and the complaisancy of their fellows. Elizabeth smiled; that one gift had never failed her. She rubbed their shaggy heads, then climbed the steps to the porch. John opened the door. 'May the Virgin be praised! It is the Little Countess!'

Elizabeth threw her arms around him and nearly burst into tears. The dogs pressed in around their feet, their long, thick tails wagging, their dirty feet slipping on the parquetry.

'I might have known, I might have known when the dogs stopped barking!' He wiped his eyes, and Elizabeth bit her lip and patted his shoulder.

'I didn't think I'd see you again,' she said. 'Is everyone still here? Is everyone all right?'

'Those that are here are well, but the young ones have been taken for labour in Germany. Zofia and Marie and I are all that's left in the house and we have to help with the farm.' He shook his head and said quietly, 'The requisitions have been very severe. The farms have been all but stripped. We try to keep back what we can.'

'In Warsaw, they are short of food,' Elizabeth said.

'Then we must count our blessings, Countess. I will tell your mother you are here.'

'I was going to surprise her,' Elizabeth said.

'I think it best she be prepared, Countess. The war has brought too many surprises.'

Elizabeth felt the truth of that and waited. She heard the murmur of voices in the drawing room and then John's tall figure was silhouetted against the faint light. Elizabeth crossed the hall. The only lights in the drawing room came from the fire and from a small oil lamp next to her brother's chair. She saw André's smile, her mother's more ambiguous expression. Then she went forward and embraced them both.

'Where did you come from?' her mother asked.

'Warsaw. I can't stay long. There would be questions asked and I'm using false papers.'

'Your last letter was from France,' her brother said. His face was pale and thin, and his shoulders stooped.

'I never knew if you got them.'

'You said little enough to us before you left,' her mother said. 'All the letters in the world couldn't make up for that.'

'You didn't even tell me Father was ill.'

'And what caused his illness but shame and heartbreak and financial worry? Could you have made him better after that?'

'Please,' said André. 'Liz's come such a long way. How did you get here? We're told the borders are all sealed.'

Elizabeth rubbed her cold hands and went to stand near the fire. 'We went to London, and London sent us to Budapest. It has taken me months to arrange the crossing.'

'And Jozef?'

'He is safe in Budapest.'

André sighed and Elizabeth went over to his chair and took his hand. 'Tell him I miss him,' he said.

Her mother turned away and wiped her eyes. For André she would swallow her anger, but it was a sour and bitter thing and it took her a moment to find her voice. When she did she spoke of the estate. 'It has been very difficult. And now they tell us we may have to take a German manager — I don't know. I am afraid for Lev Weisenov. He has sent his grandchildren to the Russian zone. Think of that!'

'He is wise,' Elizabeth said. There was another long pause. 'It would be wise for you and André to leave as well. I think it could be managed in the spring. We could forget diplomatic papers or make you both *volksdeutsch* – there are always ways.'

'That is impossible,' the Countess said. 'How can I leave our people? And André is not strong enough for the journey.'

'You will be in danger,' said Elizabeth. 'And if you get a German manager, the estate will be out of your hands anyway.'

'We have a flat in Warsaw. I will be taking André there for treatment next month.'

'That is the worst place for you both! Promise me you will stay on the estate if you do not try to leave the country!'

'It's rather late in the day to be extracting promises,' the Countess said. 'We have managed all right without your advice.'

'You know we will all be classified as Jews. You know that. Belief makes no difference. And the rumours about the Jews are all bad.'

'If André needs to go to the hospital, I will take him,' the Countess said, her voice rising.

'If he is found in hospital, he will never leave it,' Elizabeth burst out. 'For his own sake, he must stay away from Warsaw and out of sight of the Germans.'

'They will not harm him,' said the Countess, touched to the quick. 'They will not, it is impossible.' She flung her arms around her son. And nothing Elizabeth could say, not even privately to her later, could shake that determination.

Elizabeth and André sat together by the fire in the old schoolroom, where they had listened to Zofia's stories, grotesque and supernatural, and met Jozef, heard their lessons, memorised verses from the Bible and Mickiewicz. Their books lined the shelves, and a few drawings, papers and maps were still pinned to the walls, breathing memories. Elizabeth traced the large regular letters of Czeslaw's name, tempted to take the paper down and keep it as a talisman, as a sign he would return. Outside, the sky was high and blue and a wind from the steppes blew snow off the tops of the crested drifts like foam from the sea.

'It is you who are in danger,' said André. 'You who will tell us nothing of where you live or who you are working with or where you are going. At least we are with friends, with the servants and tenants.'

'I believe I could get you to the west,' she said, putting her hand on his shoulder. 'I know what papers would be needed. Once you are in Hungary, you could go anywhere. America, even. It's said the American President has the same disease.'

André heard her optimism and enthusiasm and saw she still had illusions. She had not been home quite long enough. 'Liz, we're not going anywhere. Mother will stay as long as she can protect our people; as long as there is a chance of hearing from Czeslaw. She has been very brave.'

'And you, André?'

'It does not matter,' he said. 'I will stay with her. Someone must wait for Czeslaw — and for the others. It is all I can do.'

'Don't talk like that. The war will not last forever; the British and French will come. You'll see.'

André took her hand and kissed it softly. He could not tell her what he knew, what future he read, and it was just as well, for she would need all her hope and courage. 'I pray you will see it. Try to make up the quarrel with Mother and I will be content.'

Elizabeth saw that for the moment argument was useless and did not raise the subject again. The next morning she left, and three days later, accompanied by two pilots and a navigator, she took the train for Zakopane.

Chapter Thirteen

In Budapest, the mirrors of the cafés and coffee houses reflected a plump and prosperous clientèle. Gypsy fiddlers strolled among the tables, their violins throbbing with sorrow and delight, while laughter, entwined with the smoke of expensive cigars and cigarettes, mounted to the chandeliers. The rooms were hot, boiling after heatless Warsaw, and blazing with light. Outside the streets were clear; the buildings unmarked. People spoke of holidays, considered the price of a fur coat, ordered a leg of lamb for dinner. There were no candles flickering on the street corners, no mounds of rubble, no corpses under the paving. Elizabeth saw the city as a dream in which the inhabitants moved like sleepwalkers, unaware of fate and futurity.

'I hate it here,' she said to Marek. His apartment was in a cramped, dark and rather dirty block on the edge of the redlight district.

'I couldn't afford the Metropole forever.'

'The apartment's ideal. I meant the city, I meant Hungary.'

Marek shrugged. There was a period of adjustment for everyone coming from disaster.

Elizabeth ran her finger idly along the window casement where the ancient brown paint was thick with dust. Her head ached and she was tired, more exhausted than she had been on the trip over the Tatra. It was the strain of the city, the strain of ordinary life, of food, cafés, theatres, wealth, trams with seats; of peace; of safety, of content. She had crossed with a different guide the second week in March, and the weather had been cold but fair all the way. One of the pilots was an excellent skier, but the other two airmen had reached the border in a state of near collapse. She'd hidden them in Kosice for Marek to pick up and brought the pilot on into Budapest. Since then there had been meetings and reports and negotiations with guides, with the British minister, with a variety of Polish politicians in exile – all serving as distraction from the shock of peace which had illuminated the appalling possibilities of war. Since her journey home, Budapest had become transparent; she saw the Vistula through the Danube, the shattered citadel behind the Parliament Buildings. She had absorbed Warsaw so that it was present to her in exile with a vividness greater than reality, like the memory of some loved one, dead. She had known Marek would understand.

His apartment was cold the day she arrived. Elizabeth let herself in with the key he'd left and went up the dirty stairs, the boards creaking in protest against the freezing weather. It was a sorry, sordid district. The door of his apartment stuck, and she had to kick the bottom panel and pound on the top to loosen it. Inside, the flat was clean, almost Spartan, with nothing but a table, a few mismatched wooden chairs, a stove, a sink, a metal bed, stark against the whitewashed walls. Elizabeth walked around, a vacuum in her heart. Marek possessed the usual exile's kit: a hairbrush and razor, an English phrasebook, a Hungarian dictionary, a road map of the country and, thrown carelessly on the bed, a thick navy pullover. Elizabeth held the rough wool to her face. It had some of the faint, soldiery, leather and tobacco and gunpowder smell she associated with her cousin Czeslaw, and she sat down on the bed, holding it in her arms. After a few minutes, she wiped her eyes and got up to begin heating a little water. She was standing drinking coffee by the table, when she heard the key turn in the lock.

'So you got in all right,' Marek said. His eyes, his smile, were brilliant, his felt hat and thick brown coat dusted white with snow. Elizabeth sat down the coffee cup, slopping some on the table, and Marek stepped across the room. 'I missed you,' he said. His face was cold, even his lips, and there was snow on her hands when she touched his back. He smelled of tobacco, of snow, of damp wool; she could say nothing. Marek drew back from her. 'You really managed? You've seen Warsaw?'

'I've seen everything.' She could have told him about the line, the guides, the number of the safehouses, The Fraternity, the Professor's schemes, Czacki's paper; she could have told him about the ruins, the graves, the armbands on the Jews; about Czeslaw lost, Charlie dead, about Félicie's fox coat, André's stoop, her mother's stubbornness, about refugees frozen in the snow. Instead, she drew his face down against hers, felt his thick, unruly hair, his wide shoulders, the buttons on his coat and then the smooth, hot skin of his body burning her like the fiery furnace and reducing her brain to cinders. His bed was freezing, the sheets like ice, but his dark hair fell into his eyes and his eagerness filled her with madness, with the desire to be impaled, to devour him, to lose all mind, all memory, everything but the sound of his breath, the motion of his body, the touch of his mouth as the dream city dissolved into darkness, tinged red and green at the edges like the eye of the storm.

The snow whispered against the windows, the fire hissed in the stove and the hard orange wax squeaked softly against the runners. Jozef slept on his chair, tired after waiting up all night with 'parcels' in transit. As Elizabeth worked on her skis, she thought that they must press some of the rich émigrés, or perhaps the British again, for a truck of their own.

She ran her fingertips up and down the underside of the runners, testing the wax, then bundled the skis together and carried them to the bedroom cupboard. Jozef woke up as she passed and said, 'You're going back.'

He had not asked before nor had she discussed her plans, tact and prudence converging.

'Yes.'

'When?'

'In a couple of days. Whenever the guide shows up. We're going to look at another route this time. The weather will be better; it shouldn't be too bad.'

'I don't want you to go. Once is enough.'

'Someone has to,' Elizabeth said, coming to sit on the arm

of his chair. 'It's vital that we maintain contact. After the thaw it will be different.'

'There are others who can ski.'

'Men?'

'Male couriers are not exactly unheard of,' Jozef said drily.

'They're needed for the army, and, besides, the Germans take less notice of a "mere woman".'

Jozef leaned back in his chair and began to fiddle with his pipe. 'Marek agrees, you know.' He looked out of the corners of his eyes to see her reaction.

'Yes, Marek would just as soon I stayed.' She jumped up, annoyed. 'But if I wouldn't stay for you, I'll not stay for him, either. You're my husband, after all.'

Jozef felt his heart accelerate with pain, with anger. 'And he's your lover.'

'The first,' she said, flushing. Lacking the treacherous gift of imagination, she did not see how painful it was for him to let her go and concentrated on his breach of their unspoken compact.

'First, last? Does it matter?'

'I tried with you,' she said. 'Two years. That matters.'

Bitterness filled his mouth. 'You could have married Janusz,' he said. 'A respectable man. Wealthy, *szlachta* like yourself. More suitable than a tutor. More acceptable. Even if he did beat you. Which he would have.'

'I would not have stood that for two years,' Elizabeth said. 'I would have left him the first time he raised his hand.'

'You left him before that, as I recall.'

'And you were willing to go with me.'

'I loved you,' said Jozef. 'Enough to leave everything else I cared for.'

'You show it in odd ways.'

'By trying to keep you from dying in the mountains or being shot by the Gestapo? Or, for that matter, by feeling jealous when you sleep with handsome young lieutenants?'

'If you had not saved me on the mountain, I would have left you in Greece. Now I intend to go where I want and with whom I choose.' She snatched her coat from the hook and banged out of the door, down the stairs and into the sleety rain that burned on her face like cold fire, like her mother's anger, her father's despair, Jozef's bitterness. She hated the beautiful, intact, complacent city; hated the crowds, hated the filthy chocolate paint on the casement of Marek's windows. She had to go back.

'You'll see Bratek tomorrow?' she demanded.

'I can.'

'Tell him I want to leave immediately. Once the melt starts, it will be neither so easy nor so safe.' Her face was closed and determined.

'Very well. If you are ready.'

'It will be harder later. One can get used to anything — even Budapest.'

They went this time through Nowy Sacz, to the northeast of Zakopane, a run longer but easier. She travelled with a guide named Bratek and with Andrzej, a political courier who had been with the Seventh Uhlans. But when she asked about Czeslaw's chances, he shook his head. 'Not good. We were trapped by the panzers. The tanks just blasted us all to hell. Andrzej's horse had been killed beneath him, and he had been left for dead with a concussion. 'I was lucky,' he said matter-of-factly, and Elizabeth nodded. She knew all about luck. Luck was more vital than skill, as vital as patience, as caution, as a self-abnegation that would have pleased the good Sisters.

Had anyone asked Elizabeth what had prepared a wilful, impulsive and frivolous young woman for a life of fear, boredom and fatigue, she would have answered. 'A convent education.' But where else had she learned the patience to sit in cramped rooms amidst the lives of strangers? And where had she learned self-control, so that she could conceal her horror, her anger? And self-abnegation, so that the Countess, proud and commanding, was submerged in the mousy Anglo-Polish journalist, Elizabeth Andrews, or the insignificant Anna Dabrowska? She had learned these things at the convent. During the interminable waits and the cold, exhausting journeys, she often wondered what Sister Margaret was doing during the occupation and whether she, too had seen the similarity between the poverty, obedience and chastity of religious vows and the prudent counsels of the Underground. The price of the action and camaraderie that enlarged the soul was the often cruel discipline of clandestine life and, like the good sisters, the resistants kept the Four Last Things in mind. There were, Elizabeth thought, as she walked under the arches of the bomb gutted Philharmonic Hall, plenty of pertinent reminders.

The lobby was still full of rubble and the top floors were roofless, but the lower regions of the enormous hall were sound enough to house the new Café Arkadia. Inside, a pianist swept through one of the forbidden Chopin Ballades to a thunder of applause, and immediately launched into another. Elizabeth felt her spirits rise, though she knew it was safer to meet people on the street or, for serious contacts, the Rio Rita, a bar full of German agents and practically raid-proof. But everyone needed a moment of defiance. All over the city people scrawled the anchor symbol of Fighting Poland, torched German posters and snatched 'Germans Only' signs from the trams, parks and hotels for remounting on the lamp posts. Without some outlet, there was always the danger of uncontrollable anger. On her arrival in Warsaw, Elizabeth had taken a horse cab from the station. When they were delayed by a Wehrmacht motorcycle convoy, the driver had stood up, raised his arms to the heavens and shouted, 'Pray God I live long enough to kill some of these bastards.'

Elizabeth had felt her face go white, her stomach clench. She was carrying messages for The Fraternity and several political groups, plus an assortment of false papers and enough gold to send her to Pawiak Prison. She expected the hack driver to be shot on the spot, but in their battle helmets the Germans either did not hear or did not understand. They roared on down Marszalkowska Street and wheeled into the Old City. The driver sat down again, ran his hand over the stubble of his beard, and spat with satisfaction. He touched the horse with his whip.

'The only good thing about Germans,' he said, 'is that they're so stupid.' Elizabeth began to breathe again and touched her leather bag for reassurance. 'Courier? eh, delivering papers, maybe? You're safe with me. They think I'm crazy.' He tipped his head back and laughed uproariously.

'Marysia?'

Elizabeth turned towards the waitress, a dark distinguished-looking woman, a music critic in better days.

'At the back. The man with the light hat.'

Elizabeth was surprised. She had expected Czaki but the woman shook her head. 'Where is he? What's happened?'

'They have him in Pawiak.'

Her contact knew no more. When they had transacted their business and Elizabeth asked about the old editor, he lifted his shoulders. 'His office was raided. They found the wireless set to the BBC frequency and that was enough.'

'It could have been worse. The press wasn't there?'

'He's a former editor. The Bulletin is basically BBC news reports. At very best, it'll be the new camp at Auschwitz. When are you leaving?'

'Another week.'

'Good. The longer you stay, the more dangerous. The line is working very well. The bottleneck now is really on your side.'

'We are trying to get a truck.'

'Of the first importance,' her contact said, rising.

Elizabeth finished her coffee then left the café, passing under the massive arches to the street. A few damaged trees were coming into leaf and the April sun was warm, but the gaiety of the city had gone with its flowers. The Café Arkadia was a relic of the past; the heart of Warsaw was no longer its cafés, theatres, cinemas, sports, politics, jokes — all the things Czaki had loved. The Germans had wrought a new geography. Now the vital centres were Pawiak Prison, the Szucha Street Gestapo Headquarters and the execution grounds in Parliament Gardens and Palmiry Wood. She was not sorry to be leaving.

And yet, once away, she felt cut off from all that was most vital and missed the intensity and purpose of the resistance life. In Budapest, she was a deserter, safe but guilty, and in truth she was now restive everywhere, anxious to leave Poland, restless to get back. It was only in action, when she was too busy for fears or regrets, that she felt easy: when she had men to guide, people for whom she was responsible, she could be happy. The trains might be crowded, cold and filthy with snow and mud, the dirt roads of the lower villages a slop of mud, but when, through the spruce forests, Elizabeth saw the gleaming white crown of the Tatra, her heart lifed.

The mechanic beside her frowned. He was a slight wiry man with strong, clever hands, still stained indelibly with grease and oil. She knew he skied only poorly and gave him a smile of encouragement. If the worst happened she could leave him with Adam until the melt, for his papers described him as a forester and woodcutter. Behind them, the pilots were dozing, their blond heads rocking against the windows, while the artillery officer played cards with a cavalryman little more than a boy. She was not convinced he could ski either, though he had assured her he could. The Gurals would put him to work with the horses until spring. She took another look at the Tatra, put her head back against the seat and closed her eyes. They had stood all the way to Jedrzejow, changed at Cracow, then stood for another hour, and Elizabeth wished she could fall asleep and wake up on her skis, already on the mountain.

The train slowed, its carriages rocking and swaying. The platform check was perfunctory, and Elizabeth fussed with her baggage just long enough to be sure all the men got through. Then without another glance, she picked up her bag, went out to the street and headed towards the Market Square where she cut through an alley to a wooden shed. Within five minutes the men joined her, and half an hour later their guide appeared and gave them directions to a house on the edge of town.

With two beginning skiers, the trip went slowly, and the guide was cross and gloomy all the way. By the treeline near the Czech side, the snow turned patchy in the mild air, and they took off their skis and prepared to hike. The mechanic and the cavalyman greeted the bare ground with undisguised joy, and even the guide, who had at first refused to venture across with them, began to cheer up. After an hour's walk the forest gave way to an alpine meadow, and they were in the open, dark against a stretch of melting snow, when the guide shouted a warning. Elizabeth sprinted towards the trees, glanced back and saw the two pilots scanning the clouds. 'Run!' she shouted at them. 'Run!'

Behind them, a little black plane, innocent as a toy, grew

bigger. 'Messerschmitt!' one of the pilots called. Elizabeth swore furiously at them, and they took to their heels. The plane roared into a dive, its shadow square and ugly like the Devil's wings, its guns spattering dirt and water and rock and grass in a double line. They sprawled terrified on the ground. The Messerschmitt's engine whined as the plane began to climb.

'Go on!' screamed the guide. 'Go on, he will make another pass.'

Hampered by their ski equipment and rucksacks, they scrambled across the meadow. The sound of plane faded, almost disapperared, then gained in intensity to an open throttle roar. There was a cracking sound, like the whips of a thousand carters, and the mechanic, who had been running along beside Elizabeth, stumbled. Dropping her skis, she grabbed his arm and they staggered forward through the deep wet grass. The plane's shadow darkened the ground around them. 'Get down,' he yelled and jerked her arm so that they both fell. The plane passed over them, so low they could feel the rush of wind, sharp as the blade of a scythe, and the mechanic's scream was lost in the roar of the engine. The blood from his shattered lung drenched his back and Elizabeth's face and hands, so that when she stood up and cried for help, the others thought that they had both been hit. The guide hesitated, expecting the plane again, expecting it was hopeless, but Elizabeth, furious, began dragging the wounded man. The guide waved the others toward the shelter of the trees and had Elizabeth had a revolver, she would probably have shot him. She shouted again. This time the two pilots ran out, and the three of them managed to drag the mechanic to shelter. One of the pilots cut open the blood soaked jacket, saw the damage and began to swear.

'He is dead,' said the guide, too quickly. 'Leave him before we are all trapped.'

'He is breathing,' said Elizabeth and the man moaned, filling them all with the horror of suffering.

'While we wait, they will alert the frontier guards,' said the guide.

Elizabeth took the mechanic's arm, determined they would not leave him behind, and saw the thick bright blood coating her hands. Everything stank with its heavy, sweet-salt smell.

'It is no use,' said the pilot, touching her shoulder. 'It is no use.'

'We must go on,' said the guide in a fever of nerves, but no one paid any attention. They stood in an untidy circle watching the thin forest grasses redden, listening to the declining rasp of the mechanic's breath, the more perceptive of them aware that had he not been dying, they would have had to kill him. In the end, they covered the corpse with spruce bows and a few rocks then, in silent file, followed the guide into Slovakia.

Chapter Fourteen

Elizabeth walked home in the long spring twilight, the skis, poles and blood-stained parka an incongruous bundle on her shoulder. Early flowers bloomed in the public gardens, and lovers wandered under the trees. From the top of the street, she could see the Danube, already dark, and the barges with their running lights. A frail, unsteady woman came out into the street and began walking a little dog along the curb. Above, the sky was clear, and the new moon very thin and white. Elizabeth passed under the wide arch to the courtyard and climbed the stairs. A radio was playing in one of the apartments, but her own was both quiet and dark. She set down the skis and felt in her pocket for the key.

'Jozef.'

She stepped into the half dark and let the door slam behind her. 'Jozef?'

Not a sound. Not even the usual ticking of the clock. Elizabeth carried her skis into the bedroom. The window was closed tight, trapping the musty odour of damp stone, and she threw open one of the casements. He has gone down to the café or is out with some 'parcels', Elizabeth thought, yet neither of these explanations was quite congruent with the silent apartment and her dancing nerves. On the kitchen table was a rock hard loaf of brown bread, and, beside it, a half empty bottle of milk with a thick, sour necklace. There was no other food. In the main room, the familiar smell of tobacco was already fading, and the discarded newspaper was two weeks old. She sat back on her heels and thought of accidents, jail, worse, before her heart began to hammer and she scrambled up to look in the bedroom. Jozef's coat was gone and his case, too. Only a couple of shirts and an old sweater remained in the armoire beside her own clothes. Elizabeth covered her mouth to keep from crying out and slid to the floor in grief. They had quarrelled and he was gone. She was so tired and upset that it was several minutes before she thought to call Marek.

He answered on the second ring. 'Elizabeth? Stay there. I'll come,' he said.

'What has happened?'

'I'll come,' he said and hung up.

She leaned exhausted against the bed and was half asleep when a truck rumbled into the courtyard. A moment later, Marek tapped on the door. 'I heard a truck,' Elizabeth said.

'Yes. A fine diesel.' He put his arm around her and kissed her but felt the constraint in her greeting.

'Where's Jozef?' she asked.

'He's all right.' Marek shifted a parcel from one arm to the other. 'I brought some food. By the look of you, you need a meal.'

'Never mind that. What happened?'

'The usual,' Marek said as he went into the kitchen. 'Some fascist busybody reported that Pan Gorman had a lot of adult "pupils", some of whom stayed the night. The word got to the local Gestapo, who put pressure on the Hungarian officials.'

'Was he arrested?'

'Yes, but I got to the British Legation and he was only held overnight. I saw him to the Yugoslav border. He'll be all right; Sir Owen gave him some cash and generally pulled strings.'

'I see.' Elizabeth sat down. 'I thought the worst, naturally. After the other incident.'

'We were never connected with that.' Marek said sharply. 'A Nazi sympathiser gets drunk in a disreputable café and dies in the snow? Pretty safe.'

'He left no message.'

'There wasn't time. I packed as much as I thought he could carry and collected him from the Legation. Sir Owen had insisted he stay there in case the Hungarian Second Bureau changed its mind.'

Elizabeth looked at the floor and said nothing.

'You'll have to find another flat. It's not safe here. Do you have much to move?'

She shook her head.

'Right. Eat some of this.' He unwrapped a length of hard dry *wurst*.

'I'm not hungry.'

'Don't argue, you look half starved. And have a good shot of this.' He took a little flask of brandy from his coat pocket. 'It's how I manage to walk,' he said as he poured an inch of the amber fluid into a cup. 'That's right, drink up. I'll pack your things.'

She heard him opening the closet, and then the loose armoire doors banging against the wall. 'Your husband insisted on books,' Marek called. 'I hope you'll be content with clothes.' She heard a case set smartly on the floor and the clasps clicking open. Elizabeth cut off a piece of the sausage and began to chew it mechanically, but the dense richness turned her stomach. She took a sip of the brandy to kill the taste and thought of Jozef, who loved brandy even though it went straight to his head: he'd been drinking it the night of her engagement party. She took another drink, felt the tears burn into her eyes, then rushed to choke up the sausage in the sink. She turned on the water to run away the mess before bursting into uncontrollable tears.

For a time she hadn't wanted to go back. She dreamed of the mechanic and woke in the night smelling blood. The sight of soiled napkins when her period came made her sick; it was enough. Jozef had been right; the Messerschmitt had been a warning. But when the attack in the west came, and the panzers rolled into the low countries and France as easily as they had swept into Poland, she and Marek spent hours beside the radio, frantic for news, frantic to do something. Disasters followed, until the miracle of Dunkirk and Churchill's speech, and Elizabeth saw that she had been right. The British would fight and that was a message she was willing to take home. So one morning when the meadows were as fresh and bright as new paint, she and Stefan were again hiking through the Carpathians. Swallows hawked over the grass, swooping and twittering, and in every shrub, buntings and finches whistled. It was not five, the sun was still low, but even with the morning shadows heavy beneath each tree and bush, it was a perfect June day and Elizabeth felt like singing. She wished she had a good Carpathian pony, one of Adam's well-knit, sure-footed breed. She'd send it cantering along the hills, and make the crossing a holiday.

Beside her, Stefan walked with the mountaineer's long, easy gait. He kept looking up, alert for reconnaissance planes, but the sky was empty, the smoke, the vapour trails, the busy, dangerous planes, as absent as the clouds. 'A bit different from our last trip,' he remarked.

'I was just thinking how I'd like one of old Adam's ponies.'

'Paradise,' said Stefan.

She nodded and they walked in companionable silence until a logging road emerged from the trees, and Stefan hesitated, uncertain whether to take it or to follow the more difficult, but safer, path into the foothills. They both stood listening. Far off an eagle cried and the wind shifted a few dry leaves. Elizabeth shrugged indifferently, and Stefan chose. A thin, moutain stream ran beside the path, with miniature rapids that covered the sound of their footsteps. About a mile along, the trail made a sharp descent to a little hollow, and they had just reached the bottom when they heard a sharp click. It was the sound of a rifle bolt, and from the brush ahead two Slovak border guards jumped to their feet, nearly as surprised as the couriers.

'Halt.'

They both stopped; Stefan glanced back but, but before they had any chance to run, one of the guards stepped up to them, his rifle at the ready.

'Raise your hands.'

They obeyed, and the older of the two Slovaks, a lean, mountain type with a dirty, drooping mustache, searched them quickly for weapons. When he found only two small pocket knives, he relaxed considerably.

'Take off the rucksacks,' he said, repeating the order in broken Polish when he realised he had exhausted their Slovak. Stefan's held only clothes, blankets and provisions, but Elizabeth carried a variety of political and confidential messages, the latest propaganda from London and, around her waist, a very substantial sum of money in gold. She pretended to struggle with the straps that secured her pack and slipped her hand under the tied up bundles of propanganda leaflets to the political letters.

'Nothing but dirty socks,' the young guard said when he had finished rummaging through Stefan's things. The older guard raised his chin toward Elizabeth and his partner stepped up to search her rucksack. She enchanged a look with Stefan.

'Here,' he said, 'there was a watch in that bag!'

The young guard turned towards him to protest, and that was time enough for Elizabeth to draw out the letters and a handful of pamplets, step back and fling the lot into the stream.

The frontier police swore and the senior man jerked his rifle towards her head. Elizabeth threw up her hands. For a few seconds everything was in the balance and the only sounds were the stream and their breathing. Then the older guard shouted to his partner in Slovak, but though the young man raced down the stream and succeeded in getting a handful of paper out of the torrent, the sheets were mangled and illegible. He threw the pulpy mess down on the bank in disgust.

'So,' said the guard, 'courier,' and he put shackles on Elizabeth's and Stefan's wrists. 'You are both under arrest.' He raised his rifle and gestured for them to walk.

'Those bastards must have slept through their night patrol,' Stefan whispered.

'No talking,' said the older guard sharply. 'The commander will want to see you.'

Stefan and Elizabeth were marched back along the trail. As the shock receded, fear began to mingle with their exasperation. Stefan might have hopes of a Slovak jail; Elizabeth would almost certainly be given to the Gestapo. That idea concentrated her thoughts wonderfully and just before they reached the meadow again, she asked, 'Have you had breakfast, friends?'

'You'll eat at the guard post.'

'They'll not feed you our chocolate and brandy. It will be confiscated,' Elizabeth said.

'It will,' agreed Stefan, quick on the uptake. 'But only a real Highlander's stomach can handle brandy early.'

'Hummph,' said the guard, 'I've been on the Tatra as long as you two combined.'

'Then you'll accept the offer of breakfast,' Elizabeth said, 'before good brandy is wasted on some lowlander?' She knew the Slovak word for that and the guards laughed. After a consultation, it was agreed that Stefan and Elizabeth would have their feet tied and the four of them would take care of the provisions. They sat down out of sight under the trees, and the younger guard, whose round blue eyes betrayed his nervousness, wound a bit of climbing rope around their ankles. Stefan took off his rucksack and handed it over. The guards divided up the chocolate, sliced the dried sausage, and passed the flask around.

'A fine brandy,' the older guard allowed. 'A fine way to begin a fine morning.'

'Finer yet,' said Elizabeth, leaning casually back against a tree, 'If you hadn't searched us.'

'And why is that?' asked the older guard, stroking his yellow and grey moustache. He had piercing eyes and a long, clever face.

'If you hadn't searched our packs,' Elizabeth said, 'I'd have started to cry.'

Stefan and the young guard looked surprised, but the older guard's face showed interest. 'I do hate to see a pretty lady in tears,' he said.

'I'd have told you I was hiking to see the birds like the English and had hired an incompetent guide.'

'That has happened,' the guard said judiciously, helping himself to another slice of sausage and taking a deep, appreciative swig from the flask. 'But my job is to arrest people who are crossing illegally.'

'A man's job is worth money,' Elizabeth said.

'Indeed, lady, and you've got two men's jobs here.'

'But I have money.'

'It is for the Commander to decide.'

'Say good-bye to the cash.' Elizabeth said decisively, 'for the Commander will send it to the state — if he doesn't pocket it himself. If it can't go where it was destined, I'd rather see it stay with two honest men of the mountains.'

At this, the two guards began to talk in such rapid Slovak that Elizabeth could only understand a word or two. The young guard appeared to be an innocent, hesitating fellow, and Elizabeth fixed him with her most charming smile.

'My companion,' said the older guard finally, 'is not sure.'

'He would rather see us in jail?' Elizabeth asked. She seemed on the verge of tears, and the young guard blushed. 'I could see his hesitation if we were discussing currency. But allow me,' she said as she struggled to unfasten her money belt despite the shackles. 'There are never questions asked with gold. And in such times, gentlemen.'

Another rapid burst of Slovak followed, the argument more heated. Finally, the older guard nodded and Elizabeth passed over the money belt. 'Our documents,' she said.

'We keep the documents.'

Both she and Stefan protested, but the guard would not budge. 'You see,' he said at last, 'this is our story. We caught you crossing and took your documents, but on the way back, you escaped in the woods. That is fair,' he said, and his companion nodded so vigorously that Elizabeth simply gestured for their release. Before the Slovaks could change their minds, she and Stefan snatched their packs and set off. For the first hundred yards, they hardly breathed with the strain as each cracking twig or rustling stem of grass translated to the cocking of a Slovak rifle. By the time they crossed the first open stretch and re-entered the woods, both of them were running with sweat. Stefan risked a glance back. 'Lazy buggers!' he exclaimed. 'I don't even see them!' He clapped Elizabeth on the shoulder and kissed her on both cheeks. 'Clever girl! I could smell jail. I could smell it back there.'

She hugged him, laughing with relief, and it was only later that she realised her courier work was over. Instead of her returning to Warsaw, she and Marek passed the time in cafés and restaurants, met guides, made arrangements. Elizabeth worked late, conducting the business of the line, but Marek usually left before dark to pick up 'parcels'. Some of them were British troops now, speechless in Eastern Europe and trickier to hide. Elizabeth would burn their insignia and throw their identifying buttons into the Danube. In the dog days of August, she began to carry dynamite for a group further down the Danube who hoped to delay the Rumanian oil traffic by blocking the Iron Gates. Save for the memories of Aunt Anna, this was not very interesting work and, having only a primitive notion of chemistry, Elizabeth had no fear of the material itself. Nor did she fear getting caught. It was too unreal, like their picnics and swimming in the Danube, like all of Budapest after Warsaw. It was holiday activity, engaged in to fill up the time between real events, which took place far away in the skies over London or in the streets of Warsaw or in Palmiry Wood.

Yet there was a tension provoked by certain men in dark fedoras, so that Elizabeth would feel sweat running along her arms and know she was being followed. And sometimes a black Mercedes would linger outside the apartment to tell them they were being watched, or a café, a theatre, a restaurant, would inspire a sudden uneasiness that told her to leave, instantly, without looking back. These sudden, irrational dislikes and fears were part of the deceptive holiday excitement which lent intensity to Budapest life. When there were no risks, the daily routine became flat and boring, as if the alternative to danger and work were not rest and relaxation, but a kind of sensual death. The others felt it, too. The couriers had swift, intense affairs that faded over a week's absence, and even the most discreet underground worker was prey to sudden fits of carelessness or extravagance.

Elizabeth and Marek were no exceptions. She found herself wildly attracted to a soldier with eyes like Charlie's, and one day she found Marek in the hall with his arms around a pretty Hungarian girl. With Josef she had thrown crockery; with Marek, she just laughed. Out of the appalling seriousness of life there sprang a giddiness that roosted on first one person, then another. Some drank a fabulous amount; others danced wildly between − or on − the tables in the cafés. One refugee fell in love with Elizabeth, pursued her more relentlessly than the Gestapo and jumped off the Lanchid Bridge when it became clear she preferred Marek. He was fished out of the Danube by a passing barge and suffered only a broken arm and the loss of his illusions. When Elizabeth took him flowers in the hospital, he had already transferred his affections to one of the nurses and they met without embarrassment. In this way, summer slid into an early fall, the lindens' brown leaves littered the parks, and one day a courier in transit told her that she was worth 100,000 zlotys to the Germans.

One Thursday soon after, Elizabeth was called to the British Legation. Her usual day for exchanging information and reporting on the progress of the line was Monday, and a break in this well-established routine meant something had happened. In the tram, she worried that bad news had come about Jozef or her family, but from Sir Owen's business like greeting she knew it had not and breathed easier.

The Minister rubbed his hands and fussed for a moment with the ornate, tiled stove. 'Getting colder,' he said, 'Will there be snow in the mountains?'

'In a few more weeks. Snow, but no skiers. You've heard that the Germans are trying to confiscate all the skis in Poland?'

Sir Owen nodded briskly. 'Time is of the essence in any case. The report of last week has been confirmed. The Home Army has hidden a dozen of our POWs in a deaf and dumb asylum in Warsaw. Now there are indications that the Germans plan to close the asylums.'

Elizabeth thought of André and caught her breath.

'I promised we'd try to get them out; it means sending someone with experience across,' he said, his face serious. 'I wouldn't ask you if there was anyone else, but our informant says there are only a few weeks before the asylums are emptied.'

'Are the reports usually accurate?'

'Yes, I believe they have someone in Fischer's office. The orders will have come down from the Government-General Headquarters in Cracow.'

'I don't doubt the orders, anyway.'

'Nor I. Do you want time to think it over? I do realize the magnitude of the risk when you've been caught once. If you don't feel able to undertake it, I'd quite understand.'

The bulbous gilt clock on the mantelpiece ticked loudly in the official hush. Elizabeth could hear the sound of crickets in the hills, the faint far away sputter of a plane, the whisper of fatality. 'I'm willing to try,' she said. 'When will you have a guide?'

Sir Owen stood up and shook her hand. 'That's arranged. You must be ready tomorrow.'

It was too sudden, that was her feeling, and even the exhausting hike through the mountains had not prepared her for the misery of the capital. They were wearing clogs in Warsaw, and the people in the streets were thin and shabbily dressed. On Sienna Street, opposite Central Station, the Germans were constructing a wall out of rubble that cut like a red brick snake around the southern part of the old city and wound its ominous way towards the big rail head south of the Warsaw-Gdansk Station. There were guards with attack dogs at the gates and in the high, black watchtowers strung with barbed wire. Behind this barrier the city's 400,000 Jews were quarantined, to prevent typhus according to the hateful red and black posters layered thick in all the squares near the ghetto. And everywhere smoke still drifted in the air, awakening memories of earlier trips, of earlier dangers, tormenting Elizabeth's congested lungs and making her cough. It was not just the furtive fires made with half rotten wood and stolen coal, nor the smell of ruined buildings burning, nor the oily stink of fire bombed posters, of political vandalism. It was the funeral pyre for the hopes and work and plans of generations, and the Germans tended it with a mindless persistence that sickened and enraged the heart.

The meeting place was only a few blocks from the new wall, a choice Elizabeth thought foolish, and the contact girl was nervous, another bad sign. She was a pale blonde with dark eyes, bad teeth and long, straight, bone thin legs, who looked little more than fourteen or fifteen. Elizabeth thought they had no business using such children and was unable to suppress the sharpness in her voice. 'Well? Where do I go?'

The girl glanced around and pulled at a strand of her fair hair. 'To the Asylum.'

'Directly? It's all set up?'

The girl looked close to tears. 'Roman was arrested. You were supposed to have seen him. I've had no instructions.'

'Then you've no business keeping appointments.'

163

'I've been trying to warn people.' The girl's soft voice was sad and childish. There were transparent blue circles around her eyes and thin blue veins in her bare hands.

Poor creature! Elizabeth thought. 'If you've warned a few, the word will get around. Have you somewhere safe?'

She nodded.

'Then go there at once. Who is my contact at the Asylum?'

'The custodian and gardener. He lives in a little shack in the garden. His name is Pawel. He will know. Say you have been looking for Roman. There have been arrests,' she repeated helplessly.

'Pawel. In the garden.'

'He takes his dinner at noon. You can see him then.'

'I will. Go with God.'

She will be taken, Elizabeth thought as the girl hurried down Okopowa Street. She will be caught soon. The lifespan for contact girls was pathetically short, and this one, young as she was, was doomed already. It was probable that the entire group was finished, worn down by risks and follies, danger and bad luck and loose talk. Though the Asylum was all the way out towards Bielany, Elizabeth decided to walk. It was dangerous to go at all the way things were, and certainly too dangerous to risk the trams. She felt tired and nervous, and when she finally came within sight of the Asylum, the oppressively ugly building did nothing to raise her spirits. The high stone wall that surrounded three sides of the grounds met a wrought iron fence at the front, and through the bars, Elizabeth saw a shed well back from the street. She followed the wall to a service road of frozen mud where a stout plank gate stood ajar. Elizabeth glanced over her shoulder and stepped inside. There was a fresh pile of sawdust beside the track and a thin plume of white smoke rising from the shed. She went to the door and knocked.

'One o'clock,' a testy voice yelled.

She knocked again.

'On duty at one! A man's got to eat.'

Elizabeth looked around the edge of the shed to be sure there was no one in the rear of the Asylum grounds. 'I'm a friend of Roman's,' she said.

There was a sound within and the door opened. The

custodian was a squat, powerful-looking man with a balding head crossed ineffectually with long black and grey stands of hair. He had a grizzled beard and angry black eyes. He said nothing.

'I've come about the men,' Elizabeth siad.

'You're a day late.' He stepped back and motioned her into the dim interior. 'I told him to look sharp,' he said. 'Now it's too late. They're gone.'

'Where?'

'Out of the door. Best we could do for them. One of the nurses put them in a truck, and where she went I don't know. The Krauts were at the front door and they went out the back.'

'Roman was arrested.'

'Who told you that?'

'His contact girl. I just arrived.'

The custodian grunted. 'Roman was careless. Take my advice and steer clear of that lot.'

'I came a long way for the man.'

'I told you,' he said irritably, 'they're not here. But you wait. There's a thing or two you could manage for us. If you're smarter than Roman.'

'I'm apt to be less patient than Roman,' Elizabeth said in her best Countess voice.

'Ha,' said the custodian, 'it's not your dinner's getting cold.' But he motioned for her to wait and left the shed. A few minutes later, he returned. 'It's Sister Anastasia you want. Ask her to take you to your brother.'

Elizabeth returned to the front of the Asylum. At the top of the steps a heavy door opened on to a chill, stone-floored lobby that smelled of carbolic acid and over cooked cabbage. A young sister, in a grey habit appeared. 'I'm Sister Anastasia,' she said.

'Would you please take me to see my brother?'

'If you would come this way.' She inclined her head gracefully.

'I'm told the men are gone,' Elizabeth said when they were in the corridor. 'There is not much time before it starts snowing in the Tatra.'

'I am sorry, we had no other choice. We took them as far

as the forest and the partisans. They were healthy young men who preferred to fight.'

'I could perhaps locate them.'

Sister Anastasia's face was taut. 'Half our patients were taken two days ago. They will be killed. The other half, very soon. We will accompany the children. We have already decided.'

Elizabeth looked away in horror. How many must the Asylum hold? How many children?

'You can see,' the sister continued more gently, 'that we have no more time for the ones who are safe in the woods. For these others, perhaps, you can help us.' She led Elizabeth down a short flight of steps and pushed open a door. Inside, light filtering through heavy shutters showed four iron beds in a row, three of them occupied. Two of the men had bandages about their heads and necks. The third had bandaged hands and was breathing with a heavy, rasping sound. 'A touch of pneumonia,' Sister Anasasia said. 'Not too serious.'

It was freezing cold in the room but the men were well covered. 'Can they walk?' Elizabeth asked.

'Oh yes. Though they are not fit for a long trip just yet. They are all Tommies from Dunkirk. They got off a hospital train. Don't ask me how.' She nodded reassuringly at the men and shut the door again.

'They'll never make it over the Tatra.'

'Not now. But they must be moved. We had hoped Roman would find a place, but if he's been arrested . . .'

'I'm afraid that the whole group is compromised, but I know some other people. I'll arrange something for tonight or tomorrow — if we can get them out of here.'

'That is simplicity itself. Come with a horse and wagon, a black scarf, and three coffins.'

Sister Anastasia smiled at Elizabeth's surprise.

'The Germans fear the dead. Extraordinary, isn't it, when they are responsible for so many? They will rarely open a coffin.' She smiled again. 'These dead will walk easily in another few weeks, though they are too sick yet to send to the partisans.'

'Very well, Sister. That is how we'll do it.' Elizabeth said. She wished there was some gesture of comfort or solidarity she could make, but the nun stood still and self-contained, her hands folded beneath her habit. Like the contact girl, she carried a sense of fatality, but hers was self-chosen and she seemed completely calm.

'Go quickly,' Sister Anastasia said. 'We have very little time left.'

Elizabeth walked back across Warsaw to the Professor's apartment, although her head was beginning to pound and exertion in the raw, wet weather made her cough. She'd caught cold in the mountains, and several times she had to stop and catch her breath, a weakness that frightened her because it would be a long, hard trip over the Tatra. By the time she reached The Fraternity's headquarters, she was coughing so badly that Professor Szarmach made her drink two cups of ersatz coffee laced with homemade vodka.

'I am not in good odour with the Home Army, you know.' Szarmach said when she had explained the situation. He began poking about his chemical apparatus as if he might find the soldiers a hiding place among the retorts and beakers.

'Why is that, Professor?'

'Two reasons, Countess. One is political. The other is that I work on my own, in my own time and at my own projects. In fact, they would have liked me to take orders from our friend. Roman.' He shook his head. 'Lack of security there. I saw Pawiak for him the first time we met. A good man but careless.' He rubbed the side of his nose. 'Sister Anastasia, now, sounds like a sensible woman.'

'Without doubt, but for her plan we will need a horse and wagon – and coffins.' The number of details discouraged Elizabeth, and she wiped her damp face in anxiety.

'They can be obtained. And a driver. You cannot go alone. You will be burying your whole family: father, mother and brother. I will arrange wreaths,' Szarmach said, warming to the plan. 'Of course, they will cost money.'

Elizabeth unfastened the money belt hidden beneath her sweater. 'Modest wreaths, Professor, please. I no longer look like a rich woman.'

'It will all be taken care of. Evening will be best. Rest for a while and leave the preparations to me,' he said gently. 'All you will have to do is carry them out.'

* * *

The wagon creaked and swayed, and the strong, ill-tempered horse flung its head about and threatened to bolt whenever the thought crossed its evil mind. The driver was philosophical, alternately swinging his whip and cajoling the animal. 'Germans requisitioned the good ones,' he remarked. 'This is the strongest horse left in Warsaw. It's too mean even for the Wehrmacht.' He showed a picket fence of stumpy teeth.

Elizabeth pulled the thin black veil around her shoulders and glanced at the three coffins. The holes in the lids of the thin, cheap boxes were hidden under a heap of black ribboned wreaths. The Tommies would breathe all right, but she wondered whether they could endure the cold.

'Best weather for this work,' the driver said, seeing her shiver. 'Summer time — ' he made a face and spat over the side of the wagon — 'ugh!'

Elizabeth nodded, unsure how much he knew, and coughed every time she heard a rustle from the back. She'd given the pneumonia patient a good drink of Szarmach's home brew to quiet his lungs, and hoped for the best. If only they weren't too long. The horse favoured one speed and the streets were crowded with people on foot, many dragging small wagons and barrows. The weather was raw and cold and the whole city was robed in a smoky mist, the very miasma of defeat. Out of it, with the sudden surprise of nightmare, rolled a row of trucks and armoured cars, led by a band of roaring motorcycles. They tore north up Slowacki Street, and the driver swore eloquently.

'Wilson Square. One of their favourites. Another damn forced labour roundup.'

Elizabeth felt her chest contract. 'We must turn off,' she said. 'We must not be inspected.'

'You'd better pray to your name saint, lady.' The driver turned abruptly on to Suzina Street, scattering angry pedestrians and giving the coffins a mightly jolt. From the square they heard shouts, a loud hailer, a shot. The driver touched the horse with the whip and the animal tossed its head and kicked angrily but picked up its pace. They had almost reached Karasinski Street when sirens screamed to their right as another convoy converged on the square. The driver lashed the horse in an effort to get across before they were cut off, but this time the animal put on its brakes and began dancing angrily in the traces. In a fury the driver raised his whip, but it was already too late and Elizabeth caught his arm. A pair of motorcycles had pulled off from the main convoy and were blocking the intersection. A tall S.S. Lieutenant stepped from one of the sidecars and motioned for the traffic to proceed through the checkpoint.

'Tell me nothing,' said the driver. 'I had brought a load of salvaged wood to the city and you hired me to take the coffins to the cemetery in Praga.'

'From our house,' Elizabeth said quickly. 'Out along Marymount.'

He looked at her.

'Yes, yes, my documents agree.'

They did not speak again until a sergeant motioned for them to come forward. Elizabeth saw the soldier's appraising glance at the horse, taking in its strong legs and fine coat, then the animal shied and tossed its head and tried to get the bit out of its mouth, and he stepped back hastily.

'Your papers,' the Lieutenant demanded.

As they were handing them over, there was a soft rustle from the back and Elizabeth put her hand over her mouth and began coughing noisily. Her companion's face remained expressionless.

The officer glanced over the driver's documents and then handed them back. Elizabeth's got a closer scrutiny and the officer walked around the back of the wagon, poked at the wreaths and looked at the three caskets. He was a tall, well-made man, quite young, with a thin face and a tense, arrogant expression. 'What are these?'

His Polish was poor and Elizabeth decided to risk German. 'The bodies of my father, mother and brother,' she said.

He looked at her dubiously and Elizabeth drew herself up. 'Bad food,' she said. 'They had been ill and they took a meal of bad sausage.'

'We will have to inspect the coffins,' he said, and nodded to the sergeant who warily approached the horse to lead it to the curb.

'Just a minute,' Elizabeth said. 'I must ask to speak to your superior officer.'

The Lieutenant's face grew even stiffer, but Elizabeth could see he was nervous. Indulging their own whims, the SS all feared the mysterious impulses of higher authority.

'This is an intolerable desecration. My parents and my only brother are dead of food bought openly, vouched for by the inspectors of the General Government, and now you tell me their coffins must be opened, their bones disturbed? For what? Our papers are in order. We are on our way to the cemetery. I will lodge a formal complaint. Don't touch that horse,' she said imperiously to the sergeant. 'We are not moving until we see the *Major-Sturmbannführer*.'

The Lieutenant said nothing for a moment but looked again at her documents. Elizabeth felt her throat go dry. She prayed the Tommies wouldn't stir, wouldn't breathe, wouldn't cough.

'There is no need to be upset,' the Lieutenant said in a conciliatory tone. 'I had not noticed the date on these death certificates. There should be no delay in burying these remains. My superiors would agree.'

He handed back the documents and Elizabeth waited for several seconds, as if still tempted to lodge a complaint, before she nodded and put away her papers. 'Thank you, Lieutenant.'

He stepped back and the driver clucked to his unruly horse, which, after a terrifying hesitation, trotted across Karsinski Street. They avoided Invalidow Square and headed straight for the bridge, and didn't breathe evenly again until they had crossed the Vistula. In the Praga District, they pulled into a small courtyard, where the coffins were moved into a large two-story house and the Tommies, cold and half conscious, lifted out and put to bed in the attic. The coffins were broken up for firewood and the wreaths were burned. It was only later, when she received the terrible news from Félicie, that Elizabeth wished she had kept the wreaths, that she had gone to a cemetery – which one would not have mattered. Her father had lain for several winters in the parish churchyard; she feared that the resting places of her mother and brother would never be known.

Chapter Fifteen

The deep cough came again from the other room, and Marek, keeping watch beside the window, felt his chest tighten. She is no better, he thought, no better at all. Elizabeth did not think he noticed, being very quick to rinse out her handkerchiefs, but she had begun spitting blood. He would have to get the doctor again, the prim Viennese with his little white goatee and rimless glasses, who would insist on the hospital. Marek caught the edge of his moustache between his teeth, and moved his head so that he could see the street through the ice-encrusted window. The Mercedes was still there; the men had not moved. That made the third time in a week, and Marek was sure they were Gestapo. They had progressed from skulking about hotel corridors and occasional assassinations to open surveillance and arrests. Now whole divisions of Wehrmacht were on trains across Hungary, going, it was said, to reinforce the Rumanians and protect the oil fields, but Marek was sceptical. If the Hungarians weren't careful, they'd find themselves in *der Führer's* back pocket.

He heard Elizabeth moving around, then her cough precipitated another twinge of anxiety. They should have left a month ago, should leave now, for the ominous car remained, a grey puff of exhaust soiling the narrow street. The Gestapo men must have a good reason for waiting so long in the raw cold, but then they would be used to it, as everyone was this winter. The day Elizabeth returned, it had been cold, very cold, with heavy clouds and snow in the dirty pink sky. Marek had been sitting at the table, drinking bad coffee and resting his leg which was draining again after a long hike with some 'parcels'. He was not worrying about Elizabeth, not even anticipating her return really; she came and went as she pleased and border crossings did not run to schedule. In any case, her independence was an attraction for a man who cherished his freedom as much as Marek did. No, he was thinking about a fine goulash for dinner, or perhaps inviting his plump young landlady to eat with him, of various trivial plans and pleasures, when there was a sound at the door, less a knock than a thump, like someone's arm flung against the wood. Marek got up reluctantly to answer it. Another thump, then silence. He drew the bolt, opened the door, and Elizabeth, white as the snow, collapsed into his arms. She did not say a word; her rucksack slid from her shoulder to the floor, and Marek, with a sudden pain that ran from his heart to his loins, dragged her inside.

She had been terribly ill, half out of her head with fever, and between cursing the Tatra and the guide who had abandoned her somewhere — where, Elizabeth was incapable of conveying — Marek got her to bed, found the doctor, doled out the thin, bitter, blood red medicine, and listened with horror when she cried for a priest for her mother and André, or sometimes for children, whose and where he did not know. After the fever passed, she was prey for a time to a terrible dream that was repeated with torturous regularity. Always, she was riding in an open cart with three coffins. Out of the mist appeared a German officer who demanded to examine them. She began arguing with him in German, and it was that alien language which would awaken Marek. While the officer hesitated, a faint aqueous light flowed over the skull on his high peaked hat, over his frozen, deathly face, and, behind her, the coffins gaped open, revealing her mother and André and a multitude of small forms frozen in poses of unimaginable suffering. That was when she would scream and wake up.

Of course, it had not been that way at all. Félicie had told her how it had happened at the hospital. 'She would go,' Félicie said, looking up from the mass of silverware she was sorting. Her voice was calm, but her hands betrayed her agitation. She kept testing the weight of the spoons and knives as if she had been a pedlar all her life instead of a desperate housewife, selling the family silver to survive. 'I will tell you the truth – your mother did not have much choice. I saw that when they came here. I was shocked at the change in André.' She shook her head. 'I could not stop them, Elizabeth. They went to the hospital. There was a raid. The Germans were looking for two boys who'd been shot. It was just coincidence. They didn't find what they were looking for and thought they'd arrest some of the doctors instead. When they saw your brother, they seized him, too. Your mother tried to stop them and they shot her. There, in the hospital.'

'And André?' Elizabeth had asked, sick with horror.

'They took him away. The people I know say he would have been killed within the day.'

So she knew the truth, and when so many were left in agonising suspense and doubt, knowledge, however horrible, was a blessing. As she began to get better, Elizabeth understood that. But though the dream came less frequently, Elizabeth was still not fully recovered. The failure of her mission weighed heavily on her, and her sufferings on the return journey had left her with a violent, exhausting cough. Marek wanted her to leave in January, but she would not hear of it while the Underground was still exfiltrating men, and he had found himself unwilling to leave without her. Nor could he now, though he doubted he would be released with a warning if he were arrested again.

Elizabeth appeared in the doorway, a handkerchief over her mouth to muffle her cough. 'Our friends?'

Marek nodded. So she had noticed, too, and there was no need for secrecy.

'We will have to make arrangements. I have been burning my papers. I think we should be ready to leave as soon as we can find someone to take over the line.' She started coughing as she spoke, and though she folded the handkerchief quickly, Marek saw flecks of blood. 'It is nothing – it is since I had pneumonia as a child.' She shrugged her shoulders and moved nervously around the apartment, her arms folded.

'I thought of asking Nicholas,' Marek said. 'He has escaped surveillance so far.' Nicholas was an ex-artilleryman who had been helping with the driving.

'If he is willing. And I will speak to Sir Owen. He may have someone in mind to handle their POW's. It cannot be for long, anyway.' She gestured toward the window. 'They will swallow all of Hungary.'

'It may not happen,' Marek said to encourage her. 'The Greeks are holding strong; perhaps the Yugoslavs will stay neutral or come in against the Italians.'

'The Germans will have Hungary.'

'But not us. I didn't walk half way to Budapest to become a POW.'

She smiled, suddenly affectionate, her natural optimism breaking through depressison with the quick surprise of the winter sun. 'They certainly aren't to have you! We are expecting parcels on Thursday; I think we must be ready after that.' She put her arm around him, and Marek felt a moment's pure, irrational happiness. A beach, azure and gold, shimmered somewhere in his consciousness, and the surf whispered it was not too late.

'We'll go to the sun,' he said, kissing her. 'Somewhere warm where you'll get well and I can teach you to swim.'

A dream at first: a dream of Elizabeth's return with the thumping on the door in the pitch dark, then he felt her touch his shoulder. 'A moment,' she called in Polish, then in Hungarian.

'I'll go.'

'You're not dressed,' Elizabeth said and slipped quickly out of bed, picking up his robe as she went. The light in the hall was dazzling, a green-tinged explosion, and the hammering began again. 'A moment,' Elizabeth said, and drew the bolt. The door burst open, and three men armed with pistols pushed their way into the room.

'Police,' one said, but they were not in the uniform of the Budapest police, nor did they have the perfect speech of the Hungarian Second Bureau.

'Just a minute,' she said sharply. 'What's this all about? It is the middle of the night. I want to see your authorisation.'

Their leader lifted his pistol. 'It is here.'

'I see it is German,' said Marek.

The man pivoted with a wide, menacing gesture, swinging the gun in an arc. 'The best kind,' he said. 'Get dressed. You will come with us.'

Outside, they were bundled into a Mercedes which pulled away in a spray of frozen slush, its twin beams carving mysterious tunnels out of familiar Budapest. No one spoke. Elizabeth could feel her heart pounding slowly and steadily; Marek shifted in his seat slightly and felt his notebook in his overcoat pocket; it had the names and contact points of every guide in the network. He wrapped the little book in his handkerchief, and when Elizabeth started coughing, offered it to her.

'I am all right,' she said.

Marek smiled and slipped handkerchief and book into his jacket: he knew they would search his coat first.

Their guard jerked his head and gestured with his pistol for silence. Elizabeth coughed again, a low, harsh, monotonous sound, then leaned her head back against the leather seats and closed her eyes, against the car's vertiginous flight. When the brakes went on, they were in an unfamiliar suburban street lined with substantial villas; one, well-fenced and surrounded with trees, belonged to the Gestapo. Marek touched her hand, then the doors opened and the guard motioned for them to leave the car.

A light in the entryway illuminated the icy steps – and the bars on the basement and second floor windows. The front door was good mahogany with an insert of cut and bevelled glass; a fine house, a pre-war mansion for parties, dancing, lavish diners, now transmuted like so much else into some new and hideous useage. In the reception room, the shadows of old pictures still haunted the walls, ghosts of normalcy above the large desk, the telephones, the green filing cabinets. It was three-thirty in the morning.

'Name?'
'Lieutenant Marek Zermoski.'
'Residence?'
'Name?'
'Elizabeth Gorman.'
'Place of Birth?'
'Warsaw, Polish Republic.'
'Date of Birth?'

Over the voices, the typewriter clicked, impersonal and official.

'Religion?'
'Hang up your coat.'
'Roman Catholic.'

On the other side of the room, two of the agents had begun searching Marek's jacket, his trouser pockets. They ripped open a packet of cough lozenges and probed the bandage on his leg. Above their heads, Marek caught her eye, then there was a flurry of orders and he was hustled from the room.

Elizabeth's interrogator had fine white hair closely cut, a grey, unhealthy complexion and large, cold, bloodshot eyes. He offered her a cigarette with the professional's sinister friendliness, and when she refused, lit one himself, filling the room with smoke. His fingers were dyed yellow from nicotine. 'We know all about you,' he said.

Elizabeth said nothing.

He opened a file with great deliberation. 'How many times have you crossed into Poland?'

'Since the German invasion, you mean?'

'Since the outbreak of the war.'

'You must know I would lack the proper documents.'

'But you have attempted to cross.'

Elizabeth coughed. 'I am not well enough to cross Budapest.'

'Yes on June 18th, 1940, you were apprehended with a professional guide in the Slovakian Carpathians. Do you deny that?'

'I would have thought that a matter for the sovereign state of Slovakia to handle.'

'There is co-operation between friendly states.'

'And what state do you represent?'

'We have your documents,' he said, ignoring this. 'You recognize this, I suppose.' He handed over the papers she had lost to the Slovakian guards.

'What is a picture? This is insufficient. I could find people to swear I never left Budapest.'

'We have more,' he said, imperturbably.

The sun rose and slim bars of light appeared behind the blinds. Her interrogator, a creature of the night, did not bother to open them. They went for the dozenth time over his accusations, her denials. They discussed skiiing; he mentioned his pleasure in the runs in the Carpathians; she agreed they were marvellous and regretted her absence from Zakopane. He changed his tune then capriciously, stood up and shouted and stamped his feet in ludicrous rage. Elizabeth was exhausted and his voice hurt her ears.

'It is not far to the border,' he shouted. 'If I had you across it, you'd soon tell a different story.'

'You admit you have no evidence,' Elizabeth said. 'None at all.'

He shifted again, quick as a chameleon, to perfect calm, opened the door and sat down with a thin, glittering smile. Elizabeth could hear voices in the corridor, a cry, the sound of blows. 'Some of our guests are less co-operative than others,' he said. 'This is Lieutenant Zermoski's third visit. Without your help, we will become impatient with him.'

Elizabeth knew their impatience. She had seen their street roundups: a rifle butt smashing a woman's face, a sudden shot, a scream, a wash of blood stinking on the pavement. Of the rest she had heard, in the flat, controlled voices of the Underground: of Pawiak, of Auschwitz, of Wawer and Palmiry Wood. She must not lose that control, for those who did went mad with horror. 'Lieutenant Zermoski is a Polish military officer residing legally in Hungary,' she said. 'He is not within your jurisdiction.'

'Ours is a flexible jurisdiction, as you will see.'

He hesitated a moment, waiting, but Elizabeth kept herself still and straight, her face expressionless. The interrogator went to the door and shouted for two women to take her to the cells. Staggering with exhaustion, Elizabeth was led out of the door, down the corridor. Upstairs, a prisoner screamed, and her heart jumped with the thought that it might be Marek, but the matrons moved on as indifferent as automatons. The last door opened to dark basement steps, and Elizabeth felt such a horror of being enclosed that she shut her eyes for an instant, letting herself be steered blindly by the matrons, before she bit down on the side of her tongue with all her strength. Pain shot up the side of her head and down into her chest as her mouth filled with blood. She gave a groan and a slight cough. The women pulled her arms impatiently to move her along, and as she was jerked forward, blood spattered on the bottom steps and onto the tiled basement floor.

'What is wrong?' one of the women asked, drawing back in revulsion.

Elizabeth tapped her chest, then coughed again, blood oozing from her mouth.

The guards made her sit down on the bottom step.

'It is my lungs,' Elizabeth whispered. The blood turned her stomach, and she could barely speak.

'This has happened before?'

'I have been ill all winter. Any stress, any exertion – ' She began choking and blood dripped from her lips.

'We'd better call for the doctor,' one of the guards said in German.

The other nodded, but first they dragged Elizabeth to a damp, whitewashed cell. She sat in the darkness, sick from pain, and swallowed blood for what seemed to be hours before the door of her cell scraped open. A man wearing a white hospital coat switched on the overhead light. Elizabeth looked at his flat, trim, central Asian features and thanked the Virgin for sending a Hungarian. Then she ran her hand through her thick, beautiful hair and coughed, soaking her handkerchief in blood. They had delayed so long that she had had to bite her tongue again, and the pain made her shiver in earnest.

The doctor turned to the matrons angrily. 'What is the meaning of this? You put a woman spitting blood in a coal cellar? Aside from the danger to her health, you risk infecting the entire building! Bring me some water and towels.'

They went off, obediently, and the doctor stepped over and gestured for Elizabeth to stand up. He took out his stethescope and had her open her blouse. When he had listened to her chest, he felt her pulse and looked at her eyes and her throat, and though Elizabeth tried to distract him with coughing, she feared he had guessed the source of the blood. One of the Gestapo matrons arrived with water, and Elizabeth waited for his denunciation, but the doctor took the basin and the towels without a word. He wiped off Elizabeth's face and jacket, then washed his hands carefully. 'You have severe chest congestion,' he said when the matron had gone. 'As for tuberculosis – I must order an X-ray to be sure.' He gave an apologetic shrug. 'They will insist.'

'I am very ill,' she said calmly. 'I am sure the X-ray will bear that out.'

He gave her a long look then went to the door and called for the guards. There were orders, very loud and definite on the doctor's part, and within a few minutes Elizabeth was escorted upstairs and out to a car. She was taken several miles away to the hospital, X-rayed, then returned under guard to the Gestapo Headquarters and left locked up in an empty interrogation room. She sat down next to the stove and listened to the footsteps in the halls, the clash of reinforced doors, the sound of phones ringing, of typewriters clattering: the banal sounds of a busy office. She closed her eyes, dozed, jerked awake with a shudder, dozed again, until the door opened.

'Get up.' It was the agent who had arrested them with another man who spoke in rapid Hungarian. The agent frowned, but motioned for her to follow them to the reception area. Marek was standing near the door wearing his topcoat. Except for a swelling under his left eye he was unhurt, but when he saw Elizabeth, his face went dark.

'What has happened to the Countess?' he demanded, stepping around the table toward her.

'I am all right,' Elizabeth said, touching his arm, warning him.

'I demand to know what has happened to the Countess,' Marek said to the Hungarian.

'I regret to tell you that the Countess is in the later stages of tuberculosis. I have seen the X-rays. In light of her illness, you are both to be released.' He smiled. 'Subject to certain unavoidable conditions.'

Elizabeth was handed her coat and these conditions made clear: they were not to leave Budapest, to have contacts with foreign missions, or to be out during the hours of darkness. Marek protested without real fervour, and almost as quickly as they had come they found themselves outside in the weak sun, shaky and dazzled on an unexceptional suburban street. The Hungarian drove them home. 'They will tap your phone, of course,' he said as he let them off. 'As one officer to another, I beg you to be careful.'

Marek thanked him and bowed. When the car had driven off, he took Elizabeth's arm, his face tight. 'You've blood all over you. What happened?'

Elizabeth opened her mouth and clicked her teeth together.

'Dear God!' Marek put his arms around her, and she leaned against his shoulder, faint with exhaustion and relief. 'But how did you manage the X-rays?'

'Old scars from when I was younger. I thought it was worth a try,' she said, drawing back to look at him. 'I was afraid they would hurt you.'

Marek gave a bitter laugh, patted her shoulder, and helped her to the stairs. 'Not me. Not this time. That was the Major – Hungarian Second Bureau. They're invited in to protect officers and gentlemen.'

'There were screams.'

'The Jews they beat. One in my cell had a scrotum the size of a melon. They've had him for months.' He unlocked the door and pushed it open. The apartment had been torn apart, furniture overturned, clothes and papers scattered everywhere. The kitchen floor was covered with broken glass and dishes crunched underfoot. 'You need some brandy,' he said, 'and so do I.'

Elizabeth righted a chair and sat down, not bothering to take off her coat. 'We must plan how to get out of here,' she said. 'That is the first thing.'

It took a week: a week of watching the Gestapo cars, of mysterious calls, of listening for midnight footsteps on the stairs. They waited until they understood the routine, until they had become almost accustomed to the sentinels, the shadows, the click on the phone line; until Marek, his leg throbbing, had walked every side street and alley in the district, until Elizabeth, cloistered as an invalid, was half mad with boredom and coughing worse than ever from the damp apartment. Then they called Nicholas from the phone at the back of the neighborhood café and told him dusk would be best. Late one afternoon, as the lights were going on all over Budapest, a truck rumbled towards their apartment.

Upstairs, Elizabeth and Marek waited as long as they could for fear the landlady might raise the alarm, then took a case apiece and went downstairs, listening to the creaking stairs and unseasonable rain drumming in the gutters. There was a bad moment when the wind caught the heavy front door and slammed it shut behind them, but the courtyard was empty. The landlady and her family: the small, black haired son, the war veteran older brother, and the crotchety and malevolent aunt who was their chief danger, did not look up from their meal, though their yellow tortoise shell cat jumped suspiciously on to the window sill and stared out through the fine mesh curtains.

Elizabeth and Marek walked across the cobblestones, eased open the car doors and unlocked the back for their bags. Marek's watch read five forty-three; Nicholas would arrive with the truck in two minutes. Marek glanced at Elizabeth, took a deep breath and put the key in the ignition. The engine turned over, louder than a cement truck, and died. He pressed his lips together and tried again. Another roar, a cough, a hesitation; Marek struggled with the gas and the clutch, willing it not to fail, but the car, fast but temperamental, refused to catch. It coughed and bucked and ground to a halt.

Elizabeth could see the second hand of her watch turning inexorably. They would have heard the car in the lighted flat behind them, perhaps in the street. A thin film of sweat appeared on Marek's forehead. He swore softly and turned the key, pumping the accelerator. This time the motor came to life. Marek coaxed it like a nervous horse, listening for the smooth hum that indicated the engine was ready. There was a faint hesitation yet, although he had spent several cold and dirty afternoons tuning it. Then Elizabeth touched his arm, and truck lights burst into the court, illuminating the doorway and the sagging, ornate portico. Behind, in the street, the two Gestapo agents would be dropping their rolls and *wurst* and putting their car into gear like Marek, who, as soon as Nicholas started to back out and block the street, floored the gas pedal and raced through the narrow *porte-cochère*.

'I don't see them,' Elizabeth cried, as they shot out over the pavement and bounced into the street.

The truck was beside them, Nicholas swearing and yelling

as if he were an innocent trucker who had entered the drive to turn around. He stabbed his brakes and managed to stall the motor, while the Gestapo surveillance team shouted orders and pounded on the side of their car in frustration. Elizabeth could hear the shouts, but Marek heard nothing but the surging engine, the whine of the wipers cutting a fan of visibility out of the misty rain, the squealing tyres as he wrenched the car into the right lane of the wet, narrow street. Nicholas had gained him half a minute, and he intended to make the most of it.

He squeezed the car into a narrow alley discovered on one of his painful winter walks, barked a fender on an abandoned crate, then slid through an even narrower gap by a warehouse. The car slithered and whined on the ice, but there was no way the big Mercedes could follow and he gave a whoop of triumph. They bounced out of the warehouse yard into a maze of little side streets which Marek negotiated with cheerful recklessness, urging the battered Opel forward like a cavalry charger. His ruined knee made shifting gear a rough business and he preferred to run the car flat out whenever possible. They cut in and out of the evening traffic on Rakoczi Boulevard and headed towards the river.

Near Veres Palne Street, Elizabeth spotted a black Mercedes, but it was trapped behind them in the slow traffic at the Erzsebet Bridge, and once Marek got a clear road up the Buda rock, there was no stopping them. His exuberance made Elizabeth laugh, and in the squealing tyres and slithering turns the Gestapo were well lost. When they pulled up at the British Legation, the road behind them was dark and quiet. Elizabeth spoke to the guard, and a moment later they were parked safely in the Legation courtyard.

Chapter Sixteen

Cairo – May 1941

'Get your shoulder forward,' Lieutenant Morris shouted. 'Keep in the plane of the ball.'

'More like this?' Elizabeth asked.

'Yes, try again.'

The Lieutenant put his pony to a canter and sent the ball crisply across the field on a long diagonal towards her. Elizabeth had had trouble at first in judging the speed and position of the ball, but now her only difficulty was getting the right amount of force behind a shot. She steadied the pony, a grey spotted beast that knew its business and had a reasonable tolerance for beginners, rose out of the saddle, and swung the mallet. Across the patchy yellow polo field, Lieutenant Morris galloped on to the ball and tapped it smartly backwards, so that she had to rein in and wheel her pony to pick it up. As she reached the ball, Elizabeth heard hooves behind her and, catching a glimpse of Morris's bay charging up to intercept, urged her horse on in a mixture of Polish and English. She cut diagonally in front of her pursuer and knocked the ball forward into scoring position. Morris's horse ranged up beside hers, but as he attempted to ride her off the ball, the grey muscled clear and Elizabeth shifted her mallet as she'd been taught and sent the ball through the uprights. 'Good! Lovely goal!' Lieutenant Morris shouted before swooping behind the posts, graceful as a centaur, to retrieve the ball. 'Damn nice shot,' he said, 'though a bit of rough riding there.'

'You tried to force me off,' Elizabeth said, laughing, and Lieutenant Jack Morris showed his uneven teeth and winked.

He was a tall man who had lost boyish looks and pale skin in the western desert. Heat, thirst and hardship had thinned him down and burned him up until he looked like a desert nomad. His latest spell of active duty, coinciding with Rommel's push through Benghazi, had left him with a powerful appetite for the pleasures of neutral Cairo and a breezy disregard for the Gezirah Sporting Club's disapproval of women on the polo field. He sometimes reminded Elizabeth of her cousin and of all the young Uhlans who'd frequented the estate and Félicie's salon, but those were the only bad moments. Lieutenant Morris was playful and not serious; a man of candid appetites and abundant energy, who was amused that, in certain quarters, she was a suspected German spy.

'This is a good pony,' Elizabeth remarked as they returned across the field to the stables. The sun was low, casting long shadows through the palms, and the pink and gold sky intensified the lavender blossoms of the jacarandas, the quick, black shapes of the swallows.

'Whizzer? One of the old boy's best,' Jack said. He carried his mallet casually over his shoulder, his free hand light on his pony's reins, as completely at home on horseback as Elizabeth.

Around them rose the warm smells of dusty grass, horses, the river, and faint, but omnipresent, the pungent breath of the city. Soon the sun would dip below the west branch of the Nile, the muezzins climb their minarets to call the faithful and, moist and velvet dark, the sudden African night descend, loud with insects, cooled by breezes from the Nile. Jack Morris would invite her to drinks at the Club or the Long Bar of Shepeard's Hotel, exotic places for a Polish Countess. But then, she wasn't a countess anymore; wasn't, if her passport — accepted unhesitatingly from the Balkans through the Levant — were any indication, Polish. She was a British subject born in Warsaw, a very different item, and having doubtless a British father because she was now Elizabeth Andrews and had been ever since she climbed, stiff and cold, from the trunk of the British minister's big Chrysler just inside Yugoslavia. Marek, whose new papers were for Marek Jenkins, was waiting anxiously beside his car, and in the distance, pale against a milky blue sky, the foothills of the Balkans pointed their way.

They had set off with the minister's good wishes, new papers and a microfilm described as important. Their baggage included three bottles of strong brandy and a mass of bandages for Marek's leg, Elizabeth's last good silk dress — instrumental in convincing the Vichy Consul in Istanbul that they should be allowed into Syria — and enough money to buy their way to Cairo. Behind them was the Gestapo. They missed the Wermacht in Yugoslavia by a month and hurried through Bulgaria where the Germans were omnipresent. After bribing half of Turkey, they got themselves and their care into and out of Istanbul and started down the sun-drenched Mediterranean coast, astonished by the beauty of the sea. On the heights were brilliant white houses, and everywhere spring flowers transformed the dry land while overhead, storks soared north on the thermals. Some of the villages were settlements of pioneer Jews and, in the towns, homesick refugees listened to sad German *lieder*. Marek and Elizabeth swam in the phosphorescent night sea, visited the shrines of Jerusalem and drank pale Carmel hock with members of a Polish Brigade that had marched out of Vichy Syria.

They were happy, almost in love. The combination of beauty and danger gave them the sense of an exalted present which Elizabeth did not interpret correctly, although she sensed it clearly enough one day along the Orantes. They had stopped for lunch near a wheel that lifted water for the pool of a mosque, and the mechanism groaned and creaked so loudly that they had moved further upstream. Elizabeth laid out the bread, wine, cheese and figs, while Marek scrambled down the bank to the water. Though the screen of shrubs, she could see his white shirt and the Arab headscarf that made him look like a pirate, then he disappeared through the shadows of the scrubby trees to emerge below on the gravel shore.

His tanned arm swung against the high, white sky and a stone broke the surface of the swiftly flowing water, leaving a mesh of glitter. As Marek bent to pick up another pebble, she saw his dark profile, then he turned and waved to her up the hill: a tall sturdy man with a broad face and a quick smile; her countryman, her fellow exile. In the distance the wheel creaked, lifting water for an alien religion, and overhead were strange birds; the very earth was different. The river glittered, the water wheel laboured, and Elizabeth shut her eyes for a moment, but when she opened them it was all still true. Everything else was lost; only this remained; the sky bleached with heat, the sound of insects in the grass, a bird circling high overhead, the sounds of the wheel and of Marek climbing back up the rocky slope. They had lost their past, their future; there was only this moment and a succession of other moments requiring no thought, no regrets. She believed then that it would be enough, but it was not enough for Cairo.

In March they reached Egypt, delivered the microfilm and saw, for the first time, the contents.

'Did you know what was on this?' The man they knew as Captain Francis asked. He drew the blinds against the ferocious African sun and switched on the machine.

'No,' Marek said, 'though it's pretty clear now why we were told it was important.' Enlarged many times, the brown type sprawled over the whitewashed wall like an ancient carving: regimental manoeuvres, numbers of armoured cars and tanks shipped east, diverse regimental badges observed on Wehrmacht troops in Chelm and Bialystok and along the Bug River. Elizabeth felt a soft but immensely powerful excitement steal along her nerves: they had been given this.

'And you got this through your regular channels?'

'Yes, and from a regular courier,' Elizabeth said. 'It is from a freelance group called The Fraternity. They've been a great help. The first Tommies you got out came through them.'

The Captain nodded and made a note on a thick ruled pad. He was thin and very nervous, and kept tapping his pencil on the desk and running his hands over his sparse, sun-bleached hair. 'It makes no sense. Does it make sense to you, Lieutenant?'

'They're going for Russia,' Marek said. 'The thieves and assassins are falling out.'

'That would be madness. Madness! They must be looking at Turkey. At the back route to the Suez Canal and to the oil fields.' He glanced at the faded situation map.

'They've got enough troops in Bulgaria to take Turkey now if they want.'

'And planes, tanks. With Bulgarian insignia, of course.' Elizabeth said. She was a trifle impatient with the Captain, who treated them like children and spoke in schoolboy French. Overhead the fan whined and swished, stirring the humid air.

'It will be passed on,' the Captain said quickly. 'Everything is. I'm supposed to sort it out, but things come in, people arrive. How's one to know?'

'We've been working with your Minister in Budapest for over a year,' Elizabeth said sharply. 'Surely you can get in touch with Sir Owen.'

'Gone,' he said. 'You wouldn't have heard. He's somewhere in Russia. When the Germans came in, he preferred to try the eastern route.' He looked at the screen again and turned the knob to move the film along. 'I'm inclined to think this is important, but you never know.' He gave a helpless smile and ended their conference. It took them two weeks of snubs from the Polish émigré community and suspicion from the British before they learned the reason: the Polish Deuxiéme Bureau had declared them German agents.

'It's all politics!' Marek raged. He had a glass of brandy in one hand and despite his bad knee, he looked ready to jump on to the table and smash the glassware. 'I have told you,' he said to Elizabeth, 'it is politics! I warned you of that when you first made contact with the Professor.'

'Had we not dealt with The Fraternity, we wouldn't have got the men out.' Elizabeth said. She knew he blamed her. It broke his heart to be distrusted by old comrades from the engineers. Indifferent to regimentation herself, Elizabeth had misjudged how much he longed for another brigade, for a place in some military outfit. 'The Home Army group we were put in touch with was insecure. Badly compromised.' She threw up her hands. It was impossible to describe the Warsaw Underground. The men in London who fussed about political purity and old quarrels did not know their city now, would not recognise its geography.

'It is said that we were the source of their difficulties. Even that is said.' Marek was white around the nostrils and his cousin, Waldemar, an officer with one of the British-equipped Polish Brigades, laid a hand on his shoulder.

'No one believes that, Marek. It is politics, purely politics.'

The little group of friendly officers agreed, and, to the relief of the handsome Egyptian waiter, Marek sat down heavily in one of the wicker chairs and took a long drink from his glass.

'You must realise,' one of the others said, 'that we are cautioned to be on the alert for German agents. And *Volksdeutsh*.' He had been at Tobruk, this officer, and carried its souvenirs in his dark face and bandaged hand, in his stunned pleasure at beer, at cigarettes, at cafés and female conversation.

Marek laughed. 'We had one of those in Budapest. Madame Andrew's husband took care of him.'

'You must be patient. We are told reinforcements are coming from our Army Group in Scotland. There may be someone to vouch for you.'

'Yes, yes, you will see friends then. It will be cleared up,' Waldemar said. But April came, and May, and they remained under public suspicion in an enforced, corrosive idleness. Marek began to drink a great deal and, when he drank, awareness of his grievances made him belligerent. Elizabeth was often enlisted as peacemaker, but one night in the Egyptian Quarter the situation got out of hand.

They had been having a drink with two Polish pilots attached to a reconnaissance outfit when some Deuxiéme Bureau agents arrived. Elizabeth recognised them, but before she could persuade Marek to leave, words were exchanged, and he pitched over the café table and flattened one of them. Elizabeth and the pilots tried to get between him and the agent's three companions but it was too late. As the proprietor called on Allah as witness, the Deuxiéme Bureau attacked in force. Marek, outnumbered and slowed by his bad knee, picked up one of the light metal chairs and used it as a flail. Elizabeth caught hold of one of his assailants and was struggling to keep a grip on him, when she slipped on spilled beer and they both wound up on the floor.

By this time, more or less for the pleasure of a scrap, the two pilots had gone in on Marek's side and some of the other revellers were adding advice and beginning to swing bottles and knock over tables. Through the smoky confusion,

Elizabeth caught a glimpse of Marek standing like a bull at bay, blood streaming from one eyebrow, his shirt soaked with beer. He had his back against a post so that he would not be knocked over, and he had dispatched one of his tormentors and now appeared to be removing the head from another.

'Marek!' she shouted and, he turned, a cheerful violence in the white gleam of his teeth. Elizabeth pushed and shoved through the mob, using her sharp high heels when necessary, but before she could reach him, the MPs arrived, and the cafe emptied in a rush, Poles of every persuasion fleeing alongside ANZACs, British and Egyptians. Marek was caught almost at once but Elizabeth grabbed his arm and shouted 'Disabled Veteran' until the MPs got fed up and set off after more mobile quary.

Marek, in high good humour despite a nasty cut and the beginnings of a black eye, insited on taking a horse cab back and sang loudly all the way while Elizabeth listened with a mixture of pride and exasperation. From then on, Deuxiéme Bureau agents gave them a wide berth, and Marek confined his drinking to the Continental. He drank beer and brandy and played cards with Polish officers on leave who either did not know, or did not care, about his reputation. Elizabeth preferred to practise her English at Shepeard's and to learn polo from Jack Morris.

It might have ended then in a slow, if friendly separation, but British intelligence was hydra-headed and inconsistent. SOE thought they were spies; MI decided they were not and hired Marek, with his engineering background, to scout bridges and fortifications from Lebanon north to the Turkish border and east to the Euphrates. He and Elizabeth drove out of the delta in a gilded dawn, and all the way north the crops were gold in the fields and the bare hills stood against the empty sky as stark as the bones of the earth. South of Aleppo was land where they could breathe: a wide prairie with blood red soil that stretched to the horizons like the Polish steppe. They were happy. It was only when Marek thought of the vast ages seen by the dusty towns, of the tribes, untold, forgotten, that had passed before him, of other men like himself, wandering abroad after defeat, that he slipped into melancholy.

He felt that most keenly in Damascus, a shabby, fly-blown, magnificent place, where he watched Elizabeth handle a German agent with the indifferent dexterity of a cat with a mouse and wondered whether it would not have been better for both of them if she had treated him as lightly. In Budapest, their rapport had been based on the madness of the time, their desire to strike some blow despite her sex and his handicap. Marek had thought his heart was safe, that her marriage, if nothing else, woud stand in the way. His feelings had caught him unawares that snowy day when she returned, and he had looked to Cairo for salvation, figuring to get work, to join the motorised British Army where his leg would be no more than a minor nuisance.

He had not anticipated the delays, the suspicion, the maddening never-never land of political jealousy. He had not anticipated this mission, nor the snow-capped mountains rising behind Beirut, nor the old French hotel down near the sea, nor Damascus, nervous and bored, full of storm petrels and opportunists and sunk in desert heat. Neither had he anticipated Elizabeth's frantic letters in search of her husband. More than once in Cairo he had thought he should tell her about Jozef; each time, he could find no excuse for his long delay and thought again, as always, that they must be cleared, that he must, at last, be taken for a regiment. He had not lost hope, and so, one night in Damascus when he came out of the bath and saw her lying on the bed in a long silk nightgown, rich as cream, he ignored the fluttering pain in his heart. He sat down beside her under the yellow lamplight and read, in her neat convent hand, the boasts and ideas and indiscreet gossip of Herr Schattan, supposed trade envoy, fresh from Iran and the rebellous Raschid Ali.

'That bastard had a lot to say.'

'He needed a sympathetic ear,' Elizabeth said drily, capping her pen and moving her arm so that he could read the rest of the page. 'Now whether or not he was lying —'

'It rings true — the Vichy reprisal business does, anyway.'

'A terrible decision for those soldiers.'

'The lucky French still have families and villages to worry about. What chance did ours have?'

'We cannot risk thinking too much about what we've lost,'

she said, shifting slightly on the bed. 'We have to live for the present.' Her face was hidden by her hair and the angle of her shoulder, but Marek could see the stubborn line of her chin. He laid his hand on her back, touched the thick lace that was a last, private reminder of their old lives, and said, 'And if only now matters, what do you think?'

Elizabeth rolled on to her back so that her dark hair fanned out over the sheets. 'For now, for this moment,' she said, 'I could love you forever.'

Marek had not anticipated that, either.

So he had had his chance or seen his danger, one or the other, but when they were back in Cairo, still suspect, they grew bored and restless again. Marek's was a Viking soul; he had a lust for combat, and when that was gone, he looked for trouble. Elizabeth saw him sometimes with a cipher clerk, an English girl, small and pretty. Rather, she thought ruefully, like herself in appearance, but younger, a woman without mixed loyalties and memories that must, by awakening the past, stir old wounds. Well, she understood; were they not alike? It was just their tastes that differed: he liked brandy and compliant women and the dim bar of the Continental. What she liked was the Gezirah in the afternoon with the smell of horse and hot, dry dust and, in the evening, the officers' club where Jack was saying, 'We'll have a burra-peg, shall we?'

'All right. A burra-peg.' Elizabeth struggled to get her tongue around the phrase. Jozef's instruction had not prepared her for British military slang, well sprinkled as it was with Hindi and Arabic. They laughed about this and about the night, dropping swiftly to drench the sky in perfumed lavender, then drove out to a small restaurant where the soft pat of the waiters' slippers, the rattle of cutlery and dishes mingled with the sounds of the night birds and frogs. By the time they were finished it was nearly eleven, and after the featureless darkness of the river settlements, Cairo appeared like a desert mirage, blazing with light. Jack took the bridge to Gezirah Island and stopped at one of the large modern apartment buildings.

'British lieutenants live well,' Elizabeth remarked.

'My commander's. It comes with the polo ponies. I'll let you see how the brass lives.'

The third-floor apartment had long french windows and balconies that overlooked the polo fields of the Club. Insects buzzed and whirred in the dense scrubbery below and in the thicket of palms and jacarandas that screened the far bank of the Nile. Jack pushed aside one of the curtains and looked out. 'Convenient, isn't it? The old boy just lives for polo.'

'Where is he now?'

Jack pointed west.

'What is it like out there?'

'Like? Like nothing else. In the desert you shit sand.' He turned away from the window and switched on a light. 'Will you have a drink? It's open bar here – in moderation.' Elizabeth heard him fiddling with a bottle.

'I'm not much of a drinker,' she said.

'Well, I'll admit liquor's secondary to the real joys of life.' He was standing against the light, holding his glass, a thin, taut silhouette. Elizabeth was aware of a concentration of feeling, of a nostalgia for danger, for desire, for simpler emotions. Like Budapest, Cairo was tainted by ease, by luxury and ambiguity, floating on the desert as the city on the Danube had floated over disaster. She let the curtain drop and Jack put down his glass and held out his hand. It was a certain intensity he offered, an avidity of emotion stronger than any drug, as strong as the quick ripple of the senses in danger, in combat – not, to be sure, the combat that was written in his face – but the combat of lonely journeys, dangerous meetings, basement cells. He took her face in his hands and rested his forehead against hers for a moment.

'I have waited,' he said. She touched his hands lightly, then slipped her arms around him, and they both laughed because it was so easy, because the human body is permeable, because for a moment their very bones could touch, their cries sing with the frogs and the night insects, the bats and the jackals.

After Jack left for the front, Elizabeth and Marek sometimes drove into the desert to see the great statues, the empty pyramids and colonnades and lost cities, testing how it would be to be friends, merely that. They were returning from one of these trips when they stopped at a little fly blown café on the edge of the desert. A group of about a dozen Argyles were sitting around under the palms with a noisy yellow mutt. One had an accordion and two others were standing up with their arms around each other's shoulders, bellowing, 'Keep the Red Flag Flying'.

'Heard the news, Mac?' the sergeant called as soon as Marek and Elizabeth stepped out of their dusty car.

'What news? What's happened?'

'Jerry's gone for Russia.'

'They've attacked? A serious attack?'

'Serious enough,' their officer said. He was tanned brick red with a livid burn scar down one side of his neck. 'It's been all over the BBC. A line from the Baltic to the Urals. They crossed some Polish river this morning.'

'The Bug,' said Elizabeth looking at Marek. 'It was all true, then.'

'That's the place. The Führer's asked for it this time.'

'Aye, Uncle Joe'll sort him.'

'A chair for the lady. And a drink. What will you have?'

'To our enemies,' said Marek. 'May they devour each other.'

'Another chorus, Hamish, if you please.'

'They're all half-Red,' sighed the officer. 'Glasgow lads, mostly.'

'Another round for the Argyles,' Marek told the waiter, who wiped his hands on his stained *galabiyah* and bowed and beamed and thanked Allah for this windfall. They toasted the Argyles, who stood and sang 'The Wallace Song'; they toasted the Allies, including the Reds, the Polish Brigades, His Majesty, Churchill and Sikorski, and they didn't stop until the sun was low, its narrow beams shooting through the palm fronds like spears. Then the Argyles piled into their truck and they all began an uncertain progress toward Cairo, where 'Barbarossa' was on everyone's lips, and their Captain Francis welcomed them gleefully.

'Of course we had the information! Of course we did.' He shook their hands with un-English fervour and promised to see them cleared.

In the cafés there was endless speculation and celebration, and when an engineering battalion arrived from Scotland, Marek and Elizabeth were swept into long, convivial reunions. Even their association with The Fraternity was, if not forgotten, ignored. Marek was sent to get treatment for his knee, given an exhaustive physical and, in mid-November, accepted for a Polish Brigade. No word came for Elizabeth. She kept busy, helped a friend select volunteers for Crete, was, it appeared, trusted, but remained unemployed. Her happiness for Marek thus bore a faint shadow, but he was so busy preparing that they were not together very much.

She went to see him a few days before he was to join the Brigade. His room at the Continental was on the second floor at the back, a tiny cubicle with an iron bed, overlooking the kitchens. When she opened the door, he was at the washstand, shaving.

'Morning,' he said as he slid the long straight razor under his lower lip. Elizabeth leaned against the wall and watched the blade slip through the thick white blanket of foam. When he was finished, he rinsed his razor and dried it off before wiping the last of the bay and lemon scented shaving soap from his face.

'I've come to tell you that I've decided to leave Egypt,' she said.

At once, he became very still and alert. 'Is that wise?' he asked. 'You have contacts here.'

'I know people in London, too. And it will give me a chance to locate Jozef. Someone, somewhere, knows where he is.' She had written letters all spring, all summer. Sent them to anyone who might know, to everywhere he might show up. Those irritating letters had been the guarantee of Marek's independence, and he sometimes thought it a pity the cipher clerk hadn't been married, too — there might yet be problems there. He hung up the towel, stuck his hands in his pockets and stood looking out over the roofs of the kitchens, wondering why he felt regret. He would miss her, he realised, he would miss her the most. She started to speak, to say something else about Jozef, and he said, 'You won't find him in London.'

'What do you mean?'

'He never intended to go to England. He told me that when he left Hungary.'

'Where did he go?'

'He wanted to go back to France. He said you had a house there.' Marek glanced over his shoulder at her. 'Jozef misinterpreted us – what was between us. He thought you would be happier with me. Of course, he did not expect the disaster in France.'

'You said nothing of this! Nothing! When all year I have been writing, hoping, looking for him, asking every Englishman I meet.'

'I was like Jozef,' he said with an edge in his voice. 'I misunderstood your feelings and waited too long. Then I didn't want you to worry. Or to try to go back.'

'Liar! You thought of nothing but yourself! And then you were too preoccupied, too lazy!' Elizabeth raised her hands and cleared the bureau of his silver brushes, his shaving soap, his pipes. 'You were afraid of grief,' she said in a cold, sharp voice. 'You were afraid of loving me. You are not so brave as Jozef.'

'Don't speak to me of grief,' Marek said, grabbing her arm. 'I am sick with it. Who is left for me?' But though he twisted her wrist savagely, her face remained immobile and, for one sickening moment, Marek feared he would strike her. Then Elizabeth's knees crumpled. She dropped to the floor and scooped up his brushes and pipes and held them in her arms, her face white and stricken. Marek felt the back of his throat break and knelt awkwardly beside her.

'My Darling, my darling,' he said. Her hair was against his lips, the handles of the brushes poked his ribs. He pushed them out of her hands and tumbled against the linoleum, holding her in his arms. The blades of the overhead fan tore the light with shadows, streaking their faces, bright and dark. It would never be enough, never, never, the blades of the fan said, never, never, never, in monotonous rhythm. Marek felt Elizabeth's tears, a trickle of sweat on his back, the floor against his knees, then a mixture of sorrow and pleasure so intense that the white brightness of the room darkened and his diminished vision was ringed green and purple like an aurora. He rolled onto his back, felt the fan's warm breeze and watched the procession of the blades across the ceiling. Everything was over now.

Chapter Seventeen

Nîmes 1944

As soon as he saw Guy in the café, Jozef felt a familiar tightness in the pit of his stomach. Another one. He always promised himself and Madame Rozier that this was the last, the very last, to no avail.

'Ah, bonjour, Jozef.' Guy looked older, his face puffy and sallow, his thinning hair combed in a fussy pattern across his long skull. Jozef shook hands and sat down. He would have dearly liked a beer or better yet a brandy, but since it was one of the hateful non-alcohol days, he ordered a mineral.

'We have an emergency,' Guy said. 'Can we rely on you?'

Jozef hesitated. 'We are pushing our luck. I must remember Madame Rozier. She is not young, you know. She'd never stand questioning.'

'She has had a good run,' Guy said. 'We should live so long.' Then, in a lower voice, 'He is one of yours, a navigator – very young. And we have a doctor coming.'

'Bad?' asked Jozef. There were degrees: burns and crash injuries for airmen, bullet wounds for resisters, broken hands and torn backs courtesy of *La Gest*. So many possibilities.

Guy cupped his hands around his cigarette and leaned forward. 'I have some morphia ampoules. It will be all right.'

Jozef said nothing. That meant very bad.

'We have nowhere else,' Guy said softly. 'And he speaks no French.'

The café window was dappled with drops of water and through its aqueous well Jozef saw the cold spring rain pounding on the street. He thought of Czeslaw and Charlie and the young cavalrymen. 'I will tell Madame Rozier to visit her sister.'

'Thank you, Jozef. It will be tonight,' Guy said.

Jozef put some coins on the table and pulled his scarf around his throat. Outside a wide shallow puddle stretched across the pavement, and he crossed quickly to the other side of the street, keeping ahead of his memories. Jozef rarely visited that particular café, but, in the shelter of the news kiosk, he turned and looked back, seeing not the drab, rain-washed front, the faded paint, the rolled awnings, the new signs in both French and German, but the café of summers past with the brilliant pink awning lowered, the terrace crowded, the women's hats like bright birds, the men's light suits and felt hats a backdrop for pretty dresses, bare arms, the whole afloat on flirtation and pleasure and good wine like Cleopatra's barge. He and Elizabeth had known little, forseen less; they had talked and laughed and planned, with what touching naiveté, manageable futures. What folly. What waste. And where was she now? Guy did not know how much of Jozef's obliging courage came from that uncertainty, from the fear that Elizabeth might be one of the hunted, the lost.

He pulled down the brim of his hat and headed back into the cold rain towards the Boulevard Gambetta. There had been letters. Quite a few letters, Madame Rozier said, but she had not accepted them. 'It seemed best, Monsieur. The foreign stamps, the English words. Everything was suspect. And then, Monsieur, with your new papers . . . '

Jozef had shown her samples of Elizabeth's writing, but the old lady had squinted nearsightedly and shrugged. 'I did not study them, Monsieur. I said to René – it was René, then – I said, "There's been some mistake. I am alone," I said. "There's no one here by that name." And a good thing it was, Monsieur, since you came back with a different identity.'

That was in '42 when he had, at last, returned via Yugoslavia, Trieste and Genoa with nicely made Italian papers, crossing over from captive Nice as a salesman for a business with shops on both sides of the new border. The *padrone* had not wanted to let him go. 'You could be rich, Jozef. Rich, eh?' he'd say and clap Jozef on the back. But Jozef thought that unlikely, and the work, translating for the *padrone* when he contacted corrupt Germans, seemed certain to grow more dangerous as anti-fascist resistance grew. Jozef managed a very nice deal in stolen weapons with a homesick *volksdeutch* and took advantage of the resulting good will to ask for new papers.

'Simplicity itself,' said the *padrone*, and one morning, just after the Germans occupied the south, Jozef had knocked on the door of his own house and Madame Rozier, a bad-tempered but indispensable household deity, had let him in, having managed somehow to keep the place afloat out of the money they'd left her. She had known how to acquire his ration cards, made sure he had the proper residence permits, had generally fixed whatever had not been taken care of by his forged papers. The old lady had a talent with officialdom. She did a bit of marketeering, too, for he got the impression she had money put by somewhere and she occasionally asked him to deliver heavy parcels. They were in it together, so to speak, and when he got home and hung up his dripping coat and delivered the potatoes and turnips he'd been fortunate enough to get at the early market, she knew even before he said, 'I think you might visit your sister today,' what was up.

'Today!' she said. 'Today!'

'You know she will be glad to see you. Take her the turnip. Nice and fresh. Not a soft spot in it.'

'And you will live on air,' Madame Rozier said. She stamped around the kitchen, her stout black shoes protesting to the flagstones. She had disapproved the first time, and he had refused a refugee, a Jew on the run.

'Do not trust him,' she had said. 'He will involve you and sell you to the *Milice*. You are not French, Monsieur, and you are as much at risk as he is.'

Later, when there were deportations, Jozef had had pangs of conscience. Next, it was a boy with a broken ankle. His family were running to the mountains – there was little chance for them otherwise – and this time Jozef agreed. 'He was my student,' he told Madame Rozier.

'And for this you should risk your life?' She said the same now when he told her the latest one was a Pole. He did not say it could have been Czeslaw or Marek or even Elizabeth, any one of the people he had loved.

'I have told Guy this is the last.'

'Yes, and the Allies will come and rescue us all,' Madame Rozier said bitterly.

'I believe that will happen.'

'I would like to be alive to see it.' She set her enormous basket on the table and into it put the turnip and some flour and a few eggs he had not known they possessed. Then she looked around the kitchen and shook her head. 'There's not much left.'

Jozef shrugged, half sympathetically. With one single exception, every small thing of worth had already disappeared into that capacious hamper. Candlesticks, the few scraps of silver, Elizabeth's good dresses, a nice print. The furniture had never been valuable, but Madame Rozier had managed deals for a couple of pieces, nonetheless.

'Some will buy books,' she said dubiously.

'I can't teach without my books.' But he was already considering the remains of his diminished library.

Madame Rozier was implacable. 'Anything with maps is still selling well.'

'I will look.'

'You have some with pictures. Those are the best.'

'I have a suit. What about that instead, Madame Rozier?'

She'd had her eye on it for some time, the old witch, but now she protested that he would be cold. Jozef ran up the stairs for it while she was still worrying about his health, and had it in her hands before she could fasten on something else.

'Lovely wool, Monsieur. I believe we'll do well with this. Perhaps sell it in parts, I'll see.'

'Whatever you think best,' Jozef said, holding her coat for her as the little terrier jumped in excitement: like the rest of them, the poor brute was weary of living on bread and hungered for a scrap of liver, a stew bone.

'I'll be back tomorrow night, Monsieur.'

'*Bonne chance*, Madame Rozier.'

She took his arm for a moment by way of farewell, then shook her head angrily and stumped out the door so quickly that Jozef had to grab Frisé's collar to keep him from bolting into the street after his mistress. The housekeeper was spry for an old lady, and Jozef smiled, half amused. It must be something in his character that led him so often to fall in with sharp operators. Madame Rozier was undoubtedly cheating him, but he could not find it in himself to be angry; unlike his activities, hers risked only money.

Guy arrived in the small hours. The navigator was in the bakery truck, hidden behind a screen of bread racks. Jozef opened the door and Guy and his companions carried the injured man into the house. 'Quickly, quickly,' Guy said. Jozef put out the hall light and led them upstairs. The door to the attic was unlocked, and the bed under the eaves ready. Getting the unconscious navigator up the final steps was a struggle, and, whenever the man groaned, Guy began to swear. Jozef had never seen the baker so nervous, so chalky white in the lantern light. His companions laid the injured man on the bed as gently as they could, and Jozef saw his face. He looked like a boy — certainly not out of his teens — and his lips were bluish and the skin under his eyes, smudged black. Except for his soft moans, Jozef would have thought him a corpse.

'This man should be in a hospital. What happened to him?'

'We thought just broken ribs and a torn arm. But the doctor will come.' Guy's friends were already clattering down the steps and he started to follow them. Jozef grabbed his arm.

'I must know,' he said.

Guy lifted the blanket. Thick blood-stained bandages turned the boy's left hand and arm into a club. Dark streaks radiated from the wraping to the shoulder and Jozef smelled a foul, wet decay.

'He has gangrene!'

'Please, I promise you. The doctor will come tomorrow. And there's morphine. Plenty of it.' Guy fumbled in his pocket for a cardboard box. 'See. Give him as much as he needs to keep him quiet. If it's only in the arm, we can save him.'

'He needs an operation. They'll have to amputate the arm. Perhaps even take the shoulder! It is madness to try this in the middle of town.'

'There was nowhere else. Nowhere. Max was arrested. Cécile is under surveillance.'

'You should have warned me,' Jozef said, his voice rising. 'I have pupils. Another day and the whole house will stink. What are you trying to do to me?'

'What was I to do, keep him in the fucking bakery?'

The boy cried out on the bed behind them and Guy said, 'Just give him some morphine.'

'How long since he's had some? I don't want to kill him.'

'Three hours.'

When Jozef picked up the box of ampoules, Guy ducked down the hatchway. Jozef heard his feet on the stairs, the front door, the rough sound of the truck. He stood for a moment, sweating and furious, then the boy groaned and Jozef rolled up the sleeve of the navigator's undamaged arm and gave him an ampoule. There were nine left: a treasure on the back market, but if the navigator needed a shot every three hours — Jozef ran his hand across his face, dizzy with the smell and with fear. Please send the doctor, he thought. Please, dear God! He stood for a few minutes in the cramped space of the eaves, watching his angular shadow and the soft flicker of the lantern. Then he concealed the discarded ampoule in a piece of paper and covered the navigator with a quilt. He lay so still that for a moment Jozef feared the morphine had finished him off, but no, the thin chest was still disturbed by breath. There was a feverish sweat on the navigator's forehead and his fair hair was matted dark above his young face. Jozef felt his angry panic turn to pity. He knelt down at the side of the bed and, for the first time in years, asked the Virgin's mercy. Then he got up, leaving the lantern in case the navigator regained consciousness.

He screamed at six and Jozef almost fell getting up the stairs to give him the morphine before the neighbours heard. This time the injured man remained in a state of semi-consciousness and Jozef went down and boiled up some thin vegetable soup Madame Rozier had left.

'Try to drink this.' He blew on the hot liquid, then put the spoon to the navigator's mouth. The boy swallowed feebly. 'That's good. A little more.' But one was all he could manage. Jozef put out the lantern and opened one of the heavily shuttered windows. In the thin morning light, the navigator's skin was translucent, a mere veil over the bones, and Jozef was afraid that he was dying.

'Who?' the navigator breathed. He began to struggle against the covers, against his sickness and fever with a helpless incomprehension.

Jozef put a hand on his shoulder. 'You must stay quiet. My name is Jozef. A compatriot. You were shot down but you are safe with me. We will get a doctor.'

The sound of his own language seemed to calm the navigator. He stopped trying to sit up and closed his eyes. 'Sleep,' Jozef said. 'I will come back soon.'

The morning's lessons were agony, strained as Jozef's nerves were between the fear of hearing the navigator and the hope of the doctor's arrival. At mid-day, he ran his fingers over the diminishing rows of ampoules and wondered if he should try to find Guy, but, afraid to miss the doctor, he waited until Madame Rozier returned home. While she fixed dinner, Jozef hurried to the café but the baker was not about.

'We will get the doctor tonight,' he told Madame Rozier, but he did not need her sceptical frown to make him uneasy; Guy's white face and worn temper had already warned him. That night Jozef stayed up beside the navigator, wiping the sweat off the sick man's face, feeding him spoonfuls of clear soup and water and, at ever shorter intervals, opening the box for the ampoules of morphine. In the morning, he went to the café. Guy was sitting in the back, far from his usual table, his hands cupped around his coffee.

'Where is the doctor?'

Guy looked around nervously. 'He was arrested.'

'You must find another. We will be out of morphine in another few hours. When it is gone ...'

'Have you any other source? Have you a doctor? I've been looking everywhere,' Guy said in a low voice. He hunched his coat around him, and Jozef could see he was shivering.

'You never had a doctor,' Jozef said.

'I swear! He was arrested!'

'Find me one.' Jozef reached across the table and took hold of the smaller man's jacket. 'Today.'

'I will try.' Guy made an ineffectual motion of his hand. 'You know I have a wife,' he said. 'Children. You understand.'

'The hell with you,' Jozef said, and left the café. The previous winter a doctor on the Rue de Lampèze had treated him for 'flu, and now Jozef tried to remember if Dr. Oury had given the slightest hint of his politics. A waiting room photo of Petain? No, that was Madame Rozier's doctor; he had collected a prescription for her once. He had no way of guessing Oury's reaction, but Jozef decided that he would have to take a chance. The consulting room was over a watch-maker's shop and between nerves and weariness, Jozef was out of breath by the time he reached the foyer.

'I'm sorry Doctor isn't in this morning,' the pretty receptionist said.

A cowardly relief mingled with Jozef's exasperation. 'I can come back this afternoon. It won't take very long.'

The receptionist raised her plucked eyebrows and looked at the appointment book sceptically. 'We're really very full up.'

'I don't mind waiting. It is my chest again. Dr. Oury saw me in December.'

'Well − around four, then.'

Jozef thanked her though it meant nearly five hours to wait and said he'd return that afternoon.

The navigator was asleep when Jozef got home; Madame Rozier had given him the morphine two hours early. 'What could I do? It's a wonder the neighbours haven't called in the police already. I should have given it to him all at once and been done with him.'

'No,' said Jozef, horrified. 'We will not be his murderers. We can manage today if we can spread out the shots.'

'And tomorrow? Where is that doctor? The boy rots while we wait.'

'There is trouble. Guy's usual doctor has been arrested.'

'I warned you about that baker. They have dumped him on you.'

'That's neither here nor there at the moment. Do you know any other doctor?'

'Who would come for such a case?'

'Or give us some morphine. If we can keep him quiet until Guy finds someone.'

'Ha,' said Madame Rozier. 'Give, never. Come, no. Sell?' She pursued her mouth and concentrated. 'See Dr. Muel. Off

Avenue Feuchères.' She rubbed her fingertips together. 'They say he helps women in difficulties.'

'I will try him if my own doctor refuses.'

'There must be money,' said Madame Rozier, but Jozef knew better than to ask her. He took out his cigarette case. It was French gold, a present from the Countess when André had passed his special exams.

Madame Rozier nodded. 'It should do,' she said, but Jozef took the precaution of slipping one of her sharp pairing knives into his pockert before he went downtown.

'I am so sorry,' Oury's receptionist said. 'He has been called to the hospital. A heart patient.'

Jozef felt a flush of heat across his chest and a sudden coldness after it. 'Will the doctor be back later today? It is really vital I see him.'

'I don't know how long he will be at the hospital. You understand, Monsieur, that such emergencies do not run according to any plan.'

'Of course, forgive me,' Jozef said. 'Is there anyone who covers for Dr. Oury?'

'Dr. Burias, but he is on holiday. I am sorry, Monsieur. I am sure Doctor can see you tomorrow.'

'Yes,' said Jozef, but tomorrow would be too late. In the steep and narrow stairwell, he slipped on the worn linoleum, clutched the banister and saw the wet print of his hand on the wood. His blood jumped in his ears and its muffled thump made his head ache. He would have to see Dr. Muel. Have to. The navigator had received another of the precious ampoules after lunch and at that rate Madame Rozier would soon finish the box. Jozef took a deep breath and pushed open the heavy door to the street.

The address was far along the avenue, and he didn't reach Muel's office until after five. Jozef's breath grew short when he realised the time and though he kept assuring himself that Guy would bring a doctor soon, he did not really believe it. He rang the bell, once, twice, and, not getting an answer, tried the handle and pushed open the front door.

The entry foyer was still and gloomy. The opaque chandelier was dark and the only light came through the grudging panes of a green and maroon stained window. The receptionist's chair by the telephone was empty. 'Doctor?' Jozef called, then again. An oppressive silence flowed around him. There were two heavy doors on either side of the reception area. One was locked; the other opened on to a waiting room. 'Dr. Muel?' Jozef said as he stepped inside. There was a sound from the inner office and a short man with a square, smooth face opened the door. He wore thick round glasses that at once magnified and shielded his light eyes. 'The office is closed.'

'It is an emergency.'

The doctor waited.

Jozef's mouth was dry and the words were made of sand. 'A friend of mine has been injured. He has insisted on staying at home. A bad arm. I am worried – there are signs of infection.'

'I am a gynaecologist not a general practitioner. A case such as you describe should be taken to the hospital.'

'That is not possible.'

'I do not handle such matters,' the doctor said and turned back towards his office.

'Then some morphine,' Jozef said, reckless with anxiety. 'Please. I can pay.'

'Monsieur, what you take me for?'

'A patriot and a christian.' But, just in case, Jozef stepped closer and slid his hand in his pocket.

'You will leave, Monsieur, before I report such a request.' Dr. Muel started to close his office door, and, desperate, Jozef put the knife to his ribs.

'Be so kind as to give me some morphine. Ampoules would be best.'

The angry flush drained from the doctor's face and a film of sweat appeared on his smooth cheeks. Jozef registered the doctor's fear with a kind of surprise and, numb with terror himself, glanced around the room and saw a white metal cupboard. He looked at the doctor. After the merest hesitation, Dr. Muel took out a key and unlocked his supplies. Jozef recognized a box like the one Guy had brought with the navigator.

'Will this do?' Muel asked.

'Open it.'

The carton was packed close with smooth thin ampoules. Jozef put the carton in his pocket, then took out his cigarette case and laid it gently on the doctor's desk. 'For your trouble, Doctor.'

He crossed the waiting room and the foyer and hurried into the street. He was minutes away before he remembered the telephone, but it did not matter. With almost a sense of relief, he felt that he could do no more. Dr. Muel would call to report the incident or he would not. It was out of Jozef's hands entirely.

'Thank God, he's quiet at last,' Madame Rozier said when she opened the door. 'I have used the last of the morphine.'

'No matter.' Jozef put the box in her hands and hung up his coat.

'Dr Muel gave you this?'

'After a fashion. How long has it been?' He lifted his head towards the stair.

'Over an hour. I thought I heard him a little while ago, but it must have been children playing somewhere. Or the wind.'

'Perhaps we might try some of the soup. He needs fluids.'

Madame Rozier went into the kitchen and Jozef followed her idly. She put a few spoonfuls of soup into a little pan and turned on the gas. Then she put some coffee in another pan and heated it for Jozef. He sat and drank it slowly, as if it was the real thing and not the dreadful ersatz of acorns and sweepings. He was suddenly tired. 'Hide all your possessions, Madame Rozier. If there is trouble, you came in by days only and knew nothing.'

She looked at him, then nodded.

Jozef emptied his cup and got up. 'I will check on our guest,' he said. Yet he was reluctant; the panicked anxiety he had felt in the streets and the doctors' waiting rooms had been replaced by a heavy apprehension. He glanced at some of his students' papers lying neglected on his desk, then went to the attic door. Jozef was about to turn the handle when he heard the sound: a soft tapping, a driping like a leaky pipe. He cursed the old plumbing, opened the door and recognised the smell from slaughtering days on the estate. There was a thin red line dripping from the top of the stair.

Jozef clutched the bannister then raced, stumbling and slipping, up the steps. The attic floor was awash in blood. The young navigator lay half in and half out of bed, his legs tangled in the covers, his mangled arm exposed. There was blood all over his arm and on his throat and on his chest and running down the warped floor towards the steps. A black military knife they had not known he possessed lay bloody by his fingers. Jozef crossed himself as slowly as a man in a dream and stepped over to close the boy's eyes. The eyelids were still warm; the navigator's moment of madness or despair had come just before salvation, perhaps while Madame Rozier and he sat talking in the kitchen or while he lingered over the papers. Jozef crossed himself again, and stood for a moment, his hand frozen in space; then he understood the danger as well as the horror and stepped to the head of the stairs.

'Madame Rozier,' he called. 'Madame Rozier!'

Chapter Eighteen

Spring – 1944

The young FANY was immensely thorough. 'Just let me check the labels,' she said apologetically, turning down the band of Elizabeth's pants. 'You'd be surprised. I've had a couple all set to jump in British knickers.' Then she emptied the pockets of Elizabeth's sweater and slacks and checked the neckband on her shirt. 'Tickets are the worst. People wear their clothes to break them in and leave the stubs in their pockets.' As she handed the garments back one by one, the FANY kept chatting brightly. She knew that outgoing agents hated to be searched, hated everything except getting away quickly. 'The weather looks good anyway.'

'I've got my fingers crossed.'

The FANY nodded. This agent's jump had been postponed twice already. 'Now for your kit. You understand about the money belt? Good. Put it on first, please.' She went to the rack standing against the wall and took down a large jumpsuit.

The sight of the parachute overalls made Elizabeth's stomach tighten; they all hated the jumps. She had an unwelcome vision of the balloon going up, the platform swaying gently beneath its giant belly, before a jumper hurtled through the opening in the bottom and plummeted straight for the earth. Down on the tarmac, waiting their turn, the agents in training had held their breaths until the white flower of the chute opened. They had all been afraid. She was still afraid, though it might be better at night, without the dizzy sight of Ringway and the English countryside in miniature below. It might be.

The FANY busied herself filling the capacious pockets around the overall legs with a collapsible shovel, a commando knife, a flask, some rations. The .38 automatic she handed directly to Elizabeth.

'You might want to check this yourself,' she said, and Elizabeth dutifully weighed the hateful thing in her hand and examined the safety and the clip. It seemed to her unlikely that she would ever use such a weapon, but, though she was strongly tempted to refuse, she pocketed it without complaint. She was on her good behaviour after a row with Smathers, her conducting agent. Though he had a tremendous record in the field, Smathers had irritated her. Every briefing had been delivered from a position of such unassailable authority and with such a belief in correct systems and procedures that Elizabeth, eternal freelance and improviser, had been moved irresistibly to disagreement. He was not the only one with experience, despite the awkward dentures that concealed evidence of his stay with the Gestapo. Still, they were professionals and they had managed all right until the day that he briefed her on the political factions she would meet.

'You must realise that many of them are communists,' he said. 'You must be prepared to work with them.'

Though Elizabeth's face was eloquent she said, 'I am willing to work with anyone to defeat the Germans. Anyone,' she repeated, and gave him a straight look.

Smathers had a way of twitching one side of his upper lip like a rogue horse. 'I wanted to be sure. Some of you Poles find that a sticking point.'

'We might be excused for that.'

'Not when it makes for problems.' Since his return from Paris, Smathers had worked with a variety of touchy and demanding brothers-in-arms. Except for France, which he loved with a knight errant's passion, the rest of the Captive Nations could go hang.

'You were glad enough to see us in the Battle of Britain. When you needed our pilots.'

'I'd forgotten your particular interest in that,' said Smathers. 'Well, we've done our share. We've damn well kept our end of the bargain.'

'I've been misinformed. I'd heard that General Sikorski died in a British plane, guarded by your people.'

'Have you any idea how many planes have crashed during this war?' Smathers asked, his face red and his voice rising.

Elizabeth had things she'd wanted to say for a long time and she was prepared to outshout him if necessary. 'Don't tell me it was an accident. Wasn't it that Sikorski was a nuisance to our all-powerful ally, the Red Army?'

'I can't talk to you if you are going to accuse us of assassinating Sikorski!'

'Then let us say it was carelessness. But the latest schemes are not carelessness. Perhaps we can replace Sikorski, but can we replace Lwow, Wilno? Wilno! Pilsudski was born in Wilno!'

'This is sentiment, not politics,' yelled Smathers, but now they were both shouting at once, nerves raw from waiting, from the paranoia and sorrow of their calling.

'Now the Russians want Tarnpol and the Prypec Marshes and Pinsk. Is there no end to Russian greed or British naïveté?'

'Or Polish romanticism! Do you think you'd be here at all if . . .'

'Are you all half-Red? The Curzon Line is a British invention.'

'And what do you think will be left of Poland without our mediation? God knows why we bother, but His Majesty's Government . . .'

'His Majesty's Government would sell us all to keep that murderous sot Stalin happy!'

Two FANYs came in then and spared them the indignity of coming to blows. A few days later, they sent a major, someone quite high up, to talk to her.

'You know Smathers has had a bad time,' he said by way of apology.

This major was handsome, well-fed and polite, a powerful man who'd had a 'good war'. The Countess would have charmed such a man, but Elizabeth said, 'We've all had bad times.'

'Yes.' The Major was silent for a while, one of those long English silences more eloquent than their speech. 'Are you still willing to go?'

Her heart leapt. 'That was never in doubt, was it? I have waited nearly three years.'

'Yes. Well, this is the nervous time,' the Major said.

So right. When the FANY started explaining the purposes of the spine pad. Elizabeth resisted the impluse to ask how many times she had jumped. Instead, she zipped the remaining pockets closed and took a few experimental steps around the room. Her equipment weighed her down and made her feel so awkward and nervous that she announced she had to go to the WC and the whole kit had to come off again. The FANY was unsurprised; departing agents were all alike.

'It won't be long now,' she said when Elizabeth was once again dressed. 'Would you like a cup of tea?'

Elizabeth said yes simply for the pleasure of being alone for a few minutes. Outside, a light plane took off — a Lysander by the sound of it — before the deeper, louder sound of a bomber's engines set up a vibration in her soul. They must go this time, they must! She had waited long enough. Let Sister Margaret rejoice: she had learned patience.

How often had she leaned over the Embankment to watch the Thames and thought of the Vistula, how often had letters come with the ritual, 'nothing suitable for you at this time?' Elizabeth could have lived in peace and security, done useful things, found someone to love and forgotten the others, but that had proved impossible. She had been born for one thing — and what should it be but this? All that had made her, blood, bone, custom, belief, the steppe in spring, the Tatra in winter, a heritage of horsemen, conspirators, martyrs, murderers and saints had produced the same imperative and brought her to this ill-built hut with its blinds shut tight against the growing darkness. In a few minutes, she'd be in the plane, on her way to France, and Elizabeth thought of Jozef.

She liked to imagine him in Nîmes, taking pupils, living as he had so many years ago, though it was just as likely that he had never reached France, that he had been dead all these years, almost as long as Mother and André. At this dangerous thought, Elizabeth strained her ears towards the warming engines, glad that in a few hours her personal life would be left behind: it was not she but Madeleine Deshenes who would drop to the maquis. Madeleine Deshenes! Elizabeth had already been so many different people — Marianne and

Paulettte in training, Elizabeth Gorman and Elizabeth Andrews in Budapest and Cairo, Marisia and Anna Dabrowska in Warsaw – that with an intense, queasy anxiety, her mind went blank. Madeleine Deshenes! The name meant nothing and, for a moment, it was as though Madeleine had never existed, as though the past week had not been devoted to her biography. Then bits and pieces of personal history swam into consciousness. Madeleine Deshenes was born on May 10th, 1916, in St. Etienne. Father, August Deshenes, baker, died in the Great War. Mother, Evonne, milliner, died in 1934 of cancer. Attended school at the Convent of the Sacred Heart. Trained in secretarial work. Now employed as personal secretary to Monsieur Claude Robanne, director of a small chemical company, Chemi-Borely, near Marseilles. Relatives in eastern France, including a sister, Evonne Grivois, in Grenoble ... Like an actress readying herself for a big role, Elizabeth paced the room and tried to feel like Madeleine Deshenes.

There was a sound on the step outside and the door opened. 'We're ready, Miss.' She walked on to the tarmac, heavy in her flight kit, and the airman nodded across the field. The hulk of an American Liberator was waiting for her, drenched in moonlight like a whale at sea.

There were four agents going, a man and a woman she had trained with and another agent who had been at Ringway for the jumps. They shook hands on the tarmac and murmured, '*Bonne chance*', remembering briefly their arduous training, the daily runs, the *plastique*, single combat and wireless codes. Elizabeth had done a practice demolition with Georges one dark night and had almost been caught by a village warden. He put his arm around her for a moment, then waddled to the stair and struggled into the belly of the aircraft. Isobel was next – they had practised ciphers together – then Elizabeth grabbed the ladder and climbed on to the first rung, the shovel packed into her leg pocket making every step awkward. Inside, an airman motioned them forward and they dropped down with their backs against the fuselage like unhorsed knights.

A few minutes later, the plane roared down the runway. At the Channel, the Liberator tested its guns, then rocked and shuddered in the flack over Normandy. Beyond the batteries, there was only the sound of the engine like the approach of fate, and in its deafening monotone Elizabeth thought of the jump to come and remembered her instructor, a squat, tough, humorous man, hoarse from shouting over the sound of engines. In the eerie silence of the balloon gondola, his voice had sounded amplified. 'It's not hard, you understand,' he'd said. 'Not hard at all. It's just unnatural.' *Le mot juste*, Elizabeth thought.

It did not seem very long — not quite long enough — before the dispatcher laid his hand on her shoulder. The others were already standing up and, out of the window, Elizabeth saw the gleaming Rhône winding through the fields and woods. 'Running in,' the dispatcher shouted over the roar, and Elizabeth sat on the edge of the hole where the strong, cold current of the night wind was flowing. Time expanded, the engines throbbed, then, at last, the red warning light went on, dying their faces crimson, and the dispatcher shouted, 'Action stations!' Elizabeth slid her feet and legs into the hole and balanced there, body stiff, her hands on the metal edges. 'Don't look down,' her instructor had said. 'When you're running in for a jump, don't look down.' Elizabeth shut out everything except the dispatcher's hand, and when it fell, she slid through the open bay and the darkness of the Liberator's shadow into the wind and moonlight.

She dropped like a stone. There was a terrible instant when she knew she'd made a horrible, irrevocable mistake, when fear and the drop took the breath from her lungs. Then the chute opened above her, welcome as the wings of an angel, and, swinging in the rigging, Elizabeth was struck by the unearthly loveliness of the night, as though from this height all things were beautiful to God. The moonlight poured over the fields and woods, turning the grass to silver and the distant river to a ribbon of pure light. Beneath her, the chute with her wireless and others bearing cylindrical weapons canisters, formed a delicate pattern like flowers opening on a dark French tapestry. They were drifting away to her right towards the faint, and rapidly diminishing, pattern of the reception committee's lights, and Elizabeth realised that she was floating inexorably eastward away from the landing area. She swooped towards some trees, expecting to land in them, but continued to float over the darkness of the woods like one of Zofia's Devils until, right at the edge of a rough pasture, the ground leaped toward her and she curled over into her rigging and a cluster of bushes.

Elizabeth took a deep breath. The Liberator had gone, leaving behind silence like a vacuum. To fill it came the smell of damp pasture, woods, cattle, the call of a owl and the songs of frogs in the low places, all so familiar, so reassuringly natural and earthly, that, with a kind of stunned gratitude, she reached out her hand and touched the leaves, the earth. Then she crept out of the twigs and branches. Except for the prodigal moon, there was not a light anywhere, nor any human sound or sign. She'd been warned the Americans dropped high and here she was: miles, probably, from the reception committee, in the most exposed position possible for an agent, with no idea where help or danger might lie. She wasted a few minutes in anger, then cut loose from the rigging and struggled out of her overalls. These, the silk and lines she buried beneath the bushes, then pushed the shovel down a rabbit hole. She was tempted to discard the large and heavy .38 the same way but, unsure of her bearings, stuck it in her jacket pocket. The knife went in her belt, the rest of her possessions into a small rucksack. A faint breeze was blowing from the southwest, and, checking her compass, Elizabeth started in that direction, her scratched back throbbing.

She walked for almost an hour before she reached a road. The wood she'd crossed was on one side and a field of grain on the other. Elizabeth looked up and down, but, at after two in the morning, the road was empty. Tired of pushing across open country, she set along it; she had gone less than a mile when a sound made her stop. A farm dog was barking somewhere, but there was another sound, a crunch, a rustle. Elizabeth felt her blood begin to pound. There was someone in the wood, more than one, and seeing a light moving through the trees, she dived into the grain. The searchers were behind her, not to the west as the reception committee ought to have been. Who else had seen the chute? A car full of Gestapo; a group of Milice, maybe, alerted by some sleepless farmer? Elizabeth felt the sweat running down between her breasts. To be caught so soon! Behind her were open fields and across the road, the wood and a farm with several noisy watchdogs: she would have to stay where she was. She heard shouts, closer now, and the beams of several lights swept across the road. She flattened herself against the ground.

'*Allo,*' someone called. '*Allo, Madeleine, Allo.*' Elizabeth went cold. They knew her name; the group had been penetrated; it was all over. She felt the emphatic shape of the .38 in her pocket and took it out slowly. '*Allo,*' someone called again with a pure French country accent.

Milice, Elizabeth decided, but so noisy and unmilitary, that she risked raising her head just a little. A motley collection of farmers wearing stout boots, worn trousers, loose shirts and smocks was standing on the road. They had their hands on their hips and they were talking in loud, exasperated voices.

'*Allo, Madeleine,*' one shouted to the night.

'*Allo*' replied Elizabeth, scrambling to her feet. They all jumped and several raised hunting rifles and pointed them in her direction. Night, fear, the drop, the long walk through rough country, and now the chance of being shot by the reception committee provoked Elizabeth to a stream of military profanity.

'Madeleine?'

'Yes, Madeleine,' she said, adding a few choice phrases. 'The damn Yanks dropped me wide and I've been walking all night to find you.'

The farmers, surprised and a little shocked, were suspicious. Exasperated, Elizabeth was about to deliver a few more opinions when she remembered her password. 'Where are the snows of yesteryear?' she said.

A stout man in dark work clothes started to laugh and threw his arms around her. 'We have found Madeleine. From London.'

The faces around her broke into smiles. One by one, they extended their hands. 'We are the Maquis of Crest,' their leader announced with a flourish. 'Tomorrow we'll take you to Robert.'

Chapter Nineteen

Drôme and Isère – July 1944

It was a fine summer. In the mountains the sky was clear, blue as an aquamarine, and the hot sun on the pine forests filled the air with the scent of resin. The alpine villages and farms of the high Vercors plateau reminded Elizabeth of the Carpathians, and she loved going up to the forests where the Maquis hung out the tricolour emblazoned with the black cross of Lorraine. The invaders seemed far away, and an illusionary independence flourished in the presence of Maquisard chiefs like fiery Colonel George with his beautiful white horse; Clément, Mayor of Villard-le-Lans, recently back from consultations in Algiers; Colonel Huet, head of Vercors resistance; Colonel Descour, the French Forces of the Interior regional commander, and Yves Farge, who had arrived to be a Commissioner of the Republic on the very day of the first great air drop. Elizabeth knew them all, along with the company commanders, the cooks, nurses, arms instructors, the exiled Poles, the band of tall and exotic Senegalese, the liaison people and couriers, who, like herself, spent the summer travelling.

She loved this work and was only too glad to leave Robert's messages to the tireless and efficient Albert. Let pale Albert stay confined with the wireless. Elizabeth preferred to be out in all weathers, someimtes on a motorbike, more usually, for security's sake, on foot or on a bicycle. For distant runs, she could hitch a ride with one of the circuit's *gazogènes,* but to the cells in the small towns she travelled under her own power, walking from one village to the next, talking in cafés and workshops, kitchens, barns and gardens; visiting a doctor's office, a pimp's lodgings, a poacher's shack. The agents in Robert's far flung territory had reports to make and orders to receive on behalf of their cells. The movements of General Pflaum's 157th Division, the number of aircraft at Montelimar and Valence, the arrival of a new Gestapo figure or a company of Miliciens, as well as news of a bridge blown or a train derailed, must all be sent on to London or Algiers and to the other Maquis band and cells that might be affected. Elizabeth's job was to commit these reports and orders to memory. The agents had information for Robert; they needed ammunition or money, encouragement or advice or congratulations. She passed the messages.

Elizabeth enjoyed meeting the brave and cheerful people of the Resistance circuits, admiring not so much their courage, which was taken for granted, as the inner balance that enabled a rabbitskin merchant, a retired sea captain, an amateur musician, a secretary, an old priest, a café owner, to live both a normal and a clandestine existence. She liked the fertile country, too, with its vineyards and vegetable gardens and pastures full of fat sheep, but best, she liked the mountains with the Maquis camps, filled in the morning with the smell of the cooking fires, the bark of orders, the filtered forest light. For a brief period around D-Day, this Maquis life was glorious. Volunteers poured into the camps on the Vercors, the tricolour flew, the Free Republic of Vercors was proclaimed. The Maquisards enjoyed a dangerous Saturnalia, then, alerted by the stoppage of the tram running between St. Vizier and Grenoble, the Germans attacked the northeast corner of the fortress plateau. They advanced in strength through Guillets and attacked St. Nizier but were beaten off. The following day, the Germans moved up the slopes with artillery and mortars. The Maquis had to withdraw and St. Nizier was taken and burned.

Since then, the Germans had been nibbling at the Vercors perimeter and bombing its villages with planes from the airfield at Chabeil. Robert had become increasingly anxious about this situation, and both Elizabeth and Albert had transmitted warnings to Algiers. But so far, neither the Americans nor the British had seen fit to bomb the airstrip, and the reports Elizabeth had collected indicated that the field was still covered with Junkers. As she entered the bare, dusty yard that surrounded Robert's current safehouse, Elizabeth thought they must complain yet again to London and Algiers. But that would be Albert's worry. She had been travelling for two days, most of them on foot, and was thinking of taking a bath, washing her hair and changing her clothes. It was a relief to step from the brilliant sun to the low fieldstone-paved kitchen, cool and dim and smelling of garlic, basil, onions and tomatoes. Madame Chantrel, heavy, fiftyish, dressed in black, was cutting up a rabbit at the broad, scarred table.

'*Bonjour, Madeleine,*' she said, wiping one of her strong red hands on her apron then extending it to Elizabeth. 'Good to see you. A hot day to travel.'

'Very hot. You're in the right place here.'

Madame lifted her head delicately to indicate upstairs. 'They're waiting for you.'

Elizabeth saw any chance of a bath go out of the window and went up to a front bedroom hazy with smoke. Albert was sprawled on the bed, the omnipresent cigarette between his stained fingers, and Robert was sitting in a rocking chair, his long legs stretched halfway across the floor. Jean-Pierre, a young Maquisard from Montelimar, leaned against the window casement, the afternoon a brilliant square of light at his back. 'We can hold out if they drop either mortars and heavy artillery or paratroopers,' he said.

'And if the German planes are knocked out.' Robert turned to Elizabeth. 'What's the report? Are the planes still at Chabeil?'

'Yes. As of this morning, fifty-eight of them. Mostly Junkers.'

'Why haven't they hit them?' Jean-Pierre demanded angrily. 'What do they say, Albert?'

Albert ran his knuckles hard across his forehead. His face was puffy and pale, his eyes red from cigarettes, late nights and strain; wireless work was nerve-wracking under the best of conditions. '"Message received". How many times do you think I've sent requests? All "most urgent". And Descourt is sending on his own transmitter. Madeleine, too. Madeleine, tell him how much traffic we've sent.'

Jean-Pierre did not wait for the reply. 'They do not want us to have heavy weapons. The Right sees the end of the war already and wants the status quo. The regular boys expect to come back and step in after we've been bled white fighting the Boches. Am I right, Robert?'

'I doubt it's more than stupidity,' Robert said. He unfolded himself from the chair and put one hand on Jean-Pierre's thin shoulder sympathetically. His dark eyes were grave; his large, regular features, still. In contrast to the volatile French, Robert never hurried; he conveyed the calm seriousness of a young priest, but today Elizabeth felt his serenity was assumed. Robert had disapproved from the start of defending the Vercors as a redoubt, knowing that neither his circuits nor any other Resistance forces were sufficiently well equipped. His anxiety had increased with the unexpected arrival of an inter-Allied mission which envisioned an all out struggle on the plateau. To his protests and questions, Algiers replied that the plan had been approved at the highest levels. Then why didn't they send the reinforcements, the mortars? Why didn't they bomb Chabeil? Robert had no answers for Jean-Pierre.

'It can be done,' Jean-Pierre said stubbornly. 'You believe that, Robert?'

'If we can get the equipment and reinforcements, yes. Otherwise, it is impossible for any guerilla force to hold out against good troops with heavy artillery. The German planes represent a danger as well.'

'It depends on convincing Algiers and London, then. It all comes down to that.' Jean-Pierre looked at Albert.

'I want to see how things are on the Vercors,' Robert said to Elizabeth. 'Colonel Huet's to be at Villard-le-Lans. I want you to come. Albert will be needed to transmit messages from here.'

'I feel I should go with you,' Albert said, returning to what was obviously a previous discussion.

'No. If anything happens to us, you will be able to relay messages until the circuit can be recognised. Besides, you've hardly been out of doors for months; you're in no condition to cross the Vercors on foot.'

'Do you want me to pick up my transmitter?' Elizabeth asked.

'Yes. Jean-Pierre will go with you in the truck,' Robert said. 'Walking would take too long.'

Elizabeth knew then that the situation was serious, and her uneasiness was only increased by the delay at Die, where they were pressed to stay for the Bastille Day celebrations. With the battle in Normandy and the threats to the Vercors, these festivities had taken on an unusual fervour and poignancy. It was afternoon before they left Jean-Pierre with a group preparing to defend the town and began the exhilarating climb through the tunnels and passes to the rock girt plateau. It was a perfect day, one of a perfect summer, and then they saw the planes, the machines small and far away and clear against the blue sky. The aircraft were approaching Vassieux, a small town where one of the inter-Allied teams had constructed a landing strip, and both of them felt an irrational leap of hope: Dakotas?

'Can you see their markings?' Elizabeth asked. Robert was in the passenger seat with a sten gun on his lap. He stuck his head out of the truck window.

'Can't tell. No! There's smoke at Vassieux!'

They both swore. The Junkers from Chabeil, for sure.

'They expected a *parachutage*,' Robert said. 'The Germans must have followed our planes in.'

Elizabeth ran the *gazogène* flat out, but the air raid was over by the time they reached Vassieux and the villagers were busy beating out the fires. The Germans had been attracted by an American drop of a thousand light weapons containers. Robert congratulated the Maquisards on this stupendous haul, but when they were alone in the truck, Elizabeth saw that he was discouraged. In the weeks she'd known him, Robert had only once seemed nervous: when he'd received word that his pregnant wife was ill back in England. So far as work was concerned, he was almost unfailingly calm and confident. Like Elizabeth, he was a natural who thrived on the clandestine life, and he had made a success of it in spite of the handicap of his distinctive appearance. At well over six feet, he was a giant among the French, a man whose dark features and exceptional size were easily remembered. In compensation, he had become passionately security conscious, hiding a quick mind and prodigious organisational abilities behind the indolent façade of a convalescent school teacher. Elizabeth had recognised his qualities almost at once, and they shared a deep intellectual and emotional rapport. It amused her that he was a teacher like Jozef, and more than once she thought that their close, but quite platonic, friendship was what she should have had with her husband. 'They did not harm the landing strip,' she remarked. 'A few craters. Nothing that can't be fixed.'

Robert gave a half smile. He had not thought to ask her to check the air strip, but then her initiative and independence often surprised him.

'It is not too late if the Dakotas come, is it?' she asked, knowing how many friends he had in the villages and camps.

'If they come. I begin to wonder if Jean-Pierre isn't correct. If it isn't politics after all. Or just stupidity.'

'Or too much optimism,' Elizabeth said.

'Yes. One is always amazed at how little the situation is appreciated in London and Algiers. They are all still thinking in terms of regular forces. They have no conception of what Resistance leaders work with. None whatsoever.'

'I think there Jean-Pierre *is* right: there is a general distrust of irregulars.'

Robert sighed and leaned his head against the back of the cab. 'And perhaps rightly so,' he said in a thoughtful tone. 'What will become of us after the war? I think of some of the youngsters who've had two, three years of this gangster life; what happens to them when it's over?'

'Your profession will be needed to save us from the horrors of peace,' Elizabeth said, before Robert shouted a warning. Over the sound of the *gazogène's* engine, she heard the full-throated roar of a diving fighter and the crack of its bullets. She slammed on the brakes and they dived from the cab, rolling off the road into a ditch. The plane soared to the top of its arc and swooped again, shattering the windshield and spraying a line of bullets along the dust, while they lay pinned to the warm earth like insects, the sky huge and hostile above them. Then the sound of the plane faded, replaced by the drum of their hearts, the awakening sounds of the grasshoppers, the startled finches. Knees trembling, Elizabeth climbed into the truck to knock out the damaged glass, while Robert threw some more blocks in the boiler. To the north there was smoke, more smoke than at Vassieux, and, a few miles later, they found almost the whole of La Chapelle on fire.

'Incendiaries,' a woman shouted to them furiously. 'The Boches dropped incendiaries.' She was standing in the street, her face black with smoke and her arms blistered red. Behind her, the roof of a small house was falling in chunks into the fire. Two children clung almost unnoticed to her skirts. 'Incendiaries,' she shouted. 'Incendiaries.'

Robert swore softly. 'The second time for some of them,' he said. 'The second time in six months.'

Elizabeth swung the truck through a cloud of smoke and turned towards the hot, dusty town square, three sides of which were blazing. The flames slid along roof timbers with a sinister hiss and burst through windows to ignite curtains, furniture, woodwork. A group of men were wetting down the roof of the hotel, and when they saw the truck, they shouted and waved. Clément was in the middle, directing their operations with great energy, his cloth cap and tweed jacket filthy with soot and water. 'We need your truck. We've taken casualties. Children, too. We must get them to the hospital at Die.'

Elizabeth opened the cab door. 'Get them to load some more fuel; we almost ran out getting this far.'

Clément gave a bitter laugh. 'Fuel! We could stuff the whole town in the boiler.' He clasped her hand, then Robert's. 'Three weeks they said. It will soon be six! What am I to tell these people, Robert?'

'Vassieux was bombed as well, but they got a thousand canisters this morning. We will have plenty of small arms.'

'How can small arms defend us against Junkers? We need brens and mortars. Get some wood here for the *gazogène*,' he called to the fire fighters.

'The hotel's not empty yet,' someone said. 'The travellers say they're safer inside.'

Clément swore. 'Damn city folk! They'll be feeding their faces! Tell them to get out or they'll be washed into the fire. Where's Lucien? He can take the truck back to Die with the wounded. Is it Huet you're looking for, Robert? I can drive you north when we get this under control.'

Elizabeth opened the boiler of the *gazogène* and helped

load the fuel. Around them the square quivered in the heat, and a shifting wind brought clouds of black, acrid smoke. When the wounded were brought to the truck, they choked for breath and screamed as coughing opened their wounds. Lucien had them almost ready to go when a beam collapsed on one of the fire fighters, and the injured had to wait again until the village doctor could splint and bandage the crushed leg.

By evening, the town was glowing like a furnace with hot beds of crimson and yellow coals. Murky clouds of smoke and steam rose like a vision of hell, but the Free Republic of the Vercors was not destined to end in fire. The end came a week later when the whole situation had deteriorated beyond any hope of recovery and the plateau was lashed with a torrential rain.

Everyone was exhausted, that was part of it, from the rain and the unceasing attacks of the enemy. The men had been fighting off and on for weeks, and now, after prodigious efforts, all the news was bad. The Maquis had fallen back from the Grimone Pass, and despite an ambush and heavy losses, the Germans were still advancing towards Die. Troops from General Pflaum's 157th Division were in Valence and at the Lus-la-Croix-Haute Pass, and now the word was that a couple of thousand Germans with artillery had left St. Nizier heading south on the plateau towards Villard-le-Lans.

Elizabeth shook the rubber poncho from her shoulders and water streamed on to the stone floor and pooled around her boots. She'd managed a ride back to HQ but it had been in an open truck; before that, she'd been slogging along roads muddy as a Polish autumn. Three other Maquisards arrived behind her, soaked to the skin, red-faced, shivering and stamping their feet. They drew out their weapons from beneath sodden coats and sweaters. They were young, no more than in their middle teens, and they immediately gravitated to one of the headquarter's typists, a pretty black-haired girl thundering out a report. Who would ever read it? Elizabeth wondered. Who would ever use all that paper? It was clear now, had been clear for several days, that there could be only one course of action, only one ending.

Elizabeth hung up her rain gear and walked down the hall. In a matter of weeks, the handsome two-storey villa had taken on a military air. It smelled like a barracks – of cheap tobacco, sweat, damp leather and wool – and sounded like an office, an office oddly equipped with every sort of small arms. A few captured German helmets hung from pegs on the walls, along with a pair of sten guns, and the typists kept a couple of grenades or a pistol handy – just in case. In the back room, over a ringing phone, she could hear the Colonel speaking, his staff officer's voice high and precise, '... have done better than I believed possible.'

'We'd have done better with mortars.'

'And paratroopers. We had been promised reinforcements.'

'We were assured in Algiers. What can I say to my men? That we have been deceived?' That was Clément. Elizabeth knew that he felt responsible for the men who had been drawn to the Maquis, for all those who had followed him into resistance.

'We are soldiers,' the Colonel said with dignity. 'It was, after all, an affair of honour.'

'We must think of the villages. We have hundreds of civilians ...'

The speaker was interrupted by a ringing phone and Robert spoke up. 'You will end by losing the entire Maquis force if you try to fight a pitched battle.'

'And what are we fighting now but pitched battles?' Clément demanded. He was standing up at the table, his face flushed, and Elizabeth noticed that his hair had gone almost completely white. Colonel Huet and Robert were beside him, and then there was Colonel George and the English Major from the inter-Allied team and several others, all wreathed in smoke. 'Eh, Madeleine?' Clément called, seeing her in the doorway. 'Are we still killing the Boches?'

Elizabeth nodded. 'But there are reports the Germans have left Trièves.'

Huet jumped up and went to the large map pinned on the wall. 'What direction?' He asked sharply.

'Towards Les Pas and the Grand-Veymont.'

'The mountain,' Clément said. 'That means they are looking towards Vassieux.'

'They want to cut us in quarters,' Huet said. 'Force a way south from St. Nizier, and at the same time, push across the Vercors from east to west.'

'How many?' The English major asked. He had been dropped to build the airstrip at Vassieux, among other things.

'They were described as "several small columns". Maybe three to five hundred men.' Elizabeth pulled over one of the wooden chairs and sat down heavily, wiping the rain from her face. Robert poured a little red wine into his glass and passed it over to her.

'We can hold them,' the major said.

'And the two thousand from St. Nizier? With artillery? Our lines are too long,' Huet said. 'One hundred and ninety kilometres at least. And with the wounded ...' There was a pause. The wounded were the problem, along with the civilians. 'It would take all our forces to match them in the north.'

'Yet we have held them off. They still have not reached Die.'

'The Operation Groups have been magnificient,' Robert said. 'The Maquis has held off up to ten times its numbers. It is magnificent, but it is not guerilla warfare. Surely honour does not require a massacre.'

'It is not honour we are talking about,' said Colonel George. His voice was low, harsh and bitter. 'The men are not ready to withdraw and leave their villages to the Boches. They remember the Malleval Maquis.'

There was a moment's silence. The Malleval Maquis had been wiped out the previous January. Among the casualties were eight people burned alive in a farmhouse.

'The longer it goes one, the worse the reprisals will be,' Robert said softly.

'That's hardly the way to build morale,' complained the English major.

'We're not talking about morale here. We're talking about the lives of the villagers.'

'We may still get reinforcements,' the major said. 'We have the landing ground at Vassieux.'

'A cruel illusion,' Robert said, and the major swore, and they would have quarrelled, if Colonel Huet had not broken in. 'It is a matter for the local people and for the representatives of the Republic to decide,' he said. 'Our friends must understand that.' He looked solemnly around the table. 'I will ask each of you for a situation report and for your advice. Then we will make a decision on what we should do. Clément, we will begin with you.'

Tired and hungry, Elizabeth pushed herself away from the table and walked past the pounding typewriters of the dispatch room to the kitchen.

'Oh, it's you, Madeleine,' said Julienne. She was one of the young cooks, a tall, robust person with untidy dark hair wrapped in a blue scarf. 'Are you hungry?'

'Terribly. Did they leave anything from dinner?'

Julienne laughed. 'Not this lot. But there's some soup.'

She ladled out a thick vegetable soup, and Elizabeth ate a bowl of it with bread and cheese. When she was finished, she put her head on her arms and fell asleep at the table. She was still there when Robert woke her in the early hours of the morning: the Germans had broken through at Villard-le-Lans and he was going south to see if the Maquis could hold at Vassieux.

The rain stopped at sunrise. In the square at Vassieux, they stretched their legs, stiff after riding in the back of the *gazogène,* and had strong coffee with milk and a loaf of bread. Robert and Elizabeth and half a dozen others were standing around talking about the last drop, the air raid damage, the latest messages from Algiers and London, when a shout went up. A long line of planes was coming in low, out of the sun, each with a glider in tow. Dakotas! Or Flying Fortresses? The Maquisards started to cheer and the villagers looked out of their windows, then ran outside to greet the long promised reinforcements, the reinforcements that meant victory, or at least not defeat: not the burned, raped, mutilated villages, not the herds machine gunned in the fields, not that, not now. They ran, shouting for joy, towards the airstrip where the first glider was landing. Pray God, the field was level enough: that had been done with hand work and the horse pulled roller! A wing dipped, the glider bounced, then settled upright. And another one! Beautiful landings.

The townspeople and the Maquisards raced down the lane to the field, Robert and Elizabeth with them, running, cheering, before Elizabeth felt such a wave of fear that she stopped, clutching Robert's arm, shook her head.

'They're not,' she said, without knowing how she knew, how she had recognized, how she had remembered from the street horrors of Warsaw. Then the first shots of a powerful automatic weapon rang out, and there was a terrible moment of confusion and disbelief before people flung themselves on to the street, scuttled crabwise towards the nearest wall, covered their children, unfastened a weapon. The aviator Victor was quickest: he set up the heavy machine gun he'd been cleaning and two of the incoming crews died on the field. But the gliders were still landing, settling as smooth and fast as gulls on water, and the cockpits were disgorging black-uniformed SS who raced for cover, raced to begin a heavy automatic fire that had more range and power than anything the Maquis possessed.

In late morning, Huet sent reinforcements, as many as he could steal from other hard pressed units, but the Germans had managed to get two hundred troops on the ground, and they fought their way into the stone buildings nearest the landing strip and could not be dislodged. The Maquis radio operators called frantically for help, and Huet deployed and redeployed his slender forces, but by early afternoon, when it was clear no outside help would be forthcoming, Robert sent word to headquarters that he intended to leave. He spoke privately for a few moments with the Vassieux leaders, then he and Elizabeth were outside in the thin, drizzly rain, alone suddenly without the intense Maquis circle which had occupied every waking hour for the past weeks. Dampness magnified the moment of desertion: they could smell some spilled milk souring, manure in a farmyard, the cloying metallic stink of fuel and smoke and gunpowder. From the airstrip came the crack of rifles, the longer, lower sound of the Germans' automatic weapons. Elizabeth thought of Clément, whom she liked, a stolid, doughty countryman now faced with impossible decisions, and of the brave and charismatic Huet, dashing as an Uhlan, and was tempted to remain. Robert looked miserable. 'It has become pointless,' he said. 'I hope you understand.'

'He wants another twenty-four hours.' Robert looked around at the village. The edges of some buildings, the roofs and cornices of others were pitted from shell fire and blast. Emile's blacksmith's shop was roofless since the last air raid, and Tante Isabelle's café had lost all its glass. The village was already damaged, already fated. They both knew what would happen when the Maquis fell back. Robert's face was frozen; he had known these villages far longer than Elizabeth had and he felt more responsible, more to blame.

'You cannot stay,' she said. She might, but, as section chief, he had other responsibilities.

Robert stood for a moment looking at the ground, and Elizabeth felt a tremor of sympathy. He was one of a more optimistic, fortunate race, unschooled in inescapable defeats and lost causes. She laid her hand on his shoulder and he put his arm around her for a moment. Then he straightened up, his extraordinary self-control restored, though she could see at what cost. 'We have to decide which way,' he said, his voice low and hoarse. 'Toward Die or through the forests?'

'The forests,' Elizabeth said without hesitation. 'If the Germans have gone to this much effort for Vassieux, they will persist at Die as well.'

'That is my thought.' Still he remained, listening to the sounds of uneven battle, to the weapons of their friends.

'There is a path behind the Boissiers' farm which avoids the main road,' Elizabeth said, and at last Robert turned away. They skirted the German held quadrant of the village to reach the sodden fields. They had their side arms, two grenades, some chocolate and a pack of cigarettes. Once they were well outside Vassieux, they used the country roads and cattle tracks that led towards the forest of Lente. Twice they came upon skirmishes, isolated Maquisard bands trying to delay the German advance, and even in the depths of the forest they heard the sporadic fire of Maquis groups drifting into the woods, leaving the isolated farms and villages to fate and the imagination of the S.S.

They walked without stopping to rest, seven or eight kilometres an hour, through ambiguous landscapes of mist, fog and rain. The trees were dripping and the ground steamed with mist, as if nature had taken on the amorphous confusion of battle. The steep slopes and gorges of the western Vercors were laced with rivulets, the trails slippery and treacherous underfoot. At night fall, freezing cold, they found a logger's road full of ruts and puddles, and, splashing along it, overtook three young Maquisards who'd been separated from their unit. Two were wounded: Armand, rather badly through the shoulder, and Bernard, messily but superficially, in the face. Solange, a nurse even younger than the boys, had been taking them to shelter when their group was overrun and they'd fled to the forest.

Elizabeth and Robert rested with them for a while and shared out their chocolate and cigarettes before they set off again. By midnight, Armand was semi-conscious, and they were all exhausted. When they came across a poacher's shack, he and Solange were left with a crusty old mountaineer who said he hadn't seen a German in four years. Elizabeth gave Solange the .38 anyway and made sure she knew how to use it.

A dozen miles further on, the terrain got really rough, and Bernard left them to sleep in a thicket, but Robert and Elizabeth walked straight through that night and the next morning, scrambling down gullies, climbing over rocks and fallen trees, wading across swift mountain streams until they reached the safehouse outside Crest. Robert's feet were covered with blood, and Elizabeth's despite a summer of walking, badly blistered. They were soaked to the skin, half frozen, and so white with exhaustion that Madame Chantrel did not at first recognise them nor believe their arrival: they had covered seventy miles in twenty-four hours.

Chapter Twenty

August, Basse Alps – Italian Border

'It will rain,' the partisan said, looking to the north where swift-moving clouds swept the mountain peaks. The air was damp, the alpine meadows an expectant green against the pale rocks and purple sky.

Elizabeth pointed to the treeline a half mile away. 'A truck will meet us in the first village.'

'I know that place. My cousin grazes his sheep near here,' said Sebastian. He was short, only an inch or so taller than Elizabeth, but wide and strongly built, with a round, bold face. A true storm petrel, Sebastian had fought in Spain, joined an anti-fascist group in Italy, survived Mussolini's black shirts and now intended to fight the Nazis. His companion, Angelo, was slight and boyish with an air of irrepressible gaiety. He had whistled most of the way, producing beautiful melodic trills that carried far enough in the still alpine air to make Elizabeth nervous.

'You will know the path, then,' she said, as they scrambled down a narrow track hard and smooth as pavement from generations of hooves.

'My cousin's sheep make a beautiful sound when they travel at night with all their bells ringing.'

'Yes?'

'Each herd has its own combination, its own harmony, its own chords,' Sebastain said, and when Elizabeth smiled, he nodded his head vigorously. 'You don't believe me? Well, you are a northerner. They have no heart for beauty.'

On their right, the land dropped away to a valley with pastures, fields and small houses, but the trail squeezed west between the mountainside and a bare rock outcrop before reaching the wood. Despite the sunlit beauty of the low lands and the spectacular dark sky over the peaks, Elizabeth disliked this stretch which offered neither the cover of the woods nor the forwarning of the wide, empty meadows and the bare heights. The old herder who showed her the route said it had been a favourite with the OVRA patrols; now the frontier and the passes were manned by Germans no less careful. When the young partisan began to whistle again, Elizabeth unceremoniously told him to shut up.

There were finches and buntings in the grass and high overhead a kite, but it was quiet near the massive rock outcrop, and when they walked into its shadow, their feet scraped and clattered on loose stones. Elizabeth looked around: the diagonal shadow of the rock, the preternatural whiteness of the bare limestone against the storm sky, the green and grey grasses dotted with yellow flowers; the kite, black and solitary against the clouds – nothing else. Ahead was an alpine pasture, then the cover of the woods, where men used to hiding could disappear in seconds. It seemed safe, and Elizabeth began to consider the Italians' news that the Col de Larche garrison was manned by Poles. Something could be done there, and more efficiently and decisively than these arduous trips after wandering partisans and disaffected conscripts . . .

Behind her the men suddenly stopped. Sebastian shrugged eloquently but noncommittally, his friend pursed his lips on a silent chord: there was something in the air, the coming storm, perhaps, or something else that had stilled the small birds. They walked on, more quickly and warily, broke out of the shadow of the rocks and had started across the open meadow when a shout of *Halten sie!* stopped their hearts. Two German frontier police emerged from a cleft in the outcrop, their automatic rifles drawn.

'Don't move,' said Elizabeth, knowing they had but an ancient shotgun among them. 'We are cousins on our way to a family funeral.'

The men put their hands up, but Elizabeth bit her lip as if she were about to cry and slipped both hands into the pockets of her wide peasant skirt.

'We can make a run for it,' Angelo whispered.

'They'd shoot all three of us,' Elizabeth said. 'Let them come closer.'

Sebastian raised his straight black eyebrows quizzically and Elizabeth nodded. 'Good day,' she called to the Germans. '*Guten Tag.*' One guard kept them covered while the other, a corporal, asked for their papers. Elizabeth handed hers over, then gestured towards her companions and laughed. 'Papers for shepherds? These are my cousins. There is a funeral tomorrow in Bousieyas. What is a border to grief?'

'Partisans,' said the German, covering them.

'No,' said Elizabeth. 'On the bones of my dead aunt, I swear we are not.'

'And the shotgun?' the corporal asked, as he took it from Sebastian.

'In case of partisans, of course! Those bandits! I would be afraid to travel without it.' Elizabeth elaborated on this until the corporal, seeing he was being distracted, grew angry.

'You are all under arrest.' He slipped his rifle from his shoulder and gestured for them to walk on. Angelo and Sebastian took a step, but Elizabeth stood still.

'You don't want to do that,' she said, her voice very low and soft. 'You don't want to arrest us.'

The corporal raised his head. Beneath his grey-green cap, his eyes were a watery blue, red-rimmed as if he had tasted too much of the rough local wine, and he had a shaving nick on the right side of his chin. There was a moment's stillness, in which Elizabeth felt the inescapable intimacy that arises between people who may kill each other, who may die together, then, switching into German, she said, 'You are a young man. Today is not a good day for you to die.'

A muscle jumped in the guard's face, and the tip of his Mauser dropped until it was level with her chest. Elizabeth shook her head. 'It is no good,' she said, 'look here.' And very slowly and carefully, she drew her hands from her pockets. She was holding two grenades, her fingers through the loops that held the pins. 'If you shoot me, we will all die, so it is the same to me.'

She could hear Angelo breathing, hear the mountain wind disturb the grass, hear the way the leather of the German corporal's boots creaked as he shifted his weight. 'A pretty young girl like you,' he said, 'the worst you'll get is forced labour. Maybe nothing at all − if you agree to help us. You must know −'

But though his hands tightened on his rifle, Elizabeth could see the tremor. He still had hopes, a family, a lover, perhaps only a hoarded bottle of brandy; he was not willing to die, not today. 'All my friends in Warsaw are dead,' she said to let him know there was no hope, to watch his face stiffen. The soldier beside him sniffled as if he wanted to sneeze. 'It is simple,' Elizabeth said. 'No one need be hurt. Give my companion his shotgun and unload your weapons. You may keep your pistols, though you will unload them for now. You were surprised by a group of partisans across the Italian border,' she said as Angelo and Sebastian disarmed the Germans. 'By skill and cunning, you escaped. You will have time to invent what will satisfy your officer.'

'We can shoot them both,' Sebastian said, 'and end their troubles entirely.'

'No! They are unarmed and their deaths would bring reprisals. Go to the wood, and cover me so I can follow you.' She dared not look at them, lest they see some weakness in her eyes. Angelo and Sebastian hesitated, long enough for the cry of the kite, for a gust of wind, for the perception of the first drops of rain in the air. Then they stepped back, shouldered the Mausers and ran towards the wood. The corporal's face was glazed with sweat; the soldier with him looked dumbly toward the ground. He was the more dangerous, Elizabeth decided, a man who would react without thinking.

Sebastian shouted from the wood, and Elizabeth smiled. '*Weidersein,* gentlemen. It would be wise for you to walk slowly toward the rock and foolish for you to attempt anything with your sidearms. My companions would take the excuse to kill you.'

She stepped back softly, the grenades still in her hands, and the corporal said, 'Do be careful, *fraulein,* if you trip ...'

How strange their concern, their care; all lives are precious, even these. 'Go back,' Elizabeth said and they edged away, at first slowly, then more quickly until they broke into a run. She took her fingers from the pins, dropped the grenades into her pockets and sprinted for the pines. As she reached the edge of the thicket, Sebastian reached out and pulled her behind a tree. He ran one hand over his wide mouth and dark moustache and swore in a rich and complicated mixture of French and Italian.

'It is a fine weapon, isn't it?' Elizabeth asked. 'I promised you the best when you joined the Maquis, didn't I?'

For an instant his black eyes held all the ancient suspicion men have ever had of women, then he hugged her against a rough woollen coat that smelled of sweat and tobacco and nights spent in the open, of wine and gunpowder and mules and mountain earth.

'It is raining,' said Angelo, buttoning up the neck of his shabby jacket.

'So it is raining! So what! Whistle, Angelo. Something nice!' Sebastian clapped his friend on the shoulder and started down through the trees, noisily, carelessly. A moment later, Angelo began to whistle in the rain.

'Here comes the Apostle, a fisher of men,' Robert said, and Elizabeth laughed. It was a sound he liked. After the disaster on the Vercors, they had fled to the Basse Alpes and the little towns around Digne. Robert had taken up the rest of his damaged circuit, and, in between her duties as courier, Elizabeth had begun bringing in recruits for the various Maquis: Italian partisans driven into France like Sebastian and Angelo, conscript Poles and polyglot Russian ethnics from the German Army's Oriental Legion. Her ability to inspire confidence in rough, armed and dangerous men had cheered Robert immensely in the sad days after Vassieux and encouraged him now that D-Day in the south was approaching, when all they had built would be put to the test.

Elizabeth sat down on the wide ledge of the window and glanced over the red-tiled roofs, the blue and grey shutters, the white, cream and buff stones of Provence. A pair of doves cooed in the eaves and brilliant flowers embraced the balcony opposite. 'I discovered something yesterday,' she said. 'We can blow the German supply road into Digne.'

Robert's expression changed. When the Allies landed in the south, his circuit had to hold open the middle segment of the

Route Napoléon that ran from Cannes through Digne and Gap to Grenoble. If the Germans couldn't supply their garrisons, they would not be able to hold the road. He sat back down in his chair, and Elizabeth smiled admiringly. Robert never wasted her time by telling her things she already knew. He did not say that the road was protected by the garrison at the Col de Larche nor that the German forces were too strong for the Maquis. He simply sat down and waited.

'The garrison on the pass is now almost wholly Polish. Western Poles, not *volksdeutsch*. They are conscripts and they've already been in touch with some of the Italian partisans.'

'This is from?'

'The partisans I brought into the Maquis near Bousieyas. Good fellows. One has fought since Spain. A Red, of course,' Elizabeth added regretfully. 'They put me in touch with a comrade who trades with the garrison. The garrison feel they are not getting standard rations and have been swapping supplies with a Maquis group that has a couple of Poles in it. I spoke to them. One was a Lancer left behind after the collapse in '40. The others were working in France and feared deportation. Reliable men.'

'And you think the garrison will look the other way while we tear up the road?'

'I think we can get them to defect *en masse.*'

'That's no good if the Germans replace them.'

'We'll have to leave it as late as we can, get their cooperation, then blow the road and bring them out with us.'

Robert sighed thoughtfully and leaned back in his chair. The shutters of the other windows were closed and his face was lost in the deep shadows of the Mediterranean afternoon. 'Perhaps they would hold the garrison for us for a time,' he said.

'Perhaps.' Elizabeth felt the sun warm on her back. A fly buzzed in and out of the open window, and a motorcycle, Milice or Maquisard, roared down one of the narrow alleys towards the mountains. Robert fiddled with his pipe and asked several technical questions, but beyond the numbers of the men, the weapons and supplies needed, the precise situation of the blockhouse, there was not a great deal of discussion. Each appreciated the dangers, understood the possibilities. Though temperamentally different, their unspoken accord rested on a love of action and a hatred of bloodshed, on a preference for negotiation and subterfuge instead of destruction. The matter of the garrison of the Col de Larche was delicate but infinitely appealing. 'I think we must try,' he said at last from where he lay smoking in his chair, and Elizabeth smiled.

'I knew you would say that. I knew you'd agree.'

'How did you know?' In the dim room his voice was softly reflective, almost flirtatious. Yet he was a serious man. This sort of life, being less common among his countrymen than hers, was a more eccentric choice and he had embraced resistance with an almost monastic devotion. She understood that he was like Sister Margaret, a person who upheld his vows. He had spoken of his wife one day. They had sat like this during the long siesta hours and he had talked of Sarah, of his love for her and his anxiety for her during the blitz. It had been a declaration, an explanation, an appeal, and she had taken him at his word. But this mingling of work and affection was what she, and perhaps he, too, liked best.

She shrugged, a careless, graceful gesture. 'I always do. I always do know.' Sister Margaret would have said that that was a gift of continence, and perhaps it was, for Robert was transparent to her in a way that neither Marek nor Jozef had even been. She knew his thoughts, and the fewest, barest words sufficed for any report or plan. She could tell his mood as soon as she crossed the threshold of a safehouse, and he never surprised her as Marek had nor puzzled her like Jozef. He did not share their faith, their losses, their unspoken assumptions, not even the language which she loved and hungered to hear. Had they met in other circumstances she would have seen an Englishman, intelligent, no doubt, but a little shy and stiff, lacking the élan and elegance of her countrymen. And she? How would she have seemed to him? A foreigner: intense and dark and potentially troubling; she understood even that.

'Will it be a difficult climb?' he asked. He wanted to know what her life was like and how it was in the rough, deserted country that was the nearest thing to home for her. Robert understood to perfection the necessities and strictures of his calling. He knew that, within limits, there was a need for happiness.

Elizabeth could not see hi features, only the smoke catching the sunlight as it rose from his pipe. 'It will take a full day. I will follow the streams.' She smiled, thinking of the sun on the rocks, the groves of larches, the intense and perfect alloy of memory and sensation provoked by the mountains. And it crossed her mind that one day, in other mountains, she would remember Robert, too.

The convoy surprised them, appearing suddenly from around a blind curve, and Robert swung the wheel sharply to the left so that the car slewed on to a farm track, nearly cutting off one of the motorcyclists. He floored the accelerator, and the car, running smooth on stolen German petrol, roared away with the Commandant and Armand, the newly dropped SOE agent, hanging on grimly. There were shouts behind them, but Robert tore into a farmyard, squeezed between a pair of stone barns and gained a second track, even narrower and rougher than the first. 'Any of the Mongols behind us?'

The Commandant stuck his head out of the window and peered through the dust at the unbroken line of trucks and motorcycles on the main road. 'No. The lazy pigs! The German Army's going to pot with all these damn Tartars.'

'Don't complain. It's about time.'

'Let it be soon,' said the Commandant, wincing as the car bounced in and out of a particularly bad rut.

'Sorry,' Robert said as the car springs groaned, 'but they're so capricious, I'd rather not be stopped.' His own documents and his Red Cross worker's pass were impeccable and so were the Commandant's, but he was nervous about Armand. Though the new agent had come with highest recommendations, he had spent the war in the Balkans and his weak French might not pass unremarked.

'I'm surprised to be riding at all,' Armand said. 'Such luxury.'

The Commandant laughed. 'How long have you been with us, Robert? A year and a half? Robert and I were on foot until last week. On foot or on bicycles.'

'So we've earned a little speed,' Robert said. 'Is it the next turn for the road?'

'Yes, left again.'

They regained the main route just below the Barles Rift where the mountains squeezed the highway against the river. Desolate peaks with bald limestone summits rose steeply on either side, cutting off the light, and when they saw the roadblock, they had no chouce but to slow down and look unconcerned. Armand was pale. He had had no time to become acclimatised or to polish his neglected French, and he had been dropped with a great deal of money which, for safety's sake on the journey from Digne, they had divided. 'Say no more than you have to,' Robert warned before easing the car forward to a stop.

'Papers,' the German sergeant demanded. He was Wehrmacht, thank goodness, and Robert and the Commandant exchanged looks. The sergeant examined Robert's papers, then held out his hand for Armand's and the Commandant's. It is all right, Robert thought, it will be all right, but when he tipped his head to check the mirror, he felt his bowels clench: there was a black Mercedes behind them. Hurry up, he thought, but the sergeant poured over Armand's documents with such teutonic thoroughness that the doors of the Mercedes opened. Two men got out, both French, and that was bad luck; to *résistants,* the French Gestapo were more dangerous than their German masters.

The sergeant handed the Commandant his documents and would have returned Armand's as well if he hadn't noticed the two officers approaching. The tall one had the brutal disinterest of a man who has never been employed to think; the other, many years his junior, was as small and delicate as a girl, with white, almost translucent skin and circles dark as bruises under his eyes. His glance met Robert's for an instant in the car mirror and Robert knew, as he knew the sun would set in the evening, that his time had come.

'Who are these men, sergeant?' The Gestapo officer spoke in quick, rough German, and the sergeant offered Armand's papers.

The Gestapo officer looked them over and Robert's overstrained sense picked up the merest hint of excitement;

the officer had found something. 'Were you going to let these men pass through, sergeant?'

The sergeant shifted his weight from one foot to the other, then decided on equivocation. 'I wished to examine this man's papers more carefully, *Hauptmann.*'

'Did you?' Despite his borrowed German power, the Gestapo officer was full of contempt.

'We cannot be too careful, *Hauptmann,*' the sergeant said defensively. Between his own officers and the multitude of security organisations, a soldier could be trapped in any one of a dozen ways.

'Too careful!' the Gestapo officer shouted, drawing his pistol. 'Out of the car, get out of the car!' He wrenched open the door and Robert, Armand and the Commandant stepped out.

'What is this all about?' Robert asked.

'No talking,' the officer shouted. 'Search them. And you, Didier, check their car. These bandits may be armed.'

'You have seen our permits,' Robert began, but the officer, young and nervous, screamed for silence.

'They have no weapons, *Hauptmann,*' the sergeant said, after patting their clothes carefully.

The young officer looked up from his perusal of their wallets and smiled. 'So,' he said. 'Leave them. Didier will watch them. Help me with this.' He handed the sergeant a handful of currency. 'Put it out on the hood.' The bewildered sergeant spread the crisp, new notes into a fan. 'The numbers, sergeant.'

He started to read them off, then stopped. 'They are all consecutive, *Hauptmann.* These men are counterfeiters.'

'You fool! These men are bandits. Important bandits. We have caught some V.I.P. agents.'

Long after, she would remember the mountain trail up to the pass: the dense brush that pressed against the track, the swift, cold alpine streams rushing in torrents, the sheer rock faces, the open stands of pines, larches and firs, and over all, the mysterious perfume of the Mediterranean, the smell of thyme and lavender from upland meadows. Elizabeth always remembered it with happiness, untinged as was the memory of the Vercors with tragedy, with sordidness and butchery. She walked alone all day, leaving the switchback road north of Bouslieyas and following the course of a mountain stream north. At nightfall, she curled up in her blanket on the pine needles and listened to an owl in the black, southern night. The next morning she reached the Maquis camp in time for breakfast, curled her cold fingers around a coffee mug and passed on the news of the expanding Allied beachhead, the Red Army's successes, the Warsaw Rising.

Then Pawel, the ex-Lancer, led her up a ridge cloaked with the tender green of larches. The garrison was stationed above the pass in a concrete blockhouse surrounded by a cluster of wooden sheds and huts. Pawel had stopped on the edge of the clearing and produced a loud hailer.

Elizabeth didn't remember what she'd said. What did one say to armed men wearing the alien *feldurau*? In dreams, she heard only the wobbly echo of the loud hailer which dissolved into the wild, melancholy gaiety of an eastern violin. They had danced in the clearing, men in grey trousers with bare chests and black Maquisard armbands, danced in the sunlight until the rhythm of their feet melted into the sound of the explosions. She had been on the descent, going back to report to Robert, when she heard the vibration, soft, low and penetrating as the drumming of a grouse, then louder, a massive, wonderful explosion. Elizabeth had crossed herself and released the branch she held so that she went sliding and slipping on the loose stones and dirt, over the russet carpet of the pine needles, hurtling down like a skier, shouting in triumph, shouting over the wind, over the rattle of the bones of the mountain, shouting like the men of the garrison as they had stripped off their grey tunics and stood, half naked in the alpine sun. She could hear those wonderful explosions yet — oh, that they could hear them on the Vistula, in the birches of the Kampinsoka Forest, in the spires, the alleys of the stubborn, beloved, wounded city. She heard them pounding, pounding in her dream . . . and then, out of her dream, someone was shouting, 'Mademoiselle! Mademoiselle Madeleine!'

Elizabeth opened her eyes: a painted armoire, a heavy bedstead, ancient blue and white striped wallpaper like old mattress ticking, sun through thin, gauze curtains, a framed lithograph of the Sacred Heart. Where was she? Bouslieyas? Villard, Vassieux, Crest? So many different rooms, so many mornings of waking in strange houses, of listening to strange voices.

'Mademoiselle!'

Elizabeth sat up and ran a hand through her hair. She was in Seyne in the clear air of the mountains and her legs were streaked with welts and scratches from the climb to the Col de Larche. She fell back on the bed and studied the low beamed ceiling. What time, what day?

'Mademoiselle!' A knock at the door.

Elizabeth sat up and reached for a sweater. 'Yes. Come in.'

It was the daughter of the household, Yvonne, already a courier at fifteen. 'Oh, Mademoiselle, I'm so glad you're awake. There is terrible news! *La Gest* have arrested Robert and the Commandant and taken them to the barracks in Digne.'

Chapter Twenty-One

This was the most difficult thing. She lied when she said it was carrying dynamite, or facing machine guns, or out-skiing the frontier police – all lies. But that was later, when her heart was bitter, when she was no longer among those she trusted and respected. Nor was it the plane and the mechanic's blood on her hands; that had happened too fast. Nor the jumps, where one suffered in company. This was the thing one did alone and the most difficult moment came when she stood in the whitewashed office before the Capitaine's desk. He wore the black SS uniform and more of his midnight brethren passed along the halls: they had bayonetted the wounded Maquisards, the pretty typist had been disembowelled and left to die, the peasants had been raped, tortured, deported, and there were others; she dared not think of Poland.

'I have come to speak to you about the prisoner Robert LaVoie,' she said. Her voice scratched her throat: she had opened the door and stepped into the trap she feared most.

The local Resistance had found Robert and the Commandant with their customary efficiency. While Yvonne was waking her in Seyne, members of the Digne group were using all their contacts, and the people in the outlying area were laying up every piece of gold they could get their hands on to buy his release. By the time Elizabeth reached the green and white dappled shade of the Boulevard Gassendi, they knew where Robert was held, which gendarme was sympathetic. Elizabeth had shaken the dust out of her hair, washed her hands and arms in the fountain and passed herself off as Robert's wife.

The gendarme told her that the man to see about prison visits was this Capitaine Schram.

'Mademoiselle?' Schram looked up from his desk. He had a high forehead that emerged pale and hard as a sea rock, through the receding tide of his dark hair. Light eyes set close to a long, sharp nose gave him an alert, feral expression.

'Madame,' Elizabeth corrected sharply. 'Madame LaVoie.'

'Ah,' said Schram, showing the first signs of interest. 'Please sit down.' He gestured towards the chair nearest his desk and got up and closed the office door. 'So, Madame LaVoie, you've come to see me.'

'I was told you were the man who decided important things,' Elizabeth said. She was a busy woman, an important person, a countess; she had learned how to treat them — even if her hands were damp, her heart pounding.

Schram made a deprecating gesture.

'In these times, Capitaine, it is well to deal only with important men, men who understand the political as well as the military dimension.'

If he was surprised at being addressed in these terms by a woman, Schram concealed it well. 'You will come to the point, Madame.'

'The invasion of the south is only days away. Your own intelligence must agree with that.'

Schram pursed his lips and shrugged.

'Mine is considerably better. Within this week.'

There was silence. The Capitaine toyed with a pencil and glanced at his phone. Elizabeth knew he was wondering what her arrest would be worth. 'In this situation an intelligent man makes plans for the future,' she said.

'I feel safe at the moment, Madame. Safer than yourself.'

Schram smoothed the front of his black tunic.

'And in three days, Capitaine, in four, in a week? The local people have reason to hate you. Were your German friends to leave, you would be in a dangerous position. But perhaps you have the means to seek safety elsewhere.'

Elizabeth laid a stress on "means" and Schram's nose twitched at the scent of money.

'And you, Madame, have you the wherewithal to buy your safety?'

'Mine — and other's.'

'You are referring to the three valuable agents arrested this week?'

'How valuable you don't know,' said Elizabeth, risking all. 'They are valuable enough to buy your life.'

'With the Germans,' Schram said, and his hand touched the phone.

'The Germans are finished. And all the Germans in the world won't protect you if you call about me.'

He stopped and waited.

'Robert is important, of course, and I am married to him. But of more importance is the fact that my uncle is Field-Marshal Montgomery.'

Jackboots tapped up and down the hall outside, and in other offices, phones rang, doors opened, typewriters clattered. The metal shutters in Schram's room were closed against the hot Provençal sun and their images floated in the window glass, the Capitaine pale above his black uniform like a ghost, Elizabeth brown from the sun, her thick hair pulled back with a ribbon. She regretted that she did not look very elegant, perhaps not very convincing, and Schram was quiet so long that she was afraid that she had overplayed her hand. 'If you are not interested,' she said, 'or unable to make arrangements ...' and moved as if to leave.

'There would be money?' Schram asked.

'Yes. There would be money. In earnest,' Elizabeth added, and placed several gold pieces on the desk.

Schram slid the coins smoothly into his pocket and reached for the phone. Elizabeth felt her chest contract, felt the edges of her sight darken, before he spoke again. 'The man you must see is Max Leuven. He is a translator and can go anywhere.'

To cover her relief, she leaned back in the chair and studied the Fuhrer's portrait hanging under a pair of swastikas.

Schram dialled and waited. 'Max? Albert here. Can you be free this afternoon ... Interesting and important. But confidential, Max, you understand. At my apartment? Good.'

Schram put down the phone. 'At four, Madame, Number ten, Boulevard Victor Hugo.'

* * *

Beyond the archway was a stone courtyard where the sun was tamed by green afternoon shadows. A pretty child of four or five walked a doll along a window ledge, singing to it in a soft blurred speech between French and German. 'Is this the way to Number ten?' Elizabeth asked, but the girl did not move. Elizabeth started to repeat the question when Schram appeared in the doorway.

'She cannot hear you.' He touched the child's shoulder so that she turned and jumped into his arms. Schram hugged her, then put her down and, holding her chin so that she would look at him, said, 'Say hello, Madame.'

She got it on the second try and repeated the greeting to Elizabeth.

'Anne-Marie had measles last year,' Schram said. 'The fever . . .'

Elizabeth bent down and took the child's hand. When she spoke Anne-Marie watched her lips. 'You're a clever girl,' Elizabeth said and the child beamed.

'She understands most things.' Her father picked her up again and stroked the fine, golden hair. 'She will be able to go to school,' he said. 'She is quite bright.' Something in his voice, the merest touch of pain or dread, told Elizabeth that he knew what had happened to other deaf children.

They went upstairs to a fine large apartment, where Frau Schram, thin, fair and nervous, took the little girl into the kitchen. Beyond the open doorway, a baby sat in a high chair, banging on its little tray; on the wall to the right, Schram's black cap with its death's head insignia hung beside his pistol. The apartment smelled of sausages, milk and tobacco. Elizabeth sat down in a brown plush chair and looked through a gap in the shutters at the intense sky. The Capitaine lit a cigarette, tapping the ash into a tray balanced on his knee. When there was a sound on the stair, he said, 'That will be Max.'

Elizabeth saw him first: a man of medium height but round-shouldered, with an ordinary face, wire-rimmed glasses, protuberant eyes. He had a little Hitler moustache and his hair was swept from one side of his head to the other, smooth and dark as patent leather. He was wearing dark SS breeches and a grey Wehrmacht tunic, half unbuttoned in the heat. His peaked cap was crushed under one arm and he was carrying a large white handkerchief with which he wiped his flushed face.

'Come in, Max,' Schram said without turning around. 'this is Madame LaVoie.'

Max Leuven dropped down into one of the chairs. 'You could have put her in the cells, Capitaine, and saved me a walk in this heat.'

'Madame is a niece of the British Field-Marshal Montgomery.'

'Madame is a liar,' Leuven said. That arrogance was all that was left. Two years, a year, even six months ago, he'd have been in the cells himself for so slovenly an appearance.

'She has made me an interesting proposition.'

'Well, get me a beer if I am expected to swallow it,' Leuven said. The Capitaine went to the kitchen and returned with three glasses.

'The Capitaine and I were at the point of discussing money,' said Elizabeth.

Leuven's cold eyes took in her peasant skirt, the plain blue shirt, the tattered espadrilles. 'An officer of the SS does not take petty bribes.'

'I thought,' Elizabeth said, 'something in the order of one million francs.'

Schram sat up at that, but Leuven laughed. 'And where would you get such wealth, Madame?'

Elizabeth put her hand in her pocket and pulled out two damaged wireless crystals. She tossed one across the room to Leuven and he jumped as if it were a grenade. 'We have access to both London and Algiers,' Elizabeth said.

Leuven turned over the crystal, nervously. 'This is enough to put you before a firing squad,' he said, but his expression had undergone a subtle change. The threat was mere habit.

'The dead won't help you when the Allies land. It is said that you blinded those two boys from the Maquis near Sisteron, and that you were involved in the deportations . . .'

'These are lies,' Leuven said. Schram remained silent.

Elizabeth shrugged. 'Nonetheless, it is said. I expect you know that and understand what it means.'

In the silence, they could hear the baby hammering and

singing. Leuven muttered something in Flemish and then Schram said, 'It's different for you, Max.' Elizabeth knew what they were thinking. The odd mutilated Wehrmacht corpse turned up nowadays, and the time was coming to settle old scores. Leuven, who was the brains of the pair, began pacing the length of the room. Elizabeth sipped the cold, pale French beer, listened to the children playing and thought that unreality was the great enemy, especially for one like her with a dozen identities before this Madeleine who carried live grenades and feared capture and sat down on a sweltering afternoon to drink with men lost in the illusion of normalcy. The little deaf girl began to sing in French that sounded like German and a shadow passed over the Capitaine's face. He knows, Elizabeth thought, he knows all his masters have done, all he has done himself.

'Max,' he said, 'what do you think? We must decide.' And Elizabeth knew then that he was afraid.

Leuven sat down, pulled out a pad of paper and made some calculations with fussy care. 'Pounds,' he said at last.

Elizabeth shook her head. 'Francs are all you'll get on short notice – the money will have to come from Algiers.' Leuven pretended to balk at this, but his bluster and tempers were well calculated. At last he turned to Schram. 'Two million, Albert, between us, yes?'

'Two million French francs,' Elizabeth said, and they nodded. 'When?'

'Tomorrow.'

She looked at her watch. It was after five. Two hours to get to Seyne – more, for most of it was uphill and she could not cycle like the French who were born for bicycles as she had been for horses. Then time to ask Algiers to lay on a flight – and the money? 'The day after, gentlemen. You understand we must arrange with our contacts in Algiers.'

They argued about this for a time, but at last Max nodded. 'The day after tomorrow or your friends will be shot. Or deported to the Reich for safekeeping.'

'I will not fail,' Elizabeth said, though she was already wondering if they would attempt to follow her, if she could keep the hotheads in the Maquis from an assault on the prison, if this time – when they had not for the Vercors –

Algiers would send what was needed. 'You will have your money in two days.'

'The plane is coming, Madeleine.'

Elizabeth sat up in the back of the truck and heard the low drone from the southwest. 'How is the wind?' she asked before her eyes were fully open.

'Good. Jacques thinks maybe three kilometres due east. No problem.'

'And you have men down wind?'

'Yes, yes. It is not our first parachutage.'

'I know,' Elizabeth said. 'I asked for the best team; this is most important.'

He was mollified by that and by her exhausted face. Even Mademoiselle Madeleine's stamina came to an end; she had fallen asleep the moment she sat down in the truck.

Elizabeth slid off the tailgate. Lights were laid out in the familiar L pattern, and the signal man at the point had begun flashing the recognition code. Since the attack at Vassieux, she had been nervous about drops, and when the answering light came from the dark shape of the incoming plane, Elizabeth was relieved.

A moment later there was a shout from the end of the field, and the reception committee ran down the meadow. Dark above them in the moonlight, a black chute hovered, the long silver canister dangling incongruously below. 'Here it is! We've got it! Bring the truck. And a wrench, Jacques!' Elizabeth could not help smiling: silence and security were as foreign to them as bad meals. True individualists, they made a festival of everything, and as she ran through the damp lavender-scented night, she felt her muscles relax.

They would be in time after all; after excuses, after static and interference, after official delays that had had poor Albert in tears at the wireless, they would be in time.

The Maquisards opened the canister and began shouting the inventory. 'A bren. Stens. Ammunition.' She caught her breath. 'Chocolate. Morphine. Antiseptic. Ammunition. And for Madeleine,' Pierre said, handing her a heavy leather satchel.

The buckles and zippers were stiff; inside, rainbow notes were jammed in fat, new bundles.

'All right?' Pierre asked.
'Yes,' said Elizabeth. 'It is enough.'

She took Laurent with her in the best car they could manage, a big Citroën. Laurent stuck a sten under the seat and tucked a big Colt into his belt. He had a few grenades, too, by the bulges in his leather jacket. 'How's the arsenal?'

He smiled, showing his beautiful white teeth. Laurent was slim and graceful with black curly hair and perfect skin, dark as honey. His enemies called him the Arab, and the Germans called him a killer. He was a dangerous man, but they had been in scrapes together and Elizabeth trusted him. He had gone for her to Nîmes, to look for Jozef, and though he had not found him, she was grateful.

'We have enough to take the jail,' he said, showing his teeth again so that she would know he was joking. There had been a violent argument over the best way to recover Robert, the Commandant and the new British agent. Though Laurent would personally have preferred a fight, he had admired Mademoiselle Madeleine's calm and determination. He had seen that before, the day a frontier dog cornered them. She had spoken to the snarling brute in her own language like a gypsy and stroked its head without fear. Laurent had seen then that her will was strong despite her distaste for blood.

'When the Allies land, you will get your turn.'

'I will join the regulars, the Chasseurs,' Laurent said.

'But now we are at all costs peaceful. We will be dealing with nervous men.'

'Don't worry, Madeleine.' Laurent leaned back comfortably in the seat and wished he could have driven the fine, fast car. He'd had a look in the satchel, too, and had an idea how much money was involved. The Capitaine and that Belgian, Leuven, had better never return to Digne, for if they did, Laurent thought, it would be a pleasure and a duty to relieve them of that good French paper.

If Elizabeth guessed what was in his mind, she said nothing. She was concentrating completely on reaching Digne without being stopped. At every curve, she held her breath until she saw that the road ahead was clear and then floored the accelerator and roared down the straights fast enough to satisfy even Laurent. They must not be stopped. The rifts along the Bléone were particularly dangerous, for Robert had been caught there, and in the early morning, the limestone heights blocked the sun, darkening the valley like the psalmist's shadow of death. A few miles before the town, they came up behind a truck, and Elizabeth's heart pounded until she saw it was an old *gazogène,* hauling produce. They whipped by it and Laurent said, 'We'll be there too early at this rate,' which made her laugh. She had chosen him because he could distract her, because he was amusing.

'They will be waiting,' she said. The Bléone was on their right now and the soft pink and gold houses and red-tiled roofs of the mountain town rose straight ahead.

'This way,' said Laurent, and Elizabeth turned down a street so narrow that she could have reached out and plucked the milk off the doorsteps. At the end, they swung on to the Boulevard Victor Hugo, and Elizabeth parked the car under a massive plane tree. A narrow alley ran between two large buildings and Laurent nodded his head. He would cover her from there. '*Bonne chance,* Madeleine.'

'*Bonne chance,* Laurent.'

The car door banged. A dog barked and a couple of small boys in clogs clattered up the street. They stopped by Laurent's alley, but only for an instant: these days children knew when adults were armed, could sense when there might be trouble. Elizabeth took the package with half the notes and crossed the street. In the courtyard she heard a canary whistling and, upstairs at the Schram's, the noisy, happy baby.

Frau Schram answered the bell and stepped aside without a word. Elizabeth stopped in the dark hallway to let her eyes become accustomed to the shadows; it was possible that they planned to cut her throat and escape with whatever they could get.

'It is safe,' Frau Schram said softy, 'with the children ...' She pushed open the living room door, and Leuven and the Capitaine stood up. Elizabeth went in quickly and laid the package, wrapped in a kitchen towel, on a chair.

'Half,' she said.

Leuven tore open the bundle, handed some money to

Schram and quickly counted his own share. 'The rest?'

'You will get it when our men are safe in my car.'

'You have it with you?'

'You may see it, but you will be covered. I am not alone.' Schram went to the window and looked out. 'You are armed after all,' Elizabeth said.

'In the car?'

'No, gentlemen. That is as agreed.'

They wasted some moments in indecision, then Schram stepped out and spoke to his wife. When he returned, they went downstairs. Laurent was out of sight, but Elizabeth had no hesitation about opening the boot of the Citroën and unsnapping the satchel. When Leuven was satisfied, she locked the boot again and got into the car with the two men. She dropped Leuven at the central prison, then she and Capitaine Schram parked on a dusty side street. Beyond was a field enclosed three sides by a high board fence. Schram nodded towards it. 'That's the football ground. Your friends are fortunate not to wind up there.' He shaped his hand into a pistol and aimed for the field. Elizabeth said nothing.

A little breeze came up, disturbing the fine white dust and filling the air with the warm breath of the lavender fields. The old cathedral bell tolled the quarter hour, then the half. The Capitaine grew restless and tapped his watch and stared out of the back window. Elizabeth thought of all they had to do in the next few hours, in the next few days, to keep from thinking of what might have gone wrong.

'Start the car,' Schram said suddenly, and Elizabeth switched on the engine. In the mirror she saw Robert and the Commandant, pale and dirty but unhurt; Armand with a black eye and a cut lip, and behind them, waving his enormous service pistol, Leuven. The doors opened. Robert's eyes held surprise, anxiety. 'We are safe,' Elizabeth said.

She took the Route Napoléon northwest and once they were well out of town, Leuven told her to pull over. He and the Capitaine stipped off their uniforms and buried them in a thicket, emerging in shabby civilian clothes. They put their money in rucksacks and though the Capitaine set out immediately on foot, Leuven insisted on being driven nearer Sisteron. 'I have a long way to go,' he said. Just below the town, he tapped Elizabeth's arm and she stopped alongside the verge. Leuven got out, hitched up his rucksack and put on a cloth cap like a bank clerk off for a holiday.

'I don't believe this,' Armand said as they pulled away. 'He's waving good-bye.' He wiped his battered face. 'I don't believe this.'

'We thought we were for it, Madeleine,' the Commandant said. 'The Belgian comes with his pistol and orders, shouts at everyone, gets the whole block in an uproar. I says to Robert, "We're for the football ground".'

'I was afraid they'd taken you too; I thought we were all to be transferred,' said Robert, resting his hand on her shoulder for a moment. His face was thin and grey as if the blood had not yet come back into it. 'I thought, after all these months, to be caught now!'

'How much did we cost, Madeleine?' the Commandant asked slyly, and they all laughed. 'Eh, you English and "bad form". A man likes to know how much he's worth to his government.'

'Two million francs.'

The Commandant gave a low whistle of satisfaction. '*Magnifique*. We must celebrate.' And though there was much to be done, they drove to a little café the Commandant knew, ordered a spicy red fish soup, bread, white wine, Provençal salad and sat outside under the pink-striped awning. Above the hamlet the mountains rose in the crystalline light, the peaks white against the vivid blue sky. Sparrows and starlings twittered in the trees and swifts flashed back and forth across the square like ecstatic fighters. The men came back from the pump with wet hair, clean faces. The proprietor found them some shirts and they sat in the sun in white, like invalids, as if nearness to death had made them delicate. Elizabeth put her feet up on an empty chair and sniffed the clean air of the mountains and thought that anything was possible. Then the Commandant poured wine for everyone, including the proprietor and his wife and an ancient loafer, and made them laugh so much that Armand put his head down on the table and covered his ears.

Robert put his hand on Elizabeth's arm. 'I am profoundly grateful. For myself, I believe I was ready to die. But Sarah and the child ... I will see it now,' he said with a touch of surprise. 'I believe it will be a girl and we will name it after you.'

'What are you promising Madeleine?' the Commandant asked.

'Short term immortality.'

'For us all,' said the Commandant, raising his glass.

'To Albert,' Elizabeth said, 'who is the saint of patience.'

'Saint Albert of the wireless,' said the Commandant.

'And Pierre's team.'

'To Pierre, Lord of the Parachutage,' said Robert.

'To us all, *mes amis,* and to France.' They all stood up and the Commandant filled their glasses again. With one thing and another, their return to Seyne was delayed until late, and they were still asleep the next morning when Albert heard the news and went running from one room to the other, banging on the doors. 'They've landed along the Esterel and the Maures! French and American airborne and commandos!'

Elizabeth could hear the cheers, the cries of *"Vive la France",* then Robert came out of his room, a bathrobe thrown over his shoulders, his face transfigured with joy. 'Find us cars, Albert. And get out your uniforms. We're going to be liberated.'

Chapter Twenty-Two

Their lives contracted to the tap of the wireless key, blurred lines of cipher, hasty conferences between men ignorant of each others' languages. Only once in a while would Elizabeth look up from the handwritten messages and headquarters typing and understand the course of the war. She would hear the crack of small arms fire, the heavier burst of brens, the sustained answering fire of automatic rifles and mortars, and know that at some little crossroads town the Maquis was dug in to repel the German columns or, more valiant yet, to delay their retreat. The outcome would depend on the temper and fanaticism of both sides. Perhaps the convoy would shift to avoid the roadblocks; perhaps the commander would call up an armoured car, or a tank, and blast through the roadblock, rout the defenders, open the village to fire, rape and murder. She knew those sounds, and others: farm people herding their beasts towards a wood, the rattle of clogs on cobblestone streets, the tramp of weary, heavily armed men, the nervous hooves of commandeered horses, the sputter of worn out transport. But usually the battles were at third hand now: the tap of the morse key, the clatter of staff typewriters, the endless ringing of field telephones and the shouts that summoned her and Robert, alone or together, to duties with Allied liaison officers and commanders.

They'd started off with an irascible American general who had denounced private armies and lost his temper when Elizabeth arrived with the news that two thousand Polish prisoners had agreed to change sides. The exchange had become so heated that even the serene and unflappable Robert remarked on the range and vigour of her language. Later, after the Maquis proved staunch, they were more welcome. General Patch had reckoned on weeks to reach Grenoble and Lyons. Instead, his troops moved two hundred miles in four days and discovered that the Route Napoléon was open north and west and that the retreating Germans were being harassed and delayed along Highway Seven on the Rhône, the only important road left open to them. One of the old groups at Crest blew the bridge across the Drôme. The German retreat backed up mile after mile, easy prey for American Mustangs and bombers and for General Butler's troops, streaming northwest from the Riviera. Robert and Elizabeth saw the results from an American jeep.

'Been clearing this two days already,' said the sergeant, a loquacious fellow who'd been fighting since Sicily. Smoke ahead masked, without quite obliterating, the suffocating stench of rotting men and horses left unburied at the side of the road. Around them, dragged off, shoved aside by tanks and earth movers, were the burned out wrecks of tanks, armoured cars, trucks, stolen vans, coupés, sedans, farm wagons, bicycles: a vehicular scrapyard fifteen miles long and still impassable in a dozen places. 'The Maquis set them up for us.'

'That would be Jon,' said Robert, thinking of the early days when he and Albert had fled north from disaster and betrayal, 'and the Captain.'

'And Sylvia and Max,' said Elizabeth, 'and a few hundred more.'

The sergeant pointed to the heights overlooking Route Seven. 'You can see where General Butler put the batteries.'

'So that whole section of the Route Napoléon *was* open. The operational groups have been marvellous, Robert.'

'Like a Sunday drive,' said the sergeant. 'Fellows at the crossroads in berets waving us on when they saw the colours. We set up the guns and went to work. Between the artillery and the airforce, Old Jerry didn't have a chance.' He spoke with neither malice nor regret. 'A good many surrendered.'

The others lay where they fell, swollen and stinking and attracting flies like so many others, their poor lost beasts, dead beside them, while hecatombs of steel and rubber were rammed aside for the passage of new armies. A few miles further on, German prisoners were burying the dead in a long trench. They worked with scarves across their faces to cut out the smell and to protect their lungs from the still lingering gasoline smoke, pungent as a funeral pyre. In defeat and captivity, the Germans were exhausted but stoical. Elizabeth saw that quite a few were grey and some were almost as young as the young Maquisards.

'Poor bastards,' said the sergeant.

'You didn't see them in their days of glory,' Elizabeth said, and she thought of Warsaw, of roundups and street checks and sudden death.

'No, ma'am. And we know, "The mighty shall be made low"', the sergeant said in his soft drawl. He swung the jeep around a massive pile of wreckage, then squeezed between a burned out truck and an overturned sedan to regain the road. As far as they could see, the wreckage continued, the cratered pavement dark with oil and blood. They seemed to have entered the outflow of a nightmare factory whose products were corpses and twisted metal. This was the new world, the creation of the machine age; a complete triumph – and a disaster. At lunch Robert alternated shots of the sergeant's American whiskey with French beer. 'I hate aeroplanes,' he said, rubbing his forehead. 'Even ours.' His face was grey as it had been in Digne, his skin drained of blood beneath the tan.

The sergeant lit another cigarette and stared into the folds of the faded café awnings. He was familiar with mass death; he'd travelled similar highways up the length of the Italian peninsula and seen the starving children and famished whores along the side roads as well. It had made him careful; he knew what to see and what to forget.

'Without us, it might well have been worse,' said Elizabeth, putting her arm across Robert's shoulders. 'They would have levelled the villages and fought house to house as at Vassieux.'

He smiled at her, gently and sadly. 'I was a conscientious objector, you know.'

She had not.

'Not warrior stock at all. It was for an alternative to this,' he waved his hand back toward the road, 'that I came here.'

'You didn't see Monte Cassino,' said the sergeant. 'Not a single stone left on top of another. The Italians weren't this well organised.'

'Oh, we were organised,' Robert said, pouring out another large whiskey. 'We planned this, all of this.' He gulped the amber liquor and stared out at the road where tanks and trucks rolled by, stirring an endless dry white cloud of dust. The earth shuddered with their passage and the young soldiers hanging out of the trucks and jeeps waved and shouted as their endless train of armour, guns, tanks, artillery and supplies, swept through the ancient French countryside. Elizabeth wiped the dust from her face and wondered if the villages would hold out against this new horde as they had against the men from the east. All through the war, she had seen her trips to the villages as moments of respite from the tumult. A horse in a field, cows at a gate, peasants walking out with scythes to cut hay: a world unchanged over half of Europe. And now, today, the machine had caught up with them.

But then she'd known the villages under exceptional circumstances; her map had stops only for those remarkable people willing to defy the invaders, people outstanding in character, not class, wealth or education. Now the old order was returning and that, perhaps as much as the price of victory, made both her and Robert feel depressed and alien. Now town halls blossomed with tricolours, and politicians crept out to take up the reins of power and rebuild the barriers of class and station. And everywhere were new Maquisards in makeshift uniforms, stens slung casually around their shoulders, men she did not know, did not remember from the lean and dangerous days. Though victory had come, there were still shots in the night and beatings, violence, women with their heads shaved; there were quarrels and threats, lies and reprisals, a pent up viciousness as ugly in its way as the Occupation. But even this, Elizabeth knew, the land would survive. Beneath all the cruelty, a love of the earth abided, a love fierce enough to rebuild the shattered world, seek the lost men, harvest the crops, see the cattle safe in the fields. Countrywoman that she was, Elizabeth envied the French the priceless stability of their land and, more than once, swept up and down the highways with that restless mass of infantry, commandos, agents, Jedburghs, Maquisards, "Orientals", exiles, adventurers and spies, she asked herself, "Could I stay here and make a stand, if not against the enemy, against the future?"

But there was always a call, a message to cipher or decipher, a transmission to make, someone to see, someone, speechless, who needed words. The whole world was on the move from the west to east, and east to west — but slowly there, she feared, to let the Warsaw Rising bleed — and in the wake of those migrations, individuals were like birds in the spring, swept along with the flock. They went as far as Grenoble and Lyons; then they were out of Robert's sector and no longer knew the terrain of the secret army.

'We are to be ordered out,' he said one day. They were at Lyons, sitting in the outdoor café of a cramped, hotel. Sentimental music came from the lobby and the late summer heat lay around them like an over-friendly cat.

'Official?'

'Highest sources. The French want to run their own show.' He leaned back in his chair. His face was tired, but he was matter-of-fact; euphoria and disgust had both diminished. He was like the professional soldiers now, in control, detached, and waiting for his war to be over. He was ready to go home and Elizabeth understood that this was the first of what would probably be many differences between them.

'When?'

'A couple of days at the most. I could perhaps keep you with me — they'll be needing linguists and good liaison officers.'

Elizabeth smiled. 'I'd like nothing better but I'm hoping for Poland. They did promise me. And I must get to Nîmes. Someone there may know what has happened to Jozef.'

Robert nodded. He regretted losing her but suspected that it was for the best. The extraordinary days were over; from here on, their relationship could only become ambiguous. 'I'll see you get authorisation. They owe us that much. And there's something I'd like you to do on the way.' He raised his eyebrows quizzically, a large, handsome man with a kindly face and disillusioned eyes.

'Whatever,' said Elizbeth.
'See Frau Schram.'

Elizabeth took a breath. She had heard the news soon after they left Digne: like a fool, the Capitaine had returned to town and had his throat slit for those Resistance banknotes. By Laurent, she thought. The knife was his weapon of choice.

'I feel responsible for the family and I won't be allowed South. No good reason and too many contacts. You mentioned children. If you would take them a little money – '

There was an awkward silence. Elizabeth remembered Anne-Marie singing in the courtyard and thought of the other deaf children. 'Only for the child's sake,' she said.

The canary's song spilled over the courtyard like a fountain, and a faint whiff of tobacco lingered on the upper stair. Elizabeth rang the bell and waited a long time. She heard the children playing and rang again. This time the door opened, and Frau Schram stood in the doorway, pale and tense.

'My name is Madeleine,' Elizabeth said. 'I came once to speak to your husband and Max Leuven.'

'I knew none of his business,' Frau Schram said. The little girl had run out and she put a hand on the child's shoulder. 'Nothing.' She started to shut the door, but Elizabeth stopped her.

'May I come in?'

Frau Schram looked down into the early morning shadows of the courtyard. 'Before someone sees you,' she said, and stepped aside.

The hall was empty now except for a small mirror. In its dim reflection, Elizabeth's WAAF uniform looked black, and she had the eerie sensation that she and the Capitaine had changed places. Frau Schram sent her daughter to the kitchen, then led Elizabeth to the living room. She shut the door behind them.

'So you were British,' she said.
'I am a British officer, yes.'
'You murdered my husband.'
'No, Frau Schram. We kept our bargain. He would return here where he had been warned it was dangerous. And Digne

is dangerous for you, too. I am surprised that you have remained in France. With the children – '

'Do you think I have a choice?' the woman said, her voice tight. 'Did I have a choice before, in coming here – to be hated, to be feared, to be despised by these French? Now I cannot let my children leave the apartment for fear of what might happen to them.' She rubbed her hand across her mouth nervously.

'You did not get the money, then?' Elizabeth asked.

'Would we be here?' Frau Schram looked away, her face drawn, hard as a fist. 'He was bringing it to us,' she said with a hint of pride. 'He was willing to die for the Führer, but he wanted us to be safe. He was a good man.'

Elizabeth though of the boys mutilated at Sisteron, of the Capitaine's cold, greedy eyes and of his hand stroking his deaf daughter's hair. She opened her purse; she had agreed to this; it was not for her to judge. She took out some notes and laid them on the arm of the overstuffed chair. 'Leave here.'

Though her hands trembled, Frau Schram did not take the bills. 'It is blood money.'

Elizabeth was tempted to anger: there were other families in need.

'It is blood money for my husband's death,' Frau Schram said, her voice leaping to the edge of hysteria.

'It is money to save your children.'

Frau Schram went white around the lips and clenched her fists, her impotence turning to anger. She would kill me if she could, Elizabeth realised, and, sickened at the futility and waste and horror of the last six years, she spoke rapidly in Polish.

Frau Schram gave a little start but understood nothing.

'I said that in my country the SS murdered the deaf children. Every one. Now, for your daughter's sake, Frau Schram, take the money and leave this place.' Without waiting for an answer, Elizabeth walked out of the apartment, out of the courtyard, out of the green dappled shade into the white dust and white light of Provence. She was trembling and covered with sweat. I have been at war a long time, she thought.

* * *

A thunderstorm ended as the train pulled into Nîmes, leaving pools of water, sodden papers and a faint, indefinable freshness in the air. There were no taxis at the station, just a few pedal cabs, but Elizabeth was in no hurry. She slung her bag over her shoulder and walked along the edge of the old town, past the rain-darkened Arena and the Maison Carrée. She bought a baguette and ate it as she walked, breaking off little pieces to throw to the pigeons. She wished she were a soldier with a few days' leave and nothing to do but potter through the ruins or sit beside the fountains in the sun. But the arches, the columns, the porticoes, the massive, vainglorious inscriptions all reminded her of Jozef, who loved such things, knew their names and genealogies, had run off with her to see them. She did not feel he was dead, did not want, however much she longed for news of him, to know that, but still she began to walk faster as she neared the street. There was the *boulangerie* on the corner, and the *boucherie* with the carved horses' heads on the second floor, and holes gouged by bullets in the stones. There was the untidy garden, the high iron fence, then the front of the pink house, intact, faded, shuttered tight. But, of course, it had been hot. She went to the door and knocked. The apartments reverberated with a hollow sound. Elizabeth dropped her bag and went down the alley at the side. Six feet along the garden wall, fifth stone up. She opened her pocket knife, pried loose the stone and felt for the key. If it was there, Jozef was alive; if it wasn't, he was dead; if it was there ... she felt among the wall and touched smooth metal. Perhaps he'd never come back at all.

The front door was stiff, a bit swollen from the damp, and inside the hall smelled of mildew, old dust. There were cobwebs, doubtless mice, but all Elizabeth saw was Jozef's heavy brown coat. 'Jozef! Jozef!'

She ran through to the living room, to the kitchen, upstairs, shouting. She threw open the shutters so that she could look into the garden, then ran down and opened the back door. There was only the twitter of the sparrows, the sound of children playing out in the street. She shouted again, despairing of the silence, and was answered by a noise in the garden shed. A little brown and white dog ran out, barking, and behind him, Madame Rozier, cane in hand, shouting, 'No one is to be in this garden. The house is closed. All closed up!' Then she stopped, her nearsighted eyes taking in the dog's frantic greeting, the dark-haired woman, the open shutters. 'Oh, Madame! You have come back!'

Elizabeth held out her hand, but the old woman threw both arms around her, then stepped back, looked at the uniform and nodded.

'The *Boches* were never in here,' she said proudly. 'I closed the house and lived in the shed. They never even knew I was here. *Sales Boches.*' She spat indelicately on the grass.

'I am grateful,' Elizabeth said. 'But Jozef, Madame Rozier? I know he came back. His coat is in the hall.'

The old woman took her arm and looked at Elizabeth with remote, faded eyes. 'He came back in '42. He was safe here, Madame, until this past winter. He taught German, English to patriots, French to refugees.' She shook her head. 'Until last winter.'

'Madame Rozier, please! What happened?'

'Oh, he was careful, Madame. I will say that Monsieur was careful. At first, nothing. I did the shopping and he stayed upstairs. Then, he got his papers straightened out, pretended I don't know what, and resumed his old life.' She shrugged and Elizabeth bit her tongue with impatience and waited.

'It was the Vichy men, that Darlan mob, the Milice, though the Boches were busy, too.' Madame Rozier made a face and spat again in disgust. 'They rounded up the refugees, Jews mostly. No, no,' she said, seeing Elizabeth go pale, 'Monsieur was safe, but you know how he was. It was a boy, first. The family had had warning and wanted to flee but the child had a bad leg. Your husband put him in the attic. I did not approve, Madame, though it was the right thing. I saw where it would lead.'

'How long, Madame Rozier?' Elizabeth asked, her heart sick.

'This past winter. He saw it coming and warned me. We hid in the shed, Frise and I, and old as we are, we got over the fence when he was arrested.'

'Where, Madame Rozier, what charge?'

'They said he'd helped an airman, Madame. One of your countrymen who'd been shot. Though he denied it and I cleaned up the blood. Not a drop did they find. There was no proof, but they arrested him anyway. They took him north to the prison in Lyons. I came back a week later and I've lived in the shed ever since.'

Chapter Twenty-Three

Kent – 1944

Robert took the baby and stood holding her in the ornate Victorian porch while his father fussed with the camera. Though the house behind him was shadowed, his face was touched with the strong spring light that reflected off the lacy folds curving like a shell around his daughter.

'A little to the right,' said his father and Robert looked up with a brilliant smile that reminded Elizabeth of the morning of Liberation when he'd run down the hall in his bathrobe and ordered everyone into uniform. 'Good, good. Stay still.'

The shutter clicked and they all relaxed. That was the last picture. She'd had hers taken, and Robert and Sarah together, and the infant's godfather, before the whole party had been considerately snapped by the minister.

'I can't believe how good that baby's been!' Robert's mother exclaimed as she lifted the child from his arms and held her up. The baby looked around with wise infant eyes dark as blueberries.

'She's a lady of poise like her mother and godmother,' the proud father said. They all laughed at this and Sarah turned and kissed Elizabeth again. Robert's wife was pretty in a lavish, exhuberant way with dark blonde hair and a warm, impulsive manner. When Elizabeth arrived, Sarah had taken both her hands and said, 'I almost feel I know you, Robert's told me so much. I've been waiting so long to see you, to thank you.' But she spoke in a natural way so that Elizabeth did not feel strange or embarrassed. Now she said, 'It's meant so much that you could be here.'

'I would never have missed her christening. She's a splendid baby.'

'She is, isn't she!'

'When she talks,' Elizabeth said, 'I'll see she learns some Polish.'

'You must come and stay when we've moved into the school. We are to have quite a big house. Promise you'll come.'

'Of course she'll come,' Robert's father said, putting his arms around them both. 'But now it's time for the champagne.' He was small, as short as his son was tall, and quick and lively. He had kept everyone laughing at dinner the night before and, between teasing his daughter-in-law and flirting with Elizabeth, he urged the whole party inside where the buffet was ready. Sarah laid the child in a beautiful old wicker bassinet, and Elizabeth touched her namesake's tiny fingers gently and felt a confusion of feelings rippling under the pleasure of the day and the beauty of the child. Then Robert's father called them all to order and broke open the champagne. The party grew so merry that Sarah had to move her baby to a back bedroom, and it was only later, when is was nearly time for her train, that Elizabeth found herself standing next to Robert. He was watching his father organise some dancing with a bemused expression, as if trying to remember the precise sensation of pre-war gaiety.

'What fun your father is.'

'Yes. It is his talent.'

'A precious one,' Elizabeth said. The champagne bubbles tickled her nose.

'You are very quiet,' he said.

'Having a child named for you is a serious business. I feel a little older already.'

'The last few years have aged us all, I'm afraid.' Back at school Robert had been astonished at the upper forms' youthfulness. When he left for the service, they had seemed his near contemporaries, young men like himself. Now he saw that they were children.

'Still, you look to be thriving. When do you begin your new job?'

'Not 'til autumn. I'm due back in Germany soon.'

'Will it be over by then?'

'The Germans are finished now.'

'Excuse me, Robert,' his mother said, laying a hand on his arm. 'Are you taking the car? Sue and Geoff have to catch the 4.10.'

'When's yours?' he asked Elizabeth.

'Not until after five, but I thought I'd walk,' Elizabeth said. 'It's not much over a mile and the weather is lovely.'

His mother, very much the hostess, protested, but Robert said that he'd go too. 'I'll get Elizabeth to look at that tree you've been worried about in the orchard, Mother. She knows about such things.'

'Well, we'll send your case to the station with Sue and Geoff. But are you sure? The grass will be wet.'

'Please, it will be a pleasure to be out – after all the rain we've had.'

'Well, that's true enough.'

'We'll keep to the lane,' Robert said. He fetched her case, while Elizabeth made her farewells. When they were out of sight of the house he asked, 'And you? How are you, really? You said you were in Italy and North Africa.'

A shadow crossed her face. 'I was too late,' she said.

'I gather there were a lot of delays with the Anglo-Polish Mission.'

'That is an English understatement. Too many in your government think the Russians can do no wrong.'

'Not, at least, while they have Red Army Divisions in the West.'

'I will do them the courtesy of saying it was merely expediency, for some of the Poles were no better. By the time they were in agreement, the situation was hopeless. Of course, we were shipped off anyway.' Elizabeth's mouth was a thin line. She had got as far as Bastia on the Italian coast, close enough to watch planes leave Brindisi and head north over the Adriatic to Poland. But though she had spent nearly three months on that frightful and impoverished coast, neither she nor her friends had gone, and few, too few, of the pilots that had, ever came back. The ones who survived returned with tears in their eyes: Warsaw lay as black and empty as the Ghetto after the Rising in '43, with not so much as a light in the darkness.

'Our "ally", Stalin, would not let the planes refuel. Without refuelling stops, the flights were impossible; there was no way to provision the Rising.'

'I am so sorry. I know how much you had hoped to go home.'

'I begin to think I never will.' She looked past the bare, pruned limbs of the orchard to the rolling downs beyond. 'The Reds will take over Poland. My name alone would be enough. I would be an "enemy of the people".'

A stile to negotiate spared Robert the necessity of answering. Whenever he thought of Elizabeth, he envisioned her as she had been in France: vigorous, indomitable and utterly charming, capable of changing the emotional climate with a smile, and blessed with an infallible instinct for the right gesture. But though she had seemed absolutely secure and confident, peace revealed how badly she had been wounded. 'What will you do now?' he asked.

'I don't know. I've thought of running away to sea. Seriously,' she said with the sudden, embracing smile he remembered, 'there are positions open for stewardesses. I'd like the sea, I'm afraid you were right: a gangster life ruins one for normal things. And you, will you be happy teaching?'

Robert stopped and considered this, his hands thrust into his pockets, his shoulders a little stooped. 'I'll be going back to what I knew, what I did well. And then there's the family.' Since his return Robert had often thanked God for that anchor. Living in the Resistance was like driving a fast car; when the brakes went on, you kept flying for a time. Some agents made a bad return, including some of the best and bravest. For them all, there were bad dreams, sensitive nerves, ruined digestions. 'I'll confess – but only to you – that at first I felt a stranger. I mean with Sarah, my parents even. Being at home didn't seem quite real.'

Elizabeth nodded and walked on; she knew what he meant. Nîmes was more real to her than the grass beneath their feet, Nînes where Madame Rozier said, "He was arrested," and the earth darkened like the afternoon storm. Elizabeth had sat down on the steps while Frise, the little dog, capered about her feet. The old lady patted her shoulder, fetched some strong red wine and made her drink it, and then Elizabeth had pulled herself together and visited the gendarmes, the Prefecture, everyone who might know Jozef's fate, but had learned nothing definite. Preparations for the mission to Poland had given her the illusion of usefulness, but it was an illusion, and Bastia had been frightful. Mired in idleness, the agents' lives had grown untidy. They spent the evenings in cafés, restaurants, hotels: anywhere there was music, liquor, laughter. In the mornings, everyone felt miserable for one reason or another and dragged around speechlessly. Afternoons were the time for quarrels, the time when one understood how affection was eroded by futility, and honour, by giddy nights that left everyone depressed. Elizabeth remembered visiting the ancient church and lighting candles for her parents, for André, Czeslaw and Charlie, for the dead children and lost friends from the Vercors, until the golden flames lit the gloomy altar and the Virgin's still, Byzantine face. She remembered the cold sea air that smelled of salt and kelp and crept over the pavement into her bones.

Bastia was infinitely worse than Cairo, and when, at last, she couldn't stand it any more, she fled to North Africa. Though Elizabeth saw her tanker friend Jack Morris there, she was unable to settle. 'I've been back in France,' she said.

'Any news?'

She shook her head. 'None good. I found out that Jozef was in Lyons while we were on the Vercors. I passed through the city, was within a block of the jail while he was there. Had they made the connection ...'

'That would have been most unlikely.'

'Yes – fortunately. At some point he was sent east to the Reich. All I know is that he was not in the large group executed before the Liberation. Otherwise ...' She sighed and threw up her hands. 'It is the uncertainty,' she said in a soft voice. 'Sometimes I think I will never know. That is the worst. There are so many now – my Cousin Félicie and her family, friends from the Underground – and yet to know is, so often, to lose all hope.'

'A lot of DP's are turning up – ex-slave workers and camp inmates, POWs of every nationality. It is possible that you will learn something.'

'Yes, perhaps. In the meantime, I find it hard to concentrate, to work at anything.'

Robert wondered then if she could only be happy in action, if she had been born for the one thing she did superbly well, and now that it was finished, her chance for happiness was over. But that was a hateful notion, akin to despair. He had had a touch of that periodically ever since the Vercors and knew such ideas were dangerous. 'But you'll need a job.'

'Eventually. I get a fair amount in dividends – may God preserve old Lev Weisenov – but I must keep up the house in Nîmes in case Jozef returns, and the way prices are ...'

'You know we need liaison officers desperately.'

'I don't want to go to Germany. I didn't like it even in peacetime, and I doubt they'd take me in Intelligence.' She smiled ruefully. 'I had too many opinions of my own to suit them.'

'Then consider the relief services. It's hard work and I wouldn't suggest it if you weren't at a loose end, but the country is full of refugees. A lot are Polish, more are Russian. There's a desperate need for anyone who knows languages and can handle people.'

Elizabeth was silent for a moment. Below them the little local station and track looked like a child's toy – like a plaything for the new goddaughter who was the only child she was ever likely to have. England, which she had once loved, struck her as very small, neat and foreign. The heroic days were over, she was an exile who would forever be an outsider. 'The way I feel now, I might not be much use,' she said.

'So what are you doing that is of use?'

She gave him a sly smile.

'I don't want to know about it,' Robert said with mock primness. She had a weakness for able, intelligent men – and they for her. He had known that even in France, though she was clever, discreet, completely professional. He had wondered more than once what their relationship would have been if he hadn't been married, hadn't been in love with Sarah. 'You'd be better to take up smoking.'

'Schoolteacher,' she said, and laughed with the low, joyous sound he remembered from their days together.

'It has just hit you later,' he said. 'I mean what I felt along the Drôme. Do you remember that American sergeant? I drank almost all his whiskey.'

'I remember.'

'Soon we will be different people. We will forget — or learn to manage — all this.' His gesture encompassed them and their feelings as well. 'It's the in-between period that's hard, and I think you might consider Germany. You know SHAEF has had to close the French borders to the East Europeans? You didn't know that? Just this week. The influx of refugees would have shattered the French economy. They're in camps for the moment; maybe even some of your own people. Think about coming, please.'

He did not speak about it again until the train was in the station. He lifted her bag into the doorway after her and took her hand for a moment, affectionate and concerned. 'Think about what I said.'

'I will.

'Will you come?' he asked.

The steady thump and clatter of the wheels accelerated. The platform slid away and Elizabeth reached back in farewell. 'All right,' she called. 'I'll see if they'll take me.'

Elizabeth was sure the girl had been murdered. The other woman in the hut said that there had been a fight. They had shouted and pushed and showed how it had been, and, certainly, there was a mess of overturned food and blood, and the splintery chairs and unsteady tables were all in disarray, but Elizabeth was still suspicious. The dead girl with her thin blue legs and transparent hands had been killed with one stroke of a thin-bladed knife. Most fights ended differently; Elizabeth had seen those corpses, too, but for the moment she had gone along with the story. She'd asked what the fight was about and been answered with curses and sour laughs and then an outpouring of sorrows, of monstrous losses and petty griefs in Polish, Ruthenian and Yiddish. One old lady pulled at her sleeve and whispered so softly that Elizabeth had to step into the other room with her. The dead girl was her granddaughter. She said 'A good girl.'

'Why?' asked Elizabeth.

The old lady wrapped her shawl around her until it almost

covered her face. 'They spoke against the Jews and she defended us. She said they were as bad as the Nazis. They have killed my last child,' the old woman said.

Inside, there was another tale: the girl had been a Kapo, a notorious traitor, a whore. She had struck some of the others – 'With a whip, *Kapitan,* with a whip' – and told the guards whom to beat. Were they sure? Some said they had recognised her as soon as she came in the door.

Others said they lied. The girls had fought over a piece of jewellery stolen in the town. 'Given in exchange for lifting their skirts,' a toothless woman said. 'Ask Anton, eh? Hut three.' That was likely true, but it might be mere spite.

The sullen blonde hanging back by the bunks screamed that it was all lies. Lies! She was gaunt and unkempt, and the loss of most of her teeth made her look like a woman of forty instead of the schoolgirl she had been just a few years before. Elizabeth had had her removed from the hut for questioning – the others agreed that she had begun the fight and there were bruises and scratches on her face, some old, some fresh.

As to who else had participated and their motives, good or bad, Elizabeth doubted anyone else would ever know – if they knew themselves. Suffering had unhinged so many minds, that cruel and aimless violence was a commonplace. She took the old woman and the three other Jewish DPs to another barracks and threatened the rest with a ticket east if she had to be called again.

They subsided into misery, sullen or querulous by turns. What would become of them, where could they go? Elizabeth went for the dozenth time over their options and watched their despair. The Western Europeans were shipped home by the thousands every day, but the Jews and Slavs whose homes were gone faced the squalor of the transit camps indefinitely.

'Yes, yes, I will check,' she said and listened patiently to the angers and fears which she had seen most vividly in that sad corpse, lying like a doll on a khaki army blanket.

It was probably murder, Elizabeth thought as she started across a rubble-lined canyon stinking of sewage, spilled schnapps and diesel fuel. But knowing that meant nothing. The relief team had done what they could. Another three thousand refugees had arrived that morning, eighteen hundred had been shipped off. Tonight there would be fights, rapes, robberies, but tomorrow more would go home. Though the back of her head was pounding, she must think of that, of the "overall picture" the major was so fond of discussing.

A truck loaded with troops spun around a corner and Elizabeth stepped up on to a pile of concrete slabs and covered her mouth against the boiling pink dust. The truck was followed by a flock of jeeps that swung around the bomb craters and slid sideways on the turns, then screeched to a halt at some unseen obstruction ahead. Elizabeth clambered across the hunks of brick and cement, the shattered glass, the discarded bottles. A young soldier, confused by the dust and by her long print scarf, leaned over the side of a truck and made her a proposition. Elizabeth suggested some alternatives in the vernacular and moved her scarf so that he could see her captain's bars. There was some laughter from the back of the truck and a wave of snappy salutes. Elizabeth gestured for them to carry on. The soldiers were slack but only dangerous when drunk. For those times, and for fights and riots, Elizabeth carried her service revolver.

She waited at the next intersection for another line of military transport, then stepped into the desert that had been the centre of the city before saturation bombing vaporised steel, mortar and flesh. In the soft new soil which had result, scrubby pink and purple loose strife and willow herb bloomed across the bomb craters, and hardy shoots pushed through the tiles of old lobbies and filled the cracks in the paving. Otherwise, there was no natural thing; the landscape was white and grey and pink, a rocky waste across which a line of women pulled little wagons and carried bundles of food, sticks, and hard earned cigarettes. Nearer the military track, others sorted undamaged bricks and quarrelled over any scrap of value. They were big, strong-boned women, bitter and hunted-looking, and they turned their faces away as she passed.

A vehicle rumbled behind her and Elizabeth automatically moved to the side. 'Hey, Captain! Hey, Liz! Hello.'

It was a young officer she knew only as Jimmy. He had acquired a dark green Mercedes since she'd seen him last, and it held three other officers and a journalist she recognised.

'You're coming up in the world,' Elizabeth said. Jimmy had been a bit slow. Most officers commandeered a civilian car as soon as they got into town.

'You bet. Come with us. You don't want to be walking this near dark.'

'This near the drinking hour, you mean,' said one of the others.

'I'm just going back to headquarters,' she said.

'Break, break my heart! There's a party on.' He mentioned the name of what had been the city's best restaurant, now operating out of an intact cellar with an Allied clientèle. The city was starving, and the camps scrambling for turnips and potatoes, but the big black market restaurants were thriving and the officers' mess halls were elbow deep in luxury, awash in champagne and brandy, in beefsteaks, caviar, salmon. It made Elizabeth sick sometimes, sick enough so that she could smell Warsaw; not the Warsaw she'd loved, but the wartime city where she had first seen life without limitations and power without restraint. But only sometimes.

'Come on,' said the young officer. He had a sandy moustache and freckles and eyes red from drink. When his outfit had had to send the Cossacks home to die, he had stayed drunk for a week. Elizabeth respected him for that.

'All right.'

A rear door opened but Jimmy said, 'Watch it, Moyers. Get in front, Captain, you don't want to risk your virtue with the Royal Marines.'

The back seat laughed and protested, but Elizabeth climbed in beside Jimmy and his friend, who was already drunk and lurched from side to side as the Mercedes crunched over crumbled stone and mortar.

The restaurant had music provided by three black G.I.'s in their brown uniforms and a thin white drummer in an ancient dinner jacket. The trumpeter was good, sweet and clear and loud enough to cut through the clatter of the dishes, the loud, boozy voices, the sound of nervous feet the on uncarpeted floor under the too low ceiling. A few couples were already dancing but most of the crowd was jammed around the splendid tables, eating and drinking and smoking up fortunes in Occupation currency.

'I'm meeting a friend,' Jimmy said.

'Don't let me stop you.'

He put his arm around her shoulders. 'Not that kind of friend. A business friend.'

'What other kind is there?' Elizabeth asked. There had been cocktails waiting for them at the door and though she had taken wine instead, it was doing nothing for her pounding head.

'That's bad of you,' said Jimmy. He drank too much, but he was a very pleasant drinker. Sober, he was stiff and military. He had begun to drink the minute he had seen the shooting ended. 'You'll break my heart.'

'You shouldn't have invited me.'

'Darling, I need you!'

She rolled her eyes and he added, 'In every way, as always, but tonight for a little favour.'

'I've heard that before,' she said without annoyance. He amused her and they had this in common: they hated nearly everything around them.

'I need you to *sprechen* for me. To *sprechen* in *Polnisch*. A little deal,' he said.

'These "little deals" can be dangerous.'

'Only a picture. I have small vices.'

Elizabeth shrugged, non-committally. There was steak on the table, and good potatoes and green beans and thick slices of tomato. And for later, pies and tortes and gâteaux with cream. And more wine, French, of course, the drink of conquerers, looted by the Nazis and hoarded to be looted again. It was white, strong and tinged with gold. Elizabeth danced with Jimmy and with a Royal Marine and had another glass. Then she danced again with the Marine, who was handsome but aggressive in a way Elizabeth found tiresome, and she declined another turn on the floor. As she walked back to the table, she caught a glimpse of a man in a light civilian jacket sitting talking to Jimmy. His back was to her and he didn't turn until she had almost reached the table. Then he stood up.

'A long time,' said Marek. His face was harder and a new scar angled across his forehead.

She kissed him on both cheeks, but he lifted her hand to his lips with formal politeness.

'What I want to do,' Jimmy began, but Marek laid a hand on his shoulder and shook his head.

'I want to dance with Countess Elizabeth,' he said. When she smiled and nodded, he held out his hand. They stood for a moment on the edge of the floor as Marek considered the tempo of "When They Begin the Beguine". Then he moved out at half speed, and though his leg gave a little lurch to each step, he had the athlete's perfect balance as a counter. They circled the floor in silence, once, twice. She could feel his shoulder through the soft fabric of his jacket, could feel his thigh brush hers. They might have been in Shepeards', in the lounge of the Continental, in the Damascus Orient. Everything was different and nothing had changed. When the music stopped, Marek pressed Elizabeth's hand against his chest; she could feel his heart beating through her palm, through her wrist, altering the rhythm of her blood. They were two soldiers, two exiles, two friends.

'This place is very warm,' he said.

Elizabeth suddenly felt flushed with the heat and the crush of dancers. 'Yes, it is far too hot.'

'I have a car outside.'

'We should perhaps tell Jimmy,' she said, but he only smiled. They danced from near the bandstand to the hall and glided, still dancing, into the old basement loading area, past the lobby guards, laughing now and beginning to lose the beat, and through the heavy door to the narrow, dirty steps leading up into the twilight. The door closed behind them and Marek stopped and looked into her face and she had time to read his sad and hungry eyes before he kissed her, and she remembered Budapest and happiness.

'I must tell you one thing,' he said.

She shook her heard and put her fingers over his mouth.

'I must,' he said, but instead he pressed her fingers against his lips, and at the top of the stair Elizabeth saw the big car and the man who'd been left to guard it.

She woke up out of delirium into darkness and then remembered Marek drawing the curtains on the street side so that they could make love with the light on. The lamp was made of cut crystal and its facets had shed little coloured lights over the pictures stacked against the walls, the silver plate, the heavy furniture, over Marek's strong body, his wild eyes. She remembered that now, though something in her head was pounding painfully back behind her eyes and her throat was dry.

She had noticed the knotted scars running down his side to his upper thigh with sudden fear. 'Did you think I'd have left the army otherwise?' he'd asked. 'They were through with me.' Still he had been lucky. 'So lucky,' he said. Their convoy had set off a mine just outside Rome, and he'd been hit by shrapnel and glass. He laughed then, happy with escape, with medals, with a chance meeting which have provided his new *métier* and with it the danger and excitement his soul craved. And when she touched the jagged scars and began to cry, that had pleased him, too, as if those tears were what he had most wanted. Now outside in the distance there were shots, a lot of shots, and Elizabeth closed her eyes: it was nothing, drunken Russians discharging their weapons in the wasteland.

When she woke again, she thought at first that they were still at it, but a hot yellow light showed around the curtains and the dull drumming she could hear was purely internal. Marek lay asleep on his side, his arm flung across her waist and Elizabeth wondered if she mightn't stay with him and forget the rest. She had run away once before with a man and this would be simpler yet. But when she moved closer to Marek, she felt dizzy, a sensation familiar enough since the camp was full of fevers and infections, but worse than usual. Elizabeth got carefully out of bed, put on Marek's robe and went to look for the shower.

Cold water helped. I have a slight fever, Elizabeth thought, but by the time she was dressed, she was shivering and went downstairs to make tea. No one was up. Marek said he had kept on the German owners as staff, but they were out of sight and the driver from the night before, the American with the ungrammatical Polish, had disappeared as well although the big car was still parked in the alley beside the house. Elizabeth thought of calling Headquarters on the kitchen phone and was considering what difference the absence of one relief worker could possibly make when she heard Marek on the stairs. He came into the kitchen barefoot, dressed in his bathrobe.

'You're keeping army hours,' he complained, and kissed her and ran his hands over her shoulders. Then he looked at her and put his hand to her forehead. 'You feel very hot.'

'It is nothing,' Elizabeth said, though she was beginning to feel genuinely unwell. 'Maybe a touch of the 'flu. We've all had it.'

'You're working too hard.'

She shrugged. 'I might take today off.'

'I'd like that,' Marek said, drawing her close for a minute. Then he released her and stuck both hands in his pockets. 'There is something I must tell you. You wouldn't let me last night — for which I am grateful beyond words, Elizabeth, but now I must. I'm married.'

Her throat went so dry that though she formed the word there was no sound. But he knew.

'Someone I met in Cairo.'

'The cipher clerk,' Elizabeth said.

'Yes.'

'Why?' she asked.

'Because I am still that much of a gentleman, Elizabeth.'

'Then what are you doing here? What sort of life is this for a gentleman? This gangster's job?'

'Did I have much choice, Elizabeth? You've persisted to the end with the British and has it brought you a mile nearer Warsaw? We're not home anymore, and we've all had to accept second best.'

'What about your wife, your child? I suppose there was a child.'

'A son,' he said, his face stiff.

'And your wife?' she asked, though it lacerated her heart.

'I enabled her to go home respectably. My presence wasn't required further.'

Elizabeth stood up, spilling the tea, stumbling against the chair. 'Go home to them,' she cried over the anger that roared behind her ears, and when he reached out towards her, she struck his hand away. 'Go back to your son,' she said, and then the room tipped precipitously and though Marek was calling her, calling her back, she tumbled into darkness.

Chapter Twenty-Four

Elizabeth spent two weeks in the hospital with 'flu and respiratory complications. Marek returned to Berlin, but he had huge bunches of roses, carnations and lilies delivered by the American driver. One day she was sitting up, feverless for the first time, and the man asked if these was no message in return. Elizabeth set her face and asked for a piece of paper. On it she wrote, "Find Jozef for me," and signed her name. She did this to hurt him, but also to let him know that she was better. And she was. Her illness seemed to have calmed the restlessness and sorrow that had haunted her and made her miserable, as if 'flu and pneumonia had really been unshed tears for the Vercors and for lost friends and unspeakable horrors. She had only been seriously ill three times in her life, and she understood the pattern.

Still, she was so weak that she would have been sent back to England if the relief services hadn't been desperately short-handed. Instead, she was transferred to the administrative offices of an enormous DP transit camp and assigned to collate lists of refugees by destination, and to prepare manifests for trains going west. The job was simple but tedious, and late one afternoon when she was nearly finished with the next day's train, she let herself be distracted by the sounds of the football game outside. She got up from her desk and opened the window all the way. Beyond the grey hulks of the former panzer barracks was a hill with a grove of trees, sweetly green and stirring gently in the soft breeze that swayed the sad tattered laundry and carried the sounds of children playing noisily between the buildings. Elizabeth wondered what they played, what rehearsal of escape or liberation.

Below on the parade ground, a mob of men and boys ran back and forth, atheir histories written in the soiled remnants of a dozen army uniforms, in striped prison garb, in civilian jackets and coats too warm for July, in cavalry boots and mismatched shoes and every conceivable form of headgear. A few of the players, hardier than the rest, had stripped off their shirts. Their skin was as white as milk and the bones of their shoulders and ribs stood out like polished ivory, a painful contrast to the sturdy men who had danced up on the Col de Larche or even the slim, brown bodies of the young Maquisards.

Yet they were laughing, shouting back and forth in their own languages, and the old and crippled men on the sidelines yelled encouragement and gossiped in whatever common words they had. Now and then a fresher gust of wind whirled a cloud of dust among them and, absorbed in her own thoughts, Elizabeth was surprised by the rustle of papers behind her. She turned too late to keep them from blowing off the nearest desks on to the floor, and, with a sigh of irritation, she pulled the window shut and bent to pick them up. She was trying to get the papers sorted when she noticed a list of DPs to be interviewed. One was starred in red and next to the name was the notation, "claims French residence, British papers". The print waved in and out of focus, and Elizabeth gave a little cry. She was still kneeling on the floor, holding the lists in her hand, when one of her British colleagues came to the door.

'Elizabeth, are you all right? Elizabeth?'

'My husband is alive,' she said, her voice hoarse. 'Jozef Alexis Goralski; British passport: Joseph Gorman.'

The man who might be Jozef was ten miles away in one of the auxiliary camps. Elizabeth ran outside and across the parade ground to the road. The low sun had turned the sky to clear, pale tones of lemon and lavender, and its dusty rays streamed between the pines. There was a warm smell of resin, and the sounds of the rooks reminded Elizabeth of home. She had not noticed them before, nor the shadow of the wooded hills, nor the white and yellow flowers by the roadside and the heathers in the clearings. It was as if her senses, closed since France, had opened to take in everything: the warm air, the dusty light, the noisy encampments of birds before night, the sound of a jeep rolling up behind her. The driver waved and pulled the car to the side.

'You're not going to walk, Captain,' Sylvie said. Like most of the enlisted personnel, the relief team's driver had a horror of unassisted transport.

'Sylvie, I used to do trips twice this far every day.'

'War stories, Captain. A week ago you were staggering on the parade ground. Come on. This is just one step above walking anyway. Me, I've got my eye on that Kraut Mercedes that's showed up.'

'Fat chance,' said Elizabeth as she climbed in. 'I'm surprised you got the jeep.'

Sylvie laughed. She was a tough and resourceful Londoner with an intuitive grasp of the tribal customs of the British Army. 'Anyway,' she said tactfully, 'you'll have plenty to do once you get there. Seeing about a transfer and all that.'

'If he's well enough. He's been in the hospital.'

'Ah,' said Sylvie, but she added quickly 'that's not always a bad thing. If he's out again.' She glanced away from the road and saw Elizabeth's set profile. 'You will be prepared.'

'Yes,' Elizabeth said and bit her lip. She knew she must be prepared, would be; after all, she knew. But what did she know? She knew the ribs and backbones sharp as saws, the old eyes of the children, the madness of the lost. Beyond that, she did not know, for she had been in the cells only briefly and had escaped the worst as if by the word of the Virgin. She had heard, but she did not know, not as Jozef must know. And Jozef, after all, had not intended this life, had not wished it, not at all. As Marek had seen from the start in Budapest, the clandestine life, however natural to them, was foreign country to Jozef.

'You know we sent off three thousand yesterday. Almost as many today, I'd guess. They were all fine,' Sylvie said. 'Healthier than you and me some of them.'

'I know.'

'And some of the kids! Cheeky, thieving little brats they are, despite everything. Do you know what one said to me?'

Elizabeth listened with half a mind and laughed mechanically, for she knew Sylvie was kind to try to distract her. She had never been imaginative, had never tormented herself with possibilities, alternatives, consequences. Elizabeth had been the most practical of resisters; now terrible thoughts crowded around her like flies. She was desperately impatient to get there – and Sylvie drove so slowly. She wanted to stretch out the journey forever – and Sylvie drove so fast! When they had almost reached the camp she asked, 'Do you know anything about this place?'

'Good enough as camps go. It's an old prison. Solid walls, regular water and mod cons.'

'There's a blessing.'

'You bet. I'll be thankful when I never have to see, dig or smell another slit trench.'

Ahead was a narrow drive and, when they turned in from the road, they saw meadows bordered with trees and a large stone building surrounded by tents and temporary huts. A guard directed them to the office, and Sylvie manoeuvred the jeep through a yard packed with cars and trucks, the machine as nimble in her hands as a Carpathian pony. Elizabeth felt her heart accelerate as she stepped out on to the pavement.

The prison was four storeys high, a massive pile top heavy with cornices, attics and dormers like her old convent school in Warsaw. But inside, institutional order was already crumbling. Upstairs somewhere, a violin wailed in minor modulation, a child cried, a man sang drunkenly in Russian. The marble floor was streaked and dusty, and cooking smells of cabbage, turnips and potatoes were overlaid with the warm, close smell of crowded human habitation.

Elizabeth pushed her way through a group of half wild children and entered an office very like the one she'd left. 'Yes, he's with us,' the sergeant said. 'B block, second floor. That's in the annex.'

He pointed down a labyrinth of corridors and Elizabeth made her way past rooms full of families, strangers, friends, all homeless members of the new gypsy tribes of Europe. The cells stood open, and from the narrow white-washed interiors came children running with a ball or a toy, men with pipes or cards or a bottle, young women with infants and older ones with sewing or knitting. Laundry and bedding hung on the bars and children swung back and forth on the heavy doors, endangering their fingers. The air was heavy with the smell of disinfectant, dirty babies, pipes, even furtive cooking fires, as the inhabitants recreated what they could of home. Here was a kitten, there a dog — and how had these managed to survive? A boy of maybe twelve called, 'Oh, sweetie, sweetie,' to her in an insinuating, lascivious tone, while in the next alcove an old man and woman argued furiously. The young people would be elsewhere, walking at the edge of the meadows, drifting into the dense shadows of the trees — she had more than once fallen over couples in the groves behind the barracks.

Some of her colleagues were shocked by that, they wanted the refugees chaste and clean, clean above all, and polite and kind, as if suffering made one noble. They were distressed by the noise, the arguments, the cruelty, the profane women, the larcenous children, the aggressive men, by the revelation of a human jungle far removed from nice society — as if nice society could survive the loss of all its comforts. Elizabeth herself had abandoned most of her squeamishness. She was no longer the Countess who had fussed over the collar of a dress or the colour of a sash.

She took the coarser signs of life — the jokes, the propositions, the quarrels, the drunknness — as just that, signs of life, and far better than the alternative, the death that hung everywhere on the continent like a poison cloud. So it was all right with her if the DPs hung laundry from the bars and cooked stolen *wurst* on forbidden fires. A certain amount of mess was part of life, and she had become fatalistic. The world had turned out to be like Zofia's stones after all; the superstition and "ignorance" of her childhood, more accurate than the hopes and designs of educated men. The Devil was real and his wings were black, and only the intercession of the saints had brought her through so many corridors, past so many strangers to a certain wooden passage in the brick wing of a prison, where out of all the sounds, of all the languages, of all the voices, she heard just one and stopped. Jozef was singing a song she had learned the first year they went to Zakopane. She put her hand on the wall to steady herself, then walked the last few yards to the doorway.

They were using oil lamps in the annex and a round yellow glow washed the room like the halo of a saint. Three women sewing, an old man mending a boot, two younger ones playing cards, and sitting in a straight wooden chair by the table, a man with white hair and missing teeth, holding a small girl on his lap. Another girl hung on his shoulder and they were both repeating the Gural song while he hummed the melody: "High lords you are and high lords you will remain but never lords over us here..."

Without the song, she would not have recognised his face, so thin, so worn, but now without the slightest doubt she knew it was Jozef. And standing there, unnoticed in the crush, in the constant noise and coming and going, the children running from one room to the other, the women calling news back and forth, the men, jokes, in the different languages, in the smoke, in the smell of babies and cabbages, Elizabeth knew him as she had not before. She understood in the moment of the lamplight, in the light in the childrens' hair, how very much he had loved her as a child, so much so that it had ruined their adult life. She understood but she did not speak, for she was a creature of intuition and superstition and impulse and now, though one of the women looked up, though a child tugged at her sleeve, she stood motionless and waited to see if he would know.

He corrected the child on his lap, had the two repeat a phrase, then stopped. In the yellow light Elizabeth saw his face change, saw a stillness almost like fright come over him, saw him turn then put down the child and stand up. He opened his mouth to speak, could not, then, as she stepped across the threshold, he cried out her name.

A warm wind blew through the train windows and dust from lost cities formed a fine grey coating on the seats, on their clothes and luggage. Jozef and Elizabeth shared a compartment with three journalists returning for Petain's trial, Americans who complained of the heat and threw orange peels out the window like autumn leaves. Jozef held the orange they gave him for a long time, stroking the thick, pebbled skin like a connoisseur with a gemstone until he saw that made them nervous and, polite as ever, began to eat it. What he couldn't finish, he wrapped in his handkerchief and stuffed into the pocket of his coat, where the juice would seep into the lining and make a mess. Then he put his head back against the seat and fell asleep.

He slept all afternoon with his legs stretched across the suitcases, mile after rolling, clanking mile, as the dust filtered over his hands and darkened his white hair. Jozef was really too weak to travel, but his eagerness to be home had given him no rest, and at last the camp doctor said it would be better to risk the trip than to have him so uneasy of mind. Elizabeth had used her connections to secure a seat on a fast train west, and the knowledge that they would be home in a day and a half had at last brought her husband peace. He slept off and on the whole time, and when he stirred uneasily and started out of his sleep, she took his hand. 'It is the sound of the train,' he said once, and she remembered how he had trembled at the sight of boxcars on the siding.

After dark, the journalists left off adding up their black market loot and planning French meals to join a poker game in the front of the train. Elizabeth was almost asleep in the darkened compartment, when Jozef said, 'I am a different man. You must realise that.'

Against the moonlight, she could see his profile, fine drawn as an etching. In the joy and shock of reunion, he had spoken of nothing but the future, of returning "home" to Nîmes, of being back in his dearest possession, his own house. Of his recent history, she knew only that he had been wandering the roads half dead when he was picked up and taken to the camp hospital. Now he said, 'It was luck.'

'And God's mercy.'

'I will tell you,' he said. 'You decide.' His voice was a disembodied murmur above the wheels and the night wind that blew out the stale smell of the correspondents' cigarettes and blew in the smell of the fields, the woods. She might have been listening to a ghost. 'They had no proof when I was arrested, no proof at all. I thank Madame Rozier for that. Still they wouldn't let me go, not with the Maquis running wild and the invasion expected. I was shipped to Lyons and held with another political and two thieves. Odd, how much of my life has been spent with thieves,' he said, and Elizabeth thought of the terrible night in Budapest when he had gone drinking with the German and she and Marek had waited alone. He spoke of Italy then, of his struggles after he had been expelled from Hungary, of hunger and cold and of working for smugglers and marketeers on the French border. 'I owe my life to those men,' he said and lapsed into a silence so long that Elizabeth thought he had fallen asleep. But after a time, he spoke of the end in France.

'After the invasion, the more dangerous politicals were shipped to the Reich. To be killed, I suppose. I was friends with one of the wardens and when we smaller political fry were to be shifted, he managed to leave me with my friends, the crooks. A nasty lot. I told them I was a pickpocket and filched a wallet from one of them to prove it. They believed me then left me alone.' In the half darkness, Jozef flexed his long, strong fingers and Elizabeth thought of the magic tricks he'd done to amuse them as children. He'd found coins behind her ears and tame mice in the cushions of André's chair. 'You know, I was often desperate,' he said as an aside. 'Both times getting home, I was forced to steal.'

'But why didn't you go to England? Where we had friends, people with obligations to us? I wrote to everyone, thinking you'd get there sometime. After so long, Jozef, I was almost sure you'd been killed.'

'That's another story,' he said sadly. 'That's a story about your happiness. And mine, I suppose, and my stupidity. Don't blame Marek for everything. I'd have probably done the same, and I have done other things as bad.' He stopped again, and Elizabeth felt a tremor of emotion in him, the only indication of his great suffering. Then he said, 'Just before Liberation, the jail was emptied. I'd hoped to be released with the petty crooks, but my friend the warden had been transferred — he was thoroughly corrupt, God bless him, and no doubt his masters had found him out. Instead, we were all shipped east to Buchenwald.' He ran his hand over his face. 'There is no evil men will not do if they have the power. I have seen them kill children for sport, Elizabeth. One begins to think there is no good. One wonders why one lives, what evil keeps one going.'

His voice died away, leaving the faintest vibration in the warm air of the compartment. Elizabeth was afraid to ask him more, but then, without prompting, he said, 'We thieves were lucky. While the good died, we were put on a work detail and sent to one of the outer camps. This was in the autumn and we worked in the potato fields. Then, because I was educated, I was put into the hospital, such as it was, and so I survived the winter. In the spring I was again sent out with a work detail, although I'd had dysentery and was too weak to do heavy labour. By the second day of digging in the fields, I was half dead.

'They marched us back to camp through a narrow alley, and I stepped into a half ruined shed and went to sleep. I should have been discovered and shot, but somehow I wasn't missed. When I woke up, it was night and I was alone. I walked straight through the town to the woods. For two days, I stole bread from farms and slept in the rain. Then a woodcutter found me. I told him I was a German, a refugee from East Prussia, and he took me home. After a few days I could see he was getting suspicious, so I walked west again. I met some French labourers who'd escaped from farms, and we travelled together towards the sound of the guns. The fighting passed us one night while we were sleeping in a deserted barn, and the next day we saw the Americans. One gave me an orange, like our companions here, and a coat. They wanted us to stay in one of their camps, but I wanted to go home. I was on my way to the French border when I collapsed. When I came to, I was in the British hopsital.'

'Thanks be to the Virgin,' Elizabeth said.

Jozef closed his eyes.

'When you were arrested,' Elizabeth said after a while, 'you had been working.'

'I hated all that "work". But it was safe enough. I had good clients. The *Gest* wanted to learn English by the end. You'd be surprised.'

'One betrayed you.'

'No. It was worse than that. It was an aviator with terrible injuries. I was weak, Elizabeth. I should have killed him with morphine.'

Elizabeth took his hand. 'No,' she said quickly, 'you were right.'

'Judge for yourself. We ran out of the drug and before I could get more he went mad with pain and cut his throat. Madame Rozier washed the attic floor and the stairs, and I dug a hole in the floor of the garden shed and buried him wrapped in a rug. They had no proof, you see,' Jozef said, turning to face her for the first time. His eyes glittered, large in his diminished face. 'They had no proof at all, but there was something in the air. I did not know then what I know now,' he whispered. 'Some men are attracted by the smell of blood.'

Chapter Twenty-five

Nîmes – 1946

The mild evening sky was preternaturally clear, as if the smoke and dust of war had never been and the heavens were still inviolate. Jozef could see every budding leaf on the trees, hear, as if each were amplified, dozens of small birds. He smelled the moist, secret, urgent scent of spring overlaid with the faint gasoline spoor of mopeds and of the expensive engine parked below. The car door opened and Marek stepped out, wearing a fine camel hair coat. He was a bit heavier and carried a cane now, a heavy, silver-topped item, lethal as a mace: the bandit had turned from the Resistance to the black market.

Below, the bell rang, but though Jozef heard the door and Elizabeth's greeting, he stayed by the window, a tall, raw-boned man with a lined face his French neighbours thought *distingué,* and dark, wary eyes. He was waiting for her to call him, to hear her voice; he thought he would know then how things were to be and whether or not he had a chance. But when she called, 'Jozef, Jozef, Marek's here!' he was none the wiser and closed his eyes in anguish. He was well. Yes, a glance in the mirror, showed that. Marek would clasp his shoulders, press his hand, kiss his cheek, tell him he was looking healthy and congratulate Elizabeth on his recovery. 'You don't look a year older,' he'd say. 'Except for the hair.' That's what they all said – all those who had known him before, who had seen him after the prison and the camp. And Elizabeth would say. 'Now he looks like a *professeur* and charges more,' and they would laugh. Jozef knew how to laugh. He could make conversation, tell stories. His teaching was as good as ever, his touch with children as sure, though unlike adults they understood that he was sad. Beyond that, nothing.

He called, 'I'll be right down,' but remained where he was, a dark silhouette against the glass. Elizabeth would be saying, 'He's really remarkable. Even the doctor is pleased.' She had brought him back to his own house and for that he was grateful. And now, and now? He wondered why Marek had come and concentrated on the sounds below until he felt giddy and had to take a deep breath. In the camp and in the hospital, Jozef had often felt vertigo, from hunger, weakness, from the drugs they'd given him for fever. This was of a different order. Though he clutched at the table for support and told himself it was nothing, he felt a violent lurch as if some giant had blundered amongst his bolted down emotions. All those whom he had betrayed by loving the little Countess were dead; his sins and his love were irrelevant in this new world, and therefore . . . He wiped his face with his handkerchief and stepped quickly into the hall. He would feel nothing. Nothing. As he had for so long. That was the only safe way, knowing all he knew.

'Ah, Jozef! Jozef, my old friend.' Marek threw his arms about him like a great bear and Jozef was surprised to feel tears in his eyes. It was odd, but he had always liked Marek. 'How well you look!'

'Thanks to Elizabeth,' Jozef said, and put his arm around her. And how nice Marek looked, too, in an English suit, hand made shirt, beautiful shoes, all scented with a dry, expensive cologne. He was barbered and brushed to near perfection, but though his taste was infinitely better, Lieutenant Zermoski now reminded Jozef of certain Chicago gentlemen of great wealth and ruthlessness. Still he smiled and took Marek's hand: he would not judge. Marek had lost his scruples: he, Jozef, had lost his emotions. Which was more reprehensible was for Elizabeth to decide.

At dinner they talked of the past, but lightly, remembering their days in Budapest and Warsaw. Marek had come laden with gifts, with good wine and brandy and chocolate and cigars, too, and when the meal was finished, Elizabeth was prevailed upon to allow Jozef just one. They were Havanas, worth a fortune, and Jozef sniffed the dark, fragrant weed and thought of nights in Mexico and the States, of cigars and beer and easy emotions.

Elizabeth washed the dishes while the two men indulged themselves. She knew that it was good for Jozef to see people from before; it was good for him to be happy. They had told her he would get well gradually, by fits and starts, but after many months she had not found the right way to pierce his uneasy indifference and touch his emotions. So it was partly for him that she had chanced this meeting; he had always been fond of Marek.

'Lovely,' said Jozef, tipping his head back and exhaling a long curl of smoke. 'Lovely.'

'I wish you'd been with me when I got those,' said Marek. 'I really should have taken those English lessons.' His white teeth glistened beneath his thick moustache. 'It would save me money now.'

'How do you manage?' Jozef asked.

'One of my partners is a G.I. a Polish-American. He's a good enough man in a tight spot, but for certain operations something smoother is required.'

'I'm afraid that I had enough trouble with petty crime.'

Marek laughed without taking offence. 'There's where you're wrong. If you have any kind of contacts you can hardly not make money. I clear thousands of dollars with a phone call after breakfast, because they're all waiting for us. We're essential. Without the market, the soldiers would simply waste what they now steal. And,' he said, knocking the ash from his cigar, 'they'll buy anything. Just for the pleasure of buying. Anything at all. Whatever's for sale.'

'What's left?' Jozef asked, remembering the stench and ruin of the German cities, the girders and cables braided together like tangled wool.

'You'd be surprised. After all, they looted most of Europe. Ask Elizabeth where her family's silver went. Of course, the poor and honest, they're in a bad way. They sell themselves, but I don't handle that. The danger is not so much where you draw the line, as not drawing any lines at all.' He tapped his cigar again and Jozef nodded. That he understood. The black market was a child of the camps. Marek was silent for a moment and studied Jozef thoughtfully. 'Elizabeth says you're teaching again.'

'Yes, fortunately. She has had trouble finding a job.'

'None of us will get jobs. Especially not her. A woman, foreign. She'll never work at what she can really do.'

'No, I expect not,' said Jozef. 'And you, Marek? Can this last? What will you do?'

'In another six months I'll be a rich man. I'm a rich man now, as a matter of fact.' He gave a short, bitter laugh. 'The British army made me a truck driver, and nothing I was ever taught has been so profitable as that knowledge of transmissions and engines.' There was a gleam in his eyes, a dangerous light. Then he leaned back in his chair and brushed the ash from his beautiful suit. 'You know, you can always count on me,' Marek said. 'No matter what. You can count on me for help.'

At ten, Jozef excused himself and went upstairs. He could hear the voices below, Elizabeth's laughter. It had been a long winter, and now — spring. He could not blame her, yet his heart beat wildly against his chest as if trying to attract his attention. He opened the doors of the armoire where his suit hung and his raincoat and a few threadbare shirts that gave him a little twinge of envy for Marek's snowy silk. Jozef sighed and lifted the battered canvas and leather bag from the top shelf. His books were more important, the grammars and dictionaries that formed his professional library, the favourite poems, the Mickiewicz, Shakespeare, Racine, La Fontaine, the Bible in Polish, and last, the three thin, blue-backed exercise books from the estate schoolroom, his last mementos of André and Czeslaw and now, perhaps, of Elizabeth, as well. On top of these treasures, he thrust his extra shoes, his clothes; carelessly, hastily, impatient to be done. Then he lit a cigarette, the last of his day's ration, and stretched out on top of the bed. It was absurd, of course. It was not he who would leave, after all, but Elizabeth. Still he made no move to touch the case: it was good to know that he had no ties, no feelings, that he would have no regrets.

Marek told Elizabeth about trucks and about Italy and made her laugh as she had not laughed for a long time. Then he studied the room and saw that they were poor: Elizabeth had never had any head for business. He could perhaps send Jozef some money, Marek thought, to make things easier; to Jozef, for Elizabeth would say it was not necessary. Although it would be, for she said they expected her Cousin Félicie, and she herself was thinner, pale from the winter, and like himself no longer so young, not like his girls in Berlin, in Frankfurt, who seemed younger and younger. Yet he had missed her in a way that he would never miss them, and her laugh moved him.

'You said that you were going to Marseilles.'

'I'm going to the States. A little business.'

'Very nice.'

'Do you want to come?' He was half joking, but only half. She laughed and then her face grew serious.

'Bring Jozef, too.'

'You must see that would be too much for him. In every way.'

'But he is better.'

'Physically, yes, he is fine. It is the mental wounds. The doctors warned me that it will be a long time before he has natural emotions.'

'Did he ever? For you, I mean. He didn't sleep with you.'

'That was something else again. I understand Jozef.'

'And will you stay with him? Is that what you want?'

'It's what I must do,' Elizabeth said. 'And there are other reasons.'

He lifted his head, but she ignored the warning.

'You will do what you please, of course, but you will not neglect your family for me. Not for me.'

'They care little enough for me. No more than you.' His voice was bitter.

Elizabeth shook her head. 'Please! I quarrelled with you in Germany. I wanted to see you this last time to say good-bye. And to say that I had loved you.'

'But not enough. You did warn me. Like a fool I did not take that seriously.'

Elizabeth turned her glass around and round, half the wine still left in it. 'I wanted to explain,' she said, 'that what I saw for us was Cairo — that is, dissipation and futility.'

'You do not trust me.'

'I do not trust us together. I thought – before Cairo – that we could live for the present, you and I. We were very good at that for a while, weren't we, Marek?'

'I thought so.'

'But you can go mad in the present and forget the past and forget even that there will be a future. I've met such people. I've seen what they are capable of with their unlimited possibilities and imitation tomorrows. I was one for a time. Do you understand me, Marek?' She reached across the table and took his hand, for it was desperately important that he should understand. 'Jozef is my past and that is my one treasure. Whether or not he is capable of bringing me happiness does not matter.' She bit her lip before she spoke again. 'I considered going to Berlin with you. Sitting in your kitchen that morning, I thought about it very seriously.'

'But it was too late.'

'Yes, it was too late after Cairo, perhaps even before Damascus.'

'Damascus was too soon.'

Elizabeth shrugged. 'Too soon for you; too late for me.'

'You expected too much from me,' he said. 'You offered me too little and expected too much.'

She bowed her head. 'I was unfair. But if I had gone with you to Berlin, Jozef would have died. There, you see how it is, Marek. Though I told you Jozef was for always,' she added softly and sadly, 'I will miss you more than I can say.'

The birds woke Jozef just after five, squabbling and twittering in the garden. He had forgotten to close the shutters and the pale white and gold morning light stood at the window and touched the new young leaves at the bottom of the yard with emerald and rose. He put out his hand, but the bed beside him was empty. Then he remembered that Marek had come and that Elizabeth had gone away with him. At the front window, he saw the street was empty; there was no sign of a big car. Jozef told himself that he felt nothing and went down the back stair and across the thick, irregular stone floor to the kitchen. The hall window was closed, the light a lizard glitter behind the slats, but in the kitchen the long shutters were open and the white-washed room was bathed in a pellucid, dream-like light that reminded Jozef of the mountain where his heart had opened.

He stopped in the doorway, as if to brace himself against some fearful current, then the big grey and white cat sidled over to rub against his legs and cry for its milk. Jozef went to get the dish. He was in the pantry when there was a sound at the back door. Elizabeth came in, carrying an immense bunch of tulips, daffodils and forsythia.

'You're up so early! Aren't these wonderful? We must have our own garden next year.' Her smile was radiant. If she was often restless and dissatisfied, she had never lost her gift for pleasure, and Jozef felt all his defences threatened.

'I couldn't sleep for the birds,' he said.

She looked at her watch. 'Five-thirty! Marek and I talked half the night.' She put the flowers on the table and went to get a vase. 'It was already light, so I went for a walk and found the flower market setting up.' She filled the vase with water and began arranging the blooms. 'I hope you're going to make coffee.'

'I didn't expect to find you here.'

Elizabeth looked at him.

'I thought you'd gone – with Marek. He did ask you, didn't he?' Jozef had not considered before that Marek might not have and he felt a terrible anger. He would never forgive the Lieutenant if he had disappointed Elizabeth.

'Yes, he did. You are too perceptive, Jozef, and it only brings you pain. I told him it was impossible.'

'He is a rich man,' Jozef said hoarsely, 'who loves you. And you love him.'

Elizabeth shrugged. 'I loved him once. Perhaps now, too. It is still impossible.'

She was wearing a white shirt, and the walls, the table, were white too, with only her black hair, her dark eyes as contrast. War had used her lightly, lightly. She was the same, only a little thinner, but her expression was different, harder. When she stood like that he was reminded of her mother and of Madame Anna, who had, in a sense, foreseen this, who had said theirs was a family much in need of human love. But that was nothing to him. He felt nothing, though his mouth was dry, his pulse fast in his ears, behind his eyes.

'I am not the same man,' he said. 'You have been good to me; it is enough. You will be safe with Marek. It will not matter if you can't find work.' He was pleading with her and on the edge of madness, of self-destruction, as he had been that awful day in the attic when he had understood the smell of blood.

She shook her head, serious now, but said nothing. She could not help him. Though she had waited for this, for any sign, he alone must decide; he himself must want to live.

Jozef gripped the side of the sink, afraid to look at her, afraid of the whirlwind in his soul which he feared and recognized and hungered for. She could be only what she was, Jozef saw, and though she might sleep with Marek — or others — it was ludicrous to suppose she would ever make a gangster's mistress. It was as impossible as that she would ever speak to the journalists who still came sometimes, hoping to make her a professional heroine; it was as impossible as that she would ever profit, in even the smallest measure, from all her valour. Never. Her faults, and he knew them well, did not run that way; she would die first and be a Countess to the last.

Oh, she was like her mother — something in the jaw — and his heart ached. He had wanted happiness for her, even a remembered happiness like Madame Anna's, but he did not see happiness at all for Elizabeth unless with him. And with that thought, Jozef felt his heart stop and understood, suddenly, the collapse of time, the eternal present of the psyche, the winged dove of grace. He felt the summer breeze of Vienna where desire incinerated the last of his youth, and then, in the white spring light, he felt the light and cold of the mountain where he had held life in his hands and given it to her as a gift so that she could return it to him now.

'Elizabeth,' he said. He felt an absurd joy, a happiness he had never expected to feel again, and stepped forward to take her into his arms.